Deplorable Me

Kim Cormack

Acknowledgements

To my offspring Jenna and Cameron, for being supportive and loving. You make me feel like the luckiest Mother in the world. You have grown to become outstanding human beings and I couldn't be prouder of you. To Mom and Dad for always being there with endless love and support. Love you always and forever.

To Haley, Leanne and Tasha for being such incredible sounding boards, slash editing gurus on this book. You are appreciated more than I could properly describe without pages of compliments. I'll do my best to not get carried away.

Haley McGee, I always look forward to our week of hilarious inappropriate phone calls. We always catch those big whoops moments together and that is always a good laugh. You are the Kim whisperer. Thank you for being you. You rock! XO

Leanne Ruissen, thank you so much for your always epic grammar god editing skills. You caught every one of those Canadian spelling mix ups and areas where I was unnecessarily overly descriptive like the amazing editor you are. XO

Tasha Lee, you know the storyline inside out and you managed to catch intricate things that slipped past Haley and I. Thank you so much for being an extra layer of editing awesome on this one my friend. I would also like to thank you for being part of the gruesome twosome. Those M.S infusions are far less painful with some funny conversation and a Baconator XO

To My Series Readers

You are about to start book three in Lexy's series. Thank you for coming with me on this journey. I hope this series helps you find the strength to stand back up whenever you fall. Thank you so much for being patient during this last year. I hope this book is everything you hoped for and more.

KD Cormack

Dedications

To Nana and Auntie Faye, life just isn't the same without you here. It always feels like I'm missing something. This whole world is. You were both such remarkable women. Auntie Faye, you were my biggest fan, but I was also yours. You took on both life and death, with endless humour. Your shenanigans were gloriously epic. Even when you knew you were palliative, you always found reasons to laugh and never ceased to entertain. You always cracked everyone up or make them smile and that is a truly miraculous gift. I know a large part of how I deal with life comes from you.

Nana, you were my daily morning visit and quite often, my first hug of the day. Seeing your smile started each morning off with the warmth of your embrace. I brought that flicker of joy you created within me and made sure to pass it on whenever the opportunity arose. We'd have coffee and laugh as we talked about life. I've driven to your place so many times on autopilot only to have that sinking feeling as I remember you're gone. The last years were difficult sometimes but that smile, and hug meant everything to me.

Prologue

Lexy's body and soul had always belonged to her Handler, but in the last couple of months, she'd gone from one prospect to three. She'd never found herself in this position. Grey had been everything to her for so long. She adored him, but he'd been spelled to forget intimacy between them as he slept. She would always remember every heartbreaking detail of the nights they spent professing their love. Knowing it wasn't his fault, didn't make his jealousy easier to digest. He was only ever reacting to half of the story. After forty years by Grey's side, she was ready to find a physical connection that would still be there in the light of a new day. *This was something she could never have with Grey.*

She'd accidentally started something with Orin. He was a good friend and undeniably great in the sack, but he'd been in a long-term relationship, and by long term, she meant with the same girl on and off for a thousand years. At this moment, neither one could promise more than drama-free shelter from the storm of their endless duties. Being a thousand years old gave Orin a good grasp on the realities of attractions left unfulfilled. He'd made it clear he had no intention of getting into anything more serious than booty calls and flirtations until she'd closed her book of unknowns. He was all for her taking a night to see Tiberius's chapter through till its end.

She'd known Tiberius would be here, he was the leader of Triad. Their titillating encounter at the Summit left her with an urgency to experience all their dark attraction had to offer. She hadn't been able to shake the sexually charged visions of him slicing his blade into her skin, showing her a little something she hadn't known about pain induced healing pleasure. Their brief sensually charged encounters since then had only left her yearning for more.

What Happened In The First Two Books?

After a dark past a teenage girl comes back from the dead and becomes a hitman for a Clan of immortals.

Born to a mother who dies during childbirth, Lexy begins her mortal life with nothing and no one, moving from one foster home to the next until age eleven when she decides to run away with a group of friends. After a falling out, she is left alone once again. She has the misfortune of being abducted by a stranger and is held captive on a farm for five long years. During this time, she becomes subservient, knowing if she fought back, she would join those who came before her at the bottom of the well on the property. Emotionally vacant, she meets a child named Charlotte, who teaches her to feel again. She listens to stories of Charlotte's house with the yellow door and fantasizes someday they will go there together. When Lexy's reason for living dies, something within her snaps. She's put down like a rabid dog, triggering an immortal birthright. She awakens in the slime of partially submerged corpses at the bottom of the well of children lost. As an emotionless Dragon, she climbs out and rids the word of the depraved beings with unbridled rage and an axe.

She leaves the dark farm, saving another abducted child. Lexy drops her off at the police station but doesn't know the entire town has been taken over by demons. Once again, Lexy Abrelle trusted the wrong people. She rids the town of demons but can't bring herself to rejoin humanity. Our antihero resides in an isolated cabin with a pack of stray dogs destroying all who come for her until her canine companions vanish. Surviving on what she catches in animal traps. Starving, our feral antihero is teetering on the edge of sanity when she finds a young man caught in one of her traps.

Grey is sent into the woods by Clan Ankh's Oracle to find the elusive Wild Thing. Unlucky by nature, he gets caught in her trap, breaking his leg. Even though Lexy is starving, she frees him. Grey follows her back to her cabin with a broken leg. After healing him, they bond. She agrees to come back to Clan Ankh after he vows to always be her friend. Clan Triad comes for her. She fights them off, but they capture Grey. Lexy saves him and they go back to Clan Ankh together, where he stays true to his word. She finds the family she's always wanted.

Three new Ankh go into the Immortal Testing. Lexy, Grey and Arrianna survive their personal versions of hell and become Enlightened. Grey is made Lexy's Handler as she succumbs to the Dragon within. There is a clause in the Dragon Handler agreement. Grey's memory is erased whenever they become physically intimate. This goes on for decades. Lexy fights with Tiberius at the Immortal Summit and succumbs to the volatile attraction.

Forty years after her trio of partially immortal teens survived the Testing, another group finally makes it out. Kayn is revealed to be a Dragon. Lexy isn't sure how she feels about it at first, but they become murder buddies. Lexy stretches the limits of her Handler Dragon bond as she starts something with Orin, who is also Ankh. The dark attraction she feels for Tiberius isn't easy to shake, she finds herself in inappropriate situations with her enemy. Clan Ankh begins collecting teens as they survive their Corrections for the next group to brave the Immortal Testing.

Chapter 1

Temptations

She lay there listening to thundering waves washing upon the sand. Inhaling and exhaling, attempting to calm her thoughts. There was a knock on her door. Lexy tossed off her covers and got out of bed. She ran her fingers through her crimson hair. *Nobody would visit at this hour? Maybe Grey forgot his key?* She opened the door.

Orin was standing there shirtless holding a bottle of tequila. "Feel like company?" her naughty cohort enquired as he maneuvered past her without waiting for a response.

Lexy grinned as she closed the door behind her sort of booty call. *This wasn't a great idea. Neither one of them were ready for anything but a good time.* As she saw Orin's rearview Lexy sighed. *It would be so worth it though.* She walked over, snatched the bottle of golden death from Orin's hand and took a long reckless swig. She gave it back and declared, "Grey could show up."

"We'd better go for a walk on the beach then," Orin prompted as he marched back to the door, held it open and urged, "Come on. What do you have to lose?"

Nothing. Not a damn thing. Lexy thought as she followed him out.

"It feels like you've been avoiding me," Orin commented as they wandered to the beach.

"For the record, I haven't been. Grey's been passive-aggressively demanding of my time since I told him about that night," Lexy admitted. "Well, and it's a little awkward with Jenna around."

"It doesn't need to be," he inferred as they stepped out onto the beach. "Just take what you want from me. I won't get all jealous and needy, I promise." He handed her the bottle and teased, "This might help." Orin took off his swimsuit, left it there on the sand and sprinted into the surf, naked as the day he was born.

Orin made her feel like she could just do whatever she desired. Was he a good influence or a bad one? The jury was still out. She selfishly wanted him and there appeared to be no witnesses. Why not? Lexy stripped off her bathing suit, tossed it aside and boldly stood on the beach nude, feeling a womanly sense of power she couldn't even begin to explain as Orin splashed around in the surf, tempting her with his carefree ways. He waved her in. She started laughing as she went for it and dashed into the surf. Orin opened his arms, seductively luring her in without saying a word. Lexy stepped into his embrace, pressed the length of her body against his and blissfully closed her eyes. *It felt so good to be held. Why hadn't she taken advantage of his offer sooner?* Orin nuzzled her neck as he naughtily slid his hands along her rib cage until they disappeared beneath the water's surface and seductively continued the shiver worthy voyage to the small of her back. *He wanted to play healing games with her. She knew what he was about to do.* Lexy felt his excitement against her as his palms began heating the small of her back, causing goosebumps of pleasure all over her body. She gasped his name.

Orin whispered, "Ready Hun," as his ability induced an explosion of soul-shattering bliss.

Her knees buckled as intense waves of carnal pleasure caused her to cry out between the crashing of the waves. Orin kept her secure in his arms as she basked in the delicious tingly aftermath.

He nuzzled her neck and taunted, "You're welcome."

Lexy shivered as she exhaled with her legs wrapped around his waist. He almost lost his footing. Giggling, she tried to stand up. *The motion of the water was going to be an inconvenience.* Pulling away with her hands laced behind his neck, she met his self-satisfied expression. His lips began moving towards her, and she confessed, "Not out here. I can barely stand."

"Mission not even close to accomplished," Orin naughtily seduced. "Sweetheart, we haven't even grazed the surface of what I'm capable of doing to you."

She wanted to participate. With his lips poised a breath from hers, Lexy slipped out of his embrace and giggled as she flirtatiously lured him back to the beach until there was dry sand beneath her feet. He obediently played along as she lay and summoned him to join her with a finger. Orin didn't require further persuasion. He got down on all fours, intimately kissed her ankle and began a slow sensual journey up the length of her legs, trailing seductive kisses up her salty flesh. He teased her with the heat of his breath between her thighs until she was wantonly squirming and pleading for him to take her. Grinning from ear to ear, he ceased the foreplay as his lips met hers. She gasped as he entered her aggressively, taking her hard and fast until they were both crying out with not a care in the world of who might hear their X-rated encounter. Orin only gave her a second to bask in the aftermath before he began moving within her again, whispering his naughty intentions. For hours he continued giving her what she needed until they were exhausted. The duo snapped out of their bliss induced euphoria as the tide wet their backs. Scrambling to their feet, they both spun around, looking for their suits but all they saw was the ocean. They waded out searching, but they were long gone. *Fate was on a roll tonight. A naked walk of shame. How creative.*

Giggling, he responded to her inner-commentary, "We should do the walk of shame together. We'll just own it. Stroll back to our rooms naked."

Lexy hadn't found their situation humorous, but as Orin took her in his arms and planted a long seductive kiss on her, she started to laugh. She pulled away and asserted, "I think it would be best if we walked back separately."

As they waded to dry land, her naughty companion taunted, "Everybody knows we've been… close lately. Just walk in and tell your Handler you defiled me. Grey's a big boy, he'll get over it.

If only it were that simple.

"You sure you don't want a walk of shame buddy?" Orin enquired once more as he glanced back at her and baited, "Last chance."

Lexy smiled at his sexy rear view as she countered, "I'm all good. I avoid drama like the plague." *They were going to have to streak back to their rooms. There was no way around it.*

Orin took off ahead, yelling, "Next time we'll put our clothes somewhere safe!"

And with that, he left her standing naked on the beach watching his perfect ass running away. Covering her mouth, she replayed her naughty behaviour. *That was so good. Hell, she wasn't sure she had the strength in her legs to run back to her room.* As she stepped onto the cement walkway and lost the pleasurable sensation of the sand beneath her toes, it felt like coming back to reality. Lexy was tossing around the idea of just owing it as she strutted back to her room until she heard voices on the beach and sprinted as fast as she could to her door. She'd almost made it back when someone opened a door, followed by the hum of multiple voices. *Shit! Shit!* She tried the knob directly beside her room and dove inside.

Frost's voice remarked, "As flattered as I am, I just started a relationship, and I've been gone all of twenty-four hours."

Lexy whirled around with one arm concealing her chest and the other hand in front of her unmentionables. Meeting Frost's thoroughly amused grin, she explained, "I was swimming naked and I lost my bathing suit."

"Alone?" Frost coyly asked, tossing her a t-shirt and shorts from his bag.

"Of course," Lexy huffed as she quickly put on his clothes.

Politely turning around while she dressed, Frost teased, "You know it's obvious and I'm not one to judge."

He totally knew, there was no point in trying to pretend with Frost. Lexy had his tight-fitting briefs and a t-shirt on as she confessed, "It was Orin."

"I know," Frost admitted. "While we're confessing things, I sent him to your room." Lexy noticed the pizza box on the table. He offered, "Help yourself, it's piping hot. It just arrived. Had you gone streaking five minutes earlier you would have made that pizza delivery guy's night."

Lexy took a seat at the table. Frost sat across from her as they devoured the pizza. He had the opportunity to keep teasing her but didn't bother. They just consumed an entire large pizza in comfortable silence.

When Lexy got up to leave, Frost pointed out, "You're a grown woman, you don't have to feel bad about having some fun."

"I know," Lexy confirmed. "Thanks for the pizza. I was starving." She waited for Frost's naughty comeback, but he didn't say a word as she left. Without the pressure of being naked, she casually strolled to her room, quietly unlocked the door and entered. *Grey was asleep.* She didn't want to deal with the conversation, so she tiptoed to her bag, grabbed another bathing suit to sleep in and brought it with her as she snuck into the bathroom to shower. As she stepped under the spray and lathered up, Lexy smiled. *Orin was an insanely talented lover. Maybe, that's why Jenna kept going back for a thousand years? She really shouldn't do this again. Not until she was past her Tiberius fixation.* She opened the shower curtains to find Grey grinning, leaning against the sink holding Frost's underwear. *Shit.*

Grey placed the underwear on the counter, tossed her a towel and ribbed, "Someone's been rather naughty. Have a good night?"

Lexy casually wrapped the towel around herself as she baited, "I had a great night."

"Whose underwear are those? I thought Orin was a boxer guy?" Her Handler impishly sparred.

She opted for the truth, "I went skinny dipping with Orin and lost my bathing suit. So, I had to streak back to the room. I ended up hiding in Frost's room because people were coming. He gave me clothes and we ate pizza."

Confused emotion filled Grey's eyes as he gave her honesty back, "I'm sorry. I'm in a weird place. I shouldn't have asked, but this whole thing with Orin is new. I'm trying to be happy for you, but I'm finding myself feeling sad. I don't know if jealous is the word…territorial might be more accurate."

Was she making a mistake pretending they were more than just a casual fling? It felt like it. "Where were you tonight?" Lexy enquired.

"I was at the bar with Jenna, Mel and Lily. It was quite innocent. I spent the whole night talking about you," he disclosed.

It felt like she was cheating. Her heart ached as he left the room. She sat on the edge of the tub and covered her face with both hands as she teared up. *If they would just let them be together, they'd both be happy at the same time, it wouldn't always be one of them hurting as the other tried to move on.* She wiped the moisture from her eyes as she put on her bathing suit. It was most comfortable to sleep almost nude in this heat, but tonight she put on Frost's long t-shirt before leaving the bathroom. She slipped into bed next to Grey, feeling emptiness so deep it felt like she might slip into her Dragon self as she slept.

Chapter 2

Minty Fertile Moose

Lexy opened her eyes to a new day, feeling like she was still stuck in the last because she hadn't awoken in Grey's arms. *He'd slept as far away from her as he could. She didn't blame him. She understood how he was feeling. She'd felt that way a thousand times.* Lexy swung her legs over the edge of the bed and wandered to the bathroom. When she stepped out ready to go, *Grey was gone. So was his bag. This hurt. He was the only thing capable of hurting her. He knew that. Sober, in the light of day, sleeping with Orin to get over Grey wasn't a good plan at all.* A knock on the door snapped her out of her guilt. She got up to answer it. It was Grey with a coffee in each hand. As their eyes met, relief washed over her.

He passed her one and apologized, "I'm sorry. I don't want things to be weird between us. If you want Orin and this is going to make you happy, I'll just suck it up and get used to it. Let's go for breakfast."

It was time to tell the truth. Lexy disclosed, "It's nothing serious. He's still in love with Jenna, and I'm…"

"You're what?" her Handler questioned as he leaned in to smell a fragrant flower.

"Lonely," she replied. "I have needs too, and while you're off dealing with yours, I'm…" She paused again, not wanting to reveal too much.

"I'm?" Grey probed.

Meeting his eyes, she confessed, "I'm waiting for you." Her feelings for him washed over her as she changed the subject, "I could keep it outside of the Clan if that would be easier." *What was she doing? Why was she offering him something he'd never thought to offer her?*

"If you like Orin, you should just go for it," he asserted.

He was a horrible liar. The idea of her with someone else hurt him, she could see it. "Don't read too much into this. It's not serious," Lexy affirmed as she took a sip of her coffee. *He'd put cinnamon in it. She loved cinnamon.* She plucked a tiny white feather out of his hair. *Weird? Their pillows weren't goose down.* They spent a peaceful morning hanging out in their room before abruptly packing to leave for a job. They received the details via text. It was the Correction of an eighteen-year-old female marked as a vessel for Abaddon. Soon, her soul would vacate her body and become collateral damage. *Her mortal shell would house a demon. If they took her out first, she'd be funnelled through the hall of souls. The mortal would be given another chance and Abaddon's evil plot would be stopped. She didn't like these Corrections. They were basically rehoming the soul of an innocent. Abaddon would just go out and find another one.* They arrived at the girl's work address. *It was a shoe store. Excellent.* Looking at Grey, Lexy questioned, "No home address?"

"We got the same text. Your guess is as good as mine," Grey declared. "I feel like the scent of that beef jerky we ate during the drive is following me around." Grey cupped his mouth and exhaled. He grimaced as he dug gum out of his pants, grabbed one and offered her a piece.

Lexy put the gum in her mouth. *Mint...Awesome.* She chewed it for a second and sneezed loud enough to summon a fertile moose.

Grey chuckled, "That just never gets old."

She gave her Handler a good shove. He snickered as they got out of the car and strolled towards the store. He passed her the Aries Group card. Grinning, Lexy snatched it and instructed, "I'm your sister. It's my birthday, I'm buying anything I want. Work your magic. Flirt some information out of the girl while I shop."

"Right Sis. Got it. I know the drill, we're going to be here for a while," Grey chuckled as he followed her into the store.

Lexy surveyed the room and out of the two staff, there was only one girl with a mortal aura. She scanned the shelves. *Bingo. She had a thing for boots.* She strolled up to the rack and enquired about some in her size as Grey began chatting up the girl. Lexy slipped on one of the knee-high black leather boots from the box the man brought her and zipped it up. *It fit perfectly. She was obviously supposed to buy these.* Feeling bold in her sexy boots, Lexy began sizing up her attractive salesperson whose name tag read, Mike. He appeared to be in his mid-twenties and suspiciously well-groomed. She announced, "I'll take them."

Mike asked, "Are you and your boyfriend just passing through town?"

Glancing in Grey's direction, she clarified, "Brother."

Mike grinned and whispered, "Bridgette isn't into guys."

Interesting…They would have to improvise. Lexy smiled as she gave Mike her card and said, "Tell my brother I'll be waiting in the car when he figures it out."

"If you find yourselves bored, there's a pub on Main Street with good tapas," Mike offered up. "It's the only one in town, it shouldn't be difficult to find," he added as he gave Lexy back her card.

"We'll probably end up there. Thanks, Mike." Lexy answered as she waved, turned around and shoved open the door. *He was nice. With her luck, he'd get in the way somehow and she'd have to kill him too.* She wandered out to the car. *They had to confirm the girl's identity.*

A few minutes later, Grey emerged from the store, looking frustrated. He got into the car, mumbling, "She's not remotely interested in me, I tried every move I have."

Lexy turned the key in the ignition as she announced, "She's into girls. I've got this."

"Well, you definitely bought the right boots. These are hot. They could lure in anyone," he pestered, snooping through her bag. "Are you sure you're up for this?" Grey enquired as he tossed her bag on the backseat.

"Why wouldn't I be?" Lexy countered as they pulled into the hotel.

Grey grinned as he got out and coyly replied, "Never mind."

She knew what he was hinting at but wasn't about to give him the satisfaction of a response. Someone had to search this girl for the mark. One of them had to see it. She'd been doing this job for more than forty years. It didn't matter who they were, vessels had to be disposed of.

After checking in, they ordered room service and snuggled under the covers to watch a movie. At some point, they drifted off to sleep. After a long luxurious nap, Lexy awoke in Grey's arms, grateful he'd put his jealousy to rest. In those precious moments, before he woke, she usually allowed her heart to imagine what it would be like to awaken in his arms after a night spent professing their feelings. *An alternate universe where he wasn't spelled to forget.* He snuggled against her. *It felt so perfect.* She swallowed her emotions down, knowing she would never move on if she kept pretending it was possible to be something more than a one-night stand, he was spelled to forget. She rolled over and looked at the clock. It was flashing 10:03 pm. She gave Grey a shake and said, "Time to go to work."

Lexy heard him grumbling as she wandered into the bathroom to get ready. She didn't have a plan per se but knew where Abaddon usually marked their prospects. It was a crescent-shaped birthmark behind the left ear, or on the chest above their heart in the same spot where Triad was branded. On a rare occasion, it was on their back. She unwrapped a plastic cup, filled it with water, raised the glass and saluted her reflection above the sink. *She wasn't nervous, she'd kissed a girl before.* Her mind travelled back to Glory, walking her back to the RV and planting one on her before they'd gone into their Testing. *It had been forty years, but it was a memorable kiss.* Loud bangs on the bathroom door startled her back to reality, "I'll be out in a second."

"Are you decent?" Grey countered.

"Come in, I'm almost ready," Lexy answered as she carefully applied her cherry red lipstick.

He marched over shirtless with scruffy bedhead, stuck his neck in her personal space, and asserted, "Honest truth, is it too strong?"

What in the hell, Grey? Oh, he was talking about his new cologne. She preferred his usual fragrance. It was nice though. Lexy lovingly patted down Grey's messy hair as she declared,

"It's very sexy, you'll be swatting them away like flies tonight."

Grinning, Grey provoked, "I have a feeling, I'll be far too interested in what you're doing to care."

She passed him his deodorant and remarked, "Put on a fresh layer, I have to sleep next to you."

He snatched it out of her hand and taunted, "Yes, mom."

Shaking her head, smiling as she strolled out, Lexy sat on the bed to put on her new boots. *She had to shut his warm fuzzies down.*

Grey followed her out, knelt by her and offered, "Helping you put them on is the least I can do. This job is all on you tonight." He slipped one on and slowly zipped it up. As he did the same with the other, he teased, "These aren't glass slippers, don't get drunk and lose one at midnight."

He was still cupping her leather-bound calf with his hand. *She could see it in his eyes. They were having a moment. Not a Dragon Handler moment, a romantic one. She had to snap him out of it before it turned into more.*

"What if we just took a night to ourselves and stayed in? The girl will probably still be there tomorrow," Grey tempted as he cupped her calf, massaging the leather encasing it.

She felt the changing tide. He was trying to decipher the feelings that kept washing him back to her shore. It was his duty to wear down the rough edges of her heart. She loved him too much and he wasn't allowed to love her back. Lexy shifted her leg out of his hand and asserted, "We'll take a night off after we've dealt with this Correction." *She was going to have to do something shockingly out of character tonight to snap him out of it.*

They only had to drive around for a few minutes to find the pub. The bouncer at the door greeted them by moving the rope and saying, "We're officially at our limit."

His eyes flirtatiously looked Lexy over as he professed, "I totally would have let you in anyway."

She winked at him and walked away. Lexy scanned the crowded pub for the girl from the shoe store. *She knew her name but didn't want to use it. A nameless person was easier to see as a job.*

"There she is," Grey whispered as he pointed her out. "You'll need to get her alone, so there's less collateral damage. Keep her occupied. I have to use the little boy's room."

This was inconvenient. Her mark was sitting at the bar, chatting up a girl. Fingers crossed it was just an acquaintance. Her phone buzzed. *Weird.* She dug it out of her jacket. The unknown number's message read, 'Hey stranger.' *It was probably Orin.* She smiled as she texted, 'Hey stranger,' back and shoved her cell in her pocket. She had to stay on task. *Now, wasn't the time for flirtatious messages.* Lexy made her way through the crowd with no idea what she was going to do. She got as close as she could without making her intentions obvious and listened in on her conquest's conversation. Her back was exposed. *There was no mark of Abaddon.* Someone shoved past her. Lexy lost her balance and grabbed the girl's shoulder to stop herself from going down. *Shoot.* Lexy apologized, "Sorry." The girl sitting beside Bridgette offered up her seat because she had to leave. Lexy sat down. *Convenient. Her complication had removed itself.* Her phone buzzed again. Lexy looked at the message. 'Those boots would have looked better in red.' She shook her head, glanced around the pub and shoved her cell back into her pocket.

"I saw you buy those earlier, they're sexy as hell but deadly," the girl she was supposed to kill interjected.

"They are quite the death trap," Lexy admitted with a grin.

The girl introduced herself, "I'm Bridgette, and you are?"

"Lexy," she responded as she politely shook the girl's hand, stealing one of Grey's moves by holding on to it for a little longer than necessary.

"So, how long are you in town?" Bridgette probed as she continued to hold her hand.

This girl was smooth. "Another day, maybe two," Lexy replied, keeping hold of Bridgette's hand and gazing into her eyes. The bartender arrived. Lexy squeezed Bridgette's hand before letting it go, so she could pay for her drink. She took a sip of her Long Island Iced Tea as she stared at the girl's chest. *Her top wasn't low cut enough. She could see the top of what looked like a tattoo. It probably was... There was a visible one on her arm. Maybe this was the wrong girl?*

Bridgette took her continued gaze as an invitation. She leaned in, caressed Lexy's leather-bound thigh and whispered, "Want to go somewhere and talk?"

"Sure, I'll let my brother know I'm leaving." Lexy seductively kissed Bridgette's cheek and snuck a peek behind her ear as she whispered, "I'll be right back." Lexy left, feeling proud of herself as she walked away.

Bridgette called after her, "Don't trip in those. You'll break an ankle."

"I'll try not to," Lexy teased, knowing breaking bones was only temporary for her. She looked back through the crowd at Bridgette, watching her walk away. *This might be an interesting evening.* She saw Grey walking towards her.

As they embraced, he whispered in her ear, "We're not alone on this job. Just thought you should know."

"Abaddon?" Lexy mumbled, feeling strange. *Something was off, her vision was blurry.*

"Are you alright," her Handler enquired as she staggered.

The room was spinning as Lexy slurred, "I think I've been drugged."

"Let's get out of here before you pass out," Grey whispered as he led her out the door into the street.

It felt like she was still in the pub as she looked up at the swirling streetlamp and lost consciousness.

Chapter 3

Make Me Want You

As Lexy came too, she felt around with her hands. *She was on a bed with soft sheets. Grey must have carried her back to the room.* She cautiously opened her eyes, expecting to see Grey. Her eyes focused on Tiberius, standing beside the bed in just his jeans. She scrambled away and leapt to her feet on the other side of the bed, ready to rumble.

"You are always eager to kick my ass, aren't you?" Tiberius chastised as he turned and wandered away. He casually asked, "What do you take in your coffee?"

Lexy took in the untidy kitchenette. *This was a lived-in motel room.* "What did you do with Grey?" Lexy demanded, unwilling to play games with her shirtless captor.

"Your Handler's fine. He wouldn't come willingly, so we were forced to knock him out. He's sleeping it off. Sugar and cream or just cream?"

Intrigued by the situation, Lexy made her way over to Tiberius as she coolly replied, "It doesn't matter, I'm not drinking anything you give me." She joined him at the counter, scrutinizing his every move.

He prepared two cups and pointedly took a sip out of both before stepping out of the way and saying, "I get it. Anything coming from me has been sketchy in the past. I promise this is just coffee."

"Why did you drug me?" Lexy probed as she took a chance and raised the steaming liquid to her lips.

"You were walking into a trap," Tiberius revealed. "I saw you going into the shoe store as we were leaving town after a meeting and this thing we have, got the best of me."

"A meeting with?" Lexy asked, taking another sip.

"We're not in the same Clan, Lexy. I can't share all of my secrets," Tiberius flirtatiously countered as he snatched a muffin from the platter on the table.

"Why aren't you wearing your shirt?" Lexy baited, curiously.

He sat down across from her. With a knowing grin, he admitted, "You tore it off while deliriously horny."

Scattered steamy images flitted through her mind. "We didn't?" Lexy questioned, crossing her legs.

He chuckled and teased, "When I realised you were still mentally compromised, we stopped. My pants stayed on, I swear."

Lexy took another sip of coffee as she glanced at the strewn about covers on the bed and bit her lip as her mind fed her X-rated teasers.

"Remember anything?" Tiberius innocently provoked. *She didn't plan to admit a damn thing. She should just get to the point.* "So, the girl I was sitting with wasn't the right girl?" Lexy asked as she took a chance on a muffin.

"We were sent to do the same Correction. A friend filled me in on what was really going on. So, we contacted our Guardian and went in knowing Abaddon was testing an aura filter. An invention that will make it easier to hide their prospects from us. The altered job was to check it out and report back to Seth. When you two showed up, we realised Seth hadn't bothered to forward the information to the other Clans. It looked like you were going to follow through with that little seduction. I've been in your mind. I saw what they did to you on that farm. I know how far you've come and how long it's taken you to get here. I couldn't allow that part of you to be compromised by Abaddon. We only drugged you to take you out of the equation."

She'd allowed him access to her memories during the Summit, it affected his sense of reason. She didn't know what to say. What could she say? The darkness caused a connection. His need to protect her from suffering that fate again had compromised him. Lexy met his gaze as she curtly replied, "I don't need your protection, Tiberius. I would have figured it out and dealt with it."

"I don't doubt you'd kill everyone in this town before allowing an Abaddon to touch you, but the aura filters were flawless. You were getting rather cozy with that demon. I care about what happens to you even though it makes no sense to," he admitted as his hand inched closer while asking, "Were you really going to do it?"

"A part of me wanted to, when I thought she was just a girl with an unfortunate purpose," Lexy answered honestly. Tiberius threaded his fingers through hers and her emotions rushed to the surface. Confused by her response, she yanked her hand away and stated, "You know I'm going back to the bar to kill everyone, right?"

"I wouldn't expect anything less," Tiberius countered. With a knowing grin, he got up and added, "Now, you have all of the information. Do with it what you will. Send my regards to Grey. Your Handler is next door. Wait a few minutes before waking him. I'd prefer to avoid the drama." Tiberius smiled at her one last time and turned to leave.

She was supposed to hate him, but she didn't, not really…Not anymore. As Tiberius started to walk away, Lexy stood up. Every part of her wanted to go after him, but she knew she shouldn't, so she just remained where she was as he left. She sat back down at the table and took an enormous bite out of a banana chocolate chip muffin. *She'd made a lot of mistakes, letting Tiberius leave without sentiment didn't feel like one. He'd needed her to let him walk away. It felt like the right thing to do. She didn't love him. That's not what this was. It was a connection built on traumatic events. The last thing either needed was for one of them to confuse their roles by making an attraction into something more. She was sent here to do a job, she planned to finish it. She'd earned Abaddon's fear with her strength. They'd forgotten who she was…Game on!*

She grabbed the doorknob. Her mind prompted, *Tiberius just touched this, his hand was right here.* "Shit," Lexy cursed as she opened the door. *Get a hold of yourself. Tiberius doesn't matter, find Grey.* She tried the door next to her room, it was locked. She backed up a step, booted it open and saw Grey in bed sleeping. *Someone had rather adorably tucked him in.* She crawled up on the bed, pulled down his covers and placed her palms on his chiselled chest. She paused as curiosity took hold, lifted his sheets, and knit her brow. *He was naked.* She gave him a smack. *You predictable tool! Obviously, he'd had the same response to being drugged and one of the Triad had taken him out for a spin.* She sat there for a moment as her mind fed her more X-rated snippets of her steamy make-out session with Tiberius. *It made no sense to be mad at Grey when she'd done the same thing.* Lexy shook her head as she placed her palms on her Handler's chest and gave him a quick jolt of healing energy.

Grey yawned, opened his eyes and groggily commentated, "Nice room." He knit his brow as he peeked under the covers and stammered, "I'm naked. We didn't?"

"Not me, lover boy. It looks like you slept with a Triad," Lexy provoked. She bent over, grabbed his pants and tossed them at his face.

"Wait. What happened?" Grey grilled as he caught the shirt, she'd rifled at him next.

Lexy found his underwear and launched them directly at his face as she explained, "We were drugged by Triad because we were walking into a trap. Abaddon has an aura filter. It's an invention that makes auras impossible to detect the usual way. You're going to call the Aries Group for a clean-up while I go kill everyone in that bar."

Grey leapt out of bed, stammering, "You can't! You'll kill mortals too!"

"I don't care," Lexy countered.

"We have to call Markus!" Grey prompted as he pursued Lexy into the hall, hastily doing up his pants.

Lexy clutched both of Grey's shoulders as she calmly declared, "The dice have already been tossed. This is personal. You know I can't allow Abaddon to think they have the upper hand, not even for a second. I have an idea. You don't have to come, but I have to go. It's my move."

Grey asserted, "You know there's two of us. Give me a second. I'm coming with you." He was texting someone as Lexy walked away. He shoved his phone into his pocket and raced after her saying, "We need weapons!"

Silly boy. She was the weapon. If she took even the slightest amount of energy from a mortal, they'd be rendered unconscious. Either the Abaddon would have to be wearing something that altered the colour of their aura, or there would have to be an object capable of concealing the whole town. She had an idea.

Grey kept pace with her as they reached the line up to get into the pub. He responded to her inner-commentary, "What's the plan?"

"Bar fight," Lexy whispered. She marched up to the front of the line. The bouncer stepped aside to let her in but blocked Grey's entry.

Grey called after her, "Play nice!"

Nice...Right. Lexy touched someone on the dance floor, they passed out. A crowd gathered. *Mortal.* She carried on towards the bar. Her playmate from earlier was surprised to see her. "Having fun?" Lexy flirted as she slid into the empty seat beside Bridgette.

"I thought you left? It's almost closing time, where did you go?"

"Ex issues," Lexy disclosed as she took the girl's hand and admired her cheap inconspicuous bracelets. "These are quite lovely. Any sentimental meaning?"

"None whatsoever," Bridgette replied, seductively crossing her legs.

Miss Bridgette was just a demon trying to distract her. Lexy's eyes scanned the crowd. Even without the guidance of a visual aura, she could pick out the Abaddon. She'd always had the aura to guide her, she hadn't bothered to notice the other signs. Lexy held the demon's hand as she leaned in and seductively whispered, "You know what I want, don't you?"

Unnerved by her overly aggressive statement, Bridgette flirtatiously replied, "Let's go back to your hotel."

"Sounds like a plan," Lexy baited as she let go of Bridgette's hand. She stood up, placed her hand on a patron's shoulder, and he dropped to the floor. Lexy looked back and decreed, "That one's mortal." Bridgette's eyes widened. "So is this one," Lexy commented as she touched the first person who came to the boy's aid. They dropped. Bridgette silently stepped back as Lexy revealed, "Who do you think you're dealing with, aura filters make no difference, I see you."

"Are you going to knock out every mortal in the bar?" Bridgette countered, fascinated by Lexy's badassery.

Lexy nonchalantly touched another heroic human who was crouched over the unconscious ones. They went down. "I might," she saucily admitted as she touched a few more. *One didn't go down.* Stoked, Lexy exclaimed, "Bar fight time." She wound up and decked the guy that didn't faint, taking the Abaddon by surprise. A girl rushed at her. Lexy sent her soaring into the crowd. Suddenly, the bar was all drunken slurs, flying fists and chairs.

Bridgette picked up her barstool to use as a weapon and yelled to the brawling immortals, "The aura filter doesn't work!"

Lexy paid attention to which patrons had an, 'Oh, shit' expression as Bridgette's declaration travelled through the crowd. Lexy met Bridgette's eyes as she declared, "Sweetheart...No. I'm killing you last. Feel free to run away, I'll find you."

Bridgette dropped her stool and took off. Someone pulled the fire alarm. Lexy grinned, knowing it was Grey. *He was clearing the room of mortals for her, how sweet. Immortals didn't exit buildings for fire alarms.*

Grey grabbed her arm and towed her to the fire escape, explaining, "The police are here. The Aries Group is on their way, blend in with the crowd."

She wasn't finished fighting. Lexy caught a glimpse of Bridgette getting into a car across the street.

Someone wearing a suit asked what happened. Grey answered, "There was a weird smell. People started passing out on the dance floor. I'd get everyone out of there."

Lexy followed Bridgette's vehicle with her eyes as it drove away. The back window rolled down. Bridgette flipped her the bird. *That bitch! She was so dead!* Lexy took off on a dead run after the car.

Grey tackled her to the cement and hissed, "Stay down," in her ear as ambulance attendants rushed to her aid. Grey helped Lexy up with a firm grasp on her arm as he explained her symptoms, "She's disorientated from the gas leak. I think she needs to be checked out."

Asshole! Lexy allowed a first responder to walk her back to an ambulance, shooting daggers at her Handler with her eyes. Grey was grinning at her. *Oh, that shithead was in so much trouble.* She allowed them to take her blood pressure and ask a few questions. The ambulance door slammed with her still inside. *What the?* One of the paramedics shot her an evil grin. *Of course.* Lexy struggled as they forcefully held her down. She was stuck by a needle. *This wasn't good.* Her vision flickered, and the lights went out.

Chapter 4

Maybe?

She awoke in a minimalistic holding cell, alone. Seriously pissed, Lexy glared at the camera in the corner of the room and warned, "You have five seconds to explain yourself, or I'm coming through the wall." She started counting, "One, two, three…Oh, hell. Who gives a shit?" She punched a fist through the plaster and yanked out her bleeding broken knuckle. *Inconvenient.* She cupped the wounded hand with the other. Impatiently waiting for her healing ability to kick in, she began hostilely booting holes in the plaster. When her digits were as good as new, she looked up at the camera and coldly vowed, "When I get out of here, you're dead." Lexy leapt up, tore the camera off the wall, looked directly into it, and flipped whoever was watching the bird. She dropped it on the floor and stomped on it. Her Handler popped into her mind. *Where was he? Did they have him too?* For a split second, she regretted stomping on her only form of communication. *Grey usually fed her logic at this point. Guess she was going to have to do this her own way.* With a wry smile, she reached into the hole she'd kicked through the plaster, grabbed a handful of multicoloured wires and with her full weight, she yanked them out of the wall, ending up on her butt holding a fistful of sparking wires.

The power went out, she grinned. *She hadn't thought that far ahead.* She got up in the pitch-black room and began kicking holes in the plaster like a maniac. Something buzzed as emergency lighting turned on. *Sneaky bastards had a generator.* The light showed her she'd almost kicked her way into the next room. There wasn't even a moment of pause as she tore away the remnants and climbed through the hole. Lexy stood up, brushed herself off and noticed she wasn't alone. There was a young teenage girl strapped to a bed in the centre of the room. *Where in the hell was she?* She strolled over, removed the gag from the teen's mouth and tore away the leather straps she'd been bound with. "We're getting out of here. What's your name?"

The girl whispered, "Owen."

As the girl tried to stand, it became clear she was heavily sedated. "How old are you, Owen?" Lexy prompted as she began aggressively booting a hole into the next room.

"I'm not sure. I was thirteen, but I haven't had a calendar. I've been here for a long time," Owen answered disoriented.

Lexy stopped trying to stomp a hole through the wall. *She was a kid. Owen didn't appear to be much older than thirteen.* Lexy strolled over and said, "Well, Owen, we're busting out. We'll have a chat about why you're in here later." She touched Owen's shoulders and gave her a healing energy boost.

Owen smiled and agreed, "Fine. Let's go." As Lexy gave the wall another good kick, Owen ordered, "Open the door!"

Lexy turned around, ready to give the kid shit for bossing her around. The door unlocked from the outside and swung open, revealing nobody on the other side. Lexy stuck her head out into the hall.

Owen confidently instructed, "All of them."

Every door down the length of the hall swung open. People of varying ages in hospital gowns wandered out. *She wasn't sure how the kid did it. Magic maybe?* She grabbed Owen's arm, smiled and said, "We'll chat about how you did that later. First things first, let's go!" They raced for the main doors with a crowd in hospital gowns following them. Lexy sprinted at the glass, leapt through with her face shielded by her hands and kicked away the jagged edges. In moments they were all wandering around the lawn in front of a mental hospital. *Whoops.* Two unmarked black sedans pulled up. The back-passenger door flew open, Grey got out and sprinted towards her. She smiled and stepped into his arms as always. She felt him jiggling. *He was laughing.*

Grey whispered, "Did you really just break everyone out of an asylum?"

"I had help. There was this kid…" Lexy explained as she spun around looking for the girl who'd somehow unlocked everyone's doors… *She was gone.*

Grey led her back to the sedan as he explained, "They're flying us to our next job. The Aries Group will clean this up. Our bags are in the back. I'll fill you in on the way."

Lexy scanned the wandering pack of patients for the girl. Instinct prompted her to let her getaway. She opted to say nothing as she got into the backseat next to Grey. *She had a feeling she was going to run into Owen again. Hopefully, she was on their side.* As the black sedan pulled away from the mess she'd made, Lexy rested her head on Grey's shoulder as she whispered, "Where were you?"

He stroked her hair tenderly as he whispered back, "I'll always be right behind you. Next time maybe you could give me five minutes before you release all of the patients from a mental asylum?"

It wasn't her...She snuggled against her Handler and closed her eyes.

The sound of the barrier between them and the driver coming down woke her up as they arrived at an isolated landing strip.

"Well kids, we're here," the driver announced. "Make your way to the hangar on the left, you'll find your transportation detail in there."

They thanked him as they got out and lugged their bags over to the hangar. Lexy looked at Grey and asked, "Who had me? Do you know?"

Grey chuckled, as he explained, "Abaddon attempted to kidnap you in an ambulance. You woke up, beat the crap out of everyone and crashed it. Real first responders showed up before we could get to you. I guess you were still drugged up and hostile. They tasered you and brought you to the asylum because the holding cells were full at the station. You were only there for a couple of hours."

Lexy winced as she followed Grey into the hangar and quipped, "Self-control isn't my biggest strength."

"You don't say?" her Handler teased as they strolled towards the Aries group flight crew.

A lady she recognized shook Grey's hand and then cautiously reached out her hand. Lexy took it, gave it a firm shake and wittily greeted her, "Don't worry. There are no mental patients to break out here."

"Funny," the lady with the name tag that read Laura countered, "Pick a pod and tell me which sedation you want."

Grey climbed into one and said, "I'll take the gas."

Lexy got into a pod, and as they closed it, she declared, "I'll have the same." As gas filled her container, Lexy smiled. *She'd been knocked out a hilarious amount of times today. She forgot to ask where they were going.* Lexy was giggling as the lights went out. Dreams were always revealing things. She was in the room Tiberius brought her to. She'd been vaguely aware it was him carrying her as he placed her on the bed. He kissed her forehead. She opened her eyes, grabbed hold of him and whispered, "Don't go."

"Lexy, you're..." he attempted to say something. She cut Tiberius off by pressing her lips against his, and in seconds, he was all in. She deepened the seduction by darting her tongue between his parted lips. Tiberius groaned as he allowed her to roll him over, so she could be on top. The feverishly hot make-out session that followed was abruptly stopped by him as she undid his zipper, slid her hand into his pants and seductively slurred, "I bet you're always ready to go."

"We can't. Not like this," Tiberius mumbled against her lips as he forcefully removed her hand.

Lexy's eyes softened as she pouted, "Don't you want me?"

Tiberius kissed her forehead as he whispered, "So much it's making me lose sleep, but you're not yourself right now. Rain check?"

Her head felt heavy, so she rested it on his chest and closed her eyes. Her eyes popped open. *That's what happened. She could still hear the engine of the plane. She'd woken up way too early as always.*

A male voice spoke through the speakers of the pod, "We're only fifteen minutes out. Are you all good in there?"

"I'm alright," Lexy answered as her heart struggled to downplay what happened with Tiberius.

"Do you want to listen to music? Station preference?" The man's voice questioned.

"Surprise me," Lexy responded as music filled her pod.

She heard a male voice through the tune, "Out of sheer curiosity, why did you release all of those mental patients?"

She'd disabled the camera to her room and cut the lines, but there was a chance the Aries Group would still be able to watch footage of the hallway. For some reason, she felt obligated to protect Owen's identity. She replied, "What's your name?"

"Gary," he answered.

Lexy grinned and teased, "Do you believe in magic, Gary?"

"Let's just say my belief system has been altered by this job," Gary chuckled as he flicked a switch on the side of her pod.

A burst of cool refreshing oxygen filled her isolation chamber, making her instantly alert. They were beginning their descent. Lexy enquired, "How long have you been with the Aries Group?"

"Two years," Gary answered as she heard him messing around with Grey's chamber.

"Where are we?" Lexy laughed as the tires hit the runway.

Gary snickered, "It'll take all of five seconds to guess where we are."

Shit. They were somewhere cold, weren't they? The airplane stopped moving, her pod opened to a grinning Gary wearing a bright orange parka. *Holy shit, it was freezing.* He passed her a fluorescent orange jacket. Lexy's lips trembled as she hastily tugged on the parka and stammered, "We're in frigging Alaska, aren't we?"

Grey's voice piped in, "Gary, I'm dying over here. Pass me a coat."

She glanced over at her Handler as Gary passed him a jacket.

"Snazzy, not inconspicuous at all," Grey chuckled, zipping up his glaringly orange parka. Grey shook Gary's hand and ribbed, "It's always a pleasure flying Aries Group Air." Gary laughed as he led them out of the hangar to an idling truck.

Another guy strolled over and announced, "The keys are obviously in the ignition. You'll be staying at the Broken Mountain Inn. Your info is at the front desk. There are full Aries Group cards in the front zipper of your bags in the backseat. Gloves are inside the front seat console. Message Markus and tell him you've arrived. They ran into a glitch they need help with before you move on to your next job. The others are waiting for you guys at the hotel. The G.P.S is set up to direct you there."

With trembling lips and cold runny noses, they waved goodbye to the Aries Group agents. The men returned the gesture and hurried back to the hangar.

Chapter 5

This One Time In Alaska

Grey's lips were trembling as his voice broke through the silence, "Shit. My fingers are icicles." He slipped them into his pockets as they made their way to the vehicle. Grey asked, "Want me to drive?"

"Have at it my friend," Lexy replied as she started jogging through the snow. She quickly got into the passenger side and felt her painful face instantly defrost.

Grey pressed start on the G.P.S. On friend autopilot, he passed her gloves and a Kleenex from the console. While wiping his own nose, he enquired, "I had some weird flashes from yesterday while I was in that pod. Did I really have sex with a Triad?"

Lexy shrugged and replied, "You were naked when I woke you up. Your guess is as good as mine."

They drove for a few minutes in complete silence before he looked at her and hesitantly asked, "Did you?"

"No," she answered. "Look at the road before you get us in an accident."

He watched the road for a second before pressing the issue, "Were you naked?"

He didn't need the details, "No, Greydon! Watch the damn road!" Lexy looked away as sexy images came to mind.

"Did you see Tiberius?" he prodded.

She turned back to him and sighed, "You already know I did. Not that it's any of your business, but nothing happened." In the distance, they saw the lights from the hotel. Lexy exhaled. He'd be distracted by the others soon. *It had only really been a few days since they'd seen them, but so much had happened. It felt like longer. Orin.* As they pulled into the parking lot, Lexy got her game face on. They grabbed their bags and sprinted as quickly as they could for the lighted lobby, barely paying attention to the best part of being in Alaska.

Grey stopped her before she reached the door and laughed, "Come on, two minutes. It's incredible tonight."

Humouring him, she looked up at the breathtaking swirling display of heavenly light, as always, her eyes were drawn back to Grey. Even with unkempt hair, frozen purple cheeks and a runny nose, his joyous soul shone brighter than the northern lights.

"You're not even looking," he taunted. Grey pulled her into his puffy winter coat, and they embraced. He whispered, "The show's up there."

Lexy laughed as her heart overflowed. She answered, "For me, you're always way more entertaining than anyone or anything." Grey pulled away. Their eyes met in a moment of magic as their breath rose from their lips to the sky. *It felt like their spiritual tether was visible to the naked eye.* She'd been trying to reassure him, but those words meant so much more in her soul. *They would always belong to each other.*

Orin and Frost burst out of the lobby, raucously laughing. Her eyes met Orin's. *There was always the promise of something more in what was left unsaid.* Grey winked at her, shoved open the door and disappeared. He'd left her with nothing but his last visible breath entrusting her to his rival. The significance of what happened registered, she stared at the door for a second longer than she should. *She was being rude.* Lexy turned her gaze to her comically inebriated consort.

Orin held out his hand and urged, "Come on. Let's get you inside where it's warm."

Frost was flat on his back, making a snow angel. *She'd never seen him this happy. Frost and Kayn had felt like a bad idea, but maybe it wasn't? She'd had nights of feeling that love induced euphoria, but she deserved to make snow angels every day.*

"I know listening to your thoughts is a big no-no, but you do, you know. You deserve to make snow angels every day with someone who is also into making snow angels. See our resident playboy Frost over there, making angels like a damn fool."

She forgot how cold it was as she watched Frost enjoying the snow. *Frost was acting like her joy junkie Grey.*

Orin gave her a playful shove. Lexy wasn't prepared. She toppled over and landed on her side in the snow. Instead of helping her up, Orin laid next to her in the powdery white, and as they watched the northern lights dancing in the sky, he declared, "You know I understand this is casual. You don't have to filter yourself. We were friends for a long time before we were anything else, I respect your situation with Grey. It's complicated. Anything worth it usually is."

"That was a deep quote for your fireball whiskey level," Lexy chuckled.

"My deep thoughts are only enhanced by Fireball," Orin teased. He tossed a handful of powdery snow in her direction as he got up.

Lexy stood up, brushed herself off, and glanced at the hotel. *It was damn cold. She wasn't drunk like they were.*

"Even while drunk, I know how to decipher girl code. I'll meet you inside. I'd better go wake up Frosty, the snow angel making man. It looks like he passed out," Orin said as he waved her to the door.

Lexy laughed as she rushed towards the warmth of the lobby, but as she reached for the handle, a flicker of something made her stop. She turned back to the guy who'd become more than her friend and watched Orin's hilarious attempts to wake Frost. *Frosty the snow angel making man. That was funny.*

The door opened. Lily grabbed her jacket and towed her into the lobby, giggling, "Get in here and explain yourself. We've been making bets all afternoon as to why you did it."

Why she did what? The list was longer than usual today.

"Why in the hell would you break thirty-five people out of a mental institution?" Lily clarified.

Oh, that. Lexy inhaled the heated lobby air. Her skin felt like it was thawing. She opened her mouth wide, slapped her cheeks a couple of times to get her circulation going and sparred, "In my defence, I was drugged multiple times yesterday."

"So, is that the official story?" Lily impishly interrogated as she motioned for her to follow. "I have your room card. I was just waiting for you to come inside because it's horrific out there."

Lexy walked down the hall with Lily until she stopped moving and passed her a key card as she explained, "As per usual, you are sharing a room with Grey."

His bag was on one of the twin beds. As she took in the room's décor, her mind was flooded with incredible memories. *Everything was the same from the curtains to the bedspreads. They'd ended up in bed together the last time they stayed here.* Her mind fed her an image…*They were at a table in the pub watching the snow falling outside. Each table had a mini jukebox. She'd known what would happen as she put her quarter in and chose a song that always triggered Grey's feelings. She hadn't done that in a while.*

"I'll wait for you. Get ready," Lily announced. She flopped down on the bed and grabbed for the remote.

Lexy chucked her jacket on the bed Grey chose as she ribbed, "You guys have been drinking for hours, haven't you?"

Intently changing the channels, Lily snapped out of her electronic stupor and answered a question she hadn't asked, "Yes. Everyone is in the pub."

Lexy chuckled as she peeled off her clothes, slipped on new jeans and borrowed a black hoodie from Grey's bag. She had no intention of putting herself out there tonight in any direction. *Her heart was heavy. This room made her long for what they could never be. She couldn't go backwards anymore, but she also couldn't move forward…Not here. She'd be violating the beautiful memories they'd made. Even if, in the end, they were only hers.* Lily had followed her into the bathroom. Her stunning raven-haired friend was leaning against the door's frame, watching her get ready.

Lily marched over and taunted, "You are aware it didn't matter how much Kayn downplayed her looks, Frost still fell for her. You might as well take off that hoodie. Are you wearing it to deter Grey or Orin?"

Gazing at her reflection, Lexy messed her hair and smirked as she bluntly answered, "Both."

"We can skip the pub?" Lily offered. "Let's stay in the room, gossip and order in?"

She could avoid an uncomfortable situation. Lexy grinned at her reflection.

Laughing, Lily suggested, "Pizza?"

"Pizza sounds perfect," Lexy admitted as she wandered out of the washroom, snatched a menu off the nightstand and made herself comfy on the bed.

They ate a disgusting amount of pizza as Lexy vented about Grey's jealousy and inevitable makeup. *She opted to leave out the drug-induced X-rated make-out session with Tiberius. She wasn't sure if it was real or just a racy hallucination.* Lily regaled the exploits of the newbies. They'd been left to their own devices as a sink or swim kind of thing, and they were messing up in ridiculous ways. *There was a learning curve to this job with no easy route to experience but time.*

"How does it feel knowing you're not the only Dragon in our Clan?" Lily enquired as she passed her a tiny bottle of rum.

"I haven't had much time to think about it," Lexy admitted. She winced as she took the bottle and cracked the seal. *Rum was not her friend.* They drank the contents of the minibar, giggling about their crazy afterlives until they were tipsy. After finishing the alcohol in the minibar, she ceased to worry about awkward situations. They decided it was time to dance. Neither one had any gum, so they ate toothpaste and practically skipped down the hall to the pub. They were ridiculously wasted as they entered the bar. The girls uncoordinatedly rammed through the crowd, apologizing way too aggressively. *It was going to be too hot to wear Grey's hoodie once she started dancing.* They shimmied through the rough and tumble patrons. The Ankh boys were at the bar chatting up locals. Jenna and Arrianna were already on the dance floor, waving them over. They danced over to the guys. Lexy stripped off Grey's hoodie and loudly announced, "This is yours! I don't want it!" She launched it at Grey's face mid his attempted flirtation with a hot blonde and danced away. They were twirling around the dance floor laughing, having the best time ever when Grey grabbed Lexy and stopped her from jumping around.

Grey yelled over the music, "You're wasted!"

"Most definitely!" Lexy hollered back, focused on where his hand was touching her skin.

"Did you forget something?" her Handler interjected as the lights dimmed.

Offended by the disapproval in his tone, Lexy shoved him away and flippantly remarked, "If you want to take that thing back to the room, I'll crash somewhere else to sleep."

"How much did you drink? You can't even articulate a sentence," Grey calmly responded.

What an Asshat. "Like you even know what that word means," Lexy fired back, looking for her drunk friend back up. *They'd all scattered. Chicken shits.*

"Do whatever the hell you want. I'll do the same. Just look down at what you're wearing first," her Handler prompted.

She didn't want to look. Humouring Grey, Lexy peered down. *Whoops, she wasn't wearing a bra under her t-shirt. She recalled taking it off to get cozy.*

Grey passed her his hoodie as he questioned, "What was that all about? You show up drunk and toss my hoodie in my face? Did I do something? I thought we were all good?"

"You would," Lexy mumbled. "Just go pick up someone random and leave me alone, Greydon."

"Come on, let's go back to the room and talk this out, you're rather exposed," Grey sweetly suggested, intimately clutching her waist.

Lexy squirmed out of his sexy grasp as she countered, "Nobody cares! I may never wear a bra again!" The song changed. *Oh, no. Why was this slow song playing? She'd used this song to trigger his feelings for her in the past. She'd foolishly done this for much longer than sanity should have allowed.* Grey's eyes glinted with adoration. He smiled, and she lost the will to argue as her resolve dissipated like a warm breath in the Alaskan air. *She was changing this. She couldn't allow herself to be lured back in by his endearing ways and swoon-worthy smile. He didn't understand what he was doing to her.*

Grey pulled her close and whispered in her ear, "What did I do? Why are we fighting again?"

Emotion surged through her. Lexy swallowed it down as though it were possible to rid herself of how right it felt to be his arms. *They may argue, but in the end, he was her person. Their love couldn't be fought or bartered away. Fighting against the instinctual pull of their souls was like putting a bandage on a wound that would never stop bleeding.*

In response to her inner-commentary, Grey nuzzled her ear as he gave her his breathy confession, "I love you too, Lex... Always."

He meant as a friend, but the seeds of attraction had been planted, she felt it as the song began working its magic. They slowly swayed to the music. Out of nowhere, he dipped her, and she laughed. *Her unrestrained chest had done hilarious things. It was not sexy at all.*

"We won't do that again," Grey snickered.

What had she been thinking? Truth be told, she hadn't been thinking at all to stop herself from beating this situation to death in her mind.

He whispered in her ear, "This song always reminds me of you."

She knew this... It felt like she was fighting to swim out to sea against the waves of her emotions as they aggressively washed her to shore. Her struggle ceased, the only sensation was the beating of his heart in time with hers and the pull of their spiritual devotion erasing any form of self-preservation. *This was how it happened. She'd given herself to him completely decades ago, and she couldn't take it back.*

"Can we just go back to the room and talk?" Grey asked as a faster song began. The dance floor filled.

"Of course," Lexy replied. As he took her hand and led her through the crowd. She caught a glimpse of Orin's concerned expression as they passed. They left the pub and wandered back to the room full of memories that only she carried through time. Her heart began pleading for salvation. *Don't do this. It's not too late.* Grey opened the door to their suite and went inside, her feet remained firmly planted in the doorway. *If she entered, emotions would prevail over ration. Every time she did this, she lost a little of what she'd gained.* Suddenly sober, Lexy watched Grey rifling through his bag. *He hadn't noticed she was still in the hallway.*

Chapter 6

Plausible Deniability

They were standing just off the side of the dimly lit dance floor. Orin looked at Jenna and accused, "Why would you do that?"

"I don't need to explain myself to you, Orin," Jenna remarked and abruptly left mid-conversation.

His opinion meant nothing to her anymore. As she walked away, Orin stormed after her and vehemently barbed, "There are less shitty ways to cockblock your ex-boyfriend."

Offended, Jenna spun around and countered, "Everything isn't about you."

"How long are you going to pretend you don't love me?" he questioned.

With emotion-filled eyes, she answered honestly, "For as long as it takes."

Orin pursued her into the lobby, ranting, "Don't you dare walk away. You don't get to drop bombs anymore without explaining yourself."

"I don't have to explain shit to you!" Jenna blasted. "We broke up twenty years ago!" She hastily fumbled, trying to unlock the door to her room as she commentated, "You never listen. You never did."

"I'm listening right now," Orin calmly asserted.

Jenna looked at him and sighed, "The lock's sticking."

Orin held out his hand. *It was nice to know she still found him useful for something.* Jenna gave him her key. As he struggled to unlock her door, he explained, "A thousand years together can't be just swept under a rug. We were more than lovers, we were friends. Try treating me like one. You shut me down every time I have an opinion. We have to work together." He handed Jenna the key to her unlocked door.

Smiling, she clarified, "This is the problem, we're not together anymore. I don't have to pretend to run my visions by you. You aren't owed an explanation."

That last barb was a direct hit. She'd been placating his ego for centuries. He took a step back as he apologized, "I'm sorry being in love with me was such a horrible experience for you."

Jenna's eyes softened as she countered, "Come on, you know that's not what I meant. We loved each other, and it was incredible, at least sixty percent of the time, but that shouldn't be enough, for either of us."

She wasn't wrong. Orin nodded as he lovingly caressed her cheek, intending to voice his agreement.

Before he could, Jenna ignorantly brushed his hand away and mumbled, "Go away, Orin. This isn't easy for me either. Listen, we've had this conversation countless times. We both need to move on."

Now, he was pissed-off again. He didn't need the speech, but after that, he couldn't resist pushing her buttons. Orin placed his hand on the door to stop her from closing it and seductively asserted, "Why?"

"Because, I'm Ankh's Oracle, and it's an order," Jenna declared.

Time to give her a reality check. "If you're done with me, why are you stopping me from moving on?" Orin sparred as he removed his hand and watched his words sink in.

Visibly hurt, Jenna angrily slammed the door in his face.

Orin was giggling on the inside as he strolled away from his ex's room. *He was trying to move on. If she hadn't pulled that crap with the song... He'd always been fascinated by Lexy's aggressive nature. She was fearless, smoking hot and psychotic enough to keep it interesting.* When Orin turned down the hall and saw her standing there, it felt like fate.

Just as Lexy was about to go into the room, she saw Orin coming. *It felt like he'd tossed her a life jacket.* She called out, "Are you lost?" Curious, Grey stuck his head out as he approached.

Orin announced, "Actually, I was looking for you. I was just heading back to my room to order something to eat...Hungry?"

Instantly switching gears, Grey smiled and offered, "There's pizza in here. They must have ordered it earlier. Come in. Have some."

Lexy turned away from Grey and silently mouthed the words, "I owe you one."

Placing an arm possessively around her, Orin humorously clarified, "I'm not exactly in the mood for pizza, Grey."

"Oh...Ohhh, I get it," Grey exclaimed. He smiled knowingly and sent Lexy on her way, "We'll have that talk later. I might go back to the pub. You guys have fun. Enjoy your...Whatever." Grey chuckled as he left.

They stood there until Grey disappeared at the end of the hall. Orin removed his arm and replied, "You're welcome."

"Thank you," Lexy sighed.

Orin teased, "Grab what you need. I guess you're having a sleepover in my room. As friends, of course."

Relief washed over her. Lexy grabbed her bag and looked back at the room full of memories before closing the door on the past. They silently wandered down the hall to Orin's room. He held open the door. Without hesitating, Lexy went in, tossed her bag on the floor, and asked, "Did you purposely come looking for me?"

"I didn't care for the sentimental music ploy Jenna pulled. Yes, erasing his memory may have been the right thing to do, for Grey. I get it, he's your Handler, but it shouldn't always be you making the sacrifices. Haven't you ever just looked at him and said, listen Grey, we've been sleeping together for like thirty years. Your memory gets erased every time we do it, and I have to suffer through the aftermath?"

"Ironically, I have. Sometimes, we last a few weeks in a platonic relationship, but even if we don't consummate anything, the romantic feelings are erased as soon as he dies," Lexy explained. She patted the bed next to her and urged, "Come on, spill it. Something happened tonight, I can tell. There has to be a reason you came looking for me."

"Let me order first, I'm famished," Orin admitted as he scoured the menu on the nightstand.

"Why didn't we just take the leftover pizza?" Lexy enquired. She peered over his shoulder to see if there was anything that interested her.

Orin chuckled, "I can't take the girl and the pizza. That's a dick move." He dialled the number, and as it rang, he asked her if she'd made up her mind.

He meant about their midnight snack. His order sounded good. Lexy answered, "I'll have what you're having." As soon as Orin hung up, she urged, "Okay, spill..."

"There's really not much to tell. I was furious over that stunt Jenna pulled with the sappy love song. We ended up in our usual argument. I say, why don't you love me anymore? She reminds me that we've been broken up for decades. I don't know why I keep banging my head against the wall. It's silly, really. It's not like things were ever perfect between us. A thousand years of dysfunction with moments of amazing... That's what we were."

Giving Orin a sympathetic pat on the back, Lexy bluntly responded, "Emotions are stupid and complicated."

Orin chuckled as he got up and announced, "Hold that thought."

He disappeared into the bathroom. She looked around with a grin. *Oh, the irony!* This room was exactly like the one she had with Grey, except for the queen-sized bed. *With her luck, this was the actual room.* The burgundy comforter, curtains and rose-coloured carpeting were identical. *Orin helped her break the cycle. He'd tossed her a life preserver to save her from drowning in emotions. Dragons didn't usually need help, but tonight she had, and it had come from an unexpected place.* Lexy stroked the comforter and smiled as Orin strolled out of the bathroom shirtless. *Oh my.* The décor of the room ceased to matter. *Orin saw past her connection with her Handler, it was an appealing quality. It simplified their situation. Would he still be around when she was ready for something more? Did that matter? He had the sexiest abs.*

Orin grabbed a tiny bottle out of the minibar and teased, "I can hear you overthinking everything from here." Someone knocked on the door. Orin's eyes widened.

It wasn't Grey. Lexy suggested, "Maybe it's our room service. That was fast." As he chatted, she noticed his word search on the counter. *It was sort of endearing that he still did these.* She grabbed it, unclipped his page keeping pen and began circling words.

Catching her in the act as he wheeled the cart into the room, Orin scolded, "Hands off, Lex. I've been working on that obsessively for weeks."

"That's adorable," she provoked. He left the cart behind, leapt on the bed, and snatched it out of her grasp. "I finished the page you were stuck on," Lexy baited with a grin.

He slowly shook his head, reprimanding, "It's rude to play with other people's toys without asking."

She shrugged and giggled as Orin playfully swatted her with his rolled-up word search. He tossed it, began tickling her and they rolled around laughing. Playtime abruptly ended with him on top, pinning her to the mattress. They were both out of breath.

With eyes full of longing, Orin whispered, "It's a bad idea to do this tonight."

"We probably shouldn't," Lexy agreed as her fingertips seductively explored his muscular biceps. She felt his rigid manhood against her jeans and her resolve faltered. She exhaled his name, "Orin." He naughtily ran his thumb over the sparse material concealing her painfully erect nipples. She arched her back and gasped.

He roguishly whispered, "It was a bold move going braless tonight. Were you trying to seduce your Handler?"

The inappropriate direction of the conversation was completely doing it for her. She confessed, "I wasn't planning to go out. I was…" She cried out as he bit her nipple through her shirt. She clutched his hair as he taunted her with his teeth. He naughtily lifted her top, revealing her ample ravaged peaks. Her lips parted in anticipation. She closed her eyes as he purposely missed the mark and softly kissed her abdomen instead.

He undid her zipper, tugged her jeans down and whispered, "We have to be quiet." Orin slid his hand between her thighs as he promised, "We're leaving this underwear on. No regrets."

Her reasons for not doing this ceased to matter as her body responded to his touch. She gasped his name as he caressed the material between her thighs until she began wantonly pleading for him. Chuckling, he stopped touching her. She kept her eyes shut, willing him to keep going with every inch of her being. She felt the delicious moist heat of his breath between her legs as he continued toying with her until she felt the rising tide surging to the shore. Lexy gasped his name, clutching his hair.

Orin whispered against her panties, "Healer to Healer, I'll never leave you wanting."

His lips and tongue continued their treacherous games as his palms on her abdomen grew warmer. She was lost in rapture as his Healing ability ignited her flesh with tingling intense pleasure until she was wantonly squirming on his bed aching, writhing in ecstasy. Euphoria exploded in her core and rippled through her being, curling her toes. She loudly cried out his name.

Orin leapt up and muffled her cries with his hand, chuckling, "If everyone hears us, we won't be able to pretend nothing happened." He removed his palm, kissed her lips gently and taunted, "Baby, you were all pent up." Every inch of her was vibrating as Orin got up and declared, "I'll be right back."

"Don't go far," she flirted, keeping her eyes trained on his impressive rear as he walked away.

"It's not always easy being the good guy," Orin laughed as he closed the bathroom door.

Lexy bit her lip as she thought about how he'd unselfishly pleasured her. *She needed to use the washroom too. Her panties were soaked, and her jeans were at her knees.* She was strangely proud of herself as she squirmed out of them and removed her underwear. *Commando it is.* She heard the shower and smiled as she tugged her jeans on. *He was serious about the plausible deniability thing.* Lexy stretched on the comforter and grinned. *She wasn't the least bit concerned about the décor of the room now.* While waiting for Orin's return, she snuggled into the pillow and blissfully closed her eyes. She stirred to the warmth of Orin's arms. *She must have dozed off. It wasn't Grey, but it felt good.* She allowed herself to drift back to sleep.

Awakening to the dinging microwave. Lexy stretched as she opened her eyes. A content smile spread across her face.

Orin sang, "Rise and shine. Your late-night snack slash breakfast is heated up on the table."

That was the best sleep she'd had in weeks, maybe longer. She should be feeling rough this morning, but she felt terrific. Apparently, naughty time with a Healer cured many ills. Lexy wandered over and peeked at what they'd forgotten to eat the night before. *Microwaved steak. It might be alright.*

Orin peered over the top of his newspaper as she sat down and taunted, "Don't overthink it. We're friends. You'll have to eat quickly, we're leaving for the next job in a little over an hour. On a funny note, Jenna sent Grey over here to make sure we were up and to tell us we were leaving."

Lexy paused with a cube of steak on her fork poised in front of her open lips. *Oh no.*

"I was already dressed," he assured. "You were fully clothed and sound asleep, looking as pure as the driven snow. You're welcome, by the way. I told him I slept on the couch. There's no drama to deal with, you're in the clear."

"Do you have drama to deal with?" Lexy enquired as she devoured her breakfast, which wasn't half bad. He placed the paper down, grabbed his coffee and grinned. *Oh, that stinker came to get her to make Jenna jealous.* Lexy attempted to snatch his paper to smack him.

Maneuvering out of the way with the morning news in his hand, he swore, "I promise it was all about the song she played to trigger Grey."

Orin wasn't one to make false promises. Smiling, she said, "Thank you for having my back, both last night and this morning."

"That's what friends are for," Orin replied as he got up, walked over, gave her a buddy kiss on the top of her head and teased, "It's probably a good thing you fell asleep before I got out of the bathroom though."

Lexy looked up at him and apologized, "Sorry."

"No apologies necessary. Sleeping next to you was nice," Orin assured. He grinned as he patted down her freaky morning hair and prompted, "You should have a shower though if you don't want Frost and Lily to know everything. Those succubae, siren folk have a sixth sense about this stuff."

She swallowed her last bite of steak and couldn't resist messing with him as she walked away. Lexy stripped off her clothes and tossed them on the floor on her way to the bathroom. *It was fun playing with someone that had a reaction until she realised the door didn't lock.* She was standing there, staring at the unlockable door. *A part of her wanted him to come after her.* The hotel room door closed, she peered out of the bathroom. *The room was empty.*

Chapter 7

Unexpected Allies

Grey looked unimpressed as Lexy arrived in the lobby. He held out his hand. She assumed he was offering to carry her bag and attempted to pass it to him.

"You need to return your room key," he clarified. He pointed at the bright orange coat on the floor by the desk and curtly said, "That's yours. They're waiting for us in the RV." He walked away without another word.

Lexy placed her keys on the desk. *He was acting like a jealous tool, this ought to be fun.* She quickly did up the jacket and raced out to the idling RV.

Markus opened the door and waved her in, "Quickly! The heat's escaping!"

She darted inside. Markus slammed the door and directed her upfront as he announced, "We appear to have some drama going on this morning. Jenna and Grey have expressed interest in having some time away from their usual partners. So, we'll be switching up our driving buddies today. Lexy and Orin, you are the first, second, and third shift driving the RV. Grey and Jenna will be taking turns driving the truck. The rest of us will be trading off with only them." Markus looked directly at Lexy as he passive-aggressively stated, "You've been busy, haven't you?"

Well, she couldn't deny it. Was she in trouble for the mortals in the pub or freeing the patients in the asylum? Orin wasn't even there? Grey was upset because she'd spent the night in Orin's room. And for five hundred dollars, the definition of irony was… There was no point in reacting. "No problem," Lexy replied. *Spending a day with Orin sounded way better than a forced reconciliation with her pouty Handler.* She maneuvered her way to the front and smiled as she took the seat beside her ridiculously good-looking sleepover buddy. *This wasn't much of a punishment.*

Orin started the engine. While grinning, he whispered, "Hey there, my partner in crime."

"Why are you in trouble?" Lexy enquired as they pulled out of the parking lot.

Orin gave her a look as he whispered, "Jenna knew I didn't agree with her playing that song. She thinks I went to your room and took you out of the equation."

Gratitude was a confusing emotion, she didn't want to owe anybody anything.

Orin responded to her inner-commentary, "Selfless acts are free of charge. You really do have issues, don't you?"

That was the understatement of the year. Lexy leaned as close as she could and whispered, "I couldn't find my underwear."

"I have them," Orin whispered back as he slid his hand into his pocket and revealed a hint of her black lacy panties.

He was a kinky guy.

Orin grinned as he clarified, "They were on the floor when Grey showed up this morning. I had to hide them, and yes, I'll give them back."

They were both giggling as they began the journey to the next job. They spent a good portion of the morning, asking each other random questions. *It felt a little like what she'd imagined a first date to be. He'd taken a two-decade leave from his duties, but she'd only been around him occasionally in the twenty years prior. Healers were rarely headed to the same jobs back then. She'd always seen Jenna and Orin as a package deal. That's also probably how he'd seen her and Grey.*

"Batman or Deadpool?" Orin enquired.

She snapped out of her thoughts and countered, "Always Deadpool."

"Really? For some reason, I was certain you'd say, Batman," Orin teased as they carried on down the highway with trees in their peripheral vision.

They played this game all day long until it felt like they knew all sorts of weird random stuff about each other. *She now knew he preferred seafood to chicken or beef and that his favourite colour was green.* He'd been staring into her green eyes as he answered. She had the sense he was flirting. *She knew football was his favourite sport but suspected Orin meant the European version, which was referred to as soccer by people from North America. His favourite era of music was the same as hers. They had a lot in common. He enjoyed reading Science Fiction and Paranormal Fantasy and had absolutely no desire to be mortal again. Neither did she.* At first, the road trip purgatory had been enjoyable. After a twelve-hour stint of driving with only convenience store stops to stretch their legs, they were over the question and answer game. As they listened to music, Grey and Jenna were chatting at the table within earshot. *That would suck.* Lexy heard Orin's response in her mind, '*It definitely would. Maybe we should break it up and apologize?*' The truck ahead pulled off the highway. *Suddenly, their stubborn little stand became worthless.* Her heart ached as she heard Grey's laughter. *It was all fun and games until reality sunk in, and karma gave her heart a well-timed stomp.* They followed the truck down a precarious gravel road until they turned into a campsite. They heard Jenna telling Markus, she'd be sharing her cabin with Grey and remained seated up front. Their hearts were lodged in their throats. *Well, this backfired rather epically.*

"We're morons," Orin muttered, turning to look at her.

Lexy undid her seatbelt and sighed dramatically, "Yes, the verdict is in, we're idiots." She glanced at him. They burst out laughing as they shimmied out of the front and saw the empty RV. *Nobody bothered to wait. Alright...Okay. They'd made their point, and then some.* They opened the door to find their Clan gathered. There was a moment of peculiar silence, and then, everyone howled laughing.

Grey was beaming like a mischievous adolescent as he obnoxiously danced his way over to Lexy. He held out his hand and teased, "Come on. Did you honestly think we were just going to take off and leave you?"

Lexy was too relieved to be upset.

Thoroughly impressed, Orin commented, "Well played." He shook his head at Jenna as she motioned him over.

"Alright, everyone," Markus announced. "The practical joke's over. I instructed them to leave the keys to the cabins under each mat at the front door. Lexy, after Orin's done having a chat with Jenna, it's your turn. Make sure you do before you take off with Grey. Shake that long drive out of your system and go to sleep early. Work starts before dawn."

That practical joke had taken her resolve to move on, chewed it up and spit it out like the pure foolishness that it was. Lexy turned away from the group and took in where they were. They'd driven twelve hours south, but it was still chilly. Everything was green. Birds were chirping, there was a trickling stream close by. *She remembered this place. Truth be told, after more than forty years, she had memories' nearly everywhere.* Feeling guilty for various reasons, Lexy sat on a log, requiring a minute to regain her composure. *She wasn't going to be able to use handy life tools such as ration until she mellowed out. She was an adult. She shouldn't feel guilty, he wouldn't. It felt like there was always a war being waged within her between logic and emotion. She was so tired of feeling angry, bitter, guilty and lost.* A squirrel with full cheeks scurried up a tree, she snapped out of her frustration. *Wouldn't it be lovely to be a squirrel? She'd spend her days collecting nuts and berries. Being alone was uncomplicated, and in its simplicity was a sense of inner peace. There was nothing to lose when you were alone. Orin had joked around about her having issues, but who wouldn't if they were her. She'd been kidnapped at the tender age of eleven and managed to survive for five long torturous years held captive by Abaddon. They tried to destroy her, but she rose from the dead as a Dragon to rid the world of them all. After that, she'd lost her humanity, but perhaps she just wasn't able to believe in anyone or anything anymore. After being alone in the forest for years, humanity was a foreign concept. In the time before her Handler domesticated her, she'd been a Wild Thing.* Her eyes were drawn to Grey's, it was like she'd given the invisible rope a tug with only a glance. He left his conversation with Frost, wandered over and sat down beside her.

Grey placed an arm around her, snuggled her against him, kissed her cheek, and teased, "You didn't really think Jenna was just going to fall into bed with me, did you? She's an Oracle, she'd see me coming a mile away."

He was trying to make her laugh.

Grey started his apology, "I'm sorry, I was just trying to lighten up the situation. I've been a dick lately. Of course, Tiberius is going to flirt with you. Why wouldn't he? You're beautiful and amazing. I came back alone last night hoping you'd be there so we'd have a chance to talk this tension out. When you stayed in Orin's room, I spent the whole night overthinking everything until I made myself sick. I get it, Orin's a good-looking dude, and I've been unreasonably jealous. I wanted to kick Orin's ass this morning, but when I saw you in bed sleeping peacefully, I felt like an idiot. Jenna spent all day talking me through my irrational behaviour, I'm sorry. I've been ridiculous. We need to fix this distance between us."

"Can we talk?" Jenna interrupted Grey's apology.

Lexy got up. She looked back at Grey and suggested, "Pick a cabin and come back for me."

"On it," Grey answered. He jumped up and left the two girls alone.

As soon as Grey was out of earshot, Jenna began to explain, "I spent the last twelve hours trying to talk Grey out of his feelings."

"I know," Lexy admitted. *His feelings. His issues. What about her feelings? What about her heart?*

Jenna smiled warmly as she replied to Lexy's inner dialogue, "Resentment comes in waves and builds over time until it's an insurmountable wall. You can't build walls to keep your Handler out, or he can't fulfill his duties within the Clan."

His duties as the Dragon whisperer. She was more than just a Wild Thing. Lexy sighed as she reached down, grabbed a pebble and pitched it into the bushes. *She was a woman with wants, needs and desires. It made her want to struggle against the leash her Handler had on her soul. Yes...Resentment was what she was feeling.* They sat together in silence as Lexy continued rifling stones.

Frost's frustrated voice came from the bushes, "Stop throwing rocks, damn it!"

Awkward. Lexy mumbled, "Whoops. Didn't know he was there."

Jenna plucked a dandelion out of the ground as she started talking, "This flower has so many uses. The milk treats ringworm and eczema without the hormonal side effects of prescription drugs. The flower itself helps control blood sugar levels, it's a diuretic. It's really a miraculous plant, but the milk stains your clothes, and the seeds can aggressively take over a lawn."

Where was she going with this?

"I'm getting to the point," Jenna laughed as she passed the flower to Lexy. "We all have our purposes even though sometimes they're unclear. Grey is the stem, and you, are the flower."

This better not be a Sex ED speech.

Jenna smiled as she continued to talk, "You've needed Grey for a long time. I know you feel like you're finally ready to float away like a dandelion seed on the wind, but eventually, you'll have to land. Your flower needs roots to attach to the earth. Your love for Grey is what solidifies your connection to us when the Dragon takes over. It's unfortunate that fate keeps changing the rules, but you were granted a second chance at life because you vowed to act as sacrificial lambs for the greater good. Personal growth isn't in your contract. Last night, I was fed a vision that prompted me to create a scenario where you'd willingly press Grey's reset. I know you've been trying to move on, but ultimately, I also have orders to follow. I felt bad about it. I know how it must have looked, and Orin's reaction didn't help, but I need you to understand that my choices are based on visions and I'm supposed to react accordingly."

This made sense. Jenna was their Clan's version of a magic eight ball. It wasn't fair, but it didn't have to be. Lexy met Jenna's eyes as she asked, "Is this ever going to get easier?"

"Yes… But first, it's going to get much worse," was the Oracle's brutally honest reply. Jenna gave Lexy's leg a reassuring squeeze and stood up just as Grey appeared in the distance. She smiled and added, "For the record, it's been over two decades since we broke up. It took leaving the Clan for twenty years and a lot of counselling from Azariah to find the strength within myself to permanently pull the plug on our relationship. We weren't right for each other. It was a daily struggle for both of us. It wasn't an easy decision, but I'm confident it was the right one. This thing with Orin could turn out to be a good thing when the timing is right. Orin can do relief pitcher, just be blunt about other attractions and try to be patient with your Handler."

Oh, good, Dragons were well known for their patience. Jenna smiled back at her as she wandered away. *She'd totally heard her inner dialogue. That wasn't the ex-girlfriend conversation she'd expected. Orin really didn't give Jenna enough credit.*

Grey walked over, took her hand and asked, "Ready to go?"

She took Grey's hand, struggling to shut the replay of their conversation down in her head.

As they strolled down the oddly peaceful trail, he lightheartedly placed his arm around her and apologized, "For what it's worth, I know I've been a complete shithead."

Her eyes darted his way, Lexy grinned, opting out of a response. *The forest smelled amazing.* Magical looking particles of dust were floating in the sun's rays as they passed through streams of light, filtering through the branches. As they approached the cabin, Grey released her hand to open the door. He gallantly stood aside as she walked in. "I'm curious…Why this one?" Lexy innocently enquired.

Grey placed his hand against the wall as he answered, "I don't know. They're all the same on the inside, aren't they?" He leapt onto the queen-sized bed and made himself comfortable.

They weren't. Not really. She searched through the cupboards, stocked with canned soups, stews and fresh bread. The fridge was full of groceries. *The Aries Group had gone all out, she was too hungry to decide.*

Wandering up behind her, placed his hands intimately on her hips, peered over her shoulder and asked, "Does anything look good?"

Relaxing against him, she sighed, "I can't decide."

He maneuvered past her, snatched a bag of chips off the shelf, grabbed drinks from the fridge and declared, "I brought a laptop. Let's have a snack and leave the big decisions until after we've taken the edge off. I have some DVDs from the RV. I had a feeling there was no cable."

How fascinating, he always retained the most peculiar pieces of wiped memories. She brought the fruit bowl with her, placed it on the nightstand and ate grapes as Grey held up each DVD. *They were all gratuitously violent, slasher films. He knew how to seduce a Dragon, he'd been doing it for decades.* "You decide," Lexy announced as she sauntered off to the bathroom.

"Don't spend all night in there!" He hollered after her.

"I'll only be a minute," Lexy countered as she closed the door, and right at eye level was G R adores L A. She wistfully traced their initials with her finger, recalling the night he'd carved it. *Grey Riley adores Lexy Abrelle.*

He knocked on the door and asked, "Would you rather watch something funny?"

Lexy placed the palm of her hand over their initials and responded, "I'll watch anything." The doorknob turned, she stepped back as he barged in.

"You're not even using the washroom," he humorously accused as he looked at the back of the door, and right away, he noticed their initials. Grinning, Grey affirmed, "Well, that goes without saying, I've always adored you, but I totally don't recall carving our initials into this door. Weird. How drunk were we last time we stayed here?" He gave her hair a brotherly tussle.

Lexy swatted him away and countered, "We weren't drunk when you carved it." *Sometimes, she just couldn't help herself.*

The sentiment was lost on Grey. He was fiddling with his phone. He looked up and declared, "Everyone's in Frost's hot tub. Why does he always get the best cabin?"

"Seniority," Lexy replied. On autopilot, she grabbed a towel, knowing Grey usually wanted to hang out with everyone else.

He looked up from his phone and exclaimed, "I thought we were watching a movie?"

She put her towel back and teased, "Then stop playing with your phone."

Grey grinned, and she knew what he was going to do. He sang, "The first one under the covers picks the movie!"

They raced out of the bathroom, playfully shoving each other, giggling like children as they scrambled under the covers. They snuggled under the blankets and settled in with their munchies. Grey won by a hair, so he chose.

Chapter 8

Dragon Munchies

Before the movie was done, they'd devoured a few large bags of chips and almost everything in the fruit bowl. She'd just taken a bite of the last golden delicious apple when her stomach cramped. *She'd eaten a lot.* Her gut twisted again. *This time it was obvious. Shit.* She looked at Grey and confessed, "I think the job might be starting early."

"Oh, you can't be serious?" Grey complained.

She held her breath to see if he felt it.

"Nothing's happening to me yet. Are you sure it's not indigestion?" Grey answered. He placed a hand on his stomach and winced.

The expression on his face told her everything she needed to know. "What are we doing? What's the job?"

"It's for the Aries Group. We're supposed to be clearing out an infestation. Campers have been going missing. They sent in a search team and received disturbing footage before they lost contact. Whatever it is... It's coming."

"You think?" Lexy taunted as she leapt up, dashed over to the drawers and began rifling through them for something for Grey to use as a weapon. She tossed him a potato masher and said, "Get your game face on."

"Hilarious," Grey sparred, rolling his eyes.

Jenna and Orin burst through the door. Grey was standing there, holding a potato masher.

Orin jousted, "Creative weapon choice."

"Sorry! Obviously, my timing was a touch off," Jenna apologized as she tossed a blade to Grey. It sailed past him because he was still clutching the masher.

The rest of their fully armed Clan barged in. Markus began barking out orders, "Bags of salt under the sink! Go! Now! Circle the cabin! We're not sure what we're dealing with! Healers stay in the cabin! We'll need you to find our bodies later. Grey, stay with the Healers, you'll need to bring Lexy back after this one. Nobody leaves this cabin until the siren goes off."

Grey scrambled to pick up the weapon. He caught up with Lexy, and as they embraced, he vowed, "I'll always bring you back."

"I never doubt that," she affirmed as they parted.

Markus barked out, "The force field is up! We've been told the area has been cleared of mortals, but as you know, it rarely is. As of five minutes ago, nobody comes in or gets out! All three Clans have people on the outskirts of the ten-mile radius, so we can quickly cover more ground. Lexy, it's Dragon time. We'll be shadowing you until we know what we're dealing with and how to kill it. The hunt is on!"

Hunt... Lexy's heart raced. *This was going to be fun.*

Markus met Lexy's eyes. He commanded, "Kill everyone that isn't Ankh."

She nodded. *Was Tiberius out there?*

Orin leaned in and whispered, "If he's smart, he'll steer clear."

She watched Orin jog back into the cabin. *He was right. It didn't matter. Nothing did.* Grey salted the doorway and the invisible cord attaching their souls severed. She turned away from her Handler and stared into the ominous darkness of the woods as her mind travelled back to the dark farm and flickered through the sordid devastation until she climbed out of the well and reached for the axe. *This was how she resurrected the Dragon within.* Her heart solidified, growing heavier until it sunk into its protective void. Free of conscience, the predatory being within her reverted to its instinct-driven self. Like a Wild Thing, she observed the position of the moon and sprinted into the darkness. In a blur of shadows, bushes and trees, she dodged each root that reached out of the dirt to thwart her. The cramping dictated her movement until an unfamiliar putrid scent slowed her pace. With her hand against a tree, she felt for movement in the woods ahead, requiring a moment to become accustomed to the vile fragrance of her foes.

A twig snapped in the forest, followed by the scent of something pleasurably intoxicating. An arrow sailed past as her mind landed on perfume. With a whoosh, the next arrow went through her shoulder, pinning her to the bark. Slightly inconvenienced, Lexy inquisitively cocked her head as Trinity stepped out of the bushes with bows drawn. Lexy emotionlessly snapped off the end of the arrow and stepped forward. *She was the queen and she couldn't allow anyone to believe her majesty could be thwarted by merely tipping her crown.* The shaft of the arrow slid out as the wound broiled with the heat of her healing ability. Trinity realised who they'd wounded and scattered into the woods. *That's right… Run away.* Adrenaline pulsed through her as she followed the scent of perfume, methodically ending each immortal she came across until she was blanketed in warm coppery sweet-scented mist.

Shrieking snapped her out of her predatory euphoria. She sprinted towards the ungodly pitch and bombed through the heavy foliage into a surprise thicket. Exposed while out in the open but not concerned, Lexy made her way into the brush. Her sense of smell was hindered by the potency of perfume and blood spray on her skin. She waded through the dry, yellowed waist-high grass until she stepped into a patch of green. Vision alone was more than enough to determine what it was as she came across a morbid mass of human flesh, chunks of meat and an eyeball. She stepped on it, squishing it like a slug beneath a sneaker. The air grew potently sour, she whirled around as loud clicking noises echoed through the forest... *She was surrounded.* The Dragon within her grinned as dozens of large glowing eyes appeared in the woods like ground-level stars. Lexy strolled out into the centre of the thicket without a speck of indecision and released an ungodly pitched battle cry. From all sides, they attacked under cover of night with blinding light emitting eyes. They were lightning fast, all teeth, fur and disjointed jaws. With unflinching bravery, she slashed and swung her weapon. *These creatures were too fast.* They continued mercilessly coming at her, rising only seconds after they fell. *They were pissing her off. Either they were immortal, or their hearts were creatively placed.* Instinct prompted each swing of her weapon as the hoard of creatures circled her clicking. The light of dawn was expanding across the horizon. *She'd be able to see what she was fighting soon.* With panicked shrieking, black scaly wings unfolded from their backs as they took off. She harnessed her last ounce of energy and leapt on one's back. With each thud of her heart, it soared higher. *She wouldn't survive this fall, but she was dead either way.* She sliced its wing with her blade as it soared into the sunrise, and in an instant, they were wildly jerking around, rapidly descending into the forest. She tried to reach for branches as she plummeted, but her injuries were too severe. She limply smoked into each limb before hitting the ground with an explosion of pain. *She was still alive. Shit.* Agony radiated through her. *This wasn't good. She'd heal faster dead.* A bone was protruding from her wrist. *There was no point in surveying the damage, it felt like she was broiling from the inside out.* Slick with perspiration and covered in blood, Lexy struggled to get up anyway. The creature had fallen close by, it wasn't dead. Its eyes were still open. Her vision grew blurry as the pain went away. She was staring at her foe as she lost consciousness and succumbed to the forced time out.

The other Ankh approached Lexy's body. Frost replaced her knife with a sword. The creature awoke, and before it could get up, Markus lopped off its head. He addressed the group, "Decapitation it is. It looks like they're nocturnal. They must have a cave." Markus squatted next to the creature's severed head and opened its jaws. As he took a look, he noted, "It looks like they have venom, be careful. Lexy's liable to be in for quite the trip when she wakes up."

Lily placed a bottle of water and a Snickers bar beside the sword. She went to walk away and opted to leave Lexy a few more chocolate bars just in case the venom gave her the Dragon munchies.

Lexy opened her eyes with her fully healed wrist in eyeshot. She smiled as she wiggled and stretched her fingers in the dirt. On the ground next to her was a sword and three chocolate bars. *She was hungry.* Lexy crawled over, tore away the wrappers, and ate all three, squatting in the shrubbery like a gigantic homicidal field rat. She finished the water before noticing the headless creature. *Had she decapitated that?* The flying, slicing off its wing and painful fall flitted through her memory. *No, she hadn't killed it.* She recalled the creature's reaction to the sun. *They didn't burst into flames as other species did, but they were sensitive to sunlight, and decapitation was their end game. All she'd had before the fall was a knife.* She picked up the sword and gave it a swing, smiling. *Her Clan had her back. Her emotions were back on. It was inconvenient but in no way a deterrent. It was time to finish this.* Lexy sprinted away from the beheaded being, each step led by instinct. She heard scattered gunshots; her palm warmed beneath her fingerless glove. *No job was more urgent than the need to protect her Clan once her symbol went off.* She altered her path and sprinted towards the next round of shots, knowing this wasn't one of the other Clans. Bringing a gun to an immortal fight showed a serious lack of class and creativity. She burst through the bushes into a standoff between heavily perspiring seriously ill mortals and Ankh. Lily was face down in the dirt with her raven hair glistening in the light filtering through the trees. Markus was also dead. Frost was trying the talk the crazies down as Lexy cockily strolled over with a sword in hand, covered in blood, looking like a slasher film escapee.

"Don't come any closer!" One of the crazed mortals warned, pointing his shaky gun at her.

Frost looked at her and explained, "They've been infected by those creatures."

If she answered, she would have to behave. She didn't stop walking.

The frenzied mortal cocked his gun and yelled, "Stop right there! Demon!"

Lexy paused. *Was there someone behind her?* She glanced back. *He was talking about her. Well, that wasn't nice?* Lexy looked at his name tag and said, "Listen, Phil, I've had one hell of a night. I was attacked by flying demons. It was brutal. It looks like you've also had a rough time. Why do you want to shoot me Phil, and why in the hell are you wearing a name tag?"

"Company hunting trip. There are only two of us left," Phil stammered, keeping his rifle trained on her.

Inching closer, she enquired, "How many were taken?"

"There were over twenty of us. Some were taken, others just turned into those flying monster things," Phil confessed. He staggered, trying to keep his balance.

The other man started choking. Blood trickled out of his nose and sputtered from his mouth. He dropped to the ground and began thrashing around, shrieking as his bones broke and distorted.

"That's how it happens! That's how! He's going to turn! We have to get out of here!" Phil panicked.

A voice in her head urged, '*It's too late. Kill them.*'

It was Frost's voice. He was right there. How long had he been there? Oh, yes. Lily and Markus's bodies were on the ground. She wasn't feeling well. Lexy wiped the sweat from her brow as she marched towards the beast-like changing man, swung her sword back, and chopped off his head. Phil started hysterically screaming, with his shaking gun pointed at her. Lexy scolded, "Damn it, Phil. Simmer the hell down before you do something stupid. If you shoot me, you're just going to piss me off."

A shot rang out. Lexy looked down and bitched, "You shot me in the stomach, Phil! That was completely unnecessary!"

Frost took the confused mortal's weapon away as he piped in, "Don't be an asshole, Phil! We're immortals."

Lexy lifted her shirt as the bullet spit out of her healed wound and plopped into the dirt. She commented, "That was a dick move, Phil. Maybe, this shirt could have been washed? Now, there's a hole in it."

Frost cleared his throat. Lexy turned as he clarified, "The back of your shirt is shredded and soaked in blood, you're going to have to throw that out."

"I was making a point," Lexy fired back.

"Also, Phil's vomiting blood," Frost stated. "Do you want to do it? You don't look like you're feeling well."

She wasn't...And for some reason, she felt a strange kinship with Phil. She was so hot. Her knees buckled, she crumpled into the dirt, clawing at the soil with an excruciating burning sensation down either side of her spine. Frost's voice was background noise in her brain, *'Lexy...Lexy, can you hear me?'* She struggled to get back up, but everything began to spin. *The sun was too bright.* She closed her eyes.

Frost was standing there, observing Lexy's healing ability fighting the change. When she stopped moving, he knelt to check her pulse. He was distracted by his friend's predicament and didn't notice Triad sneaking up behind him. Frost peered up and cursed, "Shit," as a Triad's blade slit his throat.

The rest of Triad burst through the overgrown brush, as Tiberius declared, "We appear to have an infected Dragon." He knelt by Lexy's shivering body and tenderly caressed her hair. Tiberius looked up and announced, "Bury Ankh's bodies deep enough to make it inconvenient. Except for this one. She's infected enough to lead us back to the cave system those nocturnal assholes are hiding in." They were towing the bodies away. Tiberius stood up and sighed, "I can't do it. Don't bury Lilarah, heal her."

"You big softie," one of the Triad teased.

Tiberius strolled away from Lexy as he sparred, "It's a long boring story that nobody wants to hear. We should get out of here though before that sexy rabid Dragon wakes up and kicks our asses."

"That's your definition of sexy?" Triad's Healer Aristotle ribbed. "What if the virus is too strong?"

Tiberius looked back at Lexy's blood-drenched fevered shivering form and stated, "Forces of nature do not bend to the will of fate… They evolve."

Chapter 9

Dragons, Guardians And Snacks

Lexy felt the warmth of the sun and the silky grains of sand beneath her fingertips as she woke. She smiled, opening her eyes to a multi-hued blue sky. *She was in the in-between. Her last death must have been hardcore.* She got up and brushed the sand off her short sarong, struggling to recall the details of her demise. *Her mind wasn't cooperating.*

In a flash of light, Frost appeared. He held up his hands as he cautiously approached and said, "Please don't kill me again."

Again? "I'm sorry, I'm drawing a blank," Lexy explained. "Is Grey here?"

"He's waiting for you back in the land of the living. So, no memory at all?" Her immortal Clan member enquired.

Nothing. "Why don't you begin by explaining why I'm here," Lexy politely urged.

Frost attempted to refresh her memory, "You leapt on one of those things as it took off. It was at the cloud line when you sliced through its wing with your blade. The landing was brutal, you must have broken every bone in your body. The creature also survived the fall. While it was stunned, we chopped off its head. We heard gunfire, so we left you there to heal. When you showed up, Lily and Markus were already down. Your emotions were nearly back, but you were ill. We killed the first mortal as he turned. The other one shot you, and you went down, but in all fairness, Phil was mentally compromised."

"Phil?" Lexy questioned with a smile.

Frost grinned as he explained, "Phil was on a company retreat. They were all wearing name tags. You weren't dead, but you were infected. I was the only one capable of anything. I was preoccupied, figuring out what I was going to do next when someone from Triad snuck up and slit my throat. Tiberius buried Markus and I in the forest but didn't have the kahunas to bury his precious Lilarah. He didn't bury you either. Triad tracked you to the cave once you'd healed. The others didn't leave the cabin until after the siren signalled the end of the job."

Flashes of her savage demise invaded her mind. *She'd walked right into the cave system like she'd owned the place. It had gone badly.*

"Remembering something?" Frost enquired as he placed his symbol branded hand on hers and gave it a squeeze. White light emitted from their clasped hands.

"Was there anything left of my body?" Lexy asked. *She's become quite attached to it.*

"You're already healed and cleaned up. You just haven't woken up yet," Frost commented.

Lexy looked at her nearly see-through hand. She grinned as she disintegrated into the air.

It was too bright to open her eyes. She slid her hands along the smooth interior of the rose quartz tomb encasing her body and it opened.

With open arms, Grey sang, "Welcome back." Lexy climbed out of the tomb and stepped into his warm embrace. Hugging her so tightly her feet left the ground, Grey spun her around and put her down. Gazing into her eyes, he tenderly caressed her cheek and confessed, "I'm sorry I wasn't there to bring you out. They used my energy healing the others. Lily and I were the only energy sources. Do you remember much?"

"Not much," Lexy admitted as she wiped sweat from her brow. *The tombs were in the back of a big rig. It was ridiculously hot.*

Her Handler smiled as he assured, "Good...That's a good thing, trust me."

She was always so focused on Grey's erased memories, she rarely stopped to think about her own missing pieces of time. *Orin was acting a little standoffish. He hadn't even glanced her way.*

Grey whispered, "Give him space. You were infected with a virus and you tried to eat him."

Shit. Lexy whispered, "You're joking, right?"

"Sadly...No. You tore a chunk of skin out of his forearm with your teeth while foaming at the mouth like a rabid animal," Grey quietly retorted.

She'd been fooling herself into believing that she was capable of more. Normal girls don't try to eat their dates. She wanted to apologize but knew there was no point. She would inevitably do it again.

Grey took her hand and assured, "He'll get over it. He knew what you were."

She changed the subject, "Where are we again?"

"We're in Mexico waiting for the newbies to arrive," he answered, grabbing for the floor level rope. He yanked open the door, they were blinded by sunshine. "Welcome to Mexico!" Grey sang. "Let the shenanigans begin!"

She would have been more excited for this break from the monotony of immortality if she hadn't just chowed down on her booty call. *That was going to make things awkward for a while.* As she wandered down the ramp, she saw the motel they were staying at. *They'd been here before. It was beginning to feel like they'd been everywhere.*

Arrianna placed her arm around Lexy and explained, "I wiped some of the blood off with a sponge and put clean clothes on you, but you should go have a shower. Meet us down by the pool when you're done."

Orin wandered off with the group, without even looking her way. *Well, maybe it's for the best.* Grey was still by her side as they entered their bungalow. He gave her a quick smooch on the forehead as he offered, "I'll go run you a bath."

Lexy flopped on the bed and sighed dramatically. *Being a person was hard.* She didn't remember what she did, but she was willing to bet that biting Orin's arm wasn't even the tip of the iceberg. It frustrated her to no end that she couldn't remember. Grey called her name and she toddled to the bathroom. There was an impressive amount of bubbles.

He turned around and suggested, "Get in. I won't look." She slipped beneath the bubbles as he asked, "Are you decent?"

Apparently, she just tried to eat someone, so it would be a no, to that.

Grey responded to her thoughts as he turned around, "If he's worth it, he'll stick around, but I'm hoping he doesn't." She was about to give him shit when he clarified his reason, "You promised me you would always come back, but you didn't. When I woke up and your soul hadn't returned to your body… It was terrifying. I can't live this life without you."

Lexy calmly stated, "I'm right here."

"Point taken," Grey answered. He sat down on the tile beside the tub and looked straight ahead as he confessed, "The distance between us… It hurts."

"We'll do better," Lexy confirmed. "You won't have to worry about feeling jealous anymore. Orin's definitely rethinking his options."

Grey grinned as he answered, "Orin's the lesser of the evils. It's this inexplicable attraction you have to Tiberius that makes me feel like I'm losing my grasp on reality. You know how many times he's tortured me. I hate that idiot. I actually despise the guy. I can't see one redeeming quality." Grey's phone buzzed. He read his message.

She wanted to tell Grey everything but couldn't. She'd fought at Tiberius's side during the Summit and his reaction to viewing her memories altered her perception. Her fascination with Triad's leader grew intimate as they protected Kayn from having her virginity sacrificed. It felt like following this temptation through till its inevitable demise was the only way to stop the madness. She switched subjects, "I bet Frost's stoked about seeing his girlfriend." He was grinning as he responded to the text. *He hadn't heard a word.*

Grey got up, and as he left the room, he called out, "Don't take too long. I'd like a bath before everyone else arrives."

The bathroom door closed. *Yes, there were attractive, available girls in the mix of newbies. Her Handler's behaviour was painfully predictable.* Lexy rolled her eyes as she slipped beneath the bubbles, soaking her hair. In no time at all, Lexy was wearing her bikini sprawled in the sun next to Arrianna chatting about recent events. The hot topic around the pool was how the newbies handled their first jobs. They wandered over to the bar and ordered some slushy drinks. The two were sitting at the outdoor bar teasing Frost about how excited he was, enjoying their Pina Coladas as the newbies arrived.

They all turned around and smiled. Kayn was barefoot, wearing a spaghetti-strapped summer dress overtop of her bikini. She sprinted into Frost's arms, he spun her in a circle as they joyously laughed. The others began to greet each other with warm embraces. Lexy went through the motions while avoiding eye contact with Orin.

Markus interrupted the group as he announced, "We have a couple of days here before we travel a little further inland."

Melody looked at Orin and questioned, "Tell me we're going to be in the same place for a while?"

Lexy snuck away from the group and got into the pool. She swam for a while until Grey showed up with food. They chatted about how adorable Frost and Kayn were while eating and sipping Pina Coladas. *It felt good to see her fellow Dragon. It was a unique thing to have in common.* Mel wandered over. Grey became sidetracked so Lexy placed her drink on the ledge and got into the hot tub. She closed her eyes as her thoughts darted to Tiberius. *This wasn't the place for daydreaming.* She opened her eyes as someone slid into the hot tub next to her. *It was Dean.* They began a conversation as the hot tub filled. Soon almost everyone was packed in there like sardines laughing and joking around. Frost and Grey randomly got out, raced to the pool and leapt in. Lexy nudged Kayn and teased, "It's good to be back with you guys, even Zach."

Zach was sitting between Melody and Dean. He grinned at her and sparred, "Funny Lex."

"Let's just say, you've grown on me," Lexy provoked as she splashed him.

Kayn stood up and announced, "I'm going to love and leave you. That was a long drive and bathing at random public swimming pools for a whole week doesn't leave you feeling very fresh. I need a shower."

Lexy smiled at her and instructed, "You're in bungalow five. The door's probably open. We'll tell him where you went." Kayn grabbed her backpack and wandered away. Lexy was still watching her walk away as Orin got into the hot tub and made himself comfortable. *This was awkward. What was she supposed to say? I'm sorry I tried to eat you? She wanted to run away and so she did.* Lexy politely excused herself, "Time for a swim." She got out and wandered to the pool. Her eyes darted over to the hot tub. *It was nice to have everyone here.* Zach was a peculiar choice for Kayn's Handler. Frost surfaced right in front of her, she knelt by the edge of the pool and remarked, "Kayn's in your room." She couldn't muster up an ounce of pessimism as Frost scrambled out of the water and speed-walked away, like a hair from a jog. *It was kind of adorable.* She was having a moment watching him as Grey shoved her into the pool. She bobbed to the surface, choking on a mouth full of heavily chlorinated water. Grey was cackling as he leapt in. She chased after him, grabbing for his ankles. They tried to drown each other for a few minutes until it felt like they were being watched. Soon the pool was full of Ankh. They hung onto the ledge, chatting about their plans for the evening. Grey's eyes kept darting in Melody's direction. During the course of their conversation, it became obvious he'd be bummed if she suggested a night in, so she made it abundantly clear that he was free to stick around and have fun with the others. *She just couldn't. Truth be told, she was having a hard time being a person today. It was always difficult to know what was expected of her.* Her eyes met with Orin's. *He was coming over. Shit!* Lexy scrambled out of the pool and made her escape. She pretended she didn't hear Orin coming but knew he was right behind her as she quickly shut the bungalow door and leaned up against it, hoping he'd just go away. She wasn't ready to deal with the fall out of her cannibalistic Dragon ways. He lightly rapped on the door.

She covered her mouth with her hand as though it made a difference.

"Lexy. I know you're in there. You slammed the door in my face. Come on. We should talk," Orin urged through the wooden barrier.

She didn't want to talk about it. She just wanted him to leave it alone until she felt like a person again. She needed time to figure out how she was supposed to apologize.

"I can go and get the key from Grey?" Orin sighed.

Lexy opened the door and stepped aside as she quietly countered, "It wasn't locked."

Orin strolled in. She closed the door and stared at the knob for a second, fighting the urge to just leave. He touched her shoulder. She tensed up.

He removed his hand and assured, "You were infected by a virus… You weren't yourself. I'm not one to hold a grudge."

"I tried to eat you," Lexy countered while facing the door.

Orin grinned and chuckled, "Yes. You did."

Lexy knit her brow. She spun around and replied, "I don't remember. I can't promise I won't hurt you again."

"I know," he answered with laughter in his eyes as his lips burst into a grin.

Curious, she enquired, "What's so funny."

"You infected me, and I tried to eat everyone else with you for a while…I don't remember much past you biting a chunk out of my arm," Orin chuckled.

"Why would you even be here?" Lexy questioned, moderately concerned for his mental well-being.

"I like you," he teased. "You have some sketchy cannibalistic tendencies and a possible murder addiction but I'm morally flexible."

She was waving her red flag as hard as she could, and he was just going with it? Unable to disguise how perplexed she was with his lack of concern, Lexy giggled and scolded, "What is wrong with you? Seriously, you should know better."

"Playing it safe is boring," Orin teased and flirtatiously winked.

Jenna's words echoed in her mind. *She needed to be honest about her attractions.* Lexy clarified, "I'm not ready for anything serious."

"We've already had this conversation, but for the record, I know you have a thing for Tiberius. The whole despising each other act is quite the aphrodisiac," Orin quipped. "Why do I feel like my ex gave you a speech?"

"She's just looking out for you," Lexy admitted as she opened a Corona and offered it to him. Orin took it and thanked her before chugging it back like a savage. *He was unnervingly too good to be true. She was a horrible idea.* He grinned, she knew he'd heard her inner-commentary. Lexy slowly shook her head as she urged, "You should get back to the pool before Grey tries to sleep with your daughter."

He chuckled, "That ship has sailed. Melody's a grown-up, it's a little late in the game for me to be father of the year." Orin caressed her shoulder and ran the tip of his finger seductively down the length of her arm, while adding, "I'll go throw a wrench in his plans if you need him here with you tonight though…Is that what you want me to do?"

She always wanted to wreck Grey's booty calls, but it felt like she was missing something. She wasn't in the right state of mind to decipher his flirtatious behaviour. The door opened. Orin yanked his hand away.

Grey was beaming like a cat who'd just swallowed a canary as he said, "Hey kids… Are you coming outside to play, or should I find somewhere else to sleep tonight?"

Orin stole another Corona from the case on the table and declared, "Just clearing the air. I think you should concentrate on Handler Dragon bond stuff tonight. I'm sure I'll see you both later." He gave Grey's shoulder a brotherly pat as he maneuvered past him out the door.

Without Grey having to say a word, Lexy passed him a beer, grabbed one for herself and took a seat at the table. *He obviously had something to say. It was damn hot, and she was still cranky.* Lexy popped off the cap and took a swig of her less than satisfying room temperature beer. She heard the chair scraping across the floor as Grey pulled it out to sit but didn't look.

"I was coming to check on you because I made plans, but I'll stay if you want me to?" Grey admitted as he reached across the table for her free hand.

She closed her eyes as he took it and began caressing her palm with his thumbs. She needed him tonight but wanted him to choose to stay for the right reasons. Her eyes met his as she answered, "No…I'm just going to sleep. Go have fun."

"Are you sure?" Grey pressed as he lovingly squeezed her hand.

There was no satisfaction in being right about his plans for the evening. She wanted to tell him to stay but knew she couldn't keep giving him mixed messages if she wanted to move on. Lexy smiled and clarified, "You have a key. Go have fun. I should get some sleep tonight."

Grey smiled wryly and teased, "So everything is all good with your snack? Want me to ask Orin to come back?"

Lexy sparred, "Hilarious…Snack…Nice. I think a little space is in order after the whole trying to eat him thing…Don't you?"

He stood up, tousled her hair and baited, "Those who play with Dragons get burned."

He wasn't wrong. "Go! Get out of here!" she laughed as she waved him away. He grinned and took off. She finished her beer, while quietly listening to the birds in the vibrant green flowering bush outside the window. Greydon hadn't always sucked this badly at reading her nonverbal cues. Jenna's intuition was rarely wrong. She'd put some effort into fixing the rift between them tomorrow. Lexy took her bottle with her and placed it on the ornate antique nightstand. She crawled under the covers. *It was too hot.* She kicked off the sheets and closed her eyes.

It felt like she was asleep only seconds when her stomach cramped. *What the…?* Lexy groggily opened her eyes and focused on the clock… it was twelve. *That had to be wrong.* For a second, she was confused. *The sun was shining. It was noon, not midnight… Weird? She rarely slept in this late. Had Grey even come back last night?* Lexy got up and looked around. The room was exactly as she'd left it. *He hadn't.* She got up and wandered into the bathroom to brush her teeth. She looked at her reflection. *For someone that had done nothing last night, she looked rough.* Lexy splashed some cold water on her face, and when she reached for the towel, it wasn't there. It was on the floor. *Grey had been back to the room.* She was still wearing her bikini under her sundress so there was no need to change. As she freshened up her makeup, she listened to the humming of conversation going on outside. It felt like she had one of those random naps where you wake up and don't even know what century you're in. Her stomach cramped again, she grimaced as it growled. *She was hungry.* Lexy eyed up an apple on the counter as she strolled to the door. *They were probably all out there having lunch drinking slushy drinks. She'd have to order a Pina Colada with her lunch. A Pina Colada would be perfect.* Lexy stepped out into the glorious sunshine and was distracted by the fragrant blossoms of the bush. *Something felt off. It was too quiet.* Her stomach cramped again, this time instinct gave her a good poke. She noticed a brilliant red and teal bird frozen in mid-flight. *What now? She wasn't in the mood for anyone's shit!* Lexy stormed down the path to the bar. *It looked like someone had hit pause. Everyone was frozen in place. Grey? Where was Grey?* She saw him sitting motionless at the bar. Kayn and the bartender were talking. Lexy marched over and hissed, "Who in the hell is this asshole and why isn't anyone moving?" The stranger extended his hand in Lexy's direction. She gave him a dirty look.

The stranger explained, "Let's catch you up. I'm your father and Kayn here is your sister. Everyone will start moving again as soon as we get back. I'll make sure to return you both to the second you left. Your friends won't even know you were gone."

It felt like she'd been kicked in the gut. *Father?* She looked at Kayn. *Sister? What?* Lexy glared at the stranger and questioned, "Why would we go anywhere with you?"

With an enormous grin plastered on his face, he responded, "Did I forget to tell you my name? My name's Seth. I'm one of the three Guardians. Coming with me isn't exactly a choice."

Triad's shapeshifting asshole of a Guardian could not be her father. Lexy glanced at Kayn as the scenery flashed. They disappeared and reappeared in the jungle, standing outside of what appeared to be an Ankh crypt. *Kayn couldn't really be her sister...Could she?* The Guardian Seth walked through the wall and left them standing there. She didn't enjoy having her hand forced but a Guardian's orders weren't optional. She felt compelled to follow but Kayn hadn't moved a muscle. Lexy walked over and tapped the surface of the crypt. *This was obviously one of those exercises in faith.* Seth's voice spoke in her mind, *'What are you two girls waiting for? An invitation?'* Lexy knew the drill. She walked through the wall and vanished, hoping Kayn would follow her lead. She did, the two Dragons followed the Guardian down a long flight of stairs descending into darkness.

Seth reached the bottom and spoke in the language of the Clans, "Let there be light."

The stone chamber lit up. This was an Ankh crypt. She recognized the carvings. Her eyes were drawn to three distinct handprints on the stone.

The Guardian smiled, pointed at the handprints and ordered, "Kneel and place your hands on the prints."

Her body had a mind of its own as she instinctually followed the Guardian's command. The two Dragons obediently knelt before the carvings on the wall, glanced at each other and simultaneously placed their hands on the ancient handprints. *What was she doing?* Lexy tried to remove her hands...*They wouldn't budge.* Seth knelt and placed his palms on the third set of prints and a burst of energy travelled up Lexy's arms. Her skin began to glow with shimmering golden light. As Seth removed his hands from the wall, they were able to let go. Power surged through Lexy's being. Confusing images flooded her mind, and as they ceased, she felt a sedated sense of peace. *This was real.* She looked at Kayn and then at the immortal being that claimed to be their father.

Seth placed his hands on the top their heads and announced, "You have just been granted your birthright. As the daughters of a Guardian, you will bow for no one, but the leader of your Clan and the Guardians. Your abilities have been unlocked. They should be easier to control and you will be much stronger now." He removed his hands, took a step back and commanded, "Get off your knees."

Lexy rose to stand beside her immortal sibling aware she was blindly obeying orders but secure in the knowledge that she was supposed to. The two Dragons looked at each other, and in the blink of an eye, they were back at the bar they'd been taken from. Everyone was joking around. It was as though nothing happened. The two Dragons grinned at each other and embraced. *She had a sister. She felt it in her soul. It wasn't just because they were Dragons. They were siblings.* Grey noticed her hugging Kayn. He gave her a weird look. *She wanted to tell him but was she allowed? She'd been stunned by the revelation. She might have missed something.*

Kayn whispered in her ear, "I definitely didn't see that one coming."

Lexy pulled away from her newfound sibling and whispered, "Are we really sisters? Should we tell everyone about this?"

Clearly still in shock, Kayn was as white as a ghost. She emotionlessly replied, "Yes. We should tell everyone. You start. I'll be right there. I just need a moment." Without another syllable, Kayn left her there and wandered to the beach.

Seriously Brighton?

Frost called after Kayn, "Hey, Beautiful. Your drinks melting. It must be a hot one today."

Grey strolled over, placed his arm around Lexy and questioned, "Should I be jealous?"

And the winner of the most inappropriate comment of the day goes to Grey. Kayn was standing motionless, staring at the surf. *She was going to make her tell everyone, wasn't she? Whatever.* Lexy waved her hands, effectively catching everyone's attention and explained, "Your drinks are all melted because you were all frozen by Triad's Guardian. Seth took us with him to an Ankh crypt, where he compelled us to put our hands on these prints on the wall. We just got back." Silence fell over the group as Lexy pointed at Kayn and continued to speak, "He says he's our father so... We're sisters."

Miss Brighton was lost in la-la land staring at the roaring waves as Jenna's voice boomed, "I knew it!"

Kayn snapped out of her stupor, turned around, strolled over to the bar and snatched her stupefied boyfriend's drink as she affirmed, "Lexy and I are sisters and Seth the Guardian is our father. Let's order lunch."

Grey laced his fingers with Lexy's and gave her hand a reassuring squeeze, prompting her to look at him. He quietly said, "Promise me this won't change us."

"We've been changing for a while," Lexy admitted. She hadn't intended to punish him for leaving her side the night before, but the words slipped from her lips and tact became an afterthought.

Grey released her hand, and as he walked away, she felt their attachment stretching like an elastic band. She couldn't allow their connection further stress, even for the sake of making a point. Lexy pursued Grey down to the water calling out his name until he stopped walking away. He turned to face her. She tried to apologize. He shook his head like he didn't want to hear her excuses. That's how she'd read the situation until fear flickered in his eyes. Lexy realised she'd misinterpreted her Handler's reaction. He gathered her up in his arms and time stood still as she repeated the words, "I'm sorry."

Caressing her hair, he vowed, "I've been an idiot. I'll do better. I'll try harder. I know I've been pushing you away but it's bloody impossible to filter the jealousy. I'm aware this sounds selfish, I'm feeling irrationally territorial. I just want you to need me...to love only me."

Always. She tenderly kissed his cheek, winked and teased, "I could never leave you. You'd find me."

"This is true," Grey jousted as they strolled back to the others hand in hand.

Lexy looked at the animated crowd of immortals in the distance as she smiled and stated, "I have a sister."

"Crazy, isn't it? How do you feel about that?" Grey questioned as he tugged her against him into a brotherly half hug.

"I honestly don't know," Lexy admitted. *A sister. A father.* She stopped walking as the gravity of the revelation began to sink in. Grey gently tugged her hand and led her back to the others. They ordered their lunches and ate with their Clan, eventually ending up on the beach drinking with a small group. They remained there, talking out their issues, laughing and divulging secrets until the sky became crimson, and the last rays of the sun descended into the sea and vanished at the end of the shimmering strip of light.

Chapter 10

Epically Sloshed

Lexy stirred in Grey's arms, inhaling the fragrance of his skin.

His groggy voice teased, "Are you smelling me? Because that's super creepy."

She comically continued sniffing his chest until Grey flipped her and pinned her to the mattress as they laughed. *He was hard as stone between her thighs and things got awkward.* He nervously cleared his throat.

As her cheeks tinted, Lexy flirtatiously baited, "Morning, Greydon."

"Did I sleep here last night?" Grey enquired as he quickly peeked under the covers at his situation before rolling away.

She knew the drill, and usually, she knew what happened, but not this morning. They'd been epically sloshed last night. The events were still foggy. "I'm not sure," Lexy admitted as she also peeked beneath the covers and was relieved to find her bathing suit on. She tossed the covers aside and watched relief spread across Grey's expression. *Sometimes it was difficult to suck in her response. If he only understood how beautiful they were together. But he couldn't, and this was why she had to allow her heart breathing room.* She glanced his way, shoved him onto the bed and sprinted for the washroom, cackling as she locked the door.

Out of breath, Grey called out, "You're a cheater, Lex! A dirty rotten cheater!"

After both were ready for the day, they wandered out into the pool area where everyone was already waiting.

Orin glanced up from his book and commented, "Lovely of you to join us. We've only been waiting an hour."

Grey sauntered over and provoked, "So, do Dick and Jane still fall in the well?" Orin tried to hit Grey. He ducked, laughing.

With a smug grin, Orin jousted, "At least I read."

"I can read!" Grey declared as he looked to Lexy for backup.

She leaned in and whispered, "That's not what he meant." *They'd made up after the whole cannibal snacking incident, so she didn't want to rock the boat.* Orin smirked and added nothing.

Jenna clapped her hands as she looked directly at Lexy and announced, "Alright, let's go! I'm sure our Kayn's already knee-deep in newbie corpses."

Knee deep in newbie corpses...Seems legit. She was beginning to recall the details of the conversations she'd had the night before. *She'd known they were going to the other continent. The five were running Amar's group through some stuff in the in-between. Markus told her at the beach.*

Jenna signalled for the group to follow as she explained, "Amar has a son and he's in this Testing group. I guess the bond with this group hasn't been working. Our five Testing survivors are in the in-between, doing basically what we did for our last group. Lexy and Orin, you'll be Healer backup for Amar's group when we get there."

Orin rolled his eyes, dramatically sighing, "Awesome, this shouldn't be painful at all."

What he'd said probably had everything to do with Kayn being a Dragon and nothing to do with her personally but she still felt uneasy. The group got into three parked vehicles. Orin opened the door for her. *It felt passive-aggressive, she had no idea why.* Lexy emotionlessly slid into the backseat beside Grey, and when Orin opted for another jeep, she knew her intuition was spot on.

Grey leaned in and quietly asked, "I thought you two made up? Did you do something else?"

"Probably," Lexy replied honestly.

Frost chuckled while starting the engine. He turned back to look at her while revealing, "I think it's more about what you didn't do."

She wasn't into guessing games. After driving in silence for a while, they parked at the mouth of a vaguely familiar animal path and hiked through the lush greenery and vibrant colours of the jungle to the Ankh Crypt. Lexy didn't bother trying to speak to Orin… *He was ticked about something and honestly, she couldn't care less. She'd warned him… He'd brushed off cannibalism, and now he was being pouty. Booty calls were nothing but drama.*

Lily giggled. *Her thoughts had been heard. Truthfully, she didn't give a shit. She hoped he heard everything that took a jaunt through her damn mind. Walking behind Orin was always a magnificent vantage point. His behind should be illegal. That butt was how he got away with everything.*

Orin glanced back at Lexy. He laughed and said, "Seriously?"

Lexy smiled and shrugged.

Jenna gave Orin a playful shove as she taunted, "Come on, that's so true. Frost, you too of course."

"Excuse me, it's not polite to leave out my butt," Grey sparred. He plucked a berry off a bush and popped it into his mouth.

Orin scowled at Grey and scolded, "Spit that out, you're not a child!" Grey spat the berry on the ground as Orin slowly shook his head.

Compassionately squeezing Grey's shoulder, Lily assured, "Greydon, your butt is just fine."

Everyone laughed. Grey dramatically stammered, "You know what? You guys are assholes!" A snake slithered across the path. Grey jumped around, shrieking, "Shit! Shit!"

Lily, the exotic raven-haired seductress, placed her arm around Grey and sighed, "It's harmless. Why are you so amped up today? Come on, we're going to have fun at the banquet. There'll be drinking and dancing."

"And the other Clans will be there," Jenna quietly commented.

Grey looked at Jenna. *Bingo! Their Oracle hit the nail on the head. She might see Tiberius.* Lexy tried to rid her mind of thoughts but it put a skip in her step. They made their way through the Ankh tomb and stepped out onto another continent. Even after more than forty years it was still an awe-inspiring feat. They were led through the back of a busy restaurant and split up as they got into three black sedans. After arriving at Amar's gorgeous desert compound, they were quickly escorted to their rooms and instructed to change into a preselected outfit. Lexy wandered out onto the balcony to take in the scenery wearing a sheer flowing green dress. She was only out there for a minute when somebody knocked on their door.

Grey hollered, "I'll be right out!"

Lexy was smiling as she raced to answer the door. It was a studious looking lady named Bree, wearing a lab coat with an Aries Group pin. Orin was standing beside her.

Bree from the Aries group greeted her, "You must be Lexy. Are you ready to go? There were only a few Healers left last time I looked."

Grey rushed out of the washroom and announced, "Sorry! Sorry! I'm ready!"

"I've studied pictures of you trying to memorize everyone's names. Grey, I adore your accent. You can stay here and relax. Have a glass of wine, I'll get someone to bring you a snack. I'll come and get you if we need you for anything," Bree assured. "Right now, all I need is replacement Healers."

Grey leapt onto the bed, grabbed a bountiful vine of grapes and sang, "Have fun you two and yes Bree, a snack would be lovely."

That jerk. Bree closed the door on Grey, obnoxiously waving at them beaming. *She wanted a frigging snack. She didn't even get to kill anybody today, it felt peculiar to only do a healing job.*

Orin was waiting in the hall. They didn't speak as Bree ushered the two Healers into a tomb room. Most of Amar's Healers were already down for the count. One lone girl was still alive with her hand placed on the lid of a tomb.

Bree announced, "I brought you backup, Whitney."

Relief washed over Whitney's face as she gasped, "Oh, dear lord, thank you. I only had a few minutes left in my battery. Your people are brutal. I've lost track of how many times ours have been killed."

They didn't ask her to be a responsible adult immortal often. Guess she could play along. Lexy waved the exhausted Healer away. Whitney happily let go. Lexy placed her hands on the tomb, and as her energy began draining from her body, she asserted, "Relax. Take a break, we'll trade off." Once the tomb was strobing in rhythm with the others, Lexy removed her hands and looked up. *Orin and Whitney were already working on correcting out of rhythm tombs. There was no break. Kayn was on a Dragon killing spree, she felt so close to her right now.* A tomb lost pace with the others as Whitney crumpled to the stone floor. Lexy looked at Orin and teased, "You're next."

"I'm a thousand years old," her healing buddy bantered. "You're next."

"I'm part Guardian, all bets are off," Lexy reminded as she laid her hands on the tomb that lost beat with the others.

Orin switched tombs as he countered, "You know I'm not upset."

She was trying to concentrate. Her eyes darted to Orin as she sighed, "We're working, you're not going to win by distracting me."

Orin held his hands securely to the next out of sync tomb and stated, "You are painfully stubborn."

Their witty banter and cocky shows of strength went on for a good hour before Lexy went down and shortly thereafter so did Orin.

Lexy stirred on the stone floor to Grey's voice, scolding, "You quite obviously let this training exercise get a bit out of hand."

Zach giggled, "What was I supposed to do? She was completely psychotic."

Lexy groaned from the floor, "Colour me impressed, you took out both of us." She got up, stretched, and as she cracked her neck, she looked at Kayn and directed. "I've got Orin if you've got Melody."

Kayn peeked into one of the tombs and placed her hands on Melody's chest.

Brighton was getting rather ballsy. No problem. I'll just raise someone from the dead with almost no experience.

Mel's voice mumbled, "Hope that week-long murder spree was worth it."

"Just like going to the spa," Kayn teased, helping Mel up.

Orin opened his eyes and taunted, "I won."

Lexy winked and sparred, "I came back from the dead first." The new Ankh from Amar's group were traumatized as they shimmied past Kayn. *Her sister was also good at bonding with strangers.*

Lexy strolled over and asked, "So, it went well?"

Kayn slowly shook her head and explained, "It was fun for me, but there's no way this group is going to make it. They're not attached to each other and I'm quite certain Amar's son is supposed to be Triad."

"He's not going to be happy about that," Orin confirmed, having a difficult time getting up.

Lexy helped him stand and scanned the collection of once wide-eyed innocent Ankh. *They'd officially turned a page in the immortal manual. They weren't the least bit concerned about the aftermath of what they'd done. They were just following their orders like champs.*

Grey placed his arm around Lexy and whispered, "Upset you couldn't partake in the murder-spree?"

She calmly replied, "The day is young, opportunities may arise."

Her Handler gave her a buddy-esque squeeze, kissed her head and whispered, "Promise me you won't murder anybody today. Can't we relax and have a nice dinner? Just this once?"

"I'll try," Lexy answered.

Orin boisterously laughed.

They wandered behind the five newest Ankh as they bantered back and forth about how much Amar's son sucked at being an immortal while deliberating their course of action. It sounded like Kayn was going to have to speak to Amar. "Should we help? Offer to talk to Amar?" Lexy quietly enquired.

"It's not our pile. Their duty, their bad news to tell," Grey responded. "I'm sure you can rustle up some drama of your own."

She smiled and sparred, "Probably."

Everyone went their separate ways to their rooms. Grey opened the door for her. Lexy wandered in and saw the spread of treats he'd procured in her absence. Everything appeared to be untouched. *He'd saved it to share with her. She was the asshole.*

Grey held up a carafe and offered, "Wine?"

Lexy sat on the silky sheets and smiled as she grabbed a handful of flawless grapes. She tossed one into her mouth as he passed her a half-full glass of wine and said, "Can you do me a favour?"

His fancy grapes were tainted by ulterior motives. Bribery snacks…Well played. Irritated, she placed the grapes back on the tray and downed her entire glass of wine, knowing what her Handler was going to say. She placed the empty glass on the bedside table and replied, "Do you want me to stay away from Tiberius or Orin? And before you respond, do you intend to spend your entire evening hanging out with me or does this favour only work one way, like every other time?"

"Do you want me to stay with you?" Grey asked as he got onto the bed beside her. "Because I will," he whispered as he shifted closer.

Why couldn't he understand their situation? She'd tried everything. She'd been blunt about it. She'd pussyfooted around it. She had even explained their past as lovers in detail on occasion, the result was always the same. She was tired of it always being her with the broken heart. It wasn't right. It wasn't fair! It was always her putting her life back together, and here he was, with pleading eyes needing her to confess her love for him… Again. She got up and said, "Damn it, Grey. We can't keep doing this. You don't understand. You can't keep asking me to give my heart to you when you're incapable of giving yours back."

He leapt up as she tried to storm away and blocked her escape. "I love you. I have always loved you, and in a perfect world, we'd be together. We'd be married and have a pack of kids… I would want nothing more than to live happily ever after but that's not who we are. Why can't we just be together tonight and worry about repercussions tomorrow?"

Oh no, he didn't. Fury broiled up inside of her until there was nowhere for it to go. Lexy grabbed a vase off the counter and rifled it at Grey, who managed to duck. It missed him by a hair and shattered on the floor.

"What in the hell?" he stammered as he began backing away out of self-preservation.

"Do you have any idea how many times we've had this exact conversation? Do you?" Lexy coldly accused. "I wake up in the morning still in love with you after spending a beautiful night together and you have a clean slate. You spend the day making out with someone while I spend mine dying inside!" Lexy fired another random countertop ornament at him.

He stepped out of its path and it smashed. He tried to reason with her, "Lexy. Come on. I would never intentionally do that."

"Oh…But you do," Lexy spitefully retaliated. "We love each other. Sexy hot steamy love and I know you'd never hurt me intentionally, but you are. You have before, and you will tomorrow. It's my turn to have some fun. It's my turn to break your heart!"

Grey stood there thoroughly devastated as he calmly answered, "I think Tiberius is in the next room. I just was going to ask you to do that elsewhere. I don't want to hear it. Now, at least I know why the idea of you being with someone else hurts so much. Thanks for that." He was still trying to disguise his devastation as he sauntered into the bathroom and quietly closed the door to get away. *Well, that just rather effectively snuffed out her libido.* She sat patiently on the bed, watching the bathroom door, waiting for Grey to emerge. *Thanks for that…Her reaction was a tad harsh. This was their dynamics as a couple. They were both horrible at sharing. She was an ice queen and he was overdramatic. She threw stuff and he was easily offended. The love between them was undeniable and trying to be a real person was hard.* Lexy placed her palm against the bathroom door. A part of her wanted to apologize but her inner voice was urging her to leave it alone. As soon as he slept, her confession would be erased, and they'd be fine in the light of a new day. They usually were and that was no small feat. Over the years, she'd had to suck up some seriously damaging shit for the sake of their Handler Dragon bond. Even though neither one had spoken a word, she knew his hand was on the other side of the door. She felt his energy through the wood as though nothing separated their flesh. *He'd been the one to domesticate her but it was just for show. He'd always kept her broken in some way. He was the keeper of her cage. He was her yellow door.* Lexy yanked her hand away. *The bathroom door was yellow. Who paints a bathroom door yellow?* She backed away and took it as a sign. *She wasn't supposed to be messing with her yellow door.* Lexy glared up at the ceiling and whispered, "Funny." When she looked back at the door it wasn't yellow anymore. Fear tightened her chest. *She should leave. Yes. Before he came out and she lost her resolve to move forward.* She turned and left.

Chapter 11

Cannibalism Happens

Lexy stepped out into the hall and glanced at the door next to theirs. *Tiberius was in that room. Surely, he knew she couldn't go there with her Handler in the next room.* Curiosity lured her closer, as Lexy raised her hand to knock on Tiberius' door, Frost stormed around the corner and bumped into her. She blocked his path and probed, "Trouble in paradise?"

Frost went off, "She was thinking about him while we were! You know! It's disrespectful! I deserve better, don't I? We all know we can hear each other's thoughts."

Trying to be stone-cold serious, a smile happened as she admitted, "I just had a fight with Grey, where I confessed everything about the sexual nature of our relationship and broke two vases. I'm probably the last person you should come to for relationship advice."

"How does that work when you just tell him?" Frost enquired. "If you don't seal the deal, do you have some platonic time together before his memory is wiped?"

"Sometimes… It doesn't matter," Lexy answered. "There's no fixing my situation but yours is different. Listen, you know random thoughts slip into our minds. She loves you back, what more can you ask for?"

Frost affirmed, "I'm being an idiot, aren't I?"

"You are. Let her calm down, then go back and apologize," Lexy instructed.

"Why don't you stop by? I have someone I need to speak to. I'll only be a few minutes. She is your sister," Frost countered. He smiled and walked away.

Her sister...That was the craziest revelation. She should get to know her. Logic... Go see your sister and find out if she's okay. Lexy took Frost's hint and knocked on Kayn's door. Her mind began screaming, *Abort! Abort mission!* She didn't have time to flee. Kayn opened the door, stepped aside and ushered her in with a welcoming smile. *She was in the room. She should say something.* "Your room is better than ours," Lexy remarked as she scrutinized the rich tapestries on the walls. "Did you and Frost have a fight?" Lexy innocently enquired as she wandered across the room to check out the view from the balcony. She peered over the ledge, hoping to catch a glimpse of Triad. She heard the hamster wheel between Kayn's ears spinning, so she clarified, "I bumped into him in the hall."

"If he's going to be pissed off every time he hears a thought he doesn't like, we're going to have a lot of ridiculous arguments," Kayn mumbled as she joined her on the balcony and leaned against the shiny marble railing.

They silently gazed at the hauntingly beautiful desert scenery. *Maybe, she should say something?* "If it makes you feel any better, I'm fighting with Grey too," Lexy admitted as her crimson hair shifted like the flickering flames of a fire in the warm breeze.

"You thought about Tiberius, didn't you?" Kayn teased.

Not really, but close enough. Lexy admitted, "He's in the room next to ours, Grey wasn't impressed."

"Forget about Grey for a second…How do you feel?" Kayn asked, watching for her reaction.

Lexy had the urge to be completely honest so she went with it, "Truthfully? Excited, nervous…on edge."

Kayn grinned and piped in, "Mel's having the same day. Thorne's going to be here by tonight."

"Where's Zach?" Lexy enquired.

"No idea, he was probably giving us some time alone," Kayn responded.

Smiling, Lexy added, "He'll also be in an awkward situation tonight, the four of us should stick together."

"Stephanie?" her sister questioned.

This went well. She should leave before she screwed it up. "Her too," Lexy answered as she abruptly made her way back to the door. She snatched a flawless red apple off the tray on the decorative table as she attempted sisterly advice, "Ignore Frost. He has no right to judge anyone…ever. Neither does Grey for that matter." Lexy grabbed for the doorknob, glanced back and blurted, "I deserve to have some fun too, don't I?"

"Of course, you do," Kayn assured, smiling.

She thought so. "Good talk," Lexy declared as she walked out and closed the door. She wandered back to their room. As she reached for the doorknob, the door next to hers opened. *Not now.* Her heart caught in her chest. *It was someone she didn't recognize.* Relieved, she went into her room fully prepared to deal with the aftermath of her confession. Grey was asleep. She sat by him, watching his steady, relaxed breathing. *She couldn't stay mad. She loved the stupid, arrogant fool.* She touched his hair.

He opened his eyes with oblivious warmth, smiled and whispered, "Hey gorgeous."

The slate had been cleaned, and as far as he was concerned, their argument had never happened. *This worked out well. She hadn't been using her brain at all when she picked that fight.* Lexy kissed his cheek and whispered, "Go back to sleep." She snuggled up under the covers and fell asleep in her Handler's arms.

She awoke to the aroma of coffee. *Where was she again?* Lexy opened her eyes, sat up and yawned. *Oh yes. We reset a shitty day. For the first time, his affliction had come in rather handy.*

Grey handed her a steaming cup and exclaimed, "Drink this and get ready. Your dress is hanging in the closet. I let you sleep too long. I'm sure the receiving line has already started."

"On it," she replied. She swung her legs over the side of the bed and took a sip of coffee. Just like an old married couple, they shared the mirror.

Grey asked, "How do I look?"

She stopped primping to survey his appearance, then undid the top button of his shirt and stated, "Now, you're perfect." He gave her a brotherly shove as he left the bathroom. She was momentarily overcome by relief as she stood there, staring at her reflection. *A beautiful girl was looking back at her. She knew it, but for some reason, knowing it was never enough to make her feel worthy of anything.* Grey reappeared in the mirror behind her.

He smiled, stepped forward and shifted her hair off one of her shoulders, causing her luxurious crimson waves to flow like a waterfall down her gossamer skin. "You're stunning, and that dress is...Orin will love it."

It was always difficult to know how to respond when she wasn't sure what pertinent information had been erased. So, she opted to play it safe, "I'm not overly concerned about what Orin thinks."

"Tiberius?" her Handler prompted.

He was testing her. She sparred, "Don't worry, I'll be avoiding any form of drama like the plague."

Instantly relieved, he teased, "Aww…But I was so looking forward to watching you drop kick Tiberius in the junk."

Well, she couldn't promise she wasn't going to do that.

Grey kissed her brow and held her against him as he responded to her inner commentary, "That's my girl."

Always…even when you're driving me crazy.

"I heard that," Grey laughed as he left.

She looked at her reflection one final time before turning off the light and leaving the room. Grey took her hand, she grinned, knowing he was trying to passive-aggressively stake his claim. They bumped into Melody, Arrianna and Haley in the hall and all strolled to the banquet room together. Grey placed his arm around Mel as they waited in the line, and just like that, their Handler Dragon honeymoon was over. *Grey knew Thorne was up there. Heaven forbid Trinity's leader mess with his options for later in the evening. Here she was stifling her desires to keep the newly acquired peace and he was going to spend his night playing the field. Fine then Greydon. It's on.* Grey was standing in front of her chatting with Markus with his hand possessively placed on the small of Melody's back. Their makeshift leader met Lexy's rage-filled glare.

Markus summoned her closer and whispered, "You know Tiberius always messes with you and you're looking a little murdery this evening."

She wasn't plotting Tiberius' murder. She was plotting Grey's. Markus followed her line of sight to the placement of her Handler's hand, and the lightbulb went on.

Before Markus could do anything, Orin smacked the back of Grey's head and scolded, "No!" Mel laughed as

Orin stepped in between the two just as they moved on to chat with Amar.

"Better?" Markus ribbed, giving her shoulder a squeeze.

"Much," Lexy sparred.

Amar extended his hand and preened, "Delightful to see you, Lexy. You've had quite the month… A sister, a Guardian father and why did you free all of those mental patients again?"

Lexy grinned. *She was never going to live that down.* She shook Amar's hand, admitting, "It's a long story."

"Well, I'd love to hear it, once I get this banquet underway," the strikingly handsome Amar countered. "Drinks later?"

His teeth were so white. She should switch to whitening toothpaste. "Yes. Of course," Lexy replied. Her eyes darted to Triad's leader. *Being this close to Tiberius shook her. He was chatting up people, shaking hands… Pretending to be charming.* Lexy moved on to greet Thorne, who always reminded her of one of those innately decent movie superheroes.

Grinning as he shook her hand, Thorne acknowledged, "Feel free to call me Captain America. It looks like you've recovered nicely."

He could have been referring to many things. Intrigued, Lexy countered, "Which situation are you referring to? It's been a busy month."

"It doesn't matter. You look beautiful this evening," Thorne praised. Trinity's leader released her hand and moved on to shake someone else's. She listened to the conversation without looking back. *It was Orin, he was behind her now. She was almost at Tiberius, and her Handler had already disappeared into the crowd funnelling into the hall. She needed allies. Where was Frost? He wasn't in the receiving line.* The line shifted, she found herself standing in front of Tiberius. He was undeniably attractive with his burgundy shirt unbuttoned enough to see a sexy glimpse of his chest and snug pants. *She should walk away.*

His devilish eyes travelled seductively from her feet to her eyes. Tiberius smiled as he mischievously spoke her name, "Lexy."

As he extended his hand, her mind flashed back to the pleasure he'd given her. *Underestimating their connection felt foolish. As much as she wanted to go on despising his existence, she couldn't... Not anymore. She knew one thing for sure, she couldn't touch him...Not if she wanted ration to win over her raging libido.* She stepped away, spun around and heard his laughter as she escaped into the banquet hall, painfully aware she was only postponing the inevitable. Lexy took in the breathtaking décor. Amar always went all out for these things. The tabletops were all multi-hued sheer material on contrasting backdrops of tan. The overseas banquets had always been impressive. Their decorations were rather bland in comparison, resembling more wedding reception, less swanky nightclub.

Orin remarked, "The hall looks amazing." He placed his hand on her shoulder.

Smiling as curiosity took over, she enquired, "Where's Frost?"

Her naughty companion chuckled, "Frost and your sister haven't arrived."

My sister...That idea still messed with her mind.

"Come on, let's go find somewhere to sit," Orin suggested.

"I'll be right there," she replied as he took off in the direction of their Clan's table and left Lexy standing there scanning the crowd for her always elusive Handler. She saw him at the bar chatting with Stephanie from Triad. *Why was he always drawn to the most brutal female in the room?* She shook her head and made her way to the table, finding a seat beside Zach, who was staring at Triad's table, visibly agitated. *There were many ways to decipher Kayn's Handler's irritable demeanour. If her intuition was correct it might be jealousy, Patrick appeared to have a date. He could just be concerned about his absentee Dragon.* Lexy opted to play nice. *There was no point in asking more than he was prepared to answer.* She affirmed, "She's coming. I'm sure they just got preoccupied and lost track of time."

Zach gave her the strangest look. He grinned as he chuckled, "Well said. That was G-Rated gold. Bravo."

"Once in a while, magic happens," Lexy countered, accepting a glass of wine as the tray passed by their table. She took a sip as she thought of a way to word the question on the tip of her tongue, then opted to leave it be. She glanced back at the bar. *Grey was still chatting up that heinous bitch from Triad.*

Chuckling, Zach raised his glass and saluted, "To the complicated relationship between Handlers and Dragons."

He'd heard her uncensored thoughts. Lexy wrinkled her nose as she clinked glasses with Zach and downed her drink. Her eyes darted his way as she whispered, "Is she good in bed?" Zach choked on his gulp of wine. Lexy patted his back and teased, "So, that's a yes."

Zach shook his head as Grey swooped in from behind and kissed Lexy's cheek. He looked at Zach and provoked, "Let me know if her flirting bothers you."

Funny. Lexy socked her Handler in the rib. Grey pulled out the chair beside her, still snickering like an evil sibling. She caught herself watching the entrance for a glimpse of Tiberius. *What was she doing? What was wrong with her? Even thinking of him would cause drama.* She excused herself, requiring a moment to stifle her inner commentary. She burst out of the banquet hall onto the balcony, leaned on the railing and gazed at the starry desert sky. She'd been standing in silence for a while when she heard the doors open.

Orin's voice declared, "This has to be my favourite place in the whole world to view the night sky." He leaned over the rail next to her and enquired, "Everyone is talking about the Guardian sister revelation. Is that why you're out here?"

"It wasn't, but now that I know I'm the topic of everyone's conversations, I might just stay out here all night," Lexy taunted.

With a grin, Orin baited, "I always find it best to know exactly what you're up against."

She missed a lot of insinuations, but she caught that one. Without looking at him, she responded, "I always thought saying you can't help who you're attracted to was just an excuse for naughty behaviour."

"It is, but you don't have to make excuses, I'm all for you getting down with your bad self," Orin wittily bantered.

"How are you this evolved?" Lexy enquired, grinning.

"Mistakes, my love. I've made a shitload of epically horrible choices," Orin affirmed. He placed his hand on hers and assured, "It doesn't matter who you go home with tonight. We're all good."

She looked at him and said, "I tried to eat you."

"Cannibalism happens," Orin chuckled as they stared out over the still of the desert.

He was the most laid-back bootie call ever. She quipped, "I think that needs to be a bumper sticker."

He chuckled, "You know that's totally happening now."

"Bring it on, Healer boy," she bantered.

He teased, "Go do what you need to do. After you get Tiberius out of your system, we'll talk about our wedding. I'm still available for service calls."

"What?" she laughed, certain it was a joke. "Service texts. I don't call anybody...Ever."

"Liar," Orin sparred. "I've heard you call out my name multiple times."

She had no comeback. It was true.

He stepped away from the railing and sexily sparred, "Keep me in the race and someday, I'll rock your world."

She was still laughing as Orin opened the door and disappeared inside. *What in the hell was that all about?* No longer stressed, she entered the hall just in time to see Kayn making her way to the table. *Orin was right. Everyone was staring.* She grabbed Kayn a drink. Markus was undoubtedly ticked off about Frost being a no show for the meet and greet part of the evening. Kayn sat beside Zach. Lexy maneuvered through the tables to Ankh's seating without spilling a drop. She placed her hand on Kayn's shoulder. She handed her sister a drink and teased, "Do try to catch up." Kayn accepted the glass of red wine. Her sister casually took a sip while nonchalantly scanning the banquet. Triad was sitting clear across the hall on the far side of the enormous dance floor. Trinity was seated closest to Ankh. Tiberius strolled in and made eye contact with her long enough to make her girly parts tingle. She crossed her legs to squash the hum of arousal and then realised she'd been holding her breath. She exhaled as Tiberius smirked and headed straight for the rest of his Clan without looking back. Lexy grinned. *She'd thought she was going to be able to hide the effect he had on her, but she hadn't been able to. So much for her cocky just walk away move earlier. It didn't mean anything now. He was a smart guy. Passive-aggressive magic. She was having to force herself to look at someone else... Anyone else.*

Zach stood up and asked Haley to dance. Thorne strolled over and sat down with Trinity. There were so many things she could be looking at or paying attention to but all she could think about was the overwhelming urge to be reckless and wild. *Sleeping with Tiberius was wrong. They were in opposing Clans. He was a horrible person at least eighty percent of the time. Her Handler would lose his mind.*

Astrid whispered her reaction to Lexy's thoughts, "I'm one hundred percent into girls, but Tiberius has this hard to describe dirty boy thing going on, I get it. You look amazing tonight, you're unbelievably hot. Don't worry about Grey. He's been making his rounds chatting with every female in here. I'd really prefer he didn't take that one though."

Lexy saw who Astrid was talking about. He was having an intimate conversation with Glory from Trinity at the next table. Lexy winked at Astrid and whispered back, "I've got this." *Cock blocking Grey was her specialty and heck, it would keep her Tiberius yearning mind occupied for a minute or two.* Astrid was completely intrigued as she stole her shot glass. *Whisky…This wasn't going to go well.* Lexy sniffed it, grimaced and downed it. Astrid was beaming as she got up, strutted over to Trinity's table, leaned in and whispered in Glory's ear, "I'm doing a favour for a friend, play along." She stole the bottle of tequila from in front of Grey and began chugging it right from the bottle.

Grey jumped up, snatched it from Lexy's clutches and panicked, "What in the hell are you doing?"

She sighed, "I'm having a good time Greydon. What in the hell are you doing?" Lexy slipped into the seat on the other side of Glory and whispered, "Do you remember that night after you walked me home?"

Beyond intrigued, Glory replied, "Yes…Of course I do."

"We should do it again?" Lexy seduced, playing with one of Glory's silky curls.

Grey leaned in and quietly asked, "What are you doing?"

With a naughty glint in her eye, Glory suggested, "Lexy's an incredible kisser, why don't the three of us…"

Grey got up and said, "And I'm out. Funny. You guys think you're hilarious."

They threw their heads back laughing as Grey walked away. Once he was out of earshot, Lexy explained, "I love Grey, but Astrid is into you and Grey's into everybody."

Glory shook her head and confessed, "Astrid and I had an incredible night together before she went into the Testing. We're in opposing Clans. She's been gone for decades."

"This night is destined to go into a downward spiral why not have fun while you're circling the drain?" Lexy provoked.

Glory chuckled, "I will if you will."

Lexy wasn't sure what Glory meant. She found various inappropriate things entertaining. She raised another shot of whiskey, downed it and sort of agreed, "To having fun while we're circling the drain." Lexy stood up and gave Glory's shoulder a friendly squeeze before making her way back to Ankh's table. *They were in the middle of a debate about Amar's newbies.* Lexy was able to slip back into the seat beside Astrid undetected. They'd all been too busy debating to notice she'd left, so she just sat there listening.

Astrid whispered, "I made no promise to hold my tongue. Samid can't enter the Testing with our group. There's no way he'll be compatible."

Zach scooted back into the seat beside Kayn and remarked, "I've already put in my two cents. I feel like we have the time to assimilate him to our lifestyle. We have a couple of years until our continents Testing. I told

Markus I was all for him coming with us, but if Triad steals him, he's theirs. We just won't go out of our way to get him back. At least this way we can give them all a chance. As it stands, they have no chance at all."

Kayn kept watching the entrance. *She was obviously waiting for Frost.* Lexy really had no interest in Amar's son's odds for survival. *These guys didn't understand. It didn't matter if they couldn't see any redeeming qualities in someone that hadn't gone into the Testing, they rarely came out. Kayn's group was the first in four decades. They'd have to learn the hard way.* Lexy got up without bothering to give Astrid the humorous details of her conversation with Glory and boldly opted to take her own advice.

She was planning to find Orin, knowing hanging out with him would irk multiple people. She scanned the crowd for Grey, knowing it was supposed to be his sole purpose to stop her from doing bad things. *Supposed to be. Shocker. He was otherwise occupied, whispering in some unknown girl's ear.* She caught sight of Tiberius as he disappeared out a door on the far side of the hall. *What was he up too?* Curiosity got the best of her. She made her way across the hall and slipped out through the same door into a dimly lit corridor. *She was playing with fire…She knew this.* Lexy cautiously made her way down the darkened hall until the light disappeared. She felt around for a switch, and when she couldn't find one, she opted to go back. *He could be taking a short cut to the bathroom for all she knew.* A door closed. *Crap.* She stepped back into the shadows. *Maybe, he'd just walk right past her.* The footsteps came closer. *She wasn't the girl that hid in the shadows.* "What are you doing wandering around in the dark?" Lexy boldly enquired.

"Were you following me, Lexy Abrelle? I'm honoured," Tiberius seductively countered.

His use of her full name stunned her. She felt the undeniable electricity his presence caused as every hair stood on end. He stepped closer, and like a dance, instinct prompted her to step back to avoid contact. Her back was against the wall. *That wasn't smart.*

"Did you want to be alone with me?" Tiberius huskily baited as the space between them disappeared. He pressed his body intimately against hers, she felt the heat of his breath on her neck as he whispered, "Every time we go to one of these things, you walk away without shaking my hand. But once I get you alone, you unfold for me like the petals of a rose. Why is that?"

She trembled as he began nibbling on her earlobe. *What was she doing?*

He viciously bit her neck, triggering her healing ability. Lexy felt the pleasurable healing heat as he caressed her nipples through the thin material of her dress until she was aching with need. Her arms encircled his neck like they had a mind of their own as she gave in to what she knew she wanted.

Tiberius mischievously grasped her hips and naughtily ordered, "Tell me you want me. Say it. I'll take you right here with everyone else on the other side of that door." He aggressively cupped her buttocks.

She grabbed handfuls of his hair, unable to see reason as her enemy began wickedly grinding himself against her. As the first waves of ecstasy surged within, she whimpered, "Don't stop…Please… Don't."

He chuckled naughtily as she gasped. He covered her mouth to stifle her cries of pleasure as he reprimanded, "You naughty, naughty girl." He licked the blood from her throat as she ached with desire. "I'm going to enjoy reprimanding you almost as much as you delight in your punishment but they're serving dinner. You're Handler will be coming to look for you."

For once she had no comeback, she couldn't even think, "Tiberius," she whispered.

He knelt on the cement before her and whispered, "I bet your panties are drenched. We should take those off." He roguishly slid his hands up her calves to her thighs. He nipped at the sensitive flesh of her inner thigh and she whimpered. Adrenaline pulsed through her as she realised what he was about to do to. Lexy clutched his hair as he began licking her silky panties. *What if someone came in? What if… Oh yes.* Her toes curled as the wave of ecstasy rippled through her. She released his hair to muffle herself as she cried out his name.

"Good girl," Tiberius deviously praised with his lips against her drenched panties.

He was a naughty, naughty boy. They were going to get caught. She needed him inside of her too much to care. She was still quivering as he gathered the material of her dress around her waist. *She needed him to finish this.* Tiberius traced his finger on her ticklish abdomen, promising, "If we were alone, I'd take my blade, slice you right here and…" He sensually licked her stomach. "While you healed, I'd…"

She was so turned on her knees were buckling. *Take me. Take me, please.*

Tiberius stood up, brushed himself off and curtly said, "Try to pull yourself together before you go in or it'll be obvious." He walked away and left her standing there, trembling against the wall with soaking wet panties. *That twisted asshole. Why did she keep letting him do this? She should have known better.* Livid, Lexy took off her wet panties and tossed them down the hall. *She was going to kill him.* She shoved her skirt down and grinned, unable to help it. *Guess she was going commando tonight.* She was still trying to catch her breath when Grey stuck his head through the door and declared, "There you are. What are you doing, they're serving dinner."

Her mind scrambled for a response. It landed on something moderately feasible and sort of the truth, "Somebody pissed me off, I needed to be alone."

He shrugged and beckoned her to the open door. As she walked out, he commented, "You look flushed. You should get some food in your stomach before you drink anything else."

"Probably," she replied as they strolled back to Ankh's seating. They sat at the end of the table in front of their plates of gravy slathered roast beef and devoured their meals. *What if someone found her panties?*

Grey looked up and said, "What?"

Lexy smiled and replied, "Huh?"

Her Handler shrugged and continued to eat as she tried to think about anything else. *Her meal was bland, she could really use some hot sauce. She knew better than to ask for it at one of these functions.* Kayn, was at the far end of the table chatting with their Clan's other Testing survivors. She would have liked to have a conversation with her, so they could get to know each other better, but it was best to avoid in-depth discussions about their Guardian paternity in a room full of eavesdropping immortals. She dripped gravy on her dress. *Shit.* She picked up her napkin and dipped it in her water to wipe it off.

Grey leapt up, touched her shoulder and asserted, "No, don't use water. Give it a dab but don't wipe it, you'll have little balls of napkin all over the place. I'll get you a rag and club soda. Can you be patient for two minutes?"

"No," Lexy answered honestly.

Grey laughed and teased, "Try."

She smiled as he took off. As Lexy went to place her napkin back down on the table, she saw it...*There was a tiny yellow flower beside her plate. Tiberius was a shithead. It had to be him.* She casually brushed it off onto the floor and kicked it under the table so Grey wouldn't see it. *Asshole. She'd let him...That piece of shit.* She felt hollow as she locked the reaction to the sedating flower within her, and for a second, she became lost in her Dragon self.

Chapter 12

Losing My Mind

She wasn't sure how long she'd been gapped out looking at her plate when Grey started cleaning off her dress, but the atmosphere had changed. The dance floor was packed, and the hardcore party part of the event was underway. Everyone else had left the table and disappeared into the sea of writhing immortals and smoke. She was sitting there alone, staring at her plate like a weirdo.

"Sorry, there was a lineup at the bar. I couldn't get the bartenders attention," Grey explained as he finished cleaning up her mess. "There...Good as new. I'm going to get rid of this damp towel and get you out on the dance floor."

She smiled as he walked away. She intended to pick up that flower and shove it down Tiberius' throat, but it was gone. She surveyed the bottom of each of her stilettos. *It wasn't stuck to the bottom of her shoes. Maybe, it was on the on the waiter's or Grey's? What if it hadn't really been there at all?*

Orin slid into the chair next to her and said, "Having a good night?"

She peered under the table again as she answered, "Either someone is messing with me or I'm losing my mind."

Orin stuck his head under the table and whispered, "What are we looking for?"

She could be honest with Orin. He wasn't someone that flipped his lid for no reason, so she whispered back, "There was a tiny yellow flower under my napkin. I brushed it off the table. I didn't want to give the asshole that put it there the satisfaction of my reaction. It's gone now."

"Did you check the bottom of your shoes?" Orin quietly enquired with his head still under the table.

"I already looked," she whispered.

"Somebody probably stepped on it and walked away," Orin quietly suggested. "It could be on Grey's shoes?"

Grey's head appeared under the table. He whispered, "Are we having a secret under the table meeting?"

Lexy startled and smoked the back of her head under the table as she tried to get up with a loud clang. *Son of a...*

Grey chuckled as he rubbed her wounded noggin and teased, "I'm beginning to see the family resemblance between you and Kayn."

Her sister was incredibly accident-prone. Lexy grinned as she swatted her Handler away.

"He may have a point there," Orin ribbed as he stood up and announced, "I'm going to go and grab something from the bar."

Lexy saw the lineup of ladies and started laughing.

"Check his shoes," Orin remarked as he wandered away.

"What about my shoes?" Grey enquired as he looked at the bottom of each foot.

If she told Grey the truth, he'd freak out. She whispered, "Orin thought someone stepped in poop."

"How would anyone step in it?" Grey quietly answered. "We're indoors? None of us have been outside."

She hadn't thought that excuse out. Lexy got up, held out her hand and declared, "It doesn't even matter. Let's dance."

Grey stood up and sarcastically sighed, "I thought you'd never ask. I was beginning to feel like a bit of a wallflower." He winked as he took Lexy's hand.

They danced their way into the gyrating crowd. Between the smoke show and the pulsating lights, it was easy to throw caution to the wind. They embraced the hedonistic pulsating club music as he stayed with only her. Inevitably, a slow song began, and he took her in his arms. She rested her head on Grey's shoulder as they moved together, it felt like they had gone back in time. *He was hers, she was his, and there was no way to pretend that wasn't how it really was* …The words of the song ceased to matter and the beat of their hearts in unison was all she could hear. His embrace had worked its Handler magic. Lexy felt a sense of inner peace only his arms could provide. The song ended and the duo opted to go back to the table to be social. *She wasn't angry anymore. Her Handler had handled it.*

"I'll go get us a drink or a bottle," Grey chuckled as he took off to the bar. He strolled past Kayn and tussled her hair. Her sister swatted Grey's rear end. He glanced back and pretended to be shocked.

Don't you even think about it. He was such a playboy wanna be. Lexy slowly shook her head as her Handler strutted into the crowd in front of the bar. Grey put his arm around Haley and whispered something in her ear. Haley playfully shoved him away and shook her head. Lexy silently laughed as she watched Grey trying to persevere against the odds. Lexy felt a hand on the small of her back. She was about to kick someone's ass when she saw who it was and smiled as she enquired, "Hey Orin, how's your night going?"

"It's been rather eventful. I found a stomped yellow flower on the dance floor and put it in Tiberius' drink," Orin answered.

Impressed, Lexy gawked and whispered, "You didn't? What happened?"

"As you can see, he's fine so that might not have been what you thought it was," Orin whispered.

The mere sight of Triad's tool of a leader relit the fuse of her anger.

Tiberius grabbed a chair, sat down beside Kayn and blurted, "So, you're in a relationship with my brother now... How's that going?" He grabbed a fork and dug into her cake.

Without a thought, Kayn stabbed his hand with her fork and hissed, "Get your own cake."

Laughing too hard to bother retaliating, Tiberius massaged his wound.

She felt so close to Kayn right now.

"Awe...Kayn just stabbed Tiberius, she really is your sister," Orin quietly ribbed.

Zach's attention snapped away from Triad's table as he scolded, "Brighton! What in the hell? No stabbing people!"

Idiot. Those were her favourite underwear, she'd been polite enough. Lexy aggressively yanked Tiberius's chair away from the table with him still sitting in it and sparred, "You're not bothering my sister, are you?"

Tiberius leaned back in the chair and flirtatiously greeted her, "Hey gorgeous."

He thought he'd bested her. Think again. "Hey gorgeous yourself," Lexy mumbled. She put her full weight on the back of his seat and tipped him over. With a loud thud, her naughty corridor companion was lying flat on his back on the floor. Lexy distastefully glared down at Tiberius.

"Always so deliciously volatile. You're sexy as hell… I've missed this," he flirted from his naughty vantage point, seductively caressing her calf.

"That's odd because I haven't," Lexy icily countered.

"Liar," Tiberius provoked as he held out the hand he'd been stroking her leg with. *He wanted her to help him up…Funny. All he'd done with those wandering hands was remind her of her recklessly irresponsible tendencies.* In true Dragon style, Lexy stepped away from Triad's naughty leader. Scorching flames of animosity flew from her lips as she sparred, "I wouldn't hold your breath." She left him lying there, strutted all the way to the other side of the table and sat down to make a point.

Tiberius was still lying there laughing as Orin strolled over, politely helped him up and quipped, "You just never learn."

The leader of Triad grinned at Orin and instead of leaving, he pushed his seat back up to the table and sat down.

Orin walked around to sit in the empty chair by Lexy.

Kayn shoved her cake at Tiberius like it had cooties and said, "I'll get a new one."

Unfazed, Tiberius dug into Kayn's cake as he pointedly looked directly at Orin and enquired, "How's Jenna doing with the whole Lexy thing?"

She wanted to slam Tiberius' head into the table.

Zach nudged Kayn and whispered, "This is getting good."

"I haven't asked," Orin curtly replied. "We don't discuss who we're seeing."

"How's her Handler taking it?" Tiberius probed, purposely being a dick.

He'd heard she was seeing Orin. Now, it made sense. Lexy glared at Tiberius. She booted him under the table and declared, "I'm right here. If you have any questions about my life, ask me."

"Are you coming to my room later?" Tiberius brazenly tempted.

Lexy smiled as she shook her head and reined in her reaction to his cheeky flirtation.

"That's not a no," Tiberius teased. He took a long sip of his wine, and without breaking eye contact, he naughtily added, "There's an adjoining door between our rooms if the mood strikes you."

She crossed her legs tightly, as what she allowed him to do to her in that dark hallway flashed through her mind. *He'd left that flower. Even if it was only a similar flower, it was still cruel.*

"That's my cue," Orin broadcasted. As he excused himself from the table, he bent down and whispered in Lexy's ear, "Don't do anything I wouldn't do."

She needed a drink.

Frost slid into the seat next to his brother Tiberius and announced, "Still trying to get blood from a stone?"

She heard Tiberius' thoughts loud and clear, *'The darkest part of you is drawn to me. You can't deny it.'*

She couldn't.

'You'll give yourself to me,' Tiberius thought. *'I don't care about Orin. He doesn't mean anything. The Dragon in you wants what only I can give, and that instinctual need always wins over ration.'*

Lexy replied in her mind, *The Dragon in me doesn't want anyone. The Dragon doesn't care. That's a Dragon's purpose.*

Tiberius countered in his thoughts, *'The Dragon didn't kill me when it had the chance during that last job. Nobody told you about that, did they?'*

*Nobody had...*Lexy grabbed Frost's shot and drank it without even knowing what it was. *Dear lord, it's Tequila.*

Zach caught the waiter's attention and grabbed Kayn a ridiculously large slice of replacement cake. Tiberius slid a shot glass across the table at Kayn, she snatched it. He made eye contact with Lexy as he slid one to her with a swipe of his hand. Lexy picked up her shot of Tequila and declared, "I'm going to need a lot of these to forget who you are." While grinning at her response, Tiberius slid another shot across the table to Zach, who spent the first year of his immortality in Triad. *She needed someone rational because she wasn't feeling even a touch of it right now.* Lexy's eyes darted over to Trinity's table. Orin was chatting with Thorne. *He was fine.* Melody was also sitting there. *She might be overthinking this. Thorne and Melody had undeniable chemistry and an intimate relationship before she'd been taken by Ankh. For all intents and purposes, they were also enemies, even though the spark between them was bright enough for anyone to see. Tomorrow, they'd go back to being rivals.* Tiberius was playing footsies with her. Lexy was trying to give him no reaction at all, but each time his foot brushed against her leg, it was like he was striking a match. *He was right. She could try to fight against this with hostility, but there was something between them she couldn't deny. It was like the darkness in their souls was drawing them together. He left that flower. She knew he did even though she couldn't prove it.*

Frost looked at Kayn and enquired, "How much longer do you want to stay?"

Lexy snapped out of it. *How long had she been staring at Tiberius?*

"Another hour?" Kayn suggested. Zach sighed. Kayn gave his arm a pinch. "Consider yourself off duty. Just go over there and talk to him." Zach gave her a look.

Oh, no. She didn't. Lexy did another shot. *This conversation was a perfect distraction from Tiberius's naughty beneath the table game.*

Kayn corrected herself, "Whoops, I meant her."

"You just stabbed Tiberius," Zach casually clarified. He rolled his eyes and downed his shot.

Grinning as he noticed his brother's bloody napkin wrapped hand, Frost playfully reprimanded, "Sweetheart, you're supposed to play nice."

"That was me playing nice," Kayn mumbled under her breath.

Lexy pivoted in her seat and looked Tiberius dead in the eyes as she remarked, "Stabbings happen. Tiberius makes me feel all stabby too."

Grey slid into the seat by Zach and declared, "Go. Frost is here, I'm here. Everyone wants to stab Tiberius. He's used to it. We'll keep things PG."

Shit. Her conscience was back.

As Zach got up, he looked at Kayn and asked, "Are you planning to do anything that will get me in trouble?"

"Maybe," Kayn casually replied as she devoured her massive slice of chocolate cake like a ravenous animal.

"Are you kidding? It's getting harder to tell," Zach questioned. "Promise me you won't stab him again... Or anyone else."

Lexy looked at Kayn and thought, *Tell Zach whatever he needs to hear, I'll do it.* They both smiled. *This family bonding stuff was going to be fun. Her sister had her heart set on killing Stephanie this evening. She'd seen Kayn glaring at her on multiple occasions.*

Kayn vowed, "I promise I won't stab Tiberius again. Now get over there already."

"Or anyone else," Zach clarified.

'*Party pooper,*' Kayn thought.

Lexy winked at her, *I told you I'd do it.*

"Alright, nobody gets stabbed," Kayn promised. Zach wandered away from the table.

Grey grabbed Lexy's knee and gave her the dirtiest look as he said, "I guess I'm not leaving your side tonight. Come on. Let's dance."

Oh yes. Her moral compass had arrived. She was officially too drunk to control her inner commentary. Lexy took Grey's hand, glanced back at Kayn and mouthed the words, "I'll get Stephanie." Grey's furious grasp on her wrist as he towed her out onto the dance floor made her giggle. *Her Handler never found her murder plots funny at these Inter-Clan events.*

Lexy was out and out laughing as Grey clutched both of her shoulders, stared deep into her eyes and ordered, "You will not kill Stephanie. Do you hear me?"

Lexy doubled over laughing. *She was going to pee herself.*

Grey questioned, "How much have you had to drink tonight?"

"How much have you had to drink?" Lexy saucily countered as he relaxed his grasp. "I haven't slept with Tiberius in the coat check room so I'm probably fine."

Gathering her in his arms as they moved to the music, Grey whispered in her ear, "We're in the middle east. There is no coat check room."

With her chin on her Handler's shoulder, Lexy locked eyes with Tiberius and he winked. As they waltzed, Grey snapped her out of her distracted state by twirling her around. She laughed and caught sight of the towering Killian from Amar's crew, chatting up Haley. *The height difference was rather adorable.* As Lexy faced the table again, Thorne was sitting there with everyone, and it looked like he was panicking. *They were missing something exciting.* With her lips close to Grey's ear, Lexy commented, "There appears to be drama at our table."

Grey stealthily danced her around, so he could check it out. He countered, "There's always drama." He chuckled, "I think Tiberius is messing with Thorne."

Killian left Haley's side and waved at her. "Incoming Viking guy," Lexy warned as the large muscular adonis with flowing blonde hair approached.

Grey sighed as their mountainously built Clan member exuberantly embraced them, lifting both immortals off the ground like he was the bun on a Handler Dragon sandwich. He boisterously laughed as he spun them around with their legs dangling like rag dolls. Killian announced with his undeniably unique accent, "Guess who's coming to your continent to join your crew? I have a job to complete first, then I'm off to North America to babysit young Sammy!"

Sammy? Oh… Samid. Clever Amar… They weren't going to be able to let Tiberius take the little asshole. Amar was sending his kid with a personal bodyguard.

The titan Killian freed them from his grasp while agreeing, "I know the kid seems like a complete ass but there's more to Sam than meets the eye."

There usually was.

Killian looked directly at Lexy as he said, "You kids behave yourself tonight." He was about to walk away when he enquired, "The girl I was talking to wouldn't give me her name. She's one of yours, isn't she?"

"Her name's Haley," Grey disclosed. "She's one of the two that were stuck in the Testing for decades."

"Taken?" Killian asked as he watched her dancing with Astrid and Glory.

Grey answered, "I'm not sure. Not by me."

Killian smirked and retorted, "Good to know. She's unique with the pink hair. Can you believe she wouldn't give me her name?" He looked directly at Lexy.

He wanted her input. Why? Lexy shrugged and confessed, "I don't really know her. She hasn't done anything overly scandalous."

"Well, that's a shame," Killian sighed. He was about to leave when he looked back and revealed, "For future reference, there are cameras in all of the hallways. All of them." He chuckled as he left.

They stood there curiously watching as Killian slipped out through the door into the dark hall where she'd left her underwear. *Oh no!* Lexy fought to keep her composure as she glanced back at the table and met Tiberius' cocky grin with the dirtiest look she had in her repertoire. *She was going to kick his kinky ass.*

"I knew there was a reason you were in that hallway," Grey exclaimed as he caught on to the cause of her agitation, "Damn it, Lexy. I hate him. I despise that guy. He's tortured me."

"We torture each other," Lexy rebutted as she filtered through the embarrassment. *Their encounter hadn't been private at all. She should have her way with him and then rip his head off like a praying mantis. That dirty piece of shit.*

Grey was fuming as he whispered, "He's the enemy. Don't you have any loyalty?"

She was officially too drunk to filter her comebacks. Lexy faced her Handler and sparred, "Shall we look around the room and do a Greydon of Ankh bed buddy tally?"

"Let's not and just say we did," he countered as people dancing began paying attention to their dispute.

Lexy started vehemently listing his exploits, "You've slept with Melody, Lily and Arrianna from our Clan alone. Glory from Trinity...Who is one of our... what Grey? Any idea where I'm going with this?"

"I get it," Grey stated. "Do you need to leave?"

"I dare you to try to make me," Lexy curtly replied as she spun around and pointed, "Don't you recognize that one in the silver dress over there from Triad?" Lexy asked. "She's also a notch on your bedpost. You are no better."

"Alright. You've made your point," Grey answered. "Everyone's staring."

"I've only just begun," Lexy retorted as she pointed to the bar and announced, "There's one over there wearing red from Triad. Enemy. There's another one wearing a black pantsuit, I can't recall her name or which Clan she's with, but it's not Ankh so… Enemy." She started pointing around the room at women saying, "Enemy, enemy and not so ironically another enemy. I can keep going, but honestly, after four decades, they're all just blurring together."

"Alright…Okay, I get it. I know what I've done but you're better than me. You don't have a long list of conquests, your actions mean more," Grey countered.

Lexy pulled away from him, looked into his eyes and questioned, "Why?"

"They just do," he replied, tenderly caressing her cheek.

Damn his Handler voodoo magic. Her resolve folded like a cheap deck of cards in response to his touch. They stood there staring at each other in a stubborn standoff as everyone else danced. Lexy whispered, "When you do this, it's not fair. I don't stop you."

"Um, earlier this evening, you actually hit on Glory," Grey chuckled as he took her in his arms. Unable to fight against it, they started dancing again.

She did do that, didn't she? "But I rarely do," she teased. Grey spun her and dipped her, causing laughter to erupt once again.

He swooped her back into his arms and whispered, "Please don't sleep with him. Anybody else. Literally, anyone else and I swear I'll suck it up."

The instinct to do as he requested wasn't as strong tonight. She was too drunk to ignore her lizard brain's urges. Lexy watched as Kayn left the table with her chin innocently perched on Grey's shoulder as they danced. *Her primal urges were impressively amped up this evening.* Tiberius kept making eye contact with her each time they turned while moving to the music. Their titillating encounter during the last Summit had left her aching to experience all that dark attraction had to offer. Their brief sensually charged encounters since, had left her yearning for more. She hadn't been able to shake the sexually charged visions of Tiberius slicing her with his blade. He'd shown her about pain-induced pleasure. *It surfaced in her thoughts more than she wanted to admit. She hadn't been overly conscious of Orin's feelings tonight. Being a thousand years old gave Orin a pretty good grasp on the realities of attractions left unfulfilled, and he was all for her taking the night to see Tiberius's chapter through till it's end. Orin had no intention of getting into anything more serious than booty calls and flirtations with her until she'd closed her book of unknowns.*

Grey whispered in her ear, "I'm going to need another drink if you're going to insist on thinking about that dick."

Lexy rolled her eyes and sparred, "Jealous?"

He pulled away, considered it and teased, "Maybe a little."

She playfully shoved him away, and as she strolled back to the table, she jabbed, "You'll get over it. You always do."

"What did you just say?" Grey enquired as he caught up with her.

"Nothing important," Lexy remarked as she snatched the shot from in front of Tiberius and downed it.

Triad's leader glanced at her as she sat down beside Grey. Tiberius bit his lip and grinned as he began playing footsies with her. Smiling, she countered by sliding her foot as far up his leg as she could reach. Grey was laughing with Frost. *It didn't look like he'd noticed their flirtation.*

Grey turned to look at her, smiled and said, "You know I'm not letting you out of my sight tonight. There's no point in entertaining those naughty thoughts."

Their roles were ridiculously unfair. He could do whatever he wanted, and her actions had to be monitored. This was the price of being a Dragon. Her Handler was always present to talk her down from the ledge. His job was to stop her dark impulses. She took a sip of her wine as she watched the dancers writhing in a sea of rising smoke. Everything about this continents banquet made her want to let her Dragon soar. The pulsating light show was stimulating her need for freedom. She met Tiberius's seductive gaze again. Their eyes held with the intensity of their rendezvous in the dark hallway earlier that evening. Grey countered by possessively placing his hand on her thigh under the table, tugging her heart back to where it belonged without words. Orin shifted closer, trying to make sure she understood her options. *This was getting awkward.*

Grey glared across the table at Tiberius and said, "That's me you're playing footsies with."

Tiberius winked at Grey as he countered, "I didn't want you to feel left out. Of course, you're free to join us."

Her Handler rolled his eyes. He turned to face Lexy as he warned, "I'll be upset for like a year if you do this just so we're clear."

Without offering him the sentimentality of eye contact, Lexy whispered, "Lily…Melody… Arrianna…Do I really need to keep going?"

Defeated by the reality of his own actions, Grey looked away and continued to pretend he was listening to Frost.

Out of nowhere, Grey turned to her and asserted, "One word from you and I would have walked away from all of them."

Here they were again. Her Handler's feelings for her were returning. As soon as she gave in they would be gone, and she'd be left heartbroken. Determined to stop kicking herself, Lexy didn't respond. She took a pastry from the tray as it was offered to her. As she took her first bite, her eyes were drawn to Tiberius. His foot grazed hers under the table. She bit her lip pensively. With Grey's hand rested on her thigh, she wasn't sure she could reply by action without being caught. *She wanted to, that was her truth. She'd despised Tiberius with every inch of her being for forty years, and now, every argument just felt like foreplay between Dragons. Their duelling libidos had led them into some awkward situations, but she wanted him and admitting it was half the battle. He'd been bold enough to acquire the room next to hers, with an adjoining door. Even though she'd led him to believe she wouldn't come to him during his rather public dare, she'd wanted too.* Lexy excused herself, turning back to the table when she was far enough away, she met Tiberius's intrigued gaze and winked. She intended to make her way back to her room and use that door but needed a quick detour. Lexy maneuvered through the dancing crowd and down the short hall with muted toned tapestries to the washroom. She was alone for a moment in the stall before she heard the hollow clicking of footsteps as somebody entered. *For a split second, she found herself hoping it was him.* Lexy peered through the crack of the door. *It was Stephanie. She'd been quite the bitch to Kayn...Her sister. That was still a crazy thought. She could stay in the stall until the Triad girl left or storm out and kick her ass. She was supposed to behave ... She'd do her best.* Lexy abruptly opened the stall, startling the Triad.

The petite beauty spun around and laughed nervously, "I didn't know anyone else was in here."

Lexy strolled over with plans to wash her hands and leave but there was no soap in the dispenser. This irritated her, but she was still planning to try to play nice.

"Didn't you hear me?" Stephanie prodded.

Lexy moved over to the next sink and tried the dispenser...*it didn't work. It spoke to her. It shouldn't speak to her when she was this drunk.*

"Should I grunt like a caveman? You know, speak your language? Is the soap dispenser too difficult for you to figure out? I heard you went years without bathing," the tiny Triad provoked.

Tiberius just lost his booty call. He would have been the one to tell her that story. Lexy sighed before asserting, "I'd just quietly go about whatever business you came in here to do if I were you."

Intrigued by her hostility, Stephanie poked the Dragon within her, "I was thinking about taking Greydon out for a spin. I figure it's all good if you plan on hooking up with Tiberius tonight."

She wanted to say Grey would never go there but she knew better. He so would, without batting an eye. "Do what you want," Lexy coldly responded.

"I intend to," Stephanie vowed as she gave the dispenser a shot and it worked. She smiled at Lexy as she whispered her snarky commentary, "It's not rocket science."

And that was it! Lexy shot forward and snapped her neck. Stephanie slumped to the tile. Lexy gave her body a swift boot. *What a bitch! That was satisfying.* She pranced away with a skip in her step. The sound of chaos snapped her back to reality. *Crap. Triad's symbols went off. Adding copious amounts of alcohol to her unfiltered rage issues always backfired. She might as well own it.*

Grey was already racing down the hall, absolutely livid, scolding, "Seriously, Lex! What in the hell?"

Lexy turned around and mumbled, "I'll fix it." She opened the door to Stephanie's lifeless corpse, knelt before her, laid her palms on her mortal enemy's chest, and as the warmth of her healing energy travelled down her arms into the Triad's body, Grey yanked her aside. Her vision wavered, exhausted, Lexy passed out beside the Triad on the tile.

Tiberius appeared in the doorway. Grey turned to explain, but Tiberius interrupted him, "They obviously had a tiff. I warned Stephanie about being lippy with certain people. This only explains one of the flashes."

Grey sighed as he apologized and tried to explain, "I told Zach to go have fun and that I'd watch them tonight. It was my mistake. I'm to blame."

The leader of Triad slowly shook his head as he replied, "The rules don't apply to these two, they're part Guardian. They can't be entombed. Don't take ownership of a problem that's not yours anymore."

Amar, Markus and Frost appeared in the hallway. Tiberius summoned them over with a wave. Once again, Grey tried to take one for the team. Although Markus agreed that he'd made a misstep, he wasn't about to place the blame on Grey entirely. "You should have known better Greydon, but in all fairness, this is a situation we've never encountered. We're going to have to be creative with how we deal with this. Have you noticed a change in your bond in the last couple of days?"

Grey shrugged as he admitted, "Maybe a little."

Thorne's deep superhero voice boomed down the hall, "We've found the other body! Someone tossed Tiberius's grandson over the balcony!"

Frustrated, Frost sighed, "Let me guess, Kayn and Zach are nowhere to be found."

"I saw Zach usher Kayn out during the ruckus," Lily disclosed as she peeked into the bathroom. "Who started it?"

"Probably Stephanie, but as always, Lexy finished it, "Grey admitted.

Tiberius smiled as he gazed at the crimson-haired Dragon sprawled on the tile and commented, "I can't turn anyone in. They're Seth's daughters, and although the rules don't apply, Ankh is going to have to find a way to control this situation. They can't just be running around murdering anyone that ticks them off."

Markus met Frost's eyes as he apologized, "I'm sorry, Tiberius is right. We must find a way to have control over these two. Contact Jenna, get her to speak to Ankh's Guardian and ask her what she thinks we should do about this. Grey, take Lexy to your room and wait for us to get back to you."

Grey scooped Lexy up in his arms and carried her back to their room. As he placed her on the bed, Lexy whispered, "I'm not sorry."

He grinned as he climbed into bed next to her and replied, "I know."

Chapter 13

Immortal Time Outs

Lexy awoke as the sun's warmth began crawling up her satin sheets. She stretched. For a moment, she forgot where she was. She winced as it started to come back. *The hallway with Tiberius. Her behaviour had been horrible last night.* She smiled, proud of herself for a second. *Was that her underwear on the nightstand? Awkward. Dear lord. If Tiberius gave those to Grey, she was never going to hear the end of it. Wait a minute.* She picked up the red lacy panties. *She wasn't wearing these last night? She was obviously missing a few important pieces of the evening. She really had to be more careful with her undergarments. That scared the shit out of her.* Lexy stared at the ceiling, wishing she recalled the details. She rolled over, smelled Grey's pillow and wondered if he was on the love or hate side of that invisible line this morning. *She didn't even want to get out of bed. Plausible deniability? Yes...That might work.* Like a severely hungover princess, she swung her legs over the edge of the bed in her luxurious room, moderately prepared for a new day of his judgmental bullshit. *The balcony door was open. Grey was out there mentally packing for the guilt trip he was about to lay on her.* As always, Lexy had an ominous feeling she was in trouble. *In all honesty, she usually was after a banquet.* She wandered out onto the balcony.

Grey looked at her and started to giggle, "I can't even be mad now. It looks like you already did enough damage to yourself."

She harnessed her inner teenager, sighed dramatically, turned and marched back to the bathroom. She looked at her reflection and giggled. *Wow. Just wow.*

With pursed lips to stifle his laughter, he leaned past her to wet a facecloth. She sat on the counter facing him as he wiped off her raccoon eyes and said, "I'm not going to give you a lecture, it's a waste of time. I am going to say it would be nice to go to a party where you didn't end up murdering somebody. Just one social event."

She did feel a tad guilty. True, it was unnecessary but fun.

"I tried to wash your face last night, but you hissed at me," he teased.

Wow. She must have been really drunk.

"I'm also not going to ask why Lily showed up with those panties this morning," he casually commented.

Better to give no explanation at all. Lexy shrugged.

"Did you leave your underwear in the hallway?" Grey questioned as he gauged her reaction.

This was the problem with drinking. She couldn't remember how much he knew. Lexy suggested, "Maybe, I went commando last night?"

"I was there when you got dressed, good try," he playfully bantered.

Lexy decided brutal honesty was the way to go, "I thought Tiberius was acting sketchy, so I followed him into a dark hallway. He caught me as I tried to leave and …" *This was so stupid. Why hadn't she stuck with plausible deniability?*

"Rip the band-aid off Lex," Grey prompted. "I'd rather have the whole truth, so I can react accordingly. We're alone with the new recruits to do a training exercise, but just so you're prepared, we could be alone with Kayn and Zach for months."

"What? Where is everyone else going?" Lexy enquired.

They have a series of jobs in South America. We're supposed to be helping Kayn and Zach with their Handler Dragon bond," Grey countered. "Ironic, isn't it?"

It was. "Can we talk about this later? We didn't... He was just messing with me," Lexy explained.

Grey exhaled and agreed, "We'll talk about it later. We have to go give Kayn and Zach the news."

There was a time when this scenario would have been a dream. Grey's footsteps echoed as he walked away. She slid off the counter, knowing she was supposed to go with him. "Grey!" she called. He stopped walking. "If we're supposed to be showing them the strength of our bond, you need to stop acting like my jealous boyfriend. We need to be a united front. Sit down and relax. I need to brush my teeth and get ready."

"I'm not jealous, I'm hurt, and I feel more like a disgusted friend," Grey clarified. He sat on the bed and urged, "Go, get ready."

Lexy grabbed the underwear off the nightstand herself because asking him to grab her replacement panties felt like it might add fuel to his fire. After a few minutes, she reappeared prepared to begin the day. He'd gone back out onto the balcony. She walked out, stood next to him and asked, "What's the plan?"

"We're going to stroll over to their room and fill them in," he responded, continuing to stare off into the endless desert surrounding the compound.

"What are you looking for?" she enquired.

Placing his arm around her, he answered, "Forgiveness... Listen, I've been going over everything in my head, and I need to apologize. I've done ridiculously stupid things while drunk, it's not fair of me to judge you. It feels like we're drifting apart. I've been your Handler for over four decades and you've only dated one guy. I guess I thought physical intimacy wasn't something you required. I'm just afraid of losing you to someone who can give you everything you need. You're the only person I want to wake up next to. What if this part Guardian thing means you've outgrown me? I'm afraid you won't need me anymore. I need you more than air to breathe, Lex."

She stepped into his embrace, and as they held each other, she teased, "You'll never lose me. I outgrew you ten years ago and I'm still here." They continued to hold each other while laughing. "When we start losing track of who we are, we should remember how far we've come. Do you ever think about the day we met?"

"I was taken to a remote location and ordered to go into the woods in search of a wild girl who would only come back to Ankh with me. I wasn't allowed to bring a weapon. I was lost when I got caught in one of your animal traps. I was starting to get concerned something was going to come along and eat me when you showed up with crazy caveman hair. I recall thinking, how does a girl end up living as a Wild Thing in the woods? You released me from the trap. I looked into your eyes and knew, gaining your trust wasn't going to be easy, but I couldn't leave without you. What was your first impression of me?"

"I'm not going to lie, cannibalism did cross my mind. I was starving, but your accent was entertaining," Lexy answered. "You followed me back to my cabin with a broken leg."

Smiling, he reminisced, "You let me come inside where you healed me and shared what little food you had. I ate a squirrel for the first and hopefully last time that day. We drank questionable cabin whisky as we bonded." He started laughing.

"What?" Lexy countered.

I was just remembering how we found out Triad was hiding in the bushes outside."

Lexy giggled, "You went out to get rid of the bucket of pee and tossed it on them."

"That was only funny for like five seconds, then I started freaking out because I wasn't eighteen, and Triad could take me," he confessed.

"They did take you," Lexy confirmed.

"But you saved me, and I brought you back with me to Ankh," Grey finished the story.

"The story of how we met is rather epic," Lexy stated, leaning against the railing looking at Grey.

"I'll do better," he vowed.

She nodded and agreed, "I will too."

"Shall we go tell the kids they're grounded?" Grey announced as he held out his hand.

She took it and giggled, "If Kayn is anything like me, she already knows she's grounded, but you haven't told me what she did yet?"

"She tossed Kevin over a balcony and he went splat in the courtyard," Grey responded.

Lexy was just beaming as she giggled and pretended to sob, "I'm just so proud of her right now. You might need to be bad cop this morning."

"We have to pick opposite sides, or this punishment isn't going to work," Grey complained as they left the room and headed down the hall. He paused and sighed, "Never mind, you killed someone too, you can't be the voice of reason. I'll give her the lecture, you just try not to grin. We're supposed to be the responsible adults here."

"They're also adults," Lexy baited.

"We made up, literally five minutes ago." he reprimanded as he went to knock on their door.

Zach opened it before his fist landed knock number one and invited them inside. "Kayn's in the bathroom."

"Did she explain why she tossed Kevin over the balcony?" Grey enquired as he began digging through their fruit bowl.

Zach replied, "Inconveniently timed feelings."

Seems legit. Lexy was beaming as Kayn walked out of the washroom.

Grey approached her sister and stated, "Zach says your impulse control issues were caused by inconveniently timed feelings."

Kayn glanced at her and Lexy winked.

"Stephanie also met with an accident. Apparently, she tripped and broke her neck in the bathroom," Zach explained.

"As a result, we'll be staying with your group while the others go to the Summit," Grey declared. "Melody is going with them. Astrid and Haley will be slipping away with Samid and meeting up with Jenna and Arrianna because they have Dean. We'll be staying with you guys, so we can try to connect Amar's new trio of Ankh."

Kayn asked, "How mad is Frost, on a scale of one to ten?"

"Eleven," Grey sternly retorted.

Kayn replied, "A week apart isn't that bad. I'll fix it when I see him again."

"Try two months apart. It really goes without saying that Markus isn't feeling all warm and fuzzy about your bond with your Handler. Or my bond because I was forced to admit I told Zach to go have fun while I made sure you didn't get into any trouble. I was partying when Lexy went into the bathroom and murdered Stephanie on a whim. You tossed Kevin off a damn balcony. Now, we're all in trouble... Mostly me. So, it's the four of us with no relationship disruptions for the next couple of months."

Kayn's eyes met with Lexy's and they both smiled.

"Oh, yes... one more thing," Grey announced as he snatched Zach's cell out of his hand. "Turn in your phones. I have new burner phones for all of us. Part of our punishment is having no contact with the rest of Ankh. I have the information for the next month. They'll be contacting us with any changes."

Lexy felt a twinge of remorse. *She'd planned to text Orin as soon as she was alone. Everyone probably thought she'd slept with Tiberius.*

Kayn grimaced as she handed Grey her phone and wandered out to the balcony.

Lexy whispered in Grey's ear, "Can I text someone quickly so I'm not overthinking this for a couple of months?"

"They're already gone, if you text anyone the time and date will show," Grey responded as he gave her shoulder a loving squeeze and baited, "This is why we don't murder people at banquets, Lexy. We don't get to straighten things out with our booty calls if we're being punished. We're in trouble too."

He was enjoying this far too much.

Kayn strolled back into the room and said, "Reprimanding us by sending us on a murder spree doesn't seem like punishment to me but why not? Let's get this party started."

Zach glanced at Grey as he commented, "They're not even phased by this."

"They will be," Grey replied as he struggled to pry Lexy's cell out of her fingers. "Just give it to me, Lex."

Damn it, Greydon. Lexy released her hold on the phone. She asserted, "In all fairness, we were told the rules didn't apply to us anymore."

"Come on, Lex. Did you really believe that was the case? They can't have you two running around free to do whatever crosses your mind," Zach argued as he played with his new phone. "At least these are smartphones."

Grey fiddled with his for a second before announcing, "Yes! We have data plans!"

Lexy placed her phone on the counter as she suggested, "Go change into something from the closet and fix yourself up. If we don't eat breakfast before we leave for training in the in-between, we'll still be hungover when we get back."

Kayn wandered back to the washroom. Zach and Grey were playing with their new toys and Lexy was wishing they had more grapes in the fruit bowl. There was a knock on the door. *Please let it not be Killian. Last night was awkward enough.* Grey opened the door and stepped out of the way as a lady pushed a cart with their breakfast into the room.

Amar strolled in after her and announced, "Excellent, you're all up! Eat up! We have a lot to accomplish in a small amount of time!"

Did he know about the X-rated hallway footage?

Amar looked directly at Lexy and nodded in response to her inner commentary. He didn't miss a beat as he continued speaking, "It's ten in the morning. We're not usually big on schedules around here, but today we are, for various reasons. Our Ankh are already in the in-between having some much-needed bonding time. They don't know you're coming, their response will be authentic."

As they devoured their meals, Lexy peered up at Amar and teased, "So, you don't have a lecture prepared then?"

Amar chuckled and sparred, "Why? I'd be wasting my time."

He wasn't wrong. They placed their empty trays on the cart and followed Amar to the room they'd used for travel to the in-between the day before. As they strolled down the marble-floored hallway, two giggling children raced past and disappeared around the corner at the end of the hall.

Their immortal host explained, "The Aries group headquarters for this continent is beneath this complex. The employee's families also live here. I love having little ones around. I know you probably have a lot of questions. You can ask them when you return."

Lexy and Grey had been here many times, so this wasn't a big deal, but her sister's inner commentary had millions of questions.

Amar gently took hold of Kayn's arm, allowing the others to walk in ahead, so he could answer her questions privately. Grey put his arm around Lexy as they walked in and whispered in her ear, "This is going to be fun."

Lexy took in the ornately engraved tombs, grateful she didn't recognize the Ankh in the room. One of them grinned at her and winked. *Shit. Everyone heard about her naughty hallway rendezvous.* Grey started to chuckle. She gave her Handler a shove. They all climbed into a large open tomb. Grey laid beside her and thought, *'Sinner.'*

Is it ever a good idea to piss me off?

Perfect timing, though,' Grey sparred with only his thoughts.

Zach's voice whispered, "Do you two ever stop fighting?"

Amar interrupted, announcing, "We have four Healers operating the tombs and two Ankh as an energy source for when they become weak. Let's bond these three so they have a shot at making it out of the Testing."

The lid ground shut, sealing them in as Grey mumbled, "This is way more fun with music."

Lexy smiled as the tomb shifted to lock with the one next to it. She closed her eyes as the humming strobing brilliant light grew until it became overwhelming. Even though she'd done this thousands of times, Lexy's stomach lurched as the tomb was catapulted into oblivion. Grey hooted. They were all laughing as they began spinning upwards until it paused. Their stomachs lurched as they descended into the in-between. The tomb disappeared. They were all free-falling into the place between life and death that they were granted access to only because they were Clan. They plummeted through the clouds and the endless desert was rapidly approaching below. They all slowed and landed gracefully, crouching in the warm, inviting sand. Lexy rose to stand beneath the backdrop of a flaming crimson sunset.

Grey was about to say something when a flash of blinding light took them all by surprise. Strolling through the endless desert towards them was Frost. Kayn was about to rush into his arms, prepared to spit out a thousand apologies when his form shifted to Grey.

Grey looked at his double and remarked, "Who is this asshole?"

The form shifted again to Lily with her shimmering silky raven tresses flowing behind her as her hips hypnotizing sway almost made them forget what they were there for. As Lily came closer, she started laughing and the pitch of her giggling lowered until Lily morphed into their shenanigan loving genetic sire.

Lexy glanced at her Handler and whispered, "That's Seth." *He wasn't impressive to her. He was a deadbeat dad who left his daughter to be abused on a demon farm. She had his number.* Grey stepped closer. *His Handler senses were probably off the hook tingling because she was totally contemplating kicking his slimy Triad Guardian ass.*

Ignoring her hostile inner commentary, Seth energetically announced, "Welcome! Welcome!" Seth reached for Grey's hand. Grey looked at her as he apprehensively shook the immortal's hand.

Her genetic sire extended his hand. Lexy opted out, *Only if you want me to slam your entire body against the frigging sand like you're a blanket at the beach.* Seth grinned.

The Guardian continued his attempt to befriend his daughter's Handlers as he marched over to Zach and overzealously greeted him, "I can't wait for the show. I was most impressed with the last one." Seth extended his hand to Kayn, who accepted it rather hesitantly. The Guardian leaned in and whispered to Kayn, "I apologize for not being available when you came to see me, but I did observe the training you did with those four Ankh…it was brutal."

Kayn yanked her hand away and enquired, "Are you just here for the show? Or do you have something you'd like to say to us?"

"Do you have something you need me to say?" Seth questioned as he glanced down at the sand, grinning at the strategically placed seashell.

So many things. Lexy stared Seth down as she bitterly asked, "Why didn't you save me? I was only eleven-years-old."

Emotionlessly, Seth answered, "I put you there. I was making a Dragon."

Enraged by the Guardian's brutally honest response, Lexy attacked, "I was eleven-years-old!"

Intrigued by her fury, Seth sparred, "You not only survived your Correction, but you kicked everyone's asses that came for you. You were a fighting machine. You are something very special."

Unable to stand one more second in his presence, Lexy abruptly spun around and marched away from the group, mumbling under her breath, "Piece of shit."

They were forced to jog to catch up to her. The four Ankh disappeared in a flash of light together and found themselves strolling through a field.

Kayn grabbed Lexy's arm and asserted, "Stop. Just for a second. Why are we running away from him?"

"We are not running away," Lexy curtly replied. "We're ending a conversation with someone who isn't worthy of another word."

A visibly stricken Grey urged, "Drop it, Kayn. Trust me. I've got this. We'll meet you two after we've talked things out." Grey stretched out his hand.

Lexy scowled, knowing if she took it, he'd take her somewhere wonderful with kittens, butterflies and music. She wanted to be angry. She needed to stomp around, tearing the grass from the ground, kicking down trees. *None of this would matter because it couldn't be destroyed. Another tree would grow in its place and grass would sprout in seconds from the ground. She knew this... She'd done it before.* Lexy took Grey's hand. They disappeared and reappeared in a field full of kittens. She muttered, "You suck."

Grey sprawled in the grass and chuckled as the fluff balls of adorableness began playfully pouncing on him. He called out, "Come on, Lex. You know you want to lay here with me in a field of kittens."

She couldn't help it as a smile appeared on her face. Watching him fending off ferocious teeny tiny furballs was too cute. *Oh, Hell.* Lexy got down in the fragrant grass next to Grey. The fluffy babies came springing at her and she started laughing. *He'd won this round.* Lexy complained, "You're an asshole."

Grey rolled on his side and met her eyes as he pressed, "You love me. Admit it."

"I do," Lexy confessed. Their deep conversation was interrupted by Lexy's giggles as the furballs all pounced on her at once. Grey got up, she asked, "Where are you going?"

"I feel like dancing with you," he replied.

The sun shining behind Grey's blonde hair made it look like he had a halo. *She should make him wear one of those Halloween devil horn headbands, so people could see him coming.* Grey helped her up, tugged her against him and music started. "Now, that was smooth," Lexy commented as they slowly waltzed barefoot in the grass. The kittens disappeared, and as they swayed to the music, the brilliant blue cloudless sky darkened just like someone was turning down dimmer lights to set the mood. The light disappeared and everything went dark. They remained in each other's arms, looking up at the sky as it lit up with an awe-inspiring display of glittering stars.

Overcome by the beauty, Grey flirted, "They say it's the partner that counts."

Lexy grinned and teased, "So smooth." She laughed as they started waltzing to the music again. *She couldn't stay mad at him. It was impossible.*

Grey elegantly dipped her, and as she dangled precariously, he vowed, "You'll never lose me, it's impossible."

He'd heard her inner commentary. It felt like he had more to say. He swooped her back into his embrace and held her close as he offered, "If you still want to pluck out all of the grass, I'll stand here and applaud."

Resting her head on Grey's shoulder, she whispered, "Sometimes, I wish we could stay here forever."

"In theory, we can," he whispered. Grey kissed her head lovingly and asked, "Eighties or nineties?"

"Eighties," she replied.

Video killed the radio star came on, Grey admitted, "That was me. I don't know why I thought about that." He shrugged and started dancing anyway.

He was such a dork. Lexy stood there watching his joy, feeling guilty for how she'd been treating him. He probably already felt the same way because if she was coming to an emotionally intuitive conclusion, it would be a miracle. Her younger years surfaced. She recalled the first time she danced with Grey and Arrianna. Way back before they understood what they'd gotten themselves into. He'd always amazed her with his ability to find the beauty in everything. Her yellow door was goofily boogying over to her as the song changed to another eighties tune.

Grey snatched her hand, kissed each of her fingertips, batted his eyelashes at her and tempted, "Have fun with me?"

She sighed, knowing if she didn't play along, he'd bring back the kittens, and they'd never get anything done. They childishly frolicked around the field until Grey tripped and towed her down with him.

They were laughing in the grass when he looked at her and questioned, "Want to commit murder anymore?"

"Not so much. Well done," Lexy responded.

He got up and clapped his hands. The lights turned on, revealing endless blue sky and sunshine. Grey declared, "If you start killing them now, it might be easier to get you back."

He started walking away. Lexy scrambled to her feet and followed. The scenery flashed and they found themselves standing on a mountain top with a lush, vibrant green forest below.

Grey raised his hands and said, "I didn't bring us here."

They sensed Azariah's presence and spun around as Ankh's Guardian approached. Always a sight to behold with her luminescent heavenly glow. She spoke, "It's incredible, isn't it? A world built on wishes." She swiped a hand and the forest spanning the valley below became a meadow. The magical being gestured again and a never-ending ocean appeared in its place. With a wave of her hand, it vanished and turned to an endless desert. The lady in the light directed, "Come with me my children, I have something to show you."

In the blink of an eye, they were strolling in the white silky, luxurious sand of the desert. *If Seth was really their Guardian's sibling that meant Azariah was her Aunt. Maybe they just called themselves siblings? It felt impossible. How could this majestic being be a relation of hers? Seth was a much darker entity. He made sense.*

Azariah stopped walking. The divine being faced Lexy and clarified, "Yes, you are my niece. That needed to be said. To take away any confusion as to how this came to pass, warriors must be a mix of good and evil. Without the negative, the positive ceases to exist. I may not look like it now, but I've done my time in the darkness. There are things I've had to do that make my heart feel as hollow as yours when the Dragon takes over. For me, being attached to the light was a choice. Your light resides within a person." Azariah looked at her Handler and praised, "Grey, you're doing an excellent job. Jealousy is normal. Lexy feels those same emotions when you become close to someone else. You don't have an easy road. That's not what you signed up for. Lexy is a weapon. Your duty is to bring her out of the darkness when she's finished doing whatever our Clan requires of her. Fostering your bond is more important than either one of your egos."

"I'm not jealous," Grey clarified too quickly.

"Alright, then you two should have no problems focusing on Kayn and Zach. This wasn't the original pairing, so they're bound to have growing pains. This Conduit ability is a game-changer. Keep a close eye on Kayn's energy requirements. How much does she need and how often? Until Zach gets the hang of things, you'll show him what he has to do. Against my better judgement, Seth took the second-tier cap off your abilities. Now Lexy, we have no idea what you'll be capable of. Exercise caution if a new ability surfaces and come to us with any concerns." Azariah looked distracted. She smiled and announced, "Kayn and Zach are playing with a tsunami and you four don't have time to mess around. This group's odds are slim. Don't get attached."

The scenery exploded with blinding light and they were breathing underwater. *She wasn't disturbed by much, but this was weird.*

Grey waved his hand in front of his face and spoke, "It's a hologram."

Azariah's voice instructed, "Start walking. Your reality will veto theirs."

They began walking. Lexy's eyes zeroed in on Kayn and Zach through the shifting veil of imaginary water. *This was impressively crazy.* The blue-tinted landscape vanished as they stepped out into the meadow. Kayn and Zach believed they were a split second from being smushed by a tidal wave. They were baffled as they slowly stood upright when nothing happened. They quickly gathered their bearings as Lexy loudly commanded, "We know where they are! Let's get to work!"

Zach stormed away, furiously cursing about crazy freaking Dragons. Grey chuckled, "I've got this." He sprinted and caught up with Zach.

The two Handlers wandered ahead, having an animated conversation. *Zach was livid. Brighton wasn't playing nice summoning up tidal waves and creating drama at banquets with her unfiltered responses.* Lexy understood the need to be self-destructive. *She'd wanted to tear this place up earlier and her Handler had known what to do. Azariah was right. Zach needed Grey's help. She wasn't sure how to help Kayn because she didn't know how to help herself.* Kayn looked up at the sky as raindrops began trickling from above. *She was purposely allowing it to rain on her face.* Lexy imitated her sister's carefree action. *It felt nice sprinkling on her skin.* They continued wandering through the field. *Lexy smiled while eavesdropping on Kayn's inner commentary. Hers was always entertaining. She couldn't recall it ever raining before.*

Grey marched back to the girls and sighed, "Alright, which one of you thought of rain?"

"It was me. Am I bad?" Kayn admitted as she walked in the moist grass alongside her.

Lexy squeezed Grey's shoulder and teased, "Suck it up, princess. You won't melt."

Her Handler mouthed the words, "I might."

Zach ushered Kayn away and in minutes, they were bickering. Grey was pouty. Whatever verbal advice he'd given, had bombed. They were tainting his happy place with their incessant squabbling. "We're supposed to be helping," Lexy quietly urged.

Grey hugged her from behind and sighed, "I tried. Zach wasn't listening to a word."

No matter how angry she was, dancing always worked on her.
Grey kissed her cheek and whispered, "Good idea…
We'll show them how we dance in the rain."

*He'd just used this move on her. If she was being honest, it
fixed a variety of ills. She could humour him for the greater
good.* Lexy giggled as Grey twirled her with skills rivalling
Fred Astaire and tugged her back against him. As they
seductively moved together barefoot in the grass, she
couldn't resist teasing, "There's no music." *Where's your
game?* Lexy laced her arms around his neck and grinned.

He gazed into her eyes and wittily bantered, "Suck it
up, buttercup." Background music began. They stopped
dancing, with his palm seductively against the small of her
back. He baited, "I have game you've never seen."

She knew every move in his repertoire. "Right… Sure you
do," Lexy sparred. Kayn and Zach had stopped bickering.
Kayn's head was on Zach's shoulder. They were dancing
while having a deep conversation. Lexy whispered in her
Handler's ear, "I think they've had enough time to talk it
out, don't you?"

"This dance was for me," Grey quietly confessed.

Her eyes were drawn to his. As their gazes locked, she
felt the tide shift. Grey was looking at her like he was
seeing her clearly for the first time. This spark had lit
enough times for her to understand what was happening,
so she stepped away. With perfect timing, Zach wandered
over and blew out the flame. Without missing a beat, the
two Handlers began giggling while making plans. *Like
they had any control over what Dragon's do.*

Zach suggested, "We should think of eighteen-wheeler
sized scorpions. For the record, those were terrifying."

"We usually save those for at the end when we test
their bond. At least one of them is usually weakened by
repeated deaths. If they chose to protect each other over

running away, then we know they have a shot. We can do truck-sized spider island early on," Grey compromised.

Zach kept an eye on Kayn while proposing, "We should spice things up by adding piranhas and sharks."

"That's actually a good idea," Grey replied as he knelt and plucked a dandelion from the meadow.

Kayn was still standing where Zach had left her lost in thought.

Grey sweetly tucked the dandelion behind Lexy's ear and thought, *'Ready gorgeous?'*

Zach interrupted their exchange with an explanation, "She's just upset about being separated from Frost."

Lexy remarked, "Once she goes full Dragon, it'll suck the sentiment right out of her."

Grey laced his fingers through hers, gave her hand a loving squeeze and agreed, "Let's send the Dragons on a hunting expedition. It'll take the edge off." While still gazing into Lexy's eyes, Grey warmly kissed her hand and thought, *'Go get 'em, tiger.'* As always, she felt a confusing mixture of freedom and loss when the physical connection was severed. Grey tucked a wild crimson lock behind Lexy's ear as he whispered, "Promise me you'll come back."

"Always," she affirmed, knowing it was the truth.

Kayn strutted over with a sword in her hand and announced, "Shall we get to work then?"

Daggers are easier to run with, but whatever floats your boat. Lexy enthusiastically agreed, "Let's do this." A dagger appeared in her grasp. She gave it a warm-up swing and winked at her Handler.

Grey was grinning. Zach was not on board, he was panicking. Grey grabbed his arm and stated, "Let the Dragons out to play. We'll rein them in when it's time."

Zach was nervous. He should be. Lexy looked at Kayn and assured, "He'll get used to it. You guys just need time to grow your bond free of distractions." When Kayn didn't respond, Lexy recognized the look in her sister's eyes. *This wasn't all about Frost. She was jonesing to let the Dragon loose. That, she understood.*

As the sister's wandered away in the now dry grass, Kayn shifted her sword to a dagger. Lightning crackled above as dismal ominous clouds rolled in overhead. She was an old pro at summoning the Dragon within, Lexy cracked her neck in preparation as she travelled back in time to the moment she accepted hot chocolate from a stranger. The panic she felt when her vision wavered. She'd been old enough to understand she'd made a horrible mistake as the drugs subdued her. The unforgettable scent of the potato sack. The sensation of the hay beneath her in the stall. Heartbreaking memories flooded her mind. Rage surged within her. She clenched her palm, still able to feel the yellow flowers she'd been given at the tender age of eleven to make her forget. Her heart ached with emotions too heavy for anyone to carry. Thunder boomed as the storm within her silenced. *Nothing mattered anymore...* The sky above crackled as the Dragon that protected her emerged and spread its metaphorical wings. There was a nearly undetectable fragrance on the breeze. Requiring no prompting, Lexy sprinted into the forest. The scent of their flesh became stronger. She altered her path, avoiding roots and rocks with the agility of a mountain lion. She was an instinct-driven monster, hunting for what remained of the trio's humanity. Predatory instinct slowed Lexy's pace as she crept through the woods without snapping a twig. She was aware of the other predator's presence, but as Wild Things, they required no communication. They burst out of the bushes into the meadow, the resting newbies scrambled away into the bushes. Adrenaline raced as Lexy pursued the prey with an attention-grabbing shiny black ponytail who separated from the others much like a lion would a gazelle foolish enough to split off from its herd. She tracked it through the woods and ducked into the shrubbery as it spun around with its sword drawn. Lexy grinned, soundlessly moving through the foliage on all fours, allowing the newbie to falsely assume she'd managed to lose her.

The shiny black ponytail nervously stammered, "I know you're there."

Curiosity prompted Lexy to remain hidden. She slowed her breathing while methodically observing her prey.

"I know you're there, I can feel you," the newbie stated, grasping her sword.

It would be easy to gut it like a deer or swiftly snap its neck, but like a cat, playing with her food first was most appealing. Lexy rose from the bushes and smirked as she tossed her blade aside. *She didn't need it.* As Lexy approached, the newbie Ankh swung and missed as Lexy maneuvered out of its way.

"We're probably going to die in the Testing. What's the point of killing us?" The newbie Ankh questioned, bravely standing her ground.

Lexy cocked her head. *You can't reason with a Dragon.* She easily snatched its sword as it tried to slay her and unceremoniously snapped its neck. It slumped to the dirt as the Dragon became distracted by a blackberry bush and began eating the juicy berries while waiting for the newbie to awaken. Nearby screaming caused her pulse to race. With palms stained berry red, she heard rustling in the bush and glanced back. *Her prey was attempting to flee.* She smiled as a new blade appeared in her hand. *It was always more fun when they ran.*

A boy randomly burst through the bushes, saw her and said, "Shit."

She slit its throat and took off after the one that got away. Lexy followed the scent until she came upon Kayn, feeding on her prey's energy. Incapable of empathy or trivial thought, Lexy continued to hunt as Kayn fed on anything Lexy didn't kill. They moved through the in-between as a plague, destroying all in their path, and everywhere they touched became a nightmare. The two Handlers stepped in each time the Dragons slept to give the trio reprieve. They would show the group beauty and give them hope until the Dragons awoke.

Chapter 14

Dragon Daddy Issues

The Dragons were lounging like cats in the sun's rays at the base of a tree. A twig cracked. Lexy opened her eyes as their Guardian sire stepped out of the shadows. *She was going to kill it.*

Seth, in his masculine form, inched closer as he gushed, "Dragons are such glorious creatures."

She was going to kill it and eat it. Out of the corner of her eye, she saw an orange and black fuzzy caterpillar. She wanted to touch it, and when she did, she was able to see floating particles of dust in the light that filtered through the trees. It disappeared. Disappointed, she touched the furry creature again, and this time she felt warmer on the inside. Confused, she touched her chest and then balled up her fist to squish it, but for some reason, she couldn't do it. She picked it up and it bit her. She clapped her hands to kill it and yellow flowers sprinkled into the dirt. *No. She didn't like these.* Her palm was still stinging, so she looked. *They were still on her palm.* She frantically tried to brush them off but couldn't. Emotion surged to the surface and she remembered what was missing. *They were covering her Ankh symbol. It was gone. It wasn't there anymore.* Her gut twisted as the Dragon took the backseat.

Lexy peered up and Kayn was feeding on Seth's energy. *He'd done this to her.*

Seth yanked his hands away and scolded Kayn as she creepily responded, "I need more."

The Guardian's eyes met Lexy's, and with his palms subserviently facing upwards, he offered her a taste. She rose to her feet. With forty years of ability related self-control under her belt and the visions of yellow flowers still fresh in her mind, she refused by repeating, "You left me on that farm."

"This again," Seth complained. "For heaven's sake child, it's because of that depraved place that you've survived the unthinkable. Is there no pride in that for you?"

Enraged, Lexy raced at the Guardian Seth with her weapon in hand as the scenery flashed. She was alone in the desert swiping her blade into air. Azariah regally strode towards her, trailed by the luminescent ray that attached her to the sky. The blade in Lexy's hand vanished.

Azariah scolded, "Enough child." Ankh's Guardian waved her hand.

Lexy's body felt weighted. She dropped to her knees and her palms stuck to the sand. She tried to fight against it but couldn't.

"I apologize for the flowers. I was forced to step in and free some emotion, so I'd be able to reason with you. Under no circumstances will you feed on Seth," the heavenly being ordered. "My brother has new playthings and a bad habit of bending the rules." As Azariah placed her hand on Lexy's head, the rage disintegrated into no emotion at all. Ankh's Guardian explained, "You will not be able to move a muscle until you see your Handler. Do you understand?"

Lexy submissively nodded. The weight on her ceased, and with an explosion of light, she was on her feet where she was before she'd been taken. She couldn't move a muscle.

Seth was speaking to her sister. "You carnivorous little beast. You're dying for more, aren't you?" He provoked. "Come and get it. I dare you."

Kayn lunged at Seth and swung her blade. He stepped out of her way and she narrowly missed him.

"I see you actually have skills," Seth teased as a sword appeared in his clutches with an emerald hilt. He blocked Kayn's next swing with a clink of metal and baited, "I wouldn't start a battle you can't win."

With a wave of his hand, Kayn soared through the air and landed with a thud in the muck. Kayn casually brushed the dirt from her mid-thigh length sarong as she stood up, met his eyes and imitated his movement. With a wave of her hand, her genetic sire went soaring through the air and collided with a tree.

Seth was chuckling as he got up and countered, "A quick learner, I like that." He swung his arm again, attempting to repeat the move.

Kayn countered and neither one budged an inch. They held each other in place with the force of energy. Seth wielded his sword and as Kayn looked at her knife, it elongated into a sword with a rose quartz hilt. The battle of the beasts began. With each maneuver her sire made, her sister reacted until it became clear she was his equal.

A white flag appeared at the end of Seth's sword. He waved it a few times and dropped it into the dirt to show Kayn he'd surrendered. He offered, "You've earned it. Take whatever you need from me."

Kayn released her weapon, took her genetic sire's hands and absorbed his energy until he sunk to his knees.

He looked up at her and whispered, "Aren't you the least bit curious about what you've taken?"

Kayn peered down at him as she coolly enquired, "What have I taken?"

"Control," Seth countered from his subservient position. "Use it with caution."

Just as Kayn was about to finish him off, he evaporated into thin air.

Grey's voice broke through the silence left behind by the Guardian's hasty departure, "We should get back."

Seeing Grey freed her, but she felt nothing, so the sight of him was inconsequential. Lexy walked back to the tree and climbed it.

Grey added, "After we get you both back, of course." Kayn marched away and Zach chased after her. Grey looked up and sighed, "You're going to make me climb this tree, aren't you?"

Lexy scaled the tree until she found a concealed branch to straddle. She closed her eyes and peacefully listened to the birds singing.

He climbed the tree, sat on the branch beside her and asked, "I'd like an apple. Do you mind if we change this fir tree to an apple tree?" When she didn't respond, Grey took a chance, and in a flash, they were on a branch much closer to the ground on a tree full of apples next to the pool of water that stirred up emotions. He passed her a perfect red delicious and offered, "Apple?"

Lexy took a bite without much thought as he leapt off the branch and wandered to the pool where he sat in the grass, eating his apple. She felt the urge to come down as Grey tossed his core on the grass and got into the water.

As Grey swam around, he called out, "You should come in. The water's amazing. There's lots of starfish and orbs. It's really quite beautiful."

Lexy jumped off the branch into the soft, fragrant grass and paused to wiggle her toes before strolling over to the pool to see what he was doing. He grinned at her and she felt a tickle of something in her chest as she sat on the edge with her legs dangling in the water.

He swam to the centre and prompted, "Get in."

She had the compulsion to do as he asked, this puzzled her, but it was impossible to ignore. As she slipped into the water, euphoria washed over her. It felt like her soul was singing. She didn't understand what was happening, but she liked it. She wanted to be closer to him. She smiled.

Grey whispered, "There you are." He smiled as he opened his arms.

There was no need for words as she moved into his embrace, and with an intoxicating rush of emotion, she was whole again. They were like two pieces of a puzzle that didn't fit anywhere else. He held her against his heart, affectionately caressing her hair and whispering words of adoration until every inch of her wanted to succumb to the effects of the inhibition freeing immortal trap. *He knew what this place was... It was a solid representation of everything tempting. Why had he brought her here? It was difficult enough under normal circumstances to stop herself from craving his touch.* The magic loosened her inhibitions until her self-preservation skills were close to nonexistent. It took every ounce of will power she had to pull away and admit, "We should get away from this pool."

Grey tenderly caressed her cheek. With longing, he gazed into her eyes and questioned, "Why? I need it. You need it...Give me one good reason why we shouldn't?"

She knew better. She couldn't speak as he boldly kissed her lips and pulled away in awe.

He grinned, giving her another out, "Just one reason."

She didn't have one. She wanted him to kiss her again. Her lips instinctually parted as Grey brazenly seduced her with his tongue, and as the intimacy deepened, his hands began to roam. In the blink of an eye, they were frenzied animals in heat, struggling to tear away the material blocking their union. It became funny when they couldn't. *They were naughty immortals. Azariah was putting them in the corner.* She pushed Grey away even though it killed her and gave him a dose of ration, "You don't really want me. It's the pool. Get out of the water." She scrambled out and kept walking away with tears in her eyes, knowing how much she wanted him. *It was painfully obvious that she always would.* He had to jog to catch up. *If he saw the tears in her eyes, he'd question her.*

"Lexy, slow down!" Grey called chasing after her.

"In a minute. We need to be far enough away," she explained. Lexy kept moving until she was able to blink away the tears.

Grey grabbed her arm to slow her down and said, "Enough running away. Is the thought of being with me really that horrible?"

It was the opposite. She turned and confessed, "If we could be together for longer than a night. Yes, in a heartbeat. But we can't. You know that."

"But you would want to be with me?" Grey asked as his grip on her wrist loosened.

She rolled her eyes. *He wasn't really upset.* Lexy changed the topic, "Do you still want to tear my clothes off."

Sheepishly grinning, he admitted, "Maybe… Okay… You were right. Rational thoughts are there now. Listen, I'm sorry I brought you there, I had to counteract what Azariah did to you." Grey released her wrist, held out his hand and asked, "Still friends?"

"Friends," Lexy agreed. They shook on it and strolled into the sunset, holding hands. With warm silken sand slipping between her toes and the sun's rays on her skin, she was blissfully happy.

Grey glanced at her and exclaimed, "Amar's Healers are definitely dead. The ride home promises to be a shit show."

"We can use it as a training exercise. Kayn should have plenty of energy. I'll make Brighton take the lead," Lexy answered.

He teased, "Will your ego let you go down first?"

"Only if it's on purpose," Lexy saucily bantered.

With a skip in his step, he suggested, "Superhero entrance?"

Lexy grinned and agreed, "Alright." In a flash of blinding light, they were descending from the sky, and the two immortals landed in the dirt with catlike agility. For a second, she felt like Wonder Woman until she saw Kayn and Zach. They were absolutely covered in blackberry juice. *You leave them alone for five seconds. They were headed into the immortal equivalent of social purgatory with these two. The possibilities were endless.*

Grey took in their stained skin and sighed, "You guys have the most fun." He glanced at Lexy and asked, "How come we never have blackberry battles?"

Lexy gave her Handler a playful shove as she answered, "We're supposed to be working right now but next time I see a blackberry bush it's on." She gave Kayn a curious look as she commented, "I really wish you guys could see yourselves." This opened an inter Dragon debate about forgiving their father figure. *Kayn appeared to be forming a soft spot for the shape-shifting sociopath…She was still a hard no.*

Grey put his arm around Lexy and whispered in her ear, "We need to get back. Maybe, we should just change the subject?"

Kayn made her opinion crystal clear, "For the record, I really don't care what Seth does or if I ever forgive him."

"Good," Lexy replied.

"We have to go," Grey urged as he led Lexy away, whispering, "Try to be nice."

Whatever. An explosion of light brought them all back to the white sand of the clean slated desert.

Grey took Lexy's hand and gave it a joyful swing. He turned to the other pair and announced, "Let the Dragon Handler road trip begin."

The four lurched upwards into oblivion. In moments, they were encased within the tomb, spinning at a stomach-churning rate. Hoping Kayn could take a hint, Lexy placed her hands against the strobing crypt's lid and as her Healing energy drained into the tomb, she noticed Kayn's hands next to hers. *Good. She was following along.* They were both struggling to keep their hands in place, whirling at a speed reserved for fighter pilots and certifiably insane thrill seekers. *This training exercise wasn't going well. They were in a flat spin. She couldn't regain control. They should be slowing down by now. She was losing energy at twice the speed. Shit. Oh, no. She knew what was happening. That greedy little energy siphoning thief. Kayn probably wasn't sure how to switch between siphoning energy and releasing it. She had so much to learn.* Her focus was off as she persevered, knowing if she let go too early, she'd be covered in the boy's vomit when they awoke. *What was that sound? Her brain was sizzling like bacon on a skillet. That can't be good. She felt the familiar tingling and knew she had only seconds of consciousness left. Grey, if you can hear me, I'm going down with the ship. Puke on me and I kill you.*

Grey shouted, "Brighton! Stop us! Before I hurl!"

Each strobe of light blinded her but Lexy fought to keep her hands securely connected as gravity lurched her violently from side to side. *She couldn't keep it up for much longer.*

"I don't know how! I'm not strong enough!" Kayn yelled over the repetitive, warbling hum of the rose quartz tomb.

Yes. Kayn was... She'd taken more than enough energy to get back. Sometimes it was best to just toss someone off a dock and force them to swim.

Zach mumbled, "I'm going to pass out."

She was tossing her sister off the dock in, three, two, one... Lexy's arms dropped to her side as the blinding strobing glare became darkness.

Lexy stirred within the open tomb. She opened her eyes and grinned. *They'd made it back. Her sister had learned how to swim.* She stretched, declaring, "So, everybody's obviously dead then." As she climbed out and wandered over to stand beside Kayn. Lexy smiled at the half dozen dead Healers on the floor. She started to giggle. Kayn joined in. Another teaching moment presented itself. She'd show her the most effective way to awaken a large group. Lexy grabbed one of the bodies by the legs and explained, "They all need to go into the same tomb as Zach and Grey." One by one, they towed the Healers Amar had provided into the tomb encasing their Handlers, with no further explanation required. They closed it, then laid their palms on the ancient stone, feeding their energy directly into the rose quartz lined tomb.

In minutes, they were helping each person out. *It was time to take this show on the road.* Lexy laid her hand against the stone door. *It wouldn't budge.* Kayn followed suit and nothing happened.

A vaguely familiar girl piped in, "Only Amar can open this door."

Kayn perched on top of one of the tombs and sighed, "I don't suppose any of you have a snack?"

Grey scowled at her and mumbled, "You've had enough snacks."

Kayn blew Grey a kiss and sparred, "You were delicious."

"You're welcome," Grey jousted as he began to laugh.

Zach slid up onto the tomb beside Brighton and took her hand in a show of solidarity. Kayn leaned over and whispered in his ear, "I didn't mean to take you out too."

Zach smiled knowingly as he replied, "I know."

The girl who told them about the door held out her hand to Grey and introduced herself, "My name's Aubrey."

He gave it a polite shake as he replied, "My name's Grey."

"I know," Aubrey teased. "To be honest, I'm a bit of a fan."

"Really?" Grey flirtatiously responded, "Well, I'm certainly honoured to meet you, Aubrey. That's a beautiful name. Where are you from?"

Lexy rolled her eyes so far back all you could see were the whites as Grey continued to work his game on the curvaceous raven-haired Ankh. *She wasn't jealous. It was painfully pathetic.* Kayn and Zach were laughing. *He was making a fool out of himself. She should just kill him and shut him in a tomb until Amar showed up.* Lexy snapped out of her thoughts as a guy named Mike introduced himself. *His accent made her curious. He was obviously from the states.* The group began chatting to keep themselves occupied and Mike explained that he was backpacking through Europe with his best friend when his Correction happened.

Instantly curious, Kayn enquired, "Is your family still alive?"

His expression grew solemn as he answered, "I wasn't allowed any contact with them after I became Ankh. I'd just disappeared, so they travelled here searching for me, thinking I'd been kidnapped or worse. I thought if I stayed away, they'd have a chance but, they just wouldn't give up. They kept going back to the states, regrouping and flying back here until their flight crashed."

They all had families when they were mortal. Everyone but her. Kayn's stomach growled loudly. Everyone smiled, thinking she was hungry for food. *Lexy knew better. She was a predator too. Kayn's Conduit ability was pointing out the fact that everyone here was edible. Her sister's Handler was sleeping on the job again.* Lexy didn't have enough energy left after that mass healing to tune into Kayn's thoughts but she didn't need to. *She's healed a tomb full of people. She needed energy, and if Amar didn't hurry, there was liable to be an intercontinental incident.*

Zach interrupted her thoughts by saying, "Those newbies aren't still in the tomb, are they?"

Mike answered, "We thought it might be better for their mental well-being to leave them in there until you left. You did kill them enough times to take out six of us."

Zach corrected Mike, "That was Kayn and Lexy. Grey and I played good cop. We got a chance to know them rather well."

Aubrey met Zach's eyes and probed, "And the verdict is?"

Zach's expression darkened a touch as he replied, "Separately, they're great people, but they despise each other, I'm afraid it didn't do much to take Samid out of the mix."

Aubrey nodded without saying anything else.

The door to the room slid open. Amar smiled and asked, "I hope I haven't kept you waiting long?" He waved their four to his side and directed his Healers to awaken the others.

They followed Amar out of the room and down the long marble-floored hall as Grey gave Amar a blow by blow of their attempt to attach his newbies headed for Testing. Lexy pretended to listen but didn't really care. Amar ushered them into the dining hall, where they were served a good-sized meal. A bottle of hot sauce was placed in front of Amar. *Fascinating.* He slathered his meat and passed her the bottle. *Amar just got a lot more interesting.*

After their meal, they said their goodbyes and without much fuss or muss, they stepped through the tomb onto their own continent. The others left bags with toiletries and clothes behind. They all dug through their belongings, hoping for communication from the others. *There was nothing.*

Chapter 15

Pervie Little Creeper

They really were cutting them off to make a point. The foursome climbed the stairs out of the Ankh crypt with their bags in tow and stepped out into the sweltering jungle to the musical chirping of birds. She looked for Grey and just as she suspected her joy junkie Handler was lapping this intoxicatingly memorable moment up. *Oh, to be in his soul for a day.*

"It's incredible, isn't it?" he affirmed.

Lexy nodded and changed the subject, "Do you know where we're going next?"

"Amar told me to follow the same trail out that we used to get in," Grey answered as they lugged their bags through the sweltering jungle.

Oh, the glamorous life of an immortal. She was swatting away mosquitos, sort of paying attention to Kayn and Zach's inappropriate conversation about Twinkies. When they started a deep chat about Fruit Loops, Lexy tuned them out and quickened her pace to walk in front of Grey. *She had a headache like a mere mortal. Mental note...Never drink a glass of wine before hiking through a jungle.* They'd been walking for a while when they came to a fork in the trail. Grey chose the wrong path and picked up his pace. *He was going the wrong way.* Lexy swatted another mosquito off her arm mid feast and rushed to catch up, calling out to Grey, "We're supposed to take the other trail!"

Grey laughed and explained, "I'm sorry the lights are on but nobody's home. I'm dizzy from this heat. That could have gone badly. Did anyone have a water bottle in their backpack?"

"No water bottles but I've got your back," Lexy teased as she patted his shoulder and took the lead as they doubled back.

"Do you guys even know where we're going?" Zach questioned, wiping perspiration off his brow.

"Sort of," Grey answered honestly.

"I hope we're not, sort of lost," Kayn sparred.

Something large moved in the bushes. Lexy picked up her pace. *There were only a few large jungle animals in this area. It had probably been following them for a while. Leopards only reveal themselves when they're about to pounce. She didn't feel like wrestling a leopard today, she had a headache.*

Kayn jogged to catch up and asked, "Are there tigers in Mexico?"

"That was a leopard. Don't lag behind the group," Lexy cautioned without looking at her. *Kayn didn't need to be anxious. She was a Dragon. Zach...Now, that kid needed to be concerned.* She glanced back. *He was the straggler behind the group. Oh, well. You live and learn.* After five minutes of walking in the right direction, they saw a jeep parked on the path.

Grey crouched by the wheel well and stood up with a little black box in hand. "Sweet ride Markus," Grey proclaimed as he manually unlocked the passenger door.

Kayn found a day planner in the back and passed it to her without a word. As Lexy flipped through it, she started to giggle. *Markus certainly had high hopes.* There were times and locations all over North America marked on a calendar with detailed instructions in the margins. Sixty days in brackets. *Was this supposed to be a punishment? There were some fun looking jobs. The locations were all over the place though.* At the back in the address section, it read, join us when you've finished the starred jobs. *Only the starred jobs were theirs. This agenda only worked if nothing went wrong. It was doable.*

Grey reached for the planner as he enquired, "What do you have there?"

Lexy passed the book to Grey. "It's our schedule for the next couple of months. We'll all be so burnt out we won't know our own names by the time we're finished," Lexy remarked. She looked back at Kayn and disclosed, "I'm sorry. Maybe they might have gone a little easier on us if I hadn't killed someone too."

"Maybe, what you should take away from this moment is that murder sprees are bad," Zach teased.

That whole sentence was her job description. "Oh, you have so much to learn, my hot young friend, just follow along until you get it," Lexy countered as she dug through the console for snacks.

Beaming, Zach clarified, "Did you just call me sexy, Lexy? Ha, ha…That totally rhymes."

Dear lord. "I called you hot, not sexy. There's a difference," Lexy sparred as she did up her seatbelt and slowly shook her head. They were in the shade, but this jeep's interior was damn hot, even with the windows down.

Grey turned the key in the ignition. He swore and instructed, "There's no air conditioning. Open the windows."

"The windows are already open. Can't you tell by the mosquitos feasting on your face?" Lexy exclaimed.

"Crap!" Grey cursed, frantically swatting them away. "Did anybody check the back for water bottles?" he queried.

Lexy slapped his arm and stated the obvious, "What back?" She opened the book to see where their adventure began.

Kayn asked, "Where's our first stop?"

"We're off to Kansas," Lexy declared as the jeep pulled out, beginning their Dragon Handler bonding road trip. *Murder spree.*

Kayn giggled as Grey began cursing under his breath. "I despise driving standard. Frost did this on purpose," he complained as the jeep lurched.

Lexy sighed. *Poor baby.* She volunteered, "I'll drive. I don't care if it's standard."

Grey peered over at Lexy. Her crimson locks were whipping around in the wind as he mouthed the words, "Three hours."

It was uneven terrain and the jeep was bouncing as she stowed the calendar. She gazed out the window until Grey shoved her and pointed to the back. *Their road trip buddies were out cold.* She whispered, "Aren't they adorable." They spotted a gas station and both quietly cheered. Lexy snatched the Aries Group card out of the agenda. They left them sleeping as they dashed in to grab munchies and water for everyone. In no time they were back on the road listening to music, chatting about random, inconsequential things. Grey received a text. There was an alteration to their plans. They adjusted their course and traded off every three hours as what was left of the day slipped away as quickly as sand in an hourglass. They arrived at a small luxurious resort frequented by Lampir. Lexy grinned. *They'd been here a couple of times. This restaurant had the best enchiladas.*

"Let's check-in and bring our stuff to the room," Grey announced.

As Lexy got out, she inhaled the salty humid ocean breeze and enquired, "Shall we wake up Tweedle Dee and Tweedle Dumb?"

"It's probably going to be a long night. I'll come back out if you grab us a table. We'd better get to the restaurant if we want to have a proper meal and a few drinks before the shit hits the fan," Grey suggested, with his arm around her.

As they strolled into the air-conditioned lobby, she could practically hear angels singing in her mind. They knew they were a sweaty mess, but could have cared less as Grey collected their key at the desk and they walked to their room on the main floor next to the stairs. They stepped into the suite with double beds, Grey tossed his bag down and began digging around in it as Lexy dashed into the bathroom to touch herself up. *She didn't look that bad.* Lexy took off to save a table and order, while Grey went to wake up the sleepy heads in the jeep. As Lexy walked through the torch-lit courtyard, she noticed people doing yoga. She smiled as she walked into the restaurant. She had fond memories of this place with worn red wooden chairs around small, round two-seater tables. There was colourful art on the walls and rust-hued uneven cobblestone flooring. It was nearly empty, so finding a free table wasn't difficult. *Everyone must be doing yoga.* Lexy noticed the yoga advertisement on the wall as she sat down. *It would suck if those yoga-loving mortals got caught in the immortal crossfire. They'd zen themselves right into the hall of souls.* She perused the menu. *At least they'd be killed doing something relaxing. That might be nice.* Grey strolled in. Lexy waved him over and said, "That was fast."

Her Handler sat with her and replied, "Zach was already up. I just told him to wake his better half and meet us at the restaurant. Also, I got another message from Markus.

Our Clan is meeting with the head of the Lampir to discuss some information they've received. I guess part of Lucien's crew has gone rogue. We're back up. We're supposed to act casual and do nothing unless our symbols go off." Grey handed her his phone, so she could read the text in its entirety.

Lexy scanned the message as Grey ordered and chatted with the waitress who'd brought over complimentary chips and salsa about how empty the restaurant was. Lexy tuned them out as she reread the message. *Markus wouldn't have altered their course unless he knew this job was going to go south.*

She enjoyed fighting Lampir. It was an adrenaline rush fighting something that strong. *Lily kind of liked Lucien. It would be a shame if she had to kill him.* Lexy looked up as their drinks arrived and thanked the waitress. She asked Grey to order because she didn't feel like speaking. *Any calories would do at this point.* Lexy downed her Corona.

Grey interrupted her thoughts, "I hope we don't have to kill Lily's booty call, she's rather fond of him."

She knew he meant Lucien. "You mean me. You hope I don't have to because it will cause us a shit load of drama," Lexy baited. She dug into the complimentary chips and salsa as the thought of their Clan's sexy Disney princess upset plagued her thoughts. She peered up at Grey as she swallowed her bite. *He didn't want to hurt Lily either. He'd evolved. A few years back, he would have jumped at the opportunity to mess with Lily's love life. If Lucien was involved, they wouldn't have a choice.*

Grey's cell went off again. He read it and chuckled, "Those morons."

"What?" Lexy asked as Grey handed her his phone. It was Markus ordering them back to the room to get Zach and Kayn inside before they blew the job.

Grey finished his mouth full. Lexy stared at the picture of the best enchilada in the world on the menu and sighed, "This job better not start before I have a chance to eat an enchilada."

"You have five seconds to finish the chips and salsa while I pay for our drinks. You can do it," Grey cheered with a grin as he stood up.

Lexy devoured the chips until she noticed Grey impatiently tapping one of his feet. *Time was up.*

Grey passed her another Corona and assured, "We'll go get those idiots inside and come right back."

She chugged her Corona as they walked back to the room through the torch-lit courtyard. *Things rarely went according to plan.* Kayn and Zach were out on the balcony with the lights on in the room. *Seriously?* The two were staring a floor up across the courtyard, making it completely obvious there was something to see. *They didn't even notice as they walked by. Amateurs. If even one of those people doing yoga looked up and saw what was happening, they'd need to be corrected.* They sped up their pace, knowing Markus was probably livid and quietly slipped back into their room. Lexy leaned against the open sliding glass patio door and motioned for them to come in. They ducked. It was a ridiculous move because they were trying to hide from people a floor above. She ordered them inside with her mind. They darted into the room. Lexy shook her head as she flicked off the light, hiding the group in darkness and closed the curtains. "We really can't leave you two alone for a second," Lexy remarked, waving them closer. "Is everybody feeling focused enough to pay attention?" Kayn's mind started spinning with the reasons she needed to get to Frost. *There would be no time for reunions with boyfriends tonight.* Reading her sister's thoughts loud and clear, Lexy blocked Kayn's path and warned, "I know what you're thinking. Don't even try it. I will take you down."

Out of respect for their sisterhood of Dragons, Kayn backed down, looked at her immortal sibling and curtly prompted, "Explain."

Lexy grinned as she responded, "There's been a change of plans. Grey got a text while you two were sleeping. Part of our Clan is meeting with the head of the Lampir to discuss the information they've received. Part of Lucien's crew has gone rogue. They're trying to start a war between the hives. Once they've determined who is involved, the others will leave. We'll be sent in to correct his crew and possibly him. We've had a long-standing treaty with the Lampir, so be forewarned, this promises to be a shit show." Kayn grabbed the curtains and peeked out.

"That'd be why gawking up there from our deck might seem a little suspicious," Grey clarified. "We probably have time to go to the restaurant and have a good meal before we figuratively clean house."

Brownie points for Grey. Lexy put her arm around him as the foursome left the room. Grey slipped something in her pocket and whispered, "Put it in your ear. Keep a part of you with me if you can."

Silly boy. A part of her was always with him. Lexy inconspicuously placed it in her ear as they strolled back to the restaurant.

"What if they catch on to what they're doing and take them out before they have the opportunity to call us in?" Zach enquired.

"If our symbols go off. We're on. We'll heal ours before we leave," Lexy answered.

Grey looked at Zach and suggested, "Come sit with me. Lexy can go over things with Kayn. We have a more observatory role. They're the ones doing the job." Zach glanced at Kayn and shrugged as he left.

As the two girls sat, all Lexy could hear was Kayn, worrying about Frost. *Her sister needed a drink even more than she wanted an enchilada.*

Kayn peered up and quietly asked, "So, that's all there is to the plan?"

A waiter appeared to take their drink orders, hitting pause on her response. Lexy looked around. *Where was the waitress they had ten minutes ago? Kayn needed to loosen up.* Lexy ordered, "We'll have two shots of tequila...Each." *Now, her sister's mind was in a tailspin about whether it was a good idea to drink tequila before the job.* Lexy smiled as she responded to her thoughts, "Come on. It's our first seriously sketchy Correction with less than clear details. It would be unwise not to. Plus, it'll be hilarious to watch Grey's reaction when he sees us drinking it."

The waiter reappeared with the drink tray and placed four shots of golden hellfire on the table.

Kayn passed one to Lexy and raised her shot as she saluted, "To Dragons."

Smiling at her sister, Lexy repeated, "To Dragons," as they downed their shots.

Without hesitation, Kayn raised her second shot and announced, "To Handlers." They clinked their shot glasses and downed the second one. Lexy made eye contact with Grey. He was smiling, slowly shaking his head. *Zach was concerned. He didn't need to be. Dragons were Dragons. Being drunk didn't change anything.*

"Should we order a few more?" Kayn casually enquired as salsa and chips were placed on the table.

As Lexy reached for a chip and dipped it into the salsa, her Ankh symbol went off under her fingerless glove. Lexy whispered, "Shit...Every damn time." *It was time to kill Lampir.* The waiter placed four more shots on the table before they had the opportunity to say they were leaving. Lexy signalled to their server before he walked away and instructed, "Charge this to room 15. Thank you." They downed the shots like they were at a frat party and got up. Kayn's eyes darted over to their Handler's table. They were gone. "They're probably already back at the room," Lexy explained. "Time to clean house." The two Dragons marched through the cobblestone courtyard to the other half of the hotel.

Looking both nervous and excited, Kayn asked, "Are we using special weapons like last time?"

"Kill everything with a grey or black aura. Anything wooden will do the trick," Lexy instructed. "Either their head needs to come off or a direct hit to the heart. It's rather simple and I've always found it kind of fun once you take the whole pesky humanity thing out of the situation. They used to be a touch stronger physically, but I have a sneaky suspicion, that's changed." Kayn tripped on the uneven cobblestone in her flip flops and fell flat on her face. *Scratch that...Some things never change.* With ill-equipped patience, Lexy glanced down at her clumsy sibling face down on the cobblestone. Embarrassed, Kayn peered up. They heard giggles from the peanut gallery and realised their Handlers were on the other side of the bright floral hedge to their left. Lexy's crimson locks glinted in the light of the flickering torches as she held out her hand, yanked Kayn to her feet and coldly ordered, "Everyone with a dark aura dies. We should be able to sneak up to the first floor, correct the Lampir and get out without alerting anyone." Kayn nodded as she wiped the excess blood off her knees, raised her hand to her nose and inhaled the metallic scent. Lexy watched as the light vanished from her eyes. *Fascinating, the scent was Kayn's trigger.* Lexy went back to stall eleven and saw the yellow flowers beneath the hay. Brick by brick, the wall between her and everyone else grew until it felt insurmountable. *The laughter on the other side of the bushes ceased.* She was aware of the warmth of her Ankh symbol beneath her fingerless glove, it redirected her mind to the here and now. *Vile Ankh killing Lampir.* The Dragons inconspicuously strolled through the lobby past the orange-hued auras and slipped unnoticed into the stairwell.

Grey spoke through the earbud as Lexy scaled the stairs, "Come back to me just a little honey. This job is simple, find wooden weapons and kill everything with dark auras. Repeat the instructions."

As they stepped out into the empty hallway, Lexy emotionlessly repeated her Handler's words, "Find a weapon. Wood. Only Lampir with dark auras." It was unnecessary to discuss any plan in detail. Dragons had no need for pleasantries. They would put down who they'd been ordered to kill without sentiment. The two Dragons parted ways. Lexy left the main room for Kayn and sprinted to the end of the hall as instinct lead her to Frost's crumpled form. Lexy knelt, placed her palms on the fallen Ankh's back and gave his natural healing ability a quick bump. It would be more challenging to heal him after he'd been trampled by escaping Lampir. She towed him out of the way and snatched the chair leg he'd weaponized from his grasp. She heard the commotion down the hall and knew, those with half a brain would be running for the emergency exit, where she would be waiting. Lexy swung the leg of the chair as though she were practicing on a pitching mound. Three Lampir burst out of a room and fled down the hall. *They were coming straight at her. They must be new.* Lexy kicked the first salivating Lampir with a smoky black aura away, swiftly snapped the neck of the second, knowing it was only temporarily out of the equation. She blocked the third's path of escape and menaced, "You can try to get past me, but you'd be wasting your final moments being a chicken shit." The first was back on his feet. Both Lampir opted to come at Lexy like complete morons. She booted one down, the next received a stake in the chest. It lit up, solidified and exploded into the air as a downpour of embers and ash. Lexy disposed of all who attempted to flee by staking and turning them to clouds of black soot. With no time for thought, the next pack came racing down the hall in a swarm of snapping beastly distorted jaws. She kept launching them away, staking her assailants, but there were too many. Healers made the best sacrificial lambs. Lexy was aware each time beastly venomous teeth sunk into her flesh, but she was guarding this exit. Nobody was getting past. With the Dragon at the helm of her ship, she took down every Lampir until she was rolling on sedating sexy Lampir toxin. *Her battery was low. She needed to heal. She'd given energy to Frost.* Lexy cracked her neck as more depravities attacked. Swiftly, she disposed of five and purposely missed the sixth's heart. Lexy clutched the female Lampir's shirt, looked into her eyes and smiled as she positioned her palms against its chest. *This would help.* The dark energy began draining into her, giving her fuel to operate her Healing ability. She wasn't supposed to take it all, but she didn't want to stop. Lexy shivered with pleasure as someone tried to come through the door behind her and banged into her back.

Grey hollered loud enough to make her earpiece squeal, "Lexy! Let us in!"

Party poopers. With a slight readjustment of the stake, the Lampir sprinkled to the tile as a snowfall of ash.

"Lexy!" Grey yelled again.

She moved out of the way. *Consuming dark energy was a big no-no. They almost busted her with her hand in the cookie jar.* Zach and Grey burst through the door into a mountain of ash.

"You've been busy," Grey loudly remarked. "Sorry. We need to break up murder fest. Kayn's feeding is getting out of hand, we have to step in."

He was speaking too loudly. Lexy plucked out her earpiece and pitched it into the ashy remains. It disappeared.

"Markus probably wanted that back," Grey pointed out.

She didn't give a shit. She maneuvered out of her Handler's way as he attempted to touch her to solidify their connection. *It was solid, he didn't need to touch her. She just needed a minute. Lampir venom was a titillating additive to an already confusing situation.* The hallucinogenic poison was coursing through her system, but her bite marks had vanished. She felt the heat of her healing ability fighting against the toxin in her bloodstream.

Grey reached for her again. Lexy moved out of his way. He clicked in, "How many times?"

One Lampir bite was too many. Orin's butt sprung to mind. *She couldn't think about that, she had to snap out of it.* Lexy tried to think of sexless things like cauliflower or knitting while following the two down the hall.

They were intercepted by a freshly healed Frost, who exclaimed, "I'm going to be anywhere else. Lucien triggered Kayn's pheromones, I really don't need this mental picture. Zach, do your damn job and subdue her before... Just take her out!"

Frost took off. They all knew what he was talking about, the intoxicating fragrance was drifting down the hall. It was unforgettable and difficult to resist. They came upon Kayn feeding on Lucien. *Shit.* He was caught in her intoxicating web. He began struggling and groaning in abandon. They were all too turned on to move. Her throat was dry. They were all dumbstruck by the scent, watching it go down like creepy voyeurs.

Lucien moaned as his inhibitions ceased to exist, "My turn." His eyes darkened as he sunk his teeth into the tantalizing flesh of Kayn's forearm.

"I can't stop watching," Zach whispered.

Lexy knew what the exquisite agony of fangs mixed with the sensual pleasure of feeding would do to a Dragon. Lexy felt someone behind her. *It was Markus and a hot shirtless Orin.* Lexy gapped, staring at the pheromone-induced bulge in Orin's shorts. He caught her looking and grinned. Kayn moaned as her naughty consort adjusted his teeth.

Zach yelling for Kayn to stop, snapped everyone out of their stupor. Lexy, Grey and Zach pried Kayn away from Lucien and held her down with the full weight of all three as she struggled against them. Markus and Orin grabbed the Lampir's leader and forcibly removed him from the scenario. Kayn stopped thrashing around wildly. Lexy relaxed, still watching the door Orin and Markus left through.

Zach yelled, "Kayn! Enough! Stop!"

Lexy's eyes snapped back to the situation at hand. Grey was under the spell of Kayn's sexually charged pheromones allowing her to feed. *Oh no, you don't!* Enraged, Lexy snatched Grey from Kayn's perilous grasp and physically removed her Handler. She angrily towed Grey out the door as he pathetically fought to get back to Kayn. *Frigging pheromone secreting bullshit. She did not have the patience for this crap.* Grey began slapping her away like an unruly child, so Lexy grabbed his shoulders, gave him a good shake and warned, "Snap out of it before I'm forced to kick your ass." She heard a muffled female voice followed by pitchy squealing and realised he still had an earbud in. She blocked his route up the stairs and ordered, "They're trying to give us instructions. What are they saying?"

"Let me by, maybe I'll tell you," Grey flirtatiously sparred.

Oh, lovely, he'd turned the page on her again. This so wasn't happening. "Give me the earbud or I will toss you down the stairs and take it," Lexy threatened.

With a seductive smile, he countered, "You're not going to hurt me."

He was trying to play her. She descended a step, placed her palm against Grey's chest and gazed into his eyes. As her lips slowly moved towards his, she whispered, "All's fair in love and war." She plucked the bud out of Grey's ear and held it up to her own.

It was Frost's voice, "Put her down. I know one of you can hear me. The Aries Group is here. Take her out before we have to explain."

Lexy pointed her finger at Grey and ordered, "Stay." Mysteriously, her Handler did as he was told. She raced up the stairs, shoved open the door and held her breath to avoid being rendered helpless by the pheromones. She found Zach and Kayn making out. Lexy methodically snapped her sister's neck. As she crumpled, Zach came out of the pheromone induced stupor. Lexy noticed the others in the room across the way. Mel was alone on the balcony. Lexy waved at her. She waved back. Zach overzealously waved. Mel gave him a dirty look and walked away. *She felt a little bad for him.* Lexy commented, "Those pheromones make everybody stupid. Mel will be spending time with Lily and Frost over the next couple of months, she'll get it."

"Do you think Frost saw us?" Zach enquired as they stared at the room down a floor, across the courtyard where everyone had Lucien comically restrained on the bed.

Lexy opted out of a response. *He didn't need to feel worse. Frost might be a little pissed off, but he'd understand.*

Grey burst through the door and accused, "What in the hell did you do? I couldn't even move."

"Quit being overdramatic, we don't have time for the blame game. Come on, we need to move the body. Grab her legs," Lexy asserted.

Zach questioned, "Can't you just wake her up?"

Just wake her up. Lexy answered, "No, the Aries Group is coming, we've trashed this entire floor. I need my energy and Kayn needs a time out."

Zach picked Kayn up and said, "Fine, I'll carry her out."

"Suit yourself," Lexy responded as she passed her irritated Handler his earbud.

Grey pocketed it and sighed, "I'll grab our bags. Meet you guys at the car."

Zach cradled Kayn in his arms as they descended the stairs. Lexy took the lead, watching for witnesses. She peered out the door into the lobby. *It was deserted. Nobody was behind the desk and the lights were off.* They walked right through the courtyard. *He'd said the Aries Group was already here?* Zach gently laid Kayn on the backseat as Grey arrived with their bags. Lexy tossed him keys and suggested, "You drive first."

Grey pitched them back and sparred, "You owe me one, I'm tired."

"Owe you one for what?" she questioned. Grey rifled a plastic bag at Zach and got into the backseat.

"I'll sit up front with you and do the next shift," Zach offered as he dug through the plastic bag. He peered up and added, "I'm sure it'll be a while before Kayn wakes up."

Lexy glanced at the time as she started the engine. *There was no way of knowing how long it would take. Kayn ingested a lot of energy.* As they sped down the highway, she glanced in the rear-view. *Grey was already out cold. Maybe, he meant she owed him one for killing Stephanie and separating them from their Clan?*

"Is something upsetting you?" Zach questioned.

Everything had been kind of upsetting lately. "It's alright. I'm fine," Lexy answered. Zach offered her a visibly melted Snickers bar. She smiled and asked, "Where did you get that?"

"It was in the bag Grey tossed at my face," Zach answered. "Along with these."

He revealed the items, "There's also a bag of sour cream and onion chips, hot sauce and a few teeny tiny bottles of tequila. She knew where they came from... *Orin. Her mind drifted to thoughts of that unexpectedly steamy first night with him. There had been a few uncomfortably perfect nights since then and there was no logical reason why she hadn't just let them continue to happen. A part of her wanted that... The closeness and intimacy. Maybe, she was so focused on this attraction to Tiberius because it could never really be anything?* Lexy cleared her throat and said, "I'll have a couple chips if you're still offering."

Zach gave her the whole bag and smiled knowingly.

It was her time to say, "What?"

"You've been remarkably naughty lately, it's kind of hot," Zach admitted.

Lexy grinned as she chewed her chip to the hum of spinning tires on the highway. *Wait... Was he flirting? She honestly didn't know. Forty years had passed and sometimes it still felt like she was new to this world.*

"If I was flirting, would you be into it?" Zach playfully enquired.

Pervie little creeper. Lexy tossed a chip at him. Zach snatched it and ate it. Kayn gasped as she awoke. *She'd woken up in many a backseat after being taken out for her Dragon shenanigans. Best to just rip the bandage off.* "It was me. I killed you," Lexy super casually admitted. She noticed the time. *That was pretty good for a broken neck.*

"Don't pee where you sleep," Grey mumbled as he shifted positions.

Shit. He wasn't asleep. How much had he heard?

Zach lightened the mood as he peered back at Kayn and teased, "So, does this mean we're getting married now?"

"Alright. I get it," Kayn sighed as Zach passed her a bottle of water. She removed the cap and touched Lexy's headrest as she said, "Thanks for taking me out before I broke the Handler Dragon intimacy seal."

"Not a problem," Lexy replied as she kept her eyes focused on the dark highway ahead.

Fully awake, Grey added his two cents, "You should never sleep with your Handler. I'm so grateful we've never crossed that line."

Lexy mouthed the words, "Oh my God," at her reflection in the rear-view mirror.

Zach glanced back at Kayn and assured, "I could think of worse things."

Lexy struggled to focus on the endless dark road as her co-pilot Zach searched for a new radio station. A beautiful Spanish song came on.

Kayn touched Lexy's shoulder and questioned, "Weren't the others supposed to be at the Summit?"

Lexy responded, "Yes. I'm sure they've already left."
Headlights were approaching on the other side of the road.
It was the first car they'd seen in over an hour. Lexy's
stomach cramped. *Shit.*

Kayn ominously whispered, "I have a weird…"

The vehicle veered into their lane. *Crap.* They crashed
and began flipping down the darkened highway to the
sound of crunching metal as bodies were flung out of the
wreckage. Lexy hit the pavement and toppled down the
road until her body came to rest. *Ouch. Damn it all. Who
were those assholes? She felt the heat of her concealed Ankh symbol
strobing.* She struggled to raise her pounding head to check
on the others and lost consciousness.

Chapter 16

Voodoo Pheromones

Lexy opened her eyes, unsure how long she'd been down, she sat up and stretched. *Kayn had made good use of her alone time. She had a group of men with their hands and ankles bound.* Lexy brushed herself off, got up and announced, "Well, Brighton, what are we dealing with?"

"I'm not sure what they are but they didn't hurt any of us," Kayn replied. "Lampir, maybe?"

Lexy flipped one over and checked the distorted creature's gums by its canines. *They weren't Lampir.* She inspected the predator's blackened fingernails and said, "They appear to be Lycanthrope but not fully changed. I haven't seen this before. Did you say they didn't touch us?"

"One was right by Zach. It was twitching by his neck and I thought he was being hurt by it, but when I got a closer look, he didn't appear to have any injuries that weren't caused by the accident," Kayn explained.

Crouching for a closer look at the creature's blackened nails, Lexy stated, "Either way, running us off the road violated the treaty." One of them began squirming around growling. Lexy flipped it over and looked into its eyes as she questioned it, "You've inconvenienced us. Explain yourself. You have about five seconds before I tear out your heart and feed it to your corpse."

Fear registered in the creature's eyes as it bluntly responded, "We were driving home, there was this fragrance in the air, we started to change with no lunar prompting. The next thing we knew, we'd crashed into you guys. We were frenzied by the blonde one's scent. You were all bleeding profusely, but we sensed you weren't mortal. We also detected the Lampir toxin in the blonde one's system and knew she might turn. So, we tried to keep our distance. Those pheromones are so intoxicating. What is she?"

Those voodoo pheromones. Lexy replied, "She's one of us. She's Ankh and a Conduit. She's part Guardian, as am I."

The Lycanthrope smiled as he introduced himself, "My friends call me Emerson and I give you my word, we never intended to hurt you."

"Alright then, let's get you all untied," Lexy replied. She snapped the triple tied zip-ties like they were nothing. The Lycanthrope had fully returned to their mortal state. Her sister had a million questions about their breed and what caused someone to become Lycanthrope. Lexy answered her thoughts, "Usually genetics, but in rare cases, a scratch or a bite can infect someone with the virus."

"Good to know," Kayn replied as she held out her hand to help up the now fully mortal looking man.

Emerson raised Kayn's hand to his nose and sniffed her. His eyes were flecked with glowing yellow as he awkwardly let her go and explained, "Your scent is difficult to ignore. It's still there but faintly now."

Kayn smiled and suggested, "We should wake the boys up."

Lexy glanced at her cell, peered up from the screen and declared, "No cell service. We might be stuck here until someone comes along." *She needed to heal Grey. They had places to be and duties to fulfill. No good can come from hanging out with Lycanthrope in the desert.* Lexy wandered over and squatted beside her Handler. *He wasn't dead. It wouldn't be a taxing healing job.* She called Kayn over. They both placed their hands flat on Grey's chest and released their energy into him. He opened his eyes and groaned. The healing duo moved on to Zach. It didn't take much. Lexy noticed the flickering light on the other side of the Lycanthropes wreckage. *They'd started a fire.* Zach and Grey were already being introduced to their accidental friends. One of the Lycanthrope's voices cracked as he introduced himself. *He'd barely hit puberty. For some reason, she'd thought Lycanthrope didn't turn till sixteen...or until they'd been responsible for ending a life.* She looked at the boy and stated the obvious, "You seem quite young."

"He is," one of the men replied protectively.

Lexy nodded. *She wanted to know more but didn't want to pry.*

Kayn joined the group gathered around the flickering flames. Zach smiled as she approached and enquired, "Hungry?"

"Always," Kayn admitted, taking a seat at her Handler's side. She asked, "What are we having?"

"Whatever sees this fire and comes to eat us," Zach replied. "Or we can choose the easy route."

Intrigued, Kayn responded, "What would that be?"

Grey piped in, "I'm sure you're a bit hesitant to uncork Frost's ability, but if we set those pheromones off, our friends here can change without a full moon. You'll be able to send some for help, while the rest hunt us down something to eat."

Lexy gave Kayn's shoulder a reassuring squeeze as she assured, "I'll break your neck if you get out of hand."

Kayn shrugged as she took Zach's hand and announced, "Give it your best shot, Romeo." All eyes were on the Dragon Handler duo.

Clearing his throat nervously, Zach inched closer and gave her his sexiest come-hither smile. Kayn started giggling. "Come on, Brighton," Zach complained.

"There are too many people around, this isn't going to work," Kayn countered.

"Positive thinking," Grey urged. When Zach didn't jump right in, Grey took the initiative as he declared, "Allow me to show you how it's done."

Kayn gave her a helpless look. Lexy shrugged and whispered, "I'll break his neck too."

Grey spun around, glared at Lexy and enquired, "What did you just say?"

"Nothing important," Lexy answered. When Grey turned back to Kayn, Lexy winked at her.

Grey confidently moved in, took her hand and placed it on his chest, holding it firmly in place. "What would Frost do in a moment like this?" Grey enquired.

Staring into his eyes, she divulged, "He'd probably try to kiss me." Grey leaned in. Kayn maneuvered out of the way, laughing.

Grey chuckled and teased, "Chicken."

That made her day. Lexy grinned as Kayn summoned Emerson over and without hesitation, her sister seductively kissed the attractive middle-aged Lycanthrope. As their lips parted, Kayn's pheromones released into the desert air like a blast of mystical, sexy magic. Emerson's eyes were flecked with yellow as he stood there dumbstruck. Kayn possessively ran her fingers over his defined chest as she suggested with a raspy tone, "Why don't you harness that inner beast and go catch us something to eat?"

Emerson's eyes hazed over as he obediently responded, "Yes... Of course."

Kayn faced the rest of the pack and ordered, "I'm going to need a few of you to go for help because we've had some car trouble. Would anyone like to volunteer?"

All hands raised. Some were already beginning to change. Their facial features distorted, becoming angular and savage until one by one, they galloped away on all fours.

It felt like the whole wolf army scenario could get out of hand rather easily, but she was thoroughly enjoying the show.

Grey whispered, "Another Lily...Heaven help us."

Kayn turned to Grey and suggested, "I think Lexy could use a shoulder massage... Don't you?"

"Sure," Grey answered as he dutifully began massaging Lexy's shoulders.

It felt lovely, but she couldn't allow herself to be mesmerized by a touch or a smile. Lexy knit her brow. Irritated by how easily Grey lost his senses, she shooed him away.

With an uncompromising look, Zach whispered, "I'll just agree to play along if you promise to leave me my free will."

"Deal," Kayn whispered as she walked away from the trio as she became sidetracked by the breathtaking display of the stars blanketed across the heavens.

The Succubus and Siren abilities were used to compel away free will. Lampir often had this gift. It was usually only those who were incapable of forming real bonds. Lexy wandered over and took Grey's hand, curious to the strength of Kayn's pheromone induced hold. He barely noticed. His eyes were trained on Kayn's every movement. *It was inevitable. She'd need to be the one to put her sister down again, the timing would have to be perfect. If Grey tried to stop her, she'd be ticked off for the duration of their banishment.* The howling of the returning Lycanthropes echoed through the desert, bringing Lexy back to the task at hand. *They had to eat, get a new rental car and hurry their behinds to the next job. She had something to prove…But only, to herself.* Lexy let go of Grey's hand, knowing there was no time for a Dragon pissing contest. *She'd only succeed in pissing herself off.* Kayn was kneeling in the sand, causing the delicate grains to dance beneath her fingertips. *They could all do that.* Lexy felt the reptile's presence before seeing the rattlesnake hypnotically slithering through the sand towards Kayn. It reared its head as it began its telltale rattling.

Kayn met the reptile's penetrating gaze with her own and warned, "You will not succeed in harming me. Leave."

It came at her with no restraint as predators often do. Kayn raised her hand. The reptile froze in place. She waved it and the rattler went soaring through the air. It landed in a cloud of sand and left peacefully. Kayn began to experiment. She tossed a pebble into the air and tried to stop its descent. *Grey and Zach were mindlessly mesmerized by her sister's actions. They were sitting ducks. They'd become a midnight snack the second Kayn decided she was hungry. This might be a good time to put her down. She was distracted.* Lexy inched closer as Kayn grabbed another handful of sand, chucked it into the air and this time, every grain was mystically suspended in mid-air, slowly moving clockwise like a mobile over an infant's bassinet. Zach met Lexy's determined expression with a nod. *He was coming out of the pheromone induced stupor. He understood everyone's mental state was compromised and the last thing they needed was a Dragon with minions.* Zach continued to distract her sister by urging her to keep playing with her abilities. Kayn pitched another handful into the air and stopped it for a few seconds. The grains of sand sprinkled down like summer rain. Lexy's attention was drawn to an odour, followed by heavy panting.

Zach touched Kayn's arm and instructed, "They're back. You should stop messing around. Experiment when there are no witnesses."

Time was up. That was her cue. Lexy shot in, snapped her neck and loudly declared, "Sorry creatures, your air freshener is dead." She smirked, sensing not a one of the Lycanthrope appreciated being referred to as a creature. *This was peculiar, she rather enjoyed it.*

Grey instantly snapped out of his pheromone-induced trance and sighed, "Every damn time. I have no self-control."

He didn't. He never had. He never would.

Zach cradled his Dragon's limp body in his arms as he wandered over and placed her on the ground by the light of the fire. He sat next to her and lovingly brushed her hair out of her eyes.

"Is she your girlfriend?" The youngest, now human-looking Lycanthrope asked.

"No, I'm her Handler," Zach responded as he watched Kayn lying there completely still.

"She's one of those Dragon's then... They are always telling stories about that Dragon with the crimson hair." The adolescent boy clicked in to Lexy's presence and tried to backtrack, "All good things, of course, about how strong and powerful she is."

"Good save little buddy," Grey chuckled as he reached over and messed Lexy's hair.

Lexy swatted him away and scowled as she hissed, "Do you really want to do this right now?"

Grey flirtatiously sparred, "I might."

Their gaze held for a little longer than it should. *No.* Lexy stood up and proclaimed, "Not this time Greydon," as she stormed away.

"What did I say?" Grey sighed.

What Lexy needed was space, she didn't stop walking away until she heard the rustling of sand behind her. She turned, expecting to see Grey. *Zach? She wasn't mad at Zach… Anymore.* Lexy slowed down and allowed him to catch up.

While matching his pace with hers, Zach implored, "Grey's still back there. You can talk to me."

Lexy paused mid-step and started laughing.

"What's so funny?" Zach enquired as he uncomfortably snatched a rock from the ground and pitched it into the distance.

"You are," Lexy answered as she picked up her own stone and hurled her's so far it disappeared.

He groaned and baited, "Must you ladies always stomp on my ego?"

Lexy's expression darkened as she countered, "Must Grey always stomp on mine?"

"I see your point there," Zach replied. "You two have stretched the boundaries of your relationship. He doesn't remember anything, and he keeps putting his foot in his mouth. Is that why you're upset?"

Lexy sighed as she faced him and answered honestly, "Do you know what it's like to love someone you can never be with?"

"I know what it's like to want someone who has no serious interest in me if that counts?" Zach answered.

"You mean Melody?" Lexy enquired.

Zach grinned as he responded, "It would have been extremely helpful to know she was in love with the leader of Trinity. It still kind of stings that she knew I had this crazy crush on her and she just let it simmer without bothering to fill me in. Then, there's the whole year long booty call with Grey thing that I knew nothing about. That had to suck for you."

Glancing his way, Lexy confessed, "It always sucks for me. It's a cruel karmic joke, but you know those two have nothing serious going on. Grey was just the relief pitcher. Perhaps, she needs a new one now?"

"Right... It's not like I haven't tried. We kissed, it was amazing. It was starting to feel like maybe it was going to go my way, but we met up with Trinity. Whenever Thorne's around, it's like I'm not even in the room. How am I supposed to pretend I don't know I'm expendable?"

"You're preaching to the choir?" Lexy teased, playfully nudging him. She prompted, "What about Haley? I thought I saw something happening there."

"I keep getting sucked back into my feelings for Mel," he explained. "Also, I'm Kayn's Handler, which is just as confusing because I know I'm not even the first choice for this job. I mean, she's my friend, and there's nothing I wouldn't do for her, but she has Frost. It confuses my role. Maybe, if I had someone myself, it wouldn't?"

"Maybe," Lexy repeated as she gave Zach's arm a reassuring squeeze. "I've been trying to move on from Grey for years, but every time I do, his feelings for me resurface. That's why I walked away. He's being openly flirtatious, this is how it starts. Eventually, he'll confess his feelings. I love him too much to turn him away. We're inevitable but it's torture when he wakes up and doesn't remember. For a long time, the incredible night we spent together was worth it, but now, it just feels like I'm stuck on the wrong road."

"You deserve better," Zach assured as their eyes met.

Lexy took off her shoe and dumped out pebbles as she sighed, "That's just it. There is no one better. This isn't his fault. I know girls say that all the time, but in this situation, I know he loves me with everything he is. He's my Handler. He forgets when his memory is wiped, but he's been remembering his feelings for me, more often and closer together. For me, he's everything. If there were ever a way for us to really be together, I'd be a hundred percent in, but this has been going on for so long. I'm finally ready to see my options if that makes sense."

"It does…I don't know a lot about the guy, but Orin seems nice enough," Zach remarked.

Grinning as she recalled their last encounter, Lexy disclosed, "Orin is amazing, but I'm not Jenna, and he's not Grey. I don't know where it could possibly go while we're both still in love with other people. There are other complications. Attractions to be dealt with before I can even think about it."

"Tiberius?" Zach baited as he innocently pitched another stone.

Lexy snatched herself a pebble as she chuckled, "You don't miss a thing, do you?"

"Not usually," Zach admitted.

"It's complicated," Lexy confessed as she cast her stone.

"The dark and twisty ones are always fun," Zach sparred as he grabbed another grape-sized pebble out of the sand and winged it.

"Stephanie or Patrick?" Lexy casually probed.

Immediately on the defensive, Zach disputed, "What about Patrick?"

"Nothing, it was just a vibe I got after seeing you together," Lexy countered with a sly knowing smile.

Zach's eyes grew calm as he confessed, "While we're being honest, I'll admit it, there's a strange pull there. To make it clear, I'm straight... I enjoy sex with women."

"I'm not disputing that. I'm just making sure you know it's alright to be who you are. Some people are into both," Lexy gently revealed as a commotion by the fire made them aware Kayn was awake.

"For now, I plan to stay in one lane," Zach clarified as he brushed the sand off his hands on his shorts.

"The best things come from broken plans," Lexy teased as they jogged back to the others.

Grey was just sitting there watching a cross-legged Kayn, gleefully moulding an energy ball. He mouthed the words, "Get her before she blows someone up."

How was Kayn healed? They'd only been gone for twenty minutes. She was healing faster too but didn't plan on calling attention to it. The desert air was ominously still. The stars in the sky above had ceased their twinkling. Lexy felt the darkness coming as an ache in her bones. Her mind began feeding her flickers of Dragon inducing images. A wave of nausea washed through her, and she knew it had nothing to do with her sister openly playing with one of her most perilous abilities. *Something was coming.* Lexy snapped out of her own thoughts as Kayn disclosed, "I have no ill will with the Lycanthrope. I'm going to use this on Abaddon. They'll be here soon." Kayn's eyes met with Lexy's as she questioned, "Can't you feel it?"

She could... Lexy slowly nodded. *There was no time. They were already here.*

"Shit! Everyone up! Get ready to fight!" Grey stammered as he leapt to his feet. "Does anyone have salt?"

Lexy dashed back to their barely salvageable vehicle as Lycanthrope gathered by the fire clutching their knives, prepared to rumble.

"Hey, Grey!" Emerson called out.

Grey turned just as the Lycanthrope tossed him a closed switchblade. He caught it and warned, "You should leave. You'll be killed."

"We've never run from a fight before, why start now," Emerson refuted.

Lexy rifled through the vehicle. *Their Lycanthrope friends were going to die. Sticking around was suicide.* She returned with a box of salt and a backpack full of weapons. Lexy tossed the unopened box to her Handler.

Grey quickly made a circle of salt for safety and ordered, "There's no time. I can feel it too and my radar isn't the greatest. Get in the circle!"

"Why?" Emerson asked as the Lycanthrope joined the Ankh in the safe area encircled by salt.

Grey glanced at Emerson and repeated, "Why? How do you deal with Abaddon?"

"We don't," Emerson replied. "We've heard of them, but we've been basically left alone out here."

"Aren't you in for a treat," Zach remarked. Kayn was purposely standing outside of the circle. Zach summoned her, "Get in here, Brighton!"

Kayn brazenly remained outside of the circle's protection, moulding her blue-hued orb, without a care in the world. Kayn acknowledged Zach's command with a sly smile as she replied, "That's not necessary. Lexy's in the circle."

Lexy despised the idea of standing in the circle like a wallflower at a high school dance when she could be out there destroying demons, but she would, because her sociopathic sibling was already fully armed and ready to rumble. *Oh, the things you do for family.*

Grey clutched both of Lexy's shoulders. She snapped out of her pity party as her Handler stressed, "Promise me you'll stay in the circle. There isn't anyone else who can do it."

They were immortal. Dying was merely an inconvenience but she understood what he was saying. "I'm in the circle, aren't I?" Lexy responded.

Kayn glanced at Lexy and stated, "What better time for an experiment? If my way fails, I'm sure you've got the juice to take them out old school."

Lexy shrugged her agreement. *She'd experimented on many occasions before she understood it was easier to avoid the whole painful scenario by staying in the circle. Someone needed to give the Lycanthrope a speech. If they left the protective circle of salt, they needed to understand they were on their own.*

Zach pleaded with Kayn, "Get in here. You've already ingested too much dark energy today."

The putrid scent of sulphur filled the air. *It was officially too late to alter plans.*

Kayn met her Handler's concern with a blunt, "And I plan to use it...Right now." Brighton whirled around as the cloud of smoky demonic energy descended upon the group. It passed by Kayn without even attempting to subdue her. She clapped her hands together, the orb of indigo disappeared.

"What is that?" An awestruck Lycanthrope exclaimed as he spun in a circle, trying to keep his eyes on the ominous vapour swirling around the group protected within the confines of the salt.

Well, if nobody else was going to say it. Lexy quickly schooled the Lycanthrope, "The dark fog subdues you and the monsters consume you."

"Figuratively?" Emerson enquired, making sure to remain in the circle.

"No," Grey responded. "It tears you apart and devours you. That's why we said you should leave. But that ship has sailed. You're in the eye of the shit storm now. It's happening." He nervously observed the distracting black cloud.

What was Abaddon's play here? They were usually summoned by a newbie's energy. There were no newbies here.

Zach opened the backpack, removed three blades and tossed them into the sand, saying, "Just in case Lexy can't channel our energy with the Lycanthrope in the mix."

Kayn cracked her neck like a badass as she declared, "You won't need those." She stepped into the demonic vapours path, held up her hands and shivered as she ingested the evil entity through her pores, causing her veins to darken and rise. As she exhaled, a slight puff of black smoke escaped from her parted lips. Kayn's eyes became dark pools as the sweet agony of the power she'd consumed snuffed out all mortal sentiment.

Zach loudly instructed, "Stay focused, Kayn! It's coming!"

Kayn slowly turned to face the rustling sand.

Lexy smiled. *Zach was doing better than they thought. His instructions had reached her sister while fully in the Dragon state.* A slick midnight black, scaly, tar-covered reptilian monstrosity was shuffling through the harsh grainy landscape towards the group. Saliva dripped from its jagged jaws as it reared its head, attempting to assert its dominance over the girl who stood unafraid, blocking the path to its smorgasbord. Kayn pressed her palms together and released a spine-chilling primal wail as she used every ounce of her will to create a new hypnotizing orb of energy between her palms. She began slowly maneuvering her fingers apart and back together. Each time, the iridescent blue-hued sphere grew larger. The beast let out a screech as Kayn pitched her shimmering orb. It exploded in a splat of meaty pieces that reddened the pebble-strewn sand.

The Lycanthrope who appeared to be no more than a preteen excitedly exclaimed, "That was insane!" The boy stepped out of the circle, assuming the danger had passed.

No! Lexy grabbed for him but wasn't fast enough as the black vapour descended upon him. Lexy yelled, "Get the kid!"

Somewhat removed from the situation, Kayn serenely observed the young Lycanthrope squirming on the ground fighting for his life as the black vapour devoured the boy's energy.

"Do something!" a male voice yelled.

Knowing there was little else Kayn cared about, Zach stepped out of the protection of the circle to grab for the incapacitated Lycanthrope.

The pitch of her Handler's voice calling for help brought Kayn back from the void. She darted around the circle, yanked her Handler out of harm's way and tossed him back into the salted area of protection.

Zach shouted, "Grab the boy!"

On autopilot, Kayn also yanked the Lycanthrope out of the clutches of the demonic cloud and rifled him back into the protective circle. The young Lycanthrope staggered into Grey's arms.

Lexy called out, "Behind you! There's another one!"

Kayn spun around in a blur of curly blonde mane and raced at the next merciless abomination clawing its way through the sand towards the group.

Come on. You can do this, Brighton. Kayn dove out of the way, narrowly avoiding a well-timed swipe of the depravity's claws. She skidded through the sand on her stomach. The tar black scaly abomination shifted direction and came at Kayn as she scrambled away. Another round of incapacitating onyx fog appeared. Kayn released a primal shriek as she ingested the demonic vapour through her pores. She succumbed to the euphoria. They were all screaming her name as the scaly lizard-like atrocity's claws skewered her abdomen. The monstrosity lifted her impaled body into the air. Blood spurted out of her mouth as their Ankh symbols began strobing. Lexy's adrenaline raced as she fought against the instinct to protect her own.

Grey grabbed hold of her before instinct defeated ration. He calmly assured, "She can do this. Stay with me. Don't leave the circle. We need you. I need you."

While dangling precariously from the savage beast's claws, Kayn feistily declared, "I've got this!"

Her sister's Healing ability was fighting the good fight, but it could do little more than keep her alive while impaled like meat on a skewer. Grey and Zach kept shouting at everyone to stay in the circle as Kayn choked and sputtered up blood, frantically clawing at the beast's slick impermeable scales. *There was too much blood on the ground.* Kayn stopped fighting. She was just dangling there, watching her blood saturating the sand. *Come on, Brighton. Snap out of it. Sacrificial lambs. Yes, that was their job description, but that didn't mean giving up was an option.*

"You're not done!" Zach yelled. "You're better than this! We don't give up! Dragons never give up!"

Kayn's eyes popped open. She touched the monster's scales. *Will an ability to surface. Come on, Brighton. You're on the right track. Do it. Anything will give your healing ability a bump. Think. Operate that hamster wheel between your ears. You can do it.* A potent wave of inhibition loosening pheromone was released into the air. The Lycanthrope began changing within the circle. *Crap.* Kayn gurgled as blood sputtered from her lips. Zach couldn't take it anymore. Knife in hand, he dove from the protection of the circle into the sand. The grains sprayed up, momentarily obscuring him from view. He was sprinting to Kayn's aid before the dust settled. Zach courageously leapt onto the monstrosity's back and hung on for dear life while being tossed around like he was bareback riding a rabid demonic bronco. It's maneuverable spiked tail that operated as a third arm swiped Zach off and he tumbled across the sand. Kayn gasped as the monstrosity impaled her with its other set of claws through the small of her back. She cried out in agony as the depraved creature tugged its claws in the opposite direction, opening her stomach to an unsalvageable point.

Zach began rifling stones at the monster, hollering, "Drop her! Come on! Come get me! You slimy, worthless, demonic piece of shit!"

The beast's tail coiled around Zach like a snake. It raised him into the air and pounded him into the dirt a couple of times before catapulting him a good fifty feet. *That was going to leave a mark.* Kayn shivered as another burst of pheromone released from her pores. The Lycanthrope had morphed into gigantic beastly feral wolves. They raced to Kayn's aid, attacking the beast, chomping down on its limbs with their razor-sharp fangs. The demonic monstrosity raised its spiked tail and swiped them off like bothersome flies. Some of the Lycanthrope whimpered while struggling to get back up, as each one shook off the shock of their injuries, they continued rushing at the beast.

Kayn fiercely commanded, "Release me!" The demonic manifestation of evil turned her around. It gazed deeply into her eyes as she calmly repeated herself, "Release me."

It immediately freed her from its skewer like claws, dropping her in the sand. Getting up should have been impossible but she was a Dragon. Kayn managed to find the will to stand, with her hands clasped over her stomach to keep her intestines from spilling out. *This was a game-ending injury, but the rules had changed, hadn't they?* The beast inched closer until it was only an arm's length away from Kayn. Something changed in the monster's eyes as her sister removed a hand from her stomach and reached out to touch it. The monster knelt before her. The commotion instantly ceased. *That was one hell of a plot twist. This part Guardian thing could be a bigger deal than she'd originally thought.* One of the wounded Lycanthrope had morphed back to human. He was pulling himself through the sand, still trying to come to Kayn's aid. The half-dead Lycanthrope kissed Kayn's foot. *Maybe, it was the pheromones? Either way, Kayn would need enough energy to heal. Energy, she was too injured to aggressively collect. The logical choice was the mortally wounded Lycanthrope that had given its life trying to protect her. There was also the now subservient larger demonic entity but that just felt like a horrible idea.* Kayn's eyes met with hers. Lexy remained within the confines of the circle of salt, knowing she would have to heal her Clan when this was over. Her sister was looking to her for guidance, Lexy slowly turned her head from side to side, signalling her disapproval of either choice. Kayn's attention was drawn to her Handler. Zach was lying in the sand...motionless. Kayn turned to the gigantic lizard-like being just as it evaporated into a black mist and disintegrated into nothing. Kayn held her penetrating stomach wound as her knees buckled and she crumpled to the ground.

In seconds, Grey was kneeling before Kayn urging her to use his energy, "Take mine. You two have a lot of people to heal. I'll hang out with Zach in the in-between for a while, it's all good."

Kayn was too far gone. With a final shuddering breath, she slipped away into peaceful nothing, leaving Lexy as the only living Healer.

In the aftermath of the fight, Grey and Lexy were the only ones left standing. Abaddon was gone and the Lycanthrope were mortally wounded.

Grey took her hand and urged, "We're not allowed to heal them, but with the sacrifice they made, I don't see why we can't make sure they end up in the right place."

The most difficult part of being a Healer was knowing that you could heal anyone but weren't allowed. Lexy sat in the sand next to the youngest of their accidental companions. She pulled him onto her lap and soothed him by stroking his hair. She whispered, "I would like to know the name and the age of the bravest boy I've ever met."

The boy's eyes clouded with tears as he whispered, "Gabriel... I'm almost thirteen." *He was a child with the name of an angel.* Lexy's heart shattered into a million pieces. Her eyes were leaking. She closed them and willed her tears to cease.

Grey began to speak, "You were too heroic today for a boy your age to have to be. Where is your family?"

"I had to leave when I changed," Gabriel confessed.

"Can I tell you a little secret?" Lexy whispered, "I had to leave when I changed too. So, did Grey. We all had to, and I'm so sorry, but you're going to have to change again."

"Am I dying?" the boy whispered as he looked up at the starry sky.

"Yes. You are." Lexy disclosed, lovingly stroking his hair. She smiled warmly as she whispered, "Can you keep a secret though? This is not the end. There's so much more... I promise you it's the truth."

The boy's chest heaved as reality sunk in. He looked into her eyes and asked, "Will it hurt?"

"No," Lexy vowed. "Nothing can hurt you anymore sweet one."

Gabriel's breathing slowed as he gazed into Lexy's eyes. The boy peacefully confessed, "It hurts when I change."

Lexy cradled him against her chest so he could hear the beating of her heart for comfort. Grey anointed the child's forehead with a streak of his blood as Lexy whispered the words, "From this life unto the next." The young boy convulsed and his lips parted as he released a final breath. With vacant eyes, the bravest boy in the world slipped away into his next life.

Change did hurt...For everyone. Lexy closed the child's eyes so it looked like he was sleeping. She gently placed the empty shell that had once contained the boy's beautiful soul back on the sand and whispered, "I hope he makes it through the hall of souls into a life worthy of him." She peered up at her Handler, whose eyes were also full of tears. *Even his touch wouldn't be able to heal the aching in her heart this time.*

Grey put on a fake smile as he held out his hand and said, "Stand back up."

He helped Lexy up and held her in his arms, stroking her hair tenderly as he acknowledged, "That was a tough one. What was a boy that age doing with a pack of Lycanthrope in the desert?"

"If they hadn't run into us tonight, he'd…" she cut herself off.

Grey pulled away, looked into her eyes and said, "If he hadn't run into us, he'd have a long life ahead of him breaking every bone in his body as he changed on every full moon. Now, he has a chance to start over." He kissed her forehead and offered words of solace, "Some of the Lycanthrope over there are still moving."

Relief washed over her and Lexy dared to smile as she looked up at the twinkling stars. *Everything should feel normal again, but it didn't… Not quite.* She wandered over to check out Zach's body. *He needed some help.* She got down, placed her hands on his chest and worked her magic. Kayn was healing remarkably fast. Her stomach wound was almost closed. *Impressive.*

Grey wandered over and offered, "Do you want to speed things up. Give Kayn an energy bump. I'll volunteer. Having a cocktail on a warm sunny beach in the in-between or standing in a dark desert with no ride? I'll take a Pina Colada to go."

She wasn't going to have to heal Kayn. She'd be awake soon. "That's not necessary. Look, her stomach wound's closed," Lexy showed him Kayn's nearly pristine abdomen. Lexy noticed a flash of light out of the corner of her eye. She saw it again way off in the distance. *What was that?* She pointed to it and asked, "Did you see that?"

"See what?" Grey questioned squinting.

There was nothing there now. She felt uneasy but no nausea. Mortal anxiety? It had been kind of a rough night, not really for her…Except for the young boy. Lexy shook her head and brushed it off. *It's probably just feelings.*

A shot echoed through the desert. Grey looked down at the expanding red circle on his shirt and muttered, "" Shit." He grabbed his chest and dropped.

Oh, who would be crazy enough to shoot her Handler? She *was going to play jump rope with their intestines.* Another shot rang out. Lexy looked down at the growing red circle on her own abdomen. *She really wasn't in the mood for this shit. She was already upset.* She felt her back. *It went right through. This was going to go badly for whoever shot her. She healed quickly from shots.* Another shot rang out. She felt the burning sensation and looked at her chest. *Ohhh, they were in so much trouble.* Lexy dropped next to Grey in the sand. Time slowed down as the swooshing beats of her heart warned her, she was about to be put on an immortal time out. She reached for Grey and willed her healing energy into him to shorten the duration of his Sweet Sleep.

Chapter 17

Do Your Worst

Lexy felt the glorious warmth of the sun caressing her skin as she awoke, knowing she was in Grey's arms. She opened her eyes as a gentle breeze shifted his sandy blonde hair. Lexy grinned and whispered, "You need a haircut."

Knowing she needed a distraction, Grey openly laughed as scissors appeared in his grasp. He handed them to her, turned his back and chuckled, "It's not permanent. Do your worst."

As Lexy ran her fingers through his hair, plotting out his cut, she acknowledged the reality of the situation they'd left their bodies in, "Only a professional could make a shot from that distance."

"It has been a rather shitty evening, you're probably right," Grey responded to the sound of her scissor snips. A Pina Colada with an umbrella and a curly straw appeared in his hand. Grey teased, "Want a sip in honour of the fresh hell that awaits us?"

She stopped her ridiculously timed haircut and accepted the drink. *He had a point.* "Anyone who's had experience dealing with us would have shot me first," Lexy rationalized, before taking a nice long swig from the straw.

"They'll know something happened when we're a no show at our next job," Grey remarked.

He reached over his shoulder, Lexy passed him back his drink and declared, "Kayn's almost healed and right before I died, I gave you a dose of healing energy, so your body is also on the mend."

"If Lycanthrope sense when their own are in trouble, it could have been their pack. They could have assumed we did it," Grey suggested.

"True," Lexy replied. *Cutting his hair had been oddly soothing.* She put down the scissors, grateful he wasn't sitting in front of a mirror.

He leaned back against her, kissed her cheek and teased, "Done butchering my hair? Did that make you feel better?"

"It totally did," she chuckled.

"If they bury Zach in the desert, he is going to lose it," Grey stated.

They all had sensitive areas and being buried alive was Zach's. She gave Grey's head a quick kiss and promised, "I won't try to cut your hair in real life."

"You butchered it didn't you?" he laughed. "How bad is it?"

Her fingertips started tingling. *It was time to rejoin the land of the living.* Lexy grinned and said, "See you later alligator."

"In a while crocodile," he answered as she disintegrated into the desert air.

She reappeared. *Be calm. Figure out where you are before you let anyone know you're awake. It was stiflingly hot. She was under a rough blanket on the ground. She couldn't move. She'd been restrained by somebody who knew what they were doing. It was dark... Musky. There was an agitating scent. Potatoes.* She felt nauseous and for a second, she was an eleven-year-old girl waking up in a potato sack after trusting the wrong stranger. *Snap out of it. Forty years. It's been over forty years since that girl existed.* Muffled screams, followed by a chorus of raucous laughter focused her mind. *That was Zach. She was going to dislocate her shoulder if she kept pulling against the restraints. These were Angel chains. They wouldn't budge. Assholes. She didn't know where they were, but she knew who had them. It was Abaddon. She felt it in her bones. What was their play here? She was only able to pick up pieces of the conversation. Kayn and Grey were being held at a different location. They'd separated the Dragons from their Handlers. Smart…Leverage. They had insane monster balls putting her in a potato sack. Ohhh. That was a huge mistake.* She threw her weight back, intending to purposely dislocate something. *That frigging hurt.*

Someone laughed, kicked her and yelled, "It's awake!"

It…Only she got to call people it. One voice.

"That lump of burlap is Ankh's most dangerous warrior," a girl's voice teased.

Lexy was struck by something solid. *Two voices.*

"I'm shaking in my boots," another much deeper voice chuckled.

Three voices.

"We should bury it with the guy who's afraid of dirt," a male voice bantered. He gave her a good stomp.

Four voices. She was going to hulk right out and send every one of them back to hell where they belonged. Gunshots. Kayn must be awake. Lexy grinned. *Something was happening. More shots.* Her hand warmed, she knew one of her own was wounded. The Dragon within twitched. *It was her Handler.* Everyone was screaming. *Grey was dead.* Someone else shrieked. Things smashed, crashed, followed by more gunshots. *Oh, she was done with this crap.* Lexy had been holding on by a thin thread for Grey's sake, and now instinct was prompting her to rid herself of that last pesky shred of sanity. She allowed her heart to be swallowed up by the Dragon, knowing Grey was no longer. The bag shifted. A burst of smoky rather unsatisfying air whooshed in as she saw him. *Tiberius had freed her.* Her world shifted.

Tiberius cautiously backed away, saying, "This wasn't us, it was Abaddon."

Lexy scrambled out of the burlap. Everything was on fire. Everyone was hardcore fighting. Someone flew across the barn and landed in the blaze. An Abaddon came at her covered in flames, shrieking. She maneuvered out of the way as she joined in the fight. With her bare hands, she killed every Abaddon in her path. She whirled around. *Tiberius was gone, so was Triad.* Black auras hovered around the cowering wounded they'd left behind to burn. *They were all Abaddon.* Lexy blocked their escape and coldly asserted, "Someone kicked me."

In true Abaddon form, a tiny built brunette wielding a blade stepped forward and questioned, "Will you let me go if I tell you?"

Will you let me go? Not us. Me. Dragons don't strike deals with Demons. "No. You're all going to die," Lexy coldly responded. They attacked her as a group, slicing at her flesh with their weapons. She kept tossing the Abaddon aside until the blaze engulfed everything and the heat itself became unbearable. Her arms were bubbled up with blisters, but the pain was merely an inconvenience. They kept coming at her, desperately trying to escape their excruciating demise. In a blur of fire and blood, she rid the world of her damned captors. Lexy heard Zach calling her name through the crackling flames. Lexy was staggering around quite literally melting. *This was it...She'd lost all sense of direction.* Through her hazy oxygen-deprived brain, she caught sight of a Triad waving her over through a haze of billowing smoke, screaming, "The roofs coming down! Run!"

Lexy willed her mind to continue operating even though she was on fire. She used her last ounce of energy to sprint for the voice and staggered out of the barn just as it collapsed in a mountain of flaming rubble.

Zach suffocated the flames with a blanket and urged, "Take what you need to heal from me. It's a long story. Triad's with us tonight."

She heard an engine running as her legs gave way. Zach caught her. He picked her up.

A familiar Triad yelled, "Put her on the backseat! She'll be healed before we get there! Get in! We have to go!"

As Zach placed her on the seat, Lexy whispered, "Grey?"

Zach whispered back, "Grey's okay. I know how much it hurts…Take some of my energy."

It didn't hurt anymore. Lexy blacked out.

She awoke to the humming of the engine… *All she could smell was campfire.* The memories came rushing back. She peered down at her freshly healed skin and revealing burnt clothes.

Zach handed her a t-shirt to wear over the tattered, burnt one. He passed her some wet wipes and instructed, "Wash your face and arms so you're passable to walk through the lobby."

The Triad driving announced, "We're almost there. Take the bag on the floor back to your room. I'm sure you'll find something to wear."

"Thanks for the lift," Zach replied as they arrived at the hotel.

The Triad chuckled as they got out. The unlikely trio wandered into the lobby, strode up to the desk and rang the bell. An exhausted clerk appeared, doled out their room keys and made sure they understood nobody would be at the desk during the night and that any issues wouldn't be dealt with until nine am. She noticed the Triad taking additional room keys. She'd assumed they were dropping them off and leaving but that wasn't the case. *This wasn't good, they were also staying at the hotel.* Zach and Lexy made their way upstairs to their room. She unlocked the door and allowed Zach to win the race to the bathroom, knowing he'd be fast. Lexy stepped out onto the balcony and took in the less than stellar view. They were staying at a beautiful shore side oasis, but their room was overlooking a dusty parking lot. A vision of Tiberius freeing her flashed through her mind. *The look of panic in his eyes. Was he staying here tonight? This was a horrible idea for various reasons.*

Zach stepped out onto the deck in shorts, towel drying his hair and announced, "Your turn."

Lexy left her post awaiting the others, hoping to replace the intrusive scent of soot with soap. After she'd showered, Lexy put on the t-shirt and shorts Zach left hanging on the back of the bathroom door for her. She gazed at her reflection and couldn't help but smile. *She felt rather exposed with no bra or undergarments on. She wasn't drunk enough to feel cocky while braless.* She opened one of the packaged toothbrushes and brushed her pearly whites, wishing she had makeup.

Zach lightly knocked on the door and enquired, "Are you decent?"

"That depends on who you ask," Lexy countered with a mouthful of toothpaste. The door opened as Zach slipped in. She spat out her toothpaste and rinsed the sink while asking, "Are they here yet?"

Zach fixed his hair in the mirror behind her while replying, "Not yet. Let's go wait on the balcony." He tossed her a tiny vodka from the minibar.

Toothpaste and vodka…Gross.

He casually apologized, "Sorry about the lack of underwear. I suspect there's nothing in Triad's stuff that will fit your spectacular curves."

"Good save," Lexy jousted as they stepped out onto the balcony to watch for the others.

"Stephanie's like eighty pounds soaking wet, there's no point in waiting to dig through her stuff for either one of you," Zach clarified.

Lexy turned to Zach and said, "I don't think I've ever crossed paths with the Triad who drove our getaway vehicle. Did you ask his name?"

Zach glanced her way as he responded, "Everything happened so fast, I forgot to ask, but the guy explained why Triad came. You were kind of semi-conscious, do you recall the conversation we had on the ride over? Abaddon was trying to force Kayn to put an ability into a sword, so they could pass through the hall of souls. Seth sent Triad because our Clan's too far away. Their orders were to get our bodies out and burn the place to the ground. When they arrived, Kayn and Grey had already taken themselves out of the equation."

Her sister accidentally sent a hotel full of demons through the hall of souls. That was a month or two ago, at least. I guess the word was out. Taking themselves out was rather badass. Lexy smiled and replied, "A win for the sacrificial lambs." In the distance, they noticed a cloud of dust rising into the air. *A car was coming, it was probably them.* They began jumping up and down, waving. As the car parked, they stepped back inside. She recalled the panic fuelled emotion on Tiberius' face as he freed her from the burlap sack.

Lexy raised her mini bottle and saluted, "To awkward situations."

"May this night not be hellish," Zach replied.

They clinked their tiny bottles, drank the contents, looked at each other for a second and then raced to the stairs to greet their friends. *Seeing Grey after they'd been separated for any reason, always felt like someone had just allowed her oxygen to breathe.* Lexy rushed into Grey's embrace. *Something felt off.* She let it slide as she hugged her sister. *They didn't look half bad for two people recently risen from the dead. They must have had moist towelettes in their car too.* They quickly showered and made a unanimous decision to go get something to eat. They made their way down to the restaurant. Grey seemed irritated. *What now?* Kayn and Zach were holding hands, chatting. Lexy enquired, "What did I do now?"

"Nice…Braless. Appropriate," Grey commented.

Her heart sunk. *Here we go.* Lexy tried to make light of the situation, "Kayn's not wearing one either."

"Kayn's not my responsibility," Grey countered, without even attempting to look at her.

Oh, here we go again. She was getting sick and tired of his shit. "Silly me for assuming you'd be concerned about the whole being held captive in Angel chains, inside of a potato sack situation," Lexy sighed. He didn't bother to respond. *What was he doing?* As they entered the pub, she spotted Tiberius but had no intention of going over there to start more drama.

Pointing to where Tiberius was seated, Grey ignorantly sparred, "Tiberius saved you, go thank him."

Lexy stopped cold. She spun around and declared, "Should I just go back to the room by myself and wait for you to finish up with Stephanie or whoever else you happen across like I usually do."

"You smell like vodka. Are you drunk?" He accused.

Dear lord, she didn't have the patience for this crap.

Stephanie was just walking by when Grey placed his arm around her and provoked, "Do what you want, I plan to."

Usually, Stephanie was on board for starting a fight, but she removed Grey's arm and reprimanded, "I'm not sure what's going on here but don't use me as ammo in an argument with your girlfriend, it's childish."

Stephanie was visibly embarrassed by Grey's ignorant behaviour as her Handler added more fuel to the fire by saying, "At least if you start out with no underwear, I won't have to suffer through the embarrassment of having them returned to our room in the morning."

Furious for multiple reasons, Lexy coldly stated, "I came in here with no plans to even speak to Tiberius tonight to keep the peace but now... Now, it's on. You did this. Not me... Remember that when I don't come back to our room later."

Grey stole a drink off the server's tray as they passed, raised it into the air and saluted, "Fantastic! I get to do whatever I want!"

"Fine," Lexy called her Handler's bluff by marching over to Tiberius and sitting in the booth next to him.

Tiberius was shocked she'd come over, but went with it, "Hungry? The kitchen serves breakfast all night."

She hadn't really thought out what she was going to say or do, but she was hungry, so Lexy answered, "I could eat breakfast."

Their server appeared. Tiberius ordered. Lexy hadn't even looked at the menu, so she told the waitress she'd have the same thing. *Bacon, eggs and toast sounded perfect about now.* He slid his bottle of tequila to her and she knit her brow. *Tequila, bacon and eggs was a strange mix, but she felt like living dangerously.* Lexy held up the bottle and looked at it. *There was a worm at the bottom.* She chugged it back like a high school kid who didn't know better.

Tiberius snatched the bottle away and teased, "I'd rather not spend my night holding your hair while you puke."

"I've had a crappy night," Lexy explained.

He answered quietly, "I tried to get to you as fast as I could." Tiberius handed the bottle back and asked, "How are you doing? It had to be difficult waking up there."

It was... He needed to be straight with her and tell her what he'd done. She looked into his eyes and probed, "What did you say to Grey?"

Tiberius met her gaze as he replied honestly, "Nothing he didn't already know."

"Why would you deliberately go out of your way to make this harder?" She questioned as their meals arrived.

After pleasantries were exchanged with their server, Tiberius answered, "Eat quickly so we can get out of here. I have a lot to say but not here with a table of people watching us."

Lexy's eyes darted to where her Handler was seated. Kayn and Kevin kept looking her way. Grey appeared to be distracted by Stephanie.

Naughtily touching her leg, Tiberius leaned in and whispered, "If I had you alone."

"This isn't the..." Lexy panicked, knowing what he was about to do.

He mischievously ordered, "Don't react." His hand seductively travelled up her thigh until it reached her shorts.

He wouldn't dare. Lexy's eyes widened as Tiberius intimately caressed her where he shouldn't. Her resolve to make good choices flip-flopped in the pit of her stomach. *Someone would see.*

Tiberius leaned closer and whispered, "No underwear. You're a naughty girl. I won't be able to get up now without it being painfully obvious. Baby, I'm going to spank you so hard for doing this to me."

She wanted him too. Adrenaline raced as she realised how deviously naughty he really was… *Nobody knew what was happening under the tablecloth, it was scandalously exciting. She was shameless.* The hedonistic friction of his rhythmic secret stroking caused her to tremble with anticipation. She held his hand there, needing him to finish her off even if everyone figured out what they were doing. *Even if it blew up her afterlife.* He kept up his decadently wicked feverishly paced strokes until she gasped and shuddered as internal fireworks went off. Her toes curled. She pressed her lips together, covered her mouth and whimpered.

Chuckling, Tiberius removed his hand and instructed, "Not here. Have another shot of tequila. Finish eating. I'm in cabana 14 at the end of the cobblestone path on the beach. I'll leave first. The decision is yours." Tiberius waited until nobody was looking their way, got up with a squirm-worthy bulge in his shorts and slipped out.

She quickly ate her bacon, swigged back the tequila and peered over at the other table. Nobody noticed as Lexy slipped out of the bar. *This was crazy.* She raked her hands through her crimson locks as she passed each numbered door until she reached cabana 14. She raised her hand to knock and froze. *What was she doing?* Lexy placed her palm against his door and slowly shook her head at herself, willing her libido to settle itself down, so she could summon up helpful attributes like common sense and ration. Someone cleared their throat behind her. *It was Tiberius. That was her luck.* Lexy turned around.

Tiberius grinned and teased, "I was just grabbing some ice. The door's open."

She shouldn't be here. What was she doing?

Tiberius put down his bucket of ice. He naughtily backed her against the door, gazed into her eyes and implored, "Don't leave...Stay."

She was aching to finish what they'd started. She selfishly needed this. It felt inevitable. Their eyes locked. Lexy whispered, "This is a horrible idea."

"The worst," Tiberius naughtily confirmed, suggestively caressing her bottom lip with his thumb.

No more of his erotic games. This was happening. Lexy tugged him to her, and as their lips met, hers parted like the petals of a rose for his sinfully skilled tongue. They lost their inhibitions, feeling each other up, necking against his cabana door without a speck of modesty. *He was as rigid as stone.* Lexy boldly caressed his awe-inspiring bulge. Tiberius groaned her name, fondling her breasts and roughly pinching her nipples. His lips left hers. He savagely sunk his teeth into one of her aching rosebuds through the material of her shirt, creating sweet agony as the heat of her Healing ability made her desperate for more. Lexy grabbed a handful of hair and ordered, "Take me now!" *She needed it so badly, she was about to snap.*

"Now?" Tiberius chuckled, grinding his erection against her, promising her naughty dirty things until they were too aroused to think.

She needed him inside of her so badly. "Now. Right here," Lexy asserted. Tiberius tore away her shorts as easily as wrapping paper and slid a hand possessively between her thighs. *Oh, my... He was so good at this.* She was squirming against the door with every atom humming with lust as his thrilling caresses flipped her switch to shamelessly aroused. Lexy willed him to keep going, wantonly pleading, "Don't stop. Please. Don't stop…Yes."

He muffled her naughty requests with his lips and groaned, "That's it. I'm taking you right here." Tiberius lifted her as he cupped her bottom.

Lexy cried out with carnal pleasure as he roughly entered her and gave it to her hard and fast where everyone could see. Another tidal wave of ecstasy washed over her. He stifled her squeals of hedonistic gratification with his lips as she came so hard her knees buckled. *She would have fallen if he hadn't still had his hands on her butt.*

He whispered against her neck, "We need to go somewhere a little less public if I'm going to make you scream like that." He fumbled with the knob, ushered her inside and slammed it.

She craved him in an unnerving way. In a euphoric haze of lust, Lexy stripped off her top and tossed it. *This was insane. She needed him inside her, she ached for it. This was nuts.* Grinning at her inner commentary, Tiberius brazenly peeling off his shirt and threw it. Lexy's gaze locked on his chiselled abs.

Tiberius grinned, dropped his shorts, kicked them aside and commanded, "Bend over."

Lexy bent over the bed, looked over her shoulder innocently and baited, "Like this?"

"I'm not going to last five seconds if you keep looking at me like that," Tiberius confessed. He came up behind her, spanked her ass hard enough to make her smile and vowed, "Baby, I'm going to screw you senseless. When I'm done, I'm all you're going to be able to think about."

She gasped as he roughly slid in and slapped her bare ass so hard it stung. Unable to help herself, Lexy provoked his sexy wrath by slyly glancing back. He'd all but dared her to, and it changed the game. He mercilessly pounded her into the mattress until she was squealing, whimpering and clutching onto the sheets for dear life. Bliss imploded within and surged through her entire body, curling her toes as she spasmed and cried out. *That was incredible.* Tiberius ruthlessly kept up his vigorous angry thrusting until she was shamelessly moaning and climaxing again. He instructed her to get up on the bed and roll over. She obediently did so, enjoying the role reversal.

With his lips hovering above hers, he whispered, "I know what you need."

Lexy felt something sharp against her abdomen and looked down at his blade as it sliced into her flesh. A decadent surge of intoxicating heat from her ability healed the wound as the phone rang.

Tiberius cut her again and whispered, "Ignore it. We have privacy stones. You're wearing that bracelet and I have wildly inappropriate skills to share."

He licked the evidence off her stomach and the twisted dark part of her was so impressed. *Licking someone's blood off their skin during foreplay was a bold bat shit crazy move. He'd heard her thoughts.* Tiberius chuckled as he continued the deviant trail south until his face was buried between her thighs as his tongue worked its titillating debauchery. *His phone kept ringing.* Lexy decadently writhed on the bed, drowning in the perverse pleasure of his wickedly gratifying talent. She arched her back as euphoria swept her away. She spasmed and clawed at the bedding, shamelessly climaxing over and over as his tongue gave her countless thrilling sinful lashes. The demonstration of his lustful skills ended when she became too sensitive to play his lusty oral games. Lexy was laughing nervously, swatting him away as he chuckled and altered the route of his sensual kisses.

Tiberius kissed her belly button, looked up and teased, "Did I break another doorbell?"

He'd destroyed it. He's had a millennium to learn how to break doorknobs, doorbells... Whatever. She couldn't even think. Lexy lay on her back giggling as Tiberius playfully kissed her all over. *She didn't want to really like him, but she did.* Lexy messed up his hair and confessed, "I didn't know you were like this."

"Like what," he naughtily baited, toying with her nipples.

She should go. She didn't plan for feelings. Although she might be willing to sell her soul to have him do that regularly.

With a sheen of perspiration on his skin, he chuckled and taunted, "I only take souls by donation."

Being self-destructive was her jam but this wouldn't hurt just her. "You know this has to be a one-time thing," Lexy asserted.

"But baby, I was looking forward to meeting up on a job, beating the shit out of each other and screwing like heathens in a hallway somewhere," he flirtatiously provoked, nuzzling her neck.

His version sounded way more fun.

He intimately touched her cheek, gazed into her eyes and admitted his unfiltered truth, "I've had a thing for you ever since we met."

She'd spent most of her immortal existence despising him until they'd fought together at the Summit. He'd witnessed her darkest moments while reading her mind. They were joined in a way that could never be undone. He bit her nipple, halting the sentiment. Undeniable lust smouldered as their tongues passionately entangled. He entered her, and she felt the true nature of his feelings, in every determined thrust until the intimacy was crystal clear. Ripples of ecstasy swelled into a tidal wave of euphoria as he took her over the edge. Overpowering surges of pleasure washed through her. She arched her back and loudly moaned as he pulled out and went down on her. *His phone kept going off. She didn't care. Inhabitations had ceased to be an issue.* Lexy grabbed a handful of his hair and instructed his tongue, "Faster. Right there. Yes. That's it," until she was teetering on the edge squirming around, moaning his name, clutching the sheets about to climax.

He naughtily commanded, "Stop. Not yet!"

No. Please. She was going to kill him.

Tiberius chuckled as he stretched out on his back and naughtily prompted, "Your turn."

The phone was ringing as Lexy slid onto Tiberius and aggressively rode him within an inch of his life, climaxing countless times. They continued ignoring the phone as they switched positions and he pounded her senseless into the mattress while making shiver worthy promises until they simultaneously cried out like animals.

The Triad symbol on Tiberius' chest was strobing as he collapsed on top of her and gasped, "The kids aren't getting along. I bet we're about to have company." He groaned as he kissed her and leapt up to check his messages.

Reality was about to take out her bliss. Wanting to savour the aftermath, she shut her eyes and opened them as his weight shifted. Tiberius was sitting on the bed, pulling up his shorts.

"Patrick's called a bunch of times," he explained. "Your Handler's having a meltdown. Get dressed. Nobody needs to know. Go out the bathroom window, I'll make up an excuse." He quickly kissed her again and got up.

Lexy swung her legs over the edge of the bed and assured, "He may be a drunk idiot but he's not stupid." She scrambled to get dressed. *Where were her shorts?* Someone began pounding on the door.

"Pants on Romeo. If he catches you together, he'll light your ass on fire," Stephanie warned before barging in. She grinned at Lexy's dishevelled nude appearance, tossed the torn-up shorts at her chest and prompted, "Grab a new pair from Tiberius' bag and fix yourself up. You'll do better at talking him down if he doesn't know you've just done the deed."

Tiberius casually put on his shirt as he assured, "He shouldn't be able to do much damage."

Stephanie declared, "Patrick's distracting him but we don't have much time. Are you done here?"

"For now," Tiberius answered as his eyes met with Lexy's. He mouthed the words, "I'll text you."

She wouldn't hold her breath.

Grey was obnoxiously yelling, "Get your clothes on, Lexy! We're leaving!"

She was furious as she left the room and stormed towards Grey's bellowing voice. *The idiot was yelling her name like he was holding a ghetto blaster outside of her window in an eighties movie.* Lexy walked up, saw the smouldering hut by the pool and sighed, "What in the hell, Greydon?"

"Speak of the devil," he slurred.

She noticed the burns on Patrick. *Grey was going to be so upset when he found out he hurt him.* Patrick gave her an apologetic look as he continued to clean up Grey's mess. *This was why they'd stifled his ability. He was too emotional to have it. It was too much for him. She'd always known that on some level.* "You can't do things like this, Grey. You know that," Lexy whispered as she touched his shoulder.

Grey squirmed away and fired back, "No! Don't touch me! Was it worth it? Was stomping on my heart worth it?"

Oh, the irony. Lexy calmly responded, "You are drunk and you're being silly." She heard footsteps. Lexy turned around as Tiberius and Stephanie walked over. *Oh, this was not going to go well.*

Tiberius held up his hands as he attempted to put Grey's mind at ease, "I haven't touched her. We went for walk on the beach. We're just going to clean this mess up and go."

Grey scowled at Triad's leader and growled, "You're not worthy of breathing her air."

"Agreed," Tiberius admitted as he surveyed the damage. He gave Lexy a frustrated look.

This wasn't his fault. Please, don't turn him in. Tiberius nodded, and she knew he'd heard her thoughts. *She could fix this. She had too.*

"The pool area is only the tip of the iceberg," Stephanie explained as she started helping.

Grey sunk to his knees, sobbing. *She wanted to be detached, but she'd been where he was far too many times to be unaffected. He didn't understand why he felt so devastated, but she did.*

Grey began pleading with her, "He can't love you like I do. Nobody can. We won't get over this."

She felt guilty, but she hadn't done anything wrong…Not really. "We're already over it. Let's get you back to the room. Tomorrow is a new day," Lexy consoled as she motioned for him to come. Looking back at Tiberius, she soundlessly mouthed, "Thank you."

Tiberius mumbled a farewell shot, "She's too good for you too."

Oh, shit.

Enraged, Grey spun around. Flames of fury shot out of his hands, engulfing his nemesis. Tiberius leapt into the pool. Stephanie and Patrick tackled her Handler, leaving Lexy stunned, staring at the steam rising from the water.

Tiberius bobbed to the surface and comically sputtered, "Asshole."

Apparently, someone uncorked Grey's stifled ability. Lexy grabbed her Handler's face, forced him to look at her and reprimanded, "This is a public place. We have to kill any witnesses."

Grey drunkenly hissed, "It's my job to stop you from making mistakes." He pointed at Tiberius and announced, "That dipshit's a frigging big one." His eyes rolled back and he passed out cold.

Lovely.

Tiberius was laughing as he climbed out of the pool with a blistered everything. The pain didn't appear to have any effect on him as he looked her way, winked and confessed, "Still worth it."

Lexy shook her head, knowing the level of badass you had to be to joke about third-degree burns. *She'd just been there. She had a confusing mix of guilt and pride over what she'd done. This kept her on the fence as to the worthiness of her actions. She knew one thing for sure…Grey wasn't going to let this slide.*

Tiberius slipped into leader mode and began ordering his Clan around, "I want all of the rooms thoroughly searched. Every bathroom and closet. No witnesses. Steph, what happened? What do we know?"

Stephanie cleared her throat and told the story, "Grey noticed Lexy wasn't in the bar. First, he was crying and being all dramatic, then he started threatening everyone. He was going to light us all on fire if we didn't tell him where you took her."

Even though it sounded feasible, Patrick didn't look like he was on board with Stephanie's recount of events.

"I honestly don't believe Grey knew it was going to happen," Patrick explained. "He didn't intend to hurt me. He was as shocked as we were when he lit up the tablecloth. Our drinks were on the table and it exploded. It felt like an accident."

Tiberius chuckled, "So, I have two different accounts. Mike, you're the tiebreaker. I'd imagine the truth is somewhere in the middle."

The Triad Lexy didn't know shrugged and disclosed, "The guy was really drunk. Stephanie was rubbing salt in his wounds, saying things like I bet Tiberius has Lexy bent over right now. She kept pushing his buttons until he chucked his drink at her. Fire sprayed from his hands and the table blew up."

Tiberius fake scolded Stephanie, "I get it. Drama stresses me out too, but was that necessary? I was having a good night."

"Alright, he was confused and upset. We talked him down and cleaned up the mess. There were only two witnesses, the bartender and the waiter. They've been dealt with. Mike saw a sign in the lobby earlier that said nobody will be back at the front desk until 9 am."

"That's convenient. Steph, you come with me. Everyone else, help Lexy get party boy up to his room and then go find Kevin. I'd imagine he's wherever Kayn is."

"Zach's already out looking," Patrick replied.

Tiberius shrugged and asked, "What did you do with the bodies?" He paused and recanted, "Never mind, don't tell me. I don't really want to know."

They picked up her drunken disorderly Handler and lugged him away from the scene of the crime. Once Grey was tucked in, Lexy accompanied the Triad out. She thanked them and sighed, "I'm going to need my own room. I'll see you two later." She started walking to the stairs.

"Here, take ours. We're right next door and we're leaving. There's a kitchenette," Patrick offered as he tossed her his key.

Lexy caught it and said, "Tell Kayn and Zach where I am."

"Zach was with me until the shit hit the fan. He went looking for Kayn," Patrick answered, voluntarily satisfying her curiosity.

The Triad she didn't know, disappeared into the room next door and emerged with a backpack. He left the door open and remarked, "Tiberius texted and told me to leave you my phone. There's a key for a rental car in the bag on the chair. He'll pass on the number to Markus." He handed her his phone and added, "Leave a note for the others telling them where you are. That room is going to smell like a brewery, nobody will want to sleep there."

"I'll leave a note," Lexy assured as they took off, leaving her standing by the open door. *She'd basically pulled the pin out of a grenade and tossed it at their Handler Dragon bond tonight.* Grey didn't stir as she left a note on the nightstand and took what she needed from the bag. *Grey had pushed her to the edge of the plank and she'd jumped.* She gave the room a good once over before going next door. Too mentally exhausted to shower, she locked up, got into bed and stared at the ceiling unable to fathom what she'd done. *She felt both proud of herself and uneasy. She'd known there would be consequences, she'd done it anyway.* She was just starting to drift off when they knocked on the door.

Lexy got out of bed to let them in. She got back into bed, pulled the sheets over her head and mumbled, "Turn off the lights when you're ready to go to sleep." *She didn't want to talk about anything tonight. She couldn't.*

Chapter 18

Poking Bears

Lexy awoke to a new day. Out of the corner of her eye, she noticed the flashing cell. She read the message. *They were catching an Aries group flight to Alaska. That made sense, they'd lost at least a day of driving time. They'd be there ahead of schedule. Work. Lots of distractions. That's what they needed.* She took the opportunity to shower and get dressed. *Wearing Grey's adversary's shorts felt like poking a bear.* Lexy brewed a pot of coffee and ordered breakfast from a place close by, before waking Kayn and Zach by singing, "Rise and shine!" *She wanted to be long gone before anyone started asking questions like, what happened to the hut by the pool? She hadn't gone down to the restaurant to check out the damage, she'd been smart enough to order breakfast from elsewhere.* "We're leaving in half an hour. Breakfast has been ordered, the shower is free!" Lexy poured herself a steaming cup of coffee. *She should find that key.*

Kayn stretched and yawned as she remarked, "My, don't you look vibrant this morning. Have a good night?"

"It was eventful," Lexy answered honestly as she dug through the bag on the chair searching for the key to the rental car.

"How eventful?" Zach provoked.

Unable to help herself, Lexy countered, "How eventful was your night, Zach?"

Kayn casually enquired, "I wonder what she meant by that?"

He tossed his pillow at Kayn and jousted, "Wouldn't you like to know?"

Lexy slipped the key into her pocket as Zach claimed dibs on the bathroom. She watched Kayn giggling as she sipped her delicious coffee. Someone knocked on the door. *Breakfast.* She charged the food, strolled over and sat on the other bed. Lexy passed the tray to Kayn and announced, "I ordered the same thing for everyone." Kayn frowned as she took a bite of the bland ham and cheese omelet. Lexy grinned as she revealed a bottle of hot sauce and used it, before passing it to her sister.

They were nearly finished eating when Zach appeared and groaned, "You guys should have told me it was here. Mine's going to be cold."

Lexy took the top off his and sparred, "It's been here for all of five minutes, quit whining."

Zach scrunched up his nose as he asked, "Is there one for Grey?"

"He can get his own damn breakfast," Lexy murmured as she placed her empty container on the dresser and took her coffee into the washroom with her like a weirdo. *They were having a not so quiet conversation about her naughty behaviour. This wasn't going to stay a secret. Grey would eventually find out the truth. Plausible deniability wasn't a long-term fix, but it might get them through the day.* Lexy opened the bathroom door and gave them a scathing look to silence the gossip. *She was going to have to wake Grey up.* She gave the door a good hard slam as she left to make sure Grey heard and paused in the hallway to enjoy another sip of coffee. Grey's doorknob jiggled. *Oh shit. She wasn't ready to keep a straight face.* She scurried into the stairwell and sat there drinking coffee for a while, before opting to walk out to the parking lot to see which vehicle the mystery key unlocked. Lexy stepped out into a soundless dark lobby. *This was strange. What time was it? She walked out to the almost empty parking lot. One of five cars.* She pressed the button on the key, one of the vehicle's lights flashed. Lexy shrugged as she wandered back to the room. *She wasn't going to be able to avoid Grey forever. Time to rip the band-aid off.* Kayn and Zach were walking towards her. Grey wasn't with them. *She might as well find out what she's getting herself into.* Lexy asked, "How upset is he on a scale of say…one to ten?"

Zach answered, "He doesn't appear to remember last night. He's more worried that you're angry at him."

Lexy smiled as she left and made her way back to the room. *Maybe she'd have a day or two of peace before he remembered why he was angry? That would be nice.* She bumped into Grey at the top of the stairs. A pitch shrieked, shattering her nerves. Lexy covered her ears. Grey rushed to her side. She yelled over the incapacitating frequency, "We have to go! Now! Take the key!" *The sound ceased as they hit the lobby, but it didn't matter. They knew what this was.*

"Get in the car!" Grey hollered, unlocking the one Kayn was leaning against. In seconds, they were speeding away with Grey's foot on the gas all the way to the floor. The car lurched as they peeled onto the main road tossing them all to one side.

"Go! Go! Go!" Lexy yelled, frantically smacking Grey's arm.

Zach hollered, "What's happening? I don't understand what we're doing?"

Driving like they were being chased, Lexy shouted, "Go! Go! We have to be out of range!" There was a rumbling of a plane's engine overhead. "Go! Go! We're not far enough away!" Lexy hollered frantically. They were spitting up gravel going as fast as the car could go. Suddenly, there was a deafening thunder.

Grey screamed, "Seatbelts! Now!"

A wall of wind, earth and fire surged after the vehicle. "Brace yourselves!" Lexy yelled as the cloud of dust, debris and fire pursued them.

A millisecond before it hit, Zach whispered, "Shit."

The heat of the debris surged through the shell of the vehicle scorching their flesh, followed by agonizing cries and the inability to breathe as the wreckage began tumbling down the highway. When the dust settled, what was left of the car was still upright. There was a humming pitch in Lexy's ears. *What had Tiberius told the Aries Group?* She felt her Ankh symbol going off. *I know, I get it.* Lexy glanced at her Handler. *He was out cold.* The hollow pitch ringing in her ears made it difficult to operate her thoughts. She saw the bloody interior and smashed windshield. *Someone wasn't wearing a seatbelt.*

"Crap," Kayn moaned from the backseat.

Lexy cricked her neck, groaning, "That's why Grey yelled, seatbelts."

"Did his body hit either of you?" Kayn asked as she began tugging on the door, trying to get out.

She was wasting her time, the frame was compromised. Lexy smiled as she answered, "Just Grey, I've got him, look for Zach." Kayn climbed out of the window. *She meant look, not try to walk. Kayn crumpled on the dusty gravel road, she had so much to learn.* Lexy became aware of her own broken leg. *Of course. No exposed bone.* Under normal circumstances, she would have healed herself with Grey's energy and then removed him from the car, but she could smell smoke. Lexy placed her hands on Grey, focusing her energy on healing him. She was tearing a strip from the bottom of his shirt as he opened his eyes.

"You should at least buy me a drink first," he mumbled.

Lexy instructed, "Get out. I'll be right behind you." She placed a hand on either side of the swelling and reset her leg. She wrapped the material around the swollen area, knowing broken bones usually took an hour or two to heal, but setting it sped things up. Grey managed to get her door open. As he helped her out, she was expecting a shot of pain as she put weight on her leg and was pleasantly surprised as she felt nothing but the heat of her healing ability.

Kayn called out, "I can't find Zach? Did anyone see where his body went?"

"Go help Kayn look. I'll be fine, it's healing," Lexy urged.

Strolling over to Kayn, Grey remarked, "Those assholes never give us enough warning. He went through the window with the pressure of the explosion. I'm not sure where we were when it hit. I'm still a little out of it. Lexy's going to need a minute to heal." He took her hand and gave it a casual swing as he suggested, "Shall we go look for Zach's body?"

"We shall," Kayn replied as they comically skipped down the road.

Lexy hollered, "You guys are weirdos!" They started laughing and slowed their skip to a walk. The building they'd spent the night in was smouldering in the distance. She shook her head as she made a second ill thought out attempt to put her weight on her leg again and smiled. *It felt fully healed. That was unusually fast for a bone.* The contents of the bag were scattered down the road. *She hadn't been back to the room to get the cell. Tell me they didn't just leave it behind.* She picked up everything she could find. *No phone though...* Grey was pointing at something. There was a circle of buzzards in the air. *There he was. They found him the phone could wait.* Curious, Lexy wandered over to where they vanished from sight. There was a small rolling hill obscuring her vision. She quietly joined them, looking over the edge of a cliff with roaring waves below. Zach's body was on a ledge about ten feet down. *This was super inconvenient.*

Kayn called out, "Zach! You still alive?" His body twitched in response.

Grey yelled, "Buddy that had to suck!"

"You assholes," Zach groaned.

"There look, he's fine. He still has his wits about him," Grey commented. He peered over the ledge and hollered, "Can you climb up here?"

"Bite me." Zach groaned.

They were gazing over the edge trying to figure out how they were going to get him when Lexy decided to add her two cents, "The integrity of the ledge doesn't look strong enough for one of us to jump down there." Before they had a chance to figure out a plan, the buzzards descended upon Zach. As he swatted them away, he rolled off and plummeted into the thunderous rolling waves below. Kayn took a few steps back, sprinted to the edge and leapt off after her Handler. She disappeared beneath the waves and surfaced in the churning whitecaps.

"You are a horrible babysitter," Lexy sighed.

"Noted," Grey laughed as they watched with morbid curiosity as Kayn swam against the current fighting to save her Handler. He remarked, "She needs to grab him and swim for it under the surface."

That might work. Bubbles and swirling water were all they could see now. A massive wave pummelled them into the rocks. The wave retreated, sucking them away.

Grey sighed, "She can't lose the body. She'll need to tie herself to him with something."

He was right, dying didn't matter. They could recover the bodies later. Lexy yelled at the top of her lungs, "Tie him to you and just die!"

"You give the worst motivational speeches," he chuckled as they watched Kayn persevere against insurmountable odds. Grey sighed, "Damn it. You're right, though… Tie him to you and die! We'll find you!"

"She's probably worried about losing his body. Have you ever mentioned they only need a piece?" Lexy asked, sitting with her legs dangling over the ledge. She looked up at her Handler and suggested, "You might as well sit down and get comfortable." Kayn vanished, towing Zach's limp body with her and bobbed to the surface, still in the same place.

Grey screamed at the top of his lungs, "Cut off his finger! Just snap one off!"

"Oh, my god. Stop it, I'm going to pee," Lexy laughed. She peered over the edge and exclaimed, "Look at her go. She's like the little engine that totally couldn't."

Grey sat down beside her as he joked, "She couldn't even."

Kayn sunk into the deep once more, bringing their friend's corpse along for the ride. Lexy turned to Grey and praised, "Well-timed."

They waited for Kayn to bob back up, and when she didn't, Lexy admitted, "I feel a little bad. In retrospect, that comment was badly timed. You know these things happen to us because we're on the karma train's snuff list?"

"Yeah, we're horrible people," he conceded, kicking his legs and staring at his palm, waiting for his Ankh symbol to start strobing.

Lexy got up and blocked the sun with one hand as she scanned the horizon. "Where in the hell did they go?"

Grey stood up beside her and declared, "She's not dead. Well, unless the Ankh symbols have stopped going off for you two Guardian spawn."

Lexy glanced at her Handler and said, "Funny."

He replied, "I do try."

"I know you do, Greydon," Lexy teased as she scrutinized her symbol. "What if you're right? Maybe you should kill me and check?"

He pretended to push her and sparred, "I'll just shove you off."

"Then you'll have another body to find. Be my guest," Lexy baited, pointing out the circling shark fins. They vanished beneath the water and didn't resurface. Her brain lit up as she declared, "There's an underwater cave."

Grey chuckled, "What made you think of that?"

"It's like we're living in a Scooby-Doo cartoon, there's always an underwater cave," Lexy declared.

"That's not the craziest idea ever," Grey admitted as he gave the ground a good stomp.

Coldly looking him dead in the eyes, Lexy stated, "That was ridiculous. Are you going to break right through tons of rock like a superhero?"

"I might, you don't know," Grey replied as they began searching the crash site for the phone. He disclosed, "I could have powers you can't even imagine?"

"Quit making pathetic attempts at foreshadowing and look," Lexy remarked as she crouched and picked up what appeared to be a broken screen. She passed it to Grey and sighed, "If Kayn goes down, I get to jump in."

"Alright, only if she dies," he laughed, shaking his head.

With ironic timing, their symbols went off. *Yes. Kayn was dead. Time for a swim.*

Grey sighed, "So much for our underwater cave theory."

She was so excited. "I'm going in. If I get eaten by sharks, delete the browser history on my laptop," she sang.

"If we had your laptop, you wouldn't have to go swimming with sharks," Grey countered as they sprinted back to where their Clan had gone in.

No floating bodies. That was a good sign. "I meant when you get back to the RV," Lexy clarified as she peered over the edge.

"You've got this," he encouraged.

They high fived. Lexy backed up to take a run at it to avoid hitting the rocks.

Jenna's voice piped into their subconscious thoughts, *'Don't you bloody dare!'*

"Did you hear that?" Grey asked as he slowly spun around. '

They are in a cave, Kayn will heal. Wait for the Aries Group,' Jenna's voice instructed.

She kind of wanted to jump now though.

No!' Jenna's voice clarified.

"Come on, Lex. We'll search the coastline for another way in," Grey suggested.

She still wanted to jump. He put his arm around her and made her come.

Walking the coastline was their usual cavern searching route so that's what they did while Lexy pouted and Grey laughed. *The current was too strong. She'd just end up stuck in there too. There was a mountain of stone between them and their obligations. The irony wasn't lost on her.* Lexy declared, "We need one of those fish people in our Clan."

Grey playfully put his arm around her as they walked and laughed, "Great idea. Trinity has one. Pass me your cellphone. Oh yes, it shattered into a thousand pieces during the crash. Fish person rescue mission thwarted."

"They'll come looking for us when we don't show up for that flight," Lexy answered, scanning the horizon.

Grey asked, "Who?"

"The Aries Group?" she replied, giving him a peculiar look.

"Oh yes," Grey chuckled. "Sorry, I'm still hungover dumb. My memories are rebooting. I'm getting there."

Oh goody, she couldn't wait for him to remember why he was mad. She hadn't had the opportunity to overthink her actions yet and was quite thankful he couldn't remember his. It was like she'd been granted a stay of execution on dramafest. It was then that she noticed where a flock of black birds further inland vanished. She pointed and directed, "Over there!"

They altered their route as Grey remarked, "It's probably just a bunch of crows. They're scavengers. They'll eat a dead animal."

"Do you have a better idea?" she shot back and smiled. They picked up their pace and as they came closer, another flock of black disappeared into the earth. *They weren't crows, they were bats. They'd found the opening to a cave. Was it the right one? Did it hook up with the one their fellow Ankh were trapped in? There was only one way to find out.*

Grey stepped aside, motioned for her to enter and announced, "Dragons first."

Lexy skipped through the opening, listening to her Handler's musical laughter. She wandered into the darkness, unafraid. Lexy's heebie-jeebies were sufficiently placated by the knowledge that she was more dangerous than anything they'd encounter.

Grey sparked up his ability, so they could see where they were going, but his normally stifled flame shot out like a raging inferno. He sucked the fire back into his hands, scowled at her and accused, "You took off with Tiberius."

Oh, lovely. His memory was back. Lexy stated, "I'm not having this conversation with you right now. We need to concentrate on finding Kayn and Zach."

He mumbled under his breath, "You actually did it, didn't you?"

She sighed, "Take off your shirt."

"What? Not likely," he countered.

Dear lord. "We need to make a torch, so you don't exhaust yourself," Lexy clarified. "Tell you what. Use mine." She'd fully intended on tossing her shirt in Grey's face, but as she attempted to take it off, she remembered she wasn't wearing a bra.

"Come on, Lex. I'm waiting for your shirt," Grey coldly urged.

"I don't have the patience to deal with this right now," Lexy hissed as she marched into near darkness and bit into her hand hard enough to draw blood. Both of their symbols flashed, giving them a brief glimpse of the cavern ahead.

"Shit," he whispered. "Were those bones?"

She'd seen them too. There were strewn around the entrance of two distinct caves.

He lit up a hand with a controlled flickering flame, walked over and picked up one of the smooth perfect bones. "The game just changed. These are human."

Her stomach cramped, making it unnecessary to ask if he was certain. *Yes, the karma train was coming, and their shoelaces were tied to the tracks. It was time to shut her emotions down.* She looked at Grey and advised, "Go back to what's left of the car and wait for help. One of us should be there when the Aries Group arrives." Lexy grabbed a Tibia and snapped it in half over her knee. Grey tore another strip of material off his shirt, wrapped it around a bone and lit it up, revealing his crop top. *She could see his belly button.* Even though she was still mad at him, it was adorable.

He wandered over, passed her the Tibia torch and explained, "I'm going to walk back to the car to make sure they know where to find you guys."

She was waiting for him to say, come back to me as he usually did, but this time, he just walked away. Lexy felt nauseous as she stood there holding the torch. She needed to pick a tunnel, but first, she needed to hand over the reins to the beast within. In her mind, she travelled back in time to the dark farm. Flashes of inhuman violence numbed her until she woke, choking and gasping at the bottom of the well in the sludge of decomposing corpses. She'd risen from the dead in the place where they disposed of children lost. The haunting vision of Charlotte's partially submerged corpse. Heartbreak, so devastating the soundless screaming within rippled through her soul, morphing her into a weapon of vengeance. She clawed her way up the walls of stone as the beast her captors created, grabbed an axe and disposed of the soulless monstrosities one by one in a baptizing mist of red. Her palm strobed and the attachment to Ankh tugged her back to the here and now.

She methodically gashed her flesh with the jagged bone, luring the predators to her. As she held up her hand, she heard the thudding of numerous feet coming down one of the tunnels. *The cave-dwelling depravities had caught her scent. Only one decision remained…Was she going to allow them to come to her or venture into their layer?* She cracked her neck as she emotionlessly strolled into the tunnel of thudding feet. They reached her in a hoard. Dozens of distorted salivating warped distended jaws and fangs thundered at her. She swung her torch, and they cowered, shrieking an ungodly pitch. *Ah, they were nocturnal. The odds were in their favour, but ration meant diddly squat in an immortal fight. She needed light.* She darted forward, swung the torch again and lit up the front row. Lexy boldly stepped into the screaming chaos with a bone blade clenched in one hand and a torch in the other. She took out as many as she could, ignoring the steady burn of her healing ability as their jaws tore away chunks of her flesh. *Damn it. She needed her hands, but she also had to see. She was going to have to think outside of the box.* Lexy creatively doused her macabre assailants with flames and dropped the torch to fight by the flickering light of burning corpses. She tossed a depravity aside and launched the next creature into the wall with an impressive surge of mystery strength. She staggered forward. *Crap! She was going down!* The next ravenous being raced at her. *It was time to take a page from Kayn's battle playbook.* She emptied its energy to heal with one hand while still fighting with the other. The lifeless monster dropped into the shadows. Reenergized, Lexy continued to battle her way through the tunnels. Each time she stumbled, she drained another, until her battery was fully charged. It occurred to her she wasn't seeing in the regular way. She now saw glowing heat signatures and light outlines of where the walls and other obstacles were. She had sonar and she was hungry again. They tried to flee but there was nowhere to hide. Lexy worked her way through the endless caverns until she came across numerous blinding rays of light. *She didn't like it.*

It yelled, "Ma'am! You've been infected! Drop the weapon!"

Ma'am?

It repeated, "Drop your weapon!"

She was confused but someone smelled delightful. So good.

"Drop it!" Another glowing object commanded as something clicked.

Mortals. Lexy cocked her head, wondering what people souls tasted like as she inched closer to the intoxicating fragrance. *Who was that?*

Grey's voice advised, "She knows me. Take her out."

She heard a bunch of whooshes. Irritated, Lexy looked down and casually plucked the darts from her mid-drift. She felt off and sweaty. She stumbled, keeping her eyes glued to the light that smelled good. Everything felt tingly, but she managed to regain her footing. Annoyed, she attacked the radiant spheres in the dark. All she heard was screaming orders and more whooshing darts. One hit her neck. Displeased, she tugged it out and felt the moist warmth of the blood escaping from her throat. *Whoops.* She staggered and collapsed on the stone.

Chapter 19

Aries Group Fun

Lexy opened her eyes. She was on the floor in a cube-like room. *This was new. Where in the hell was she?* Everything was sterile as a doctor's office and she appeared to be alone. *She couldn't move. They had her arms restrained but not her legs...Fools.*

Grey's voice came from a speaker in the corner, "How are you feeling?"

She responded, "Skip the pleasantries and explain."

"You were infected by those things in the caves. The Aries Group needs to run you through a decontamination process," Grey clarified. "Zach's here. He found his way out. He's sedated in cold storage. The decontamination process is brutal. I told them to wait until we captured you to bring him out. Kayn is... We'll talk about it in person once you've been cleared of infection."

Lexy sighed, "Do I have to pretend they've restrained me, or can I just snap these cuffs off?"

A female voice from a speaker answered, "If you can take those off without us having to send someone in, feel free."

Lexy gave her restraints a tug and she was free. She got up and enquired, "What's next?"

There was laughter in the lady's voice as she instructed, "Remove your clothes and seal them in that large bag in the corner."

Lexy glanced down at her tattered blood-soaked t-shirt and shorts. *Tiberius' shorts.* She smiled and announced, "If you don't want to see me naked, you'd better look away." She boldly took everything off and placed what was left of her clothes in the bag in the corner. *Her face felt stiff. She was probably impressively covered in tainted blood.* She felt her clumped hair, knowing what it was matted with. In no time at all, she was standing there naked as the day she was born, waiting for instructions. She was told to step into the next room. Lexy noticed the outline of the door but there was no handle on her side. She placed her hand against the outline and gave it a gentle push. It opened into another room. Two people in full protective gear were holding sponges. *I guess this was happening.* Lexy strolled over and sighed, "Do whatever you have to do." On the floor were two buckets filled with something that smelled like household cleaner. *Wow. She'd been asked to do some weird shit before, but this took the cake.*

"It looks like you've had a rough week. This may seem harsh, but we need to thoroughly scrub you down and if you have any open wounds, it's going to sting," a female voice warned.

"I'm fine. For future reference, whatever you dosed me with is nice… I'll just pretend I'm at the spa." She stepped under the spray as they began scrubbing her down. Lexy glanced down at the red water pooling at her feet.

While soaping her up, the lady asked, "Do you feel lightheaded? Can you tell if you have a fever?"

A voice came over the monitor, "It took a dozen acepromazine tranq darts to take this one down, and she's standing here less than an hour later… She's fine. We're going to have to use a large animal tranq like Etorphine next time. Do we have any with us?"

"I believe we do," the lady answered.

The voice instructed, "Ask that one if we can test the dosage on her after we're done?"

"I can hear you…Ask me yourself," Lexy commented.

"Sorry about that. I was thinking out loud," the voice chuckled.

Glad someone found her uncomfortable situation funny. Lexy addressed the lady who was treating her like a person, "What's Etorphine?"

The lady put down her sponge and laughed, "It's an opioid that's about a thousand times the strength of Morphine, traditionally used on large zoo animals. That can't be used. It would kill you dear."

This lady had no idea what she was dealing with. Curiosity got the best of her, Lexy questioned, "How long have you been working with the Aries Group?"

"Not that long. Why?" the lady asked.

We can't be killed. She was unceremoniously ushered into the next room. *She'd figure it out.*

Grey's voice came over the speaker, "Did you enjoy your sponge bath?"

She sarcastically responded, "It was lovely. I wish I could have random strangers bathing me every day."

"This next part is going to hurt, but after you're finished, you get a snack. You've got to be hungry, you were in there for a while," Grey announced as she was sprayed with scalding steam from all sides.

The surface of her skin bubbled with excruciatingly painful blisters. Lexy scowled but had no plans to give a reaction. *It was best if they understood their place in the food chain and she was hungry. A snack sounded nice.* Her healing ability kicked in and in seconds the blisters vanished, leaving behind only pristine flesh.

A voice instructed, "Go into the next room. Put on a gown and a mask, then please take a seat."

She obeyed the request and sat on one of the plastic-covered chairs. The people that bathed her came in. *She knew the drill, it was blood test time.*

The woman whose face was still covered except for her eyes drew some blood while explaining, "We know the virus isn't airborne. This is just a precautionary measure. You're healing ability is impressive. My name's Karen. As soon as we've finished up here, I'll grab you a snack. You've been in there for days. Were you eating anything?"

Anyone? She had no idea. "Hopefully not," Lexy sheepishly answered. Karen gave her a funny look while passing her a bottle of water. After she drank it, she was handed another one, which was also gone in a flash.

"You were thirsty," Karen laughed.

The man looked up from whatever he was doing and announced, "Okay. She's good to go."

They removed their protective gear. "Come with me, I'll take you to Grey," Karen volunteered as they unsealed a door and stepped out into the glaring sunshine.

Grey was waiting there for her and as they embraced, he whispered, "We have an issue, I'll explain later." He stepped away and spoke aloud, "They're keeping Zach sedated as they put him through what you just finished. He'll wake up after you've healed him."

"Sure, let him sleep through it," Lexy teased as she followed Grey, assuming he knew where he was going. When it became obvious he didn't, she questioned, "And our destination is?"

"It's later," he sang, doing a slow twirl in the desert.

"What in the hell did they give you?" Lexy taunted, grinning from ear to ear.

Grey stopped spinning. He was struggling to stay focused as he rather seductively disclosed, "I think you were terrifying and I was just there."

"What in the hell, Grey? That blow was so low you'd have to be doing yoga to use it."

"Yeah…Yoga in Triad!" her Handler slammed as he flamboyantly snapped his fingers and strutted away.

Stoned Grey thought he was badass. Adorable. Lexy abrasively jousted, "I don't even know what you're talking about?" He disappeared. *Where did he go?* She caught herself before stepping over the edge of a ravine and peered down. The dust was still rising from his hits to the side of the hill. *Damn it, Greydon. He'd broken something for sure.* Lexy shimmied down the steep incline. *He always got hurt and she always had to fix him. It was getting old, and then it wasn't. They'd needed to fix each other.* The realization hit her like a gut punch. When she reached Grey, she realised he wasn't hurt at all. *He just needed to see if she would still come.* She knelt next to him and as he stared up at her with his baby blues, she couldn't stop her smile. "Message received," she promised as she helped him up.

Grey cupped her face in his hands as he gazed into her soul and disclosed, "You hurt me."

"You hurt me too," was Lexy's response. *She didn't say you hurt me back, because she didn't mean it just for this once, and it needed to be said… Screamed from a cliff at the edge of the ocean so it could echo out to sea. She might as well warn the sea creatures. Who knows what he's into now? Maybe they were next?*

His cheeks slid into a grin as he accused, "Why are you thinking about me defiling sea creatures?"

"You got that all wrong," Lexy saucily answered as she avoided the conversation by hiking up the steep incline.

He was following laughing, "I did not! Liar! I have had some strange thoughts, but why? Sea creatures. Is nothing sacred?"

She turned it around on him, "Mermaids. We're on a job, and it's a Christmas miracle, mermaids are real. Are you trying to tell me you wouldn't do it?" Lexy didn't need to turn around to see his face. *He was trying to think of a response. Tick tock player.*

"Am I cold?" he chuckled, clutching shrubbery to help him climb.

Lexy smirked, trying to keep it together as she probed, "Why would you ask that?"

"You said it was Christmas," he sparred out of breath.

That's weird. Lexy turned to look at Grey. He was tumbling down the rocky hill again. *I guess he was really injured. Whoops. She'd been so pissed off, she'd completely missed that.* She laughed as she hollered, "Alive Jack?"

"Unfortunately," he struggled to yell back.

She came to his aid. "Awe sugar, broken bones suck," Lexy consoled, lording above him. "What was that you were saying about me earlier? Wait... Let me think?"

"I'm sorry. I am sorry," he groaned.

Taking pity on her painfully stubborn Handler, she knelt and placed her hands on his torso. As the warmth of her healing ability travelled down the connection of her arms into Grey, she whispered, "I don't want to spend the next week arguing. Can't we just forget about it and move on?"

He avoided answering by mumbling, "I think I'm alright now. We should get back."

A male voice came from the top of the steep incline, "Do you want us to keep your friend sedated. We can store him until he heals, or do you want to heal him yourself?"

"One second," Grey called out as they trudged back up the embankment.

The guy from the Aries group held out his hand to help Lexy up as she explained, "I thought he knew where he was going. It took me a few minutes to realise he was still drugged." They wandered back to the plastic tunnels and attached containers around the cave.

"Confession time, we've been sedating this one for days. We were warned he wasn't going to be able to act rationally until we got you out," the man from the Aries group revealed.

Grey admitted, "True. Smart move." He looked at Lexy and baited, "And you kept following me, knowing I was drugged?"

Lexy didn't look his way as she confessed, "Always." *This was where he usually took her hand, but he didn't. It was going to hurt for a while. She hadn't even had the opportunity to overthink her actions yet. She couldn't when Grey was around, and he was with her a good ninety percent of the time.* They followed the Aries Group agent back into their quarantine set up. Zach was in the final room, where they were drawing his blood. His arms, legs and face were only mildly blistered. *He was healing rather fast for an immortal without an amped-up healing ability.*

"Is this one a Healer too?" the nameless man questioned.

This guy was beginning to irritate her. Grey strolled over to look at Zach as Lexy answered, "He's Kayn's Handler, it's highly unlikely we'll get her out of there without him." *She wasn't giving a person that hadn't bothered with formal introductions any extra information.* As Karen entered the room, Lexy found herself appreciating the fact that she hadn't treated her like a science project. She placed her palms on Zach's head and attempted to concentrate as the blisters sunk back into his flesh.

The man's inner commentary began freaking out, *'Can she heal anything? Cancer? Diabetes? Multiple Sclerosis? This could change the world.'*

Lexy looked up and ordered, "That guy needs to leave. His thoughts are distracting."

"She can hear my thoughts?" the mortal questioned.

Grey calmly stated, "We all can. Before you start getting any crazy ideas. We can only heal other immortals. Any mortal meant to die or suffer will do so even after we've successfully healed them. Fate just takes them out another way. Our job is to police other entities and to sacrifice ourselves when need be, to keep the mortal population safe. Has nobody ever explained this to you?"

Well done, Greydon. He'd rather eloquently explained their job description. It was easier to call a Correction fate when speaking to a mortal.

Karen responded for the unnamed male, "They only tell us what we need to know. He'll quiet his thoughts… Won't you, Steve?"

"Yes. Of course," Steve replied. "I'm sorry this is a lot to absorb."

"I'm going to heal him and then Grey here is going to talk him down. There will be no need to drug Zach," Lexy informed as she continued doing her job.

Zach's eyes opened. He knit his brow and flirtatiously mumbled, "Why are you wearing a hospital gown?"

"There… He's fine. Grey will stay here and explain, while I allow you to test the sedatives on me. I should be fairly close to Kayn as far as dosage goes." They left Zach and Grey to have a chat and stepped out into the heat. "Have you attempted to take Kayn out yet?"

"Yes. We ran into her and used what we used on you. It barely slowed her down," Karen explained as they strolled over to a rig parked on the other side of the structure.

"I could smell Grey. Even while infected, a part of me wanted to go with you because of my attachment to him, but Kayn and Zach are a relatively new Handler Dragon pairing," Lexy explained as they entered a room full of weapons.

A serious man removed his headset and introduced himself, "Dolan. Nice to meet you. What are you three up to?"

Karen smiled as she responded, "This young lady is graciously allowing us to test sedatives on her."

Dolan got up and shook Lexy's hand as he said, "That'll help us get it right, thank you. We've tried to take her out several times. She's a strong one."

"Her name's Kayn and she's my sister. You won't be able to take a Healer down with the same drug more than once. Once exposed, a Healer's body forms an antitoxin or immunity to drugs and various venoms. You'll have to keep upping the ante."

"We're planning to try Etorphine first. Hopefully, it'll slow Kayn down long enough to be decontaminated," Karen explained as she passed a box of tranquillizers to Dolan.

Dolan shrugged as he loaded a weapon. He looked at Lexy and explained, "Etorphine is a large animal tranq. I just need an estimate of how long my guys will have to transport Kayn into containment."

"If she can't be killed, wouldn't a headshot work?" Steve enquired as Grey and Zach walked in.

Scowling, Lexy coolly clarified, "Try it. I'll rip off one of your arms and beat you to death with it."

Grey clarified, "Dude. She's not joking. She's actually done that before."

Steve's smile vanished. Dolan suggested, "Let's go outside." They all wandered out into the dusty, rocky terrain as Dolan added, "Come at me like it's real."

Standing a reasonable distance away, Lexy explained, "You'll need to start shooting from a significant distance, Kayn's fast."

Pointing his weapon, Dolan prompted, "Whenever you're ready."

Lexy sprinted at him. He shot twice before she reached him, she'd maneuvered out of the way. He'd missed her. She gave Dolan a pat on the head and teased, "That was too easy, you need more shooters."

He winked at Lexy and laughed, "Well, you weren't supposed to avoid the darts."

"Kayn's not going to just stand there," Lexy chuckled as she strutted back to where she began and announced, "I'll just stand here this time. Go ahead, dose me till I drop." The first dart whooshed through the air into her abdomen. *It kind of tickled.* She shrugged. He shot her with a second dart. *Oh, this was nice. This stuff is glorious.* The colours swirled together into black as she went down.

She awoke to the scent of food and asked, "How long was I down for?"

Grey answered, "I wasn't keeping track of the time, but you were down long enough to order lunch."

He passed her a styrofoam container. Lexy opened it. *A beef dip with gravy and fries. This was obviously Grey's doing.* It felt like the beef dip was a white flag of surrender. She devoured it. He handed her another styrofoam container and she grinned at the contents...*Apple crisp. Delicious. Wait...This felt like bribery.*

Grey explained, "They've upped the dosage and called in more men from the caverns. They'd like to try it again, and this time they want to concentrate on how long it takes to put you down versus the time it takes for you to wake up."

Her Handler was smart. She was way more pliable with a full stomach. Lexy sighed, "Alright." She smiled to herself as Grey opened the door revealing a large crowd of armed Aries Group. She strolled past the mortals with a grin on her face. *She'd already explained the whole healing ability creating an anti-venom thing. People only ever concentrate on the parts of a conversation they want to hear.* She casually wandered over to the same spot where she'd been shot the first time and enquired, "Should I just stand here? Orrr?"

"Go ahead. Come at us," Dolan countered with a grin.

Lexy shrugged and raced at the group feeling worthy of superhero applause to the sound of multiple whooshes. *Oh darn. What the? It felt like someone filled her socks with quick-drying cement.* She staggered. *Well, shit.* The colours swirled together as the lights went out.

She opened her eyes almost immediately this time, but she was higher than a kite. Lexy slurred, "I... told you... I got the second time... not."

Grey chuckled as he tugged her onto his lap. While lovingly stroking her hair, he whispered, "You're not making sense. Nighty night friend. Don't fight it."

Like hell. She tried to get up, her limbs were worthless. Her eyelids were too heavy to stay open, so she closed them. In her next somewhat conscious episode, she was aware of being carried. She opened her eyes.

Grey smiled at her and teased, "You just took enough drugs to take down a herd of elephants and still fought it. It was rather impressive."

She wasn't some damsel in distress. This touching Handler Dragon moment was totally giving these people the wrong impression. Lexy sighed, "I think I can walk. You can put me down."

"I don't think you can," Grey warned.

"I'm fine. Put me down," she curtly instructed.

"All right, Rambo," Grey teased. He put her down.

Lexy dropped like a sack of potatoes because her legs wouldn't hold her weight. *She was going to snap.*

He sat on the ground beside her, giggling, "This feels like the perfect opportunity to have that discussion, you're as harmless as a kitten."

Oh, he was in so much trouble.

"Full disclosure, I told them to burn Tiberius' tainted shorts," he declared, watching her reaction.

Funny. Lexy sarcastically baited, "I planned on keeping those."

Grey laughed as he got up and remarked, "You shouldn't piss off your temporary legs." He walked away and left her there. For a minute, she thought it was a joke. *He was going to come back. He wasn't.* She saw Zach coming. *Bold move, Greydon.*

Kayn's Handler knelt by her and said, "I heard you needed a lift?" Zach didn't wait for an answer as he picked her up and strolled back to the unit with her cradled in his arms. He whispered, "Grey will get over it. He's just jealous."

Lexy felt the heat of her blood working to counteract whatever they'd ended up dosing her with and suspected she could walk again. She smiled at Zach's attempt to be sweet and said, "I think I can walk."

He carefully placed her down, sure enough, she could. She stretched. Zach stayed there beside her in case she couldn't and teased, "Please don't kick Grey's ass, we're supposed to be professionals."

She gave Zach a wry smile as she countered, "I think no reaction at all will have a far greater impact, don't you?"

"That, it might," Zach agreed as they entered the trailer.

Grey was looking at her like he expected her to come across the room and slam his head into the metal counter. She decided his immature behaviour was unworthy of a response, but one-upping him was too hard to resist. She wandered over to Dolan and enquired, "How long was I incapacitated?"

"Thirty-five minutes," he replied, looking at the timer on his phone.

Lexy flirtatiously moved in to get a closer look.

Dolan whispered, "If you're attempting to flirt with me, I'm not into girls."

Grey started howling. Lexy glanced at Zach, he zipped his lips and tossed away the imaginary key. *Brownie points for Zach. Doghouse for Grey.* Lexy whispered back, "First and foremost, knowing who you are is undeniably awesome. I've recently started a new relationship. I was just sneaking a peek at the time." She innocently peered up and saw her dagger hit its intended target. Grey got up and left, slamming the door. *Immortal drama. How unexpected.*

"You two need to lock yourselves away for a day and have it out," Zach scolded as he went after Grey.

Karen handed her a bottle of water and asked, "Ex-boyfriend?"

Love of her life. Cross to bear. Obsession. Beginning and end of her universe. "No. He's just my Handler," Lexy quietly disclosed, ignoring her aching heart. She took the water with her as she went to find him and instantly did. *He hadn't gone anywhere.*

Grey looked into Lexy's eyes as he admitted, "I honestly don't have it in me to fight with you anymore."

She stepped down and replied, "Me either."

Grey gave her a weak smile and decreed, "Argument over, I've lost. I'm okay with that for now."

She knit her brow. *For now? What did he mean by that?*

Zach's mind was spinning like a top, *'Oh, thank God. Nobody wants to escape a crap sandwich only to be slapped into the middle of a turd burger.'*

She got it now. She saw how Zach ended up as Kayn's Handler. His thoughts were equally weird.

Dolan opened the door and announced, "We're going in after we've all had a few hours rest. If you choose to go back in without a hazmat suit, you'll need to be decontaminated again. Oh, yes…We found you some clothes." He passed them each a plastic bag and added, "These will do just fine until you guys can go shopping. Go change. We'll let you know when we're getting ready to leave."

As a group, they changed into the clothing and opted to only go in if the Aries Group failed. They were all far too exhausted to risk closing their eyes, fearing they'd sleep through a distress call. They were given earpieces, mics and a screen so they could listen in on the action and offer input if needed. It was so different from this perspective. *The sacrificial lambs were watching from a safe place while the mortals got to have fun.* They watched the Aries Group commenting as they came upon random piles of bodies. Lexy was impressed and honestly a little proud.

Dolan's voice piped in over the coms, "Your girl has been on quite the cave-dwelling cannibal murder spree. What are the odds she just comes in willingly?"

"Mighty slim. But sometimes she surprises me," Zach answered.

There was scattered, uncomfortable laughter as the group came upon Kayn absolutely drenched in blood.

Grey started to giggle. Zach covered his mic as he quietly commented, "She's gone full Carrie. Abort mission. Abort."

She's blinded by the light. Give her a second.

"Lower your weapons!" Dolan's voice commanded.

Kayn appeared to be confused. This was a good sign. Lexy covered her mic and quietly interjected, "She hasn't killed anyone, she must be able to tell they're mortal."

"Put your weapons down or we will be forced to take you out!" Dolan shouted, pointing his.

"No," Kayn coldly responded.

"You may have been infected! Weapons down!" Another terrified agent yelled.

Attempting to use ration with a Dragon...How adorable.

"They're human bones," Kayn casually corrected as she held them up.

Lexy recognized the predatory glint in her fellow Dragon's eyes. *She was observing her prey as a cougar would from a tree. Did she intend to play with them first?* "I'd subdue her," Lexy's inner commentary drifted out of her mouth. *Whoops.*

Someone jumped the gun. A tranquillizer whizzed through the air into Kayn's torso. Kayn plucked it out without flinching and calmly declared, "That was rather rude."

The culprit backed away as they explained, "You may not be in your right mind. Drop your weapons."

That drug didn't appear to be affecting her. Lexy muffled the mic with a hand so she wouldn't unintentionally tell someone to shoot again as she whispered, "We're missing something." They shot her twice more. "That wasn't my fault," Lexy explained. Kayn tugged the darts out gleefully, giggling like it tickled.

Zach spoke to only his Clan with his thoughts, *'She's been sucking back cannibal energy for nearly a week.'*

'Well, we definitely can't tell them that,' Grey responded without words.

On many occasions, she'd used immortal energy to speed up her healing ability. Kayn was a Conduit and energy was also her vice. She might be completely healed and here they were, judging a book by its cover. They had this situation all wrong. Lexy grinned and wagered, "I'll bet you that bag of chips you're eating she comes willingly."

Grey obnoxiously crunched his chip, replying, "Not a chance."

They turned their attention back to the monitor as Kayn abruptly dropped her blade and dramatically sighed, "Next time try leading with, we're from the Aries Group, lower your weapons. There's no need to shoot me again, I'll come willingly." With idiotic timing, someone tried to grab her. Kayn warned, "I wouldn't do that if I were you."

Still amped up, the woman's voice ordered, "Stand down!"

Kayn addressed the agent with common sense, "You shot me before properly identifying yourself."

"I'll be damned. You're right," Grey declared. He tossed his bag of chips at Lexy and turned off the camera as someone knocked on the door. Grey was summoned outside to receive a phone call, leaving them awkwardly sitting there together, staring at a blank screen.

Zach reached for the remote and started clicking through stations, commentating, "With the amount of money these guys have to play with, you'd think they'd have cable."

"I bet there's internet," Lexy suggested as she offered Zach a chip.

Zach took it and enquired, "Where do they get the money from?"

"I have absolutely no idea," Lexy responded as she handed Zach the bag and held out her hand for the remote.

He gave it to her and laughed, "Go for it."

Grey opened the door and came back in. He sat down and filled them in without speaking aloud, *"The boy in Alaska's Correction has already happened. He's dead. The girl in B.C. also died. We're off to Seattle."*

Zach shrugged as he ate a chip. *Yeesh, they'd already wrecked the kid.* He offered her a chip and Lexy started laughing.

In no time at all, they'd decontaminated Kayn. They embraced as though they were relatives greeting each other after a short separation. In her head, Lexy was still chuckling about the fact that Zach was just eating chips while being told of the deaths they'd caused simply by not being there. He'd had an entire year with Triad before coming to Ankh, perhaps that was a good thing while having Dragons as your playmates.

Brighton whispered, "I guess we missed our plane?"

They were packing this site up faster than a carnival on the last day. *Why were they in such a hurry?*

The lady from the lab wandered over, handed them a cooler and explained, "These are sandwiches with deli meat and cheese. Fill up during the drive. It's a short trip to the airport so eat fast. You can have something else as soon as you're off the plane in Seattle."

"You don't have meals on the flight?" Zach enquired.

Oh, they were in for a treat. They'd never been transported by the Aries Group before. Lexy nudged him and whispered, "We have to be stored in the cargo bay in containers. It's not optional." Kayn wasn't paying attention as she gobbled up the sandwiches.

A man handed them each a card along with a cell and explained, "The cards are to buy whatever you need once you arrive in Seattle. It doesn't matter which phone you use, they're not personally assigned. Text the first contact on your phone with the name of who has each number. You'll need to be sedated for the flight. I understand sedation is no longer effective for Kayn. We'll still have to dose you. It's a paperwork thing. Just think of the bright side, it'll be a relaxing trip even if you're awake. You'll be in your compartment for the duration of the flight. There's WIFI so you should be able to keep yourself entertained. Everyone else, as I've previously said, it's mandatory to sedate you."

A nap sounded nice. Maybe she'd finally have time to overthink things? They all sort of shrugged as they followed the unnamed man to one of the dark sedans. Kayn's mind was in a tailspin through a million questions. Lexy rarely asked questions anymore. *The reasons were inconsequential. None of it mattered. Mortals lived for as long as they were meant to. It was both that simple and hard. They were frail creatures that usually made a multitude of bad choices during their short lives. Perhaps, that was the point...* Lexy took a seat in the air-conditioned vehicle. *Oh, this was nice.* Her senses rejoiced as she played around with her new cellphone. She texted her name to the first number on the list. It immediately vibrated. There was a text from Markus with only one word...Okay. *Oh, they were in big trouble, Markus was usually chatty.* They parked at a deserted airfield.

The driver got out of the sedan, strolled around to open the back door and instructed, "Walk over to that first building. There should be someone waiting for you."

Kayn thanked him, they all smiled. *Canadians were cute.*

The driver gave Kayn a strange look as he replied, "You're welcome."

The immortal foursome wandered to the building in the sweltering afternoon sun and as they entered, they were instructed to get into four suntan booth sized pods by a familiar face. *It was Karen from the caves.* Lexy gave her a quick wave as she got into hers without hesitation. *Even if she wasn't out cold for the duration of the flight, the chambers were made of Sterenimite, which rather effectively blocked them from being able to hear each other's thoughts. Her Handler wouldn't be able to judge a damn thing.* She closed her pod and smiled.

Karen knocked on her container and enquired, "Gas, needle or dart?"

"Surprise me," Lexy dared with a wink.

Karen grinned through the see-through area as her pod filled up with gas. Lexy took a few deep breaths, knowing the drill. Her naughty encounter with Tiberius flooded her thoughts as she took a nap.

Awakening as oxygen was piped into her chamber, Lexy smiled as it opened. *She'd been having X-rated dreams. She had to shut her erotic thoughts down before they started more drama with Grey.* Lexy stretched, yawned and asked, "Do we need to rent a car or does the Aries Group have one waiting?"

Smiling, Karen answered, "I'm sure someone is waiting for you because you'll also need new passports and I.D."

She was always happy someone else was taking care of the details.

Grey placed his arm around her and sang, "Ready to go shopping?"

He knew she despised shopping. The fool thought he was safe because there were witnesses. Lexy whispered, "Keep it up sweetie, you have to sleep sometime."

Grey was laughing as a tall, lanky man approached and announced, "I'm your driver. I'll take you to get everything you need."

They descended the stairs into a partially enclosed enormous cargo hold and knew it was raining by the scent in the air. *She'd missed Seattle.*

Chapter 20

This One Time In Seattle

After a few hours of touring around the city, restocking toiletries and clothing, the foursome went back to the hotel room with two queen-sized beds. They had a relaxing bath and ordered dinner. They had a lovely evening of absolutely nothing planned before their next job. Kayn wandered out of the washroom with her wild mane of damp curls. Grey was gawking. Lexy bonked him on the head with the remote. He laughed as she continued to search for a movie they hadn't all seen. *She was getting hungry. The stash of movie watching snacks on the counter was calling her name.* Lexy urged, "Come on you guys, pick something. We are so ordering a movie if they're saving money by putting us all in the same room." There was a knock on the door. Zach leapt up, grabbed his card and answered it as Grey vetoed each movie she hovered over. Kayn snuggled under the covers in the bed next to theirs. Lexy nudged Grey, so he could disagree with her next choice. *It felt like they were having a sleepover.*

Zach sat down on the bed and announced, "Dinner has been served." He handed one of the pizza boxes to her.

Lexy opened the box and said, "Brilliant idea."

Zach opened their box. Kayn playfully shoved him and praised, "Thanks, buddy."

Lexy looked over, he'd loaded half of their pizza with banana peppers and jalapeños. Zach dug into a separate bag and tossed packages of hot sauce at both girls.

Zach replied, "I know what you ladies need."

"I'll tickle your back while we're watching the movie," Kayn vowed, as she dumped an impressive amount of hot sauce on one of her slices.

Grey scowled at Lexy and teased, "What? No back tickling for me?"

Lexy held up her slice, shrugged and countered, "No banana peppers. No back tickles." Grey fake pouted as he ate his slice.

Zach leaned closer and whispered, "That's why we're never sleeping together." Grey tossed an empty styrofoam cup at Zach. It landed between the beds. "Good shot," Zach mocked.

Grey slowly shook his head and sparred, "Carry on…It's not like I can't light this whole hotel on fire."

"I dare you to pull that bullshit again and see what happens," Lexy mumbled, staring at her pepper free slice.

"Alright, friends…We're all staying in the same room tonight and I really don't have it in me to continue watching this soap opera. I'll turn this drama into a horror faster than you can say don't smother me with a pillow. Pick a movie," Kayn urged.

Zach sweetly asked, "Would you like something to drink, Hun?"

"I'd love a glass of water," Kayn answered.

Their sugary sweetness was only making Grey's asshole more irritating.

"I guess nobody thought to get any beer?" Grey enquired as he wandered over to the mini-fridge.

He was pushing her buttons on purpose. "Oh, you're not drinking anywhere around me for a long time," Lexy muttered under her breath.

Grey stopped staring into the mini-fridge. He turned around, looked directly at Lexy and coldly stated, "I have to drink to be around you. Our days of cuddling in bed are done. I'm sure Tiberius can clear his schedule to cater to your every need."

It's on pansy boy. Lexy got up, met Grey's ignorant gaze and countered, "At least he'll remember doing it."

Zach jumped up, blocked Grey and exclaimed, "Let's get out of here before one of you says something that can't be taken back."

"Don't bring him back here if he's drunk," Lexy remarked.

Grey glanced back at Lexy and jousted, "Don't you worry sweetheart, it'll take me all of five seconds to find someone worthy of my company!" He stormed out and aggressively slammed the door, leaving Zach standing there.

Zach said, "I'll just go and make sure he's alright."

"He'll get over it. I always do," Lexy replied quietly as she continued to pretend he hadn't broken her heart.

Zach slipped out of the room. Kayn glanced over and asked, "Were you guys fighting the whole time I was gone?"

"Worrying. Fighting…Our symbols kept going off. We were concerned you two were going to be swept out to sea. Jenna contacted us with your location and the warning to wait for the Aries Group to arrive before attempting to go in after you. The area was shark-infested. We'd only end up making a bad situation worse."

"What are you going to do? He's your Handler," Kayn asked.

"I'm going to get over him and move on with someone else like I should have done a long time ago. This is probably a good thing. Maybe if being with him isn't an option, I'll be able to find something lasting longer than a night," Lexy replied.

"You love him," Kayn pointed out.

While lost in her thoughts, Lexy whispered, "I always will. More than anything in this world or any other, but I can't keep doing this to myself." Kayn slipped out from under the covers and got into the bed next to her. Lexy smiled as she asked, "How about this one? Do you like scary movies?"

"Sounds good," Kayn replied. They began watching an eighties slasher film, chock full of gratuitous violence. As would be expected, both Dragons fell asleep.

Lexy awoke with her sister sleeping next to her and sat up. *The other bed was empty. The boys hadn't come back to the room last night. They needed to go to high school to stalk a teenage girl today. This was completely unprofessional. She didn't get to throw a hissy fit when he slept with someone else. These double standards were pissing her off.* Lexy strolled past the backpacks full of supplies and picked up her cell to alert the Aries group that they needed to adjust the paperwork. *They were going in without their Handlers. She needed a break from Grey and he probably needed one from her.* Lexy perched on the sink in her underwear, took a tiny knife out of the backpack and stabbed herself in the thigh. Her hand flashed. *Dickhead. Enjoy your day off; you ignorant tool.* Lexy dressed as she felt most comfortable with her free-flowing crimson hair, ruby lips, heels and jeans that accentuated her curves. She'd been disappointed when she lost those sexy red heels, but yesterday, she'd found something close in burgundy. *This was something that excited her...* She slid one on each foot. *They were the colour of blood. Her shenanigans wouldn't be as noticeable. Maybe she could get away with keeping these bad boys for a while?*

She left so her sister could finish getting ready and wandered back out, half expecting to see the boys hustling around getting ready in a panic, neither one was there. She flopped on the bed and scrolled through the nameless contacts in her new phone. Her finger hovered halfway down the list. *Did Tiberius have one of these numbers?* She was tempted to text what are you wearing to everyone on the list. Lexy grinned as Kayn trucked out wearing running shoes, with only a touch of makeup on and her hair pulled into an inconspicuous sporty ponytail. *They were never going to fight over clothes.* The Dragon sisters strolled out of the room with their backpacks full of school supplies. "Shit!" Lexy exclaimed. "They have our car."

"We'll take a cab," Kayn announced, motioning to the busy street.

Lexy had only taken a few steps when she accidentally tuned into Kayn's thoughts, '*Lexy was going to have no problem waving down a taxi looking like that. She preferred to hide in the background. Lexy's preference was the waving flag approach. This could be an interesting day. No Handlers. A bonding day with her newfound sibling. What could go wrong?* When she couldn't keep a straight face anymore, Lexy responded aloud to Kayn's thoughts, "Don't even think it."

In minutes, they were in the back of a cab on their way to school. Kayn was far too excited, it was defusing her simmering rage. *If she'd known it was this easy to take a day off, she would have played hooky decades ago.* Lexy smiled as she boldly chose a random number in her phone and texted, *What are you wearing? Oh, shoot. She really pressed send. That's not good. She should erase it.* The cab stopped. *Shit. Damn it. Oh, well. Guess we'll just let that joke roll.* Lexy peered out of the window, feeling like they'd been here before.

She turned to ask Grey. *Oh yes, her Handler was playing hooky today.* She paid the driver, and as he drove away, her cell buzzed. *She'd texted a stranger. This might be interesting.* It was from the Aries Group telling her the paperwork had been changed and the details. Lexy peered up and announced, "Grey's paperwork has been replaced with yours. We are siblings from Arizona. We moved here for our Dad's job. We're using the same first names. Our last name is Smith."

They strolled to the front doors to animated humming chatter. *Everyone was always so stoked to be at high school. Maybe this was just one of those things she didn't understand because she'd never gone. Well...Not while being a person.* A beautiful knowledge free mortal...*It didn't seem fair that she hadn't ever been a normal girl, but fair wasn't a word in the immortal dictionary. It's a wishy-washy word for whiny mortals and she was bitch-slapping her afterlife.* Her attention was captured by a gorgeous turquoise swirling aura with flecks of yellow and orange. *It was the only thing out of the ordinary in the ocean of students walking ahead. No student with a yellow-hued aura.* Her sister nudged her and they stepped aside, allowing the crowd to funnel past.

Kayn whispered, "I didn't prepare for this. Their auras are quite faint."

Lexy scanned the crowd for possibilities, while casually responding, "No biggie. I stabbed myself this morning after I brushed my teeth. I'll find her."

"Of course," Kayn teased as they joined the herd of teens and did their thing in the office.

After a witty conversation with a secretary, they marched through the open double doors into the hormonal jungle with their class lists in hand. They parted ways as the warning bell rang. Lexy found her class easily enough and sat in an empty seat. She was just getting organized, when a girl with a golden-hued aura pranced in, followed by her entourage. She smiled knowingly and pretended to pay attention, so she wouldn't be singled out. In no time at all, Lexy was phallically playing with her pen, recalling the steamy highlights of her encounter with Tiberius. She snapped out of it, relieved the teacher hadn't busted her daydreaming. *Focus Lexy.* She observed the girl's judgmental looks each time a student answered a question. *Her name was Carmen. It fit. The perfectly coifed teenage dictator was belittling her flock of pristine white sheep with only her eyes like a pro. Truthfully, she'd always preferred the black ones.* By the end of one class, Lexy knew exactly who she was dealing with. *It wasn't her job to judge anyone's morality… Especially now. Thoughts of Tiberius were clouding her duties. Grey hadn't come home when she'd harmed herself to set off her symbol. What if he couldn't forgive this one thing? If she lost him, who would bring her back when she was adrift in the emotionless isolation of her Dragon self? Would rebelling against their one-sided relationship be worth it for a fling with an enemy?* Lexy crossed her legs as she recalled more of the sordid encounter. Stuck somewhere between pride and regret as the bell rang to signal the end of class, Lexy gathered her books and followed the herd of students into the hall where they fanned out in every direction. She'd been walking for a minute when she spotted her partner for the day in the hormonal herd. Lexy called her name, Kayn turned around. "I found our girl, her name's Carmen," Lexy announced.

"Awesome. So, she was in your last class?" Kayn asked as they compared their schedules.

They had the same class next. The warning buzzer sounded. They rushed to the room and were lucky enough to find two empty seats in the back. Lexy glanced at Kayn as she thought, *She's two rows ahead of us. Can you see her?*

Kayn inconspicuously peered up from behind her book. Without words, Kayn directed her thoughts to

Lexy, *'Can there be two? In my last class, there was another girl with the same aura, but she was pregnant.*

Lexy's stomach clenched as someone knocked on the classroom door. The teacher got up and wandered over with musically clicking heels. She excused herself and stepped outside. Lexy could tell Kayn felt the same internal warning.

The teacher stepped back into the classroom and addressed the class, "Is there a Kayn Smith and a Lexy Smith in this class?"

Lexy smiled as fate threw a curveball. They raised their hands like good little mortals, gathered their belongings and got up. The teacher motioned for them to follow, so they did, knowing playing along was their only option while surrounded by witnesses. The sisters stepped out into the hall and saw Abaddon disguised as officers with swirling black auras. *What were these idiots up to?*

"Ladies, we have a few questions. We're going to need you to come with us," an Abaddon in a costume asserted.

Neither one was the least bit concerned as they wandered down the hall and out a door.

Kayn thought, *'So, I take it we have to behave until we're out of sight?'*

Lexy replied without speaking, *Play along. I'll make it clear when it's time.* They stepped outside into a somewhat private area with a dumpster and no windows. Kayn looked at her. Lexy slowly moved her head from side to side. *They hadn't blown their cover yet. Why not?* One of the ineffectively disguised officers opened the sliding side door of an unmarked black van and ordered them to get in. *Ballsy approach. She couldn't help being a little impressed.*

Kayn leaned in and whispered, "I'm not sure they know who they're dealing with?"

Brighton had so much to learn. Lexy grinned as she responded, "They know exactly who they're dealing with. We're undercover and they have the power to blow it." Lexy got into the van. There was a barrier that looked like plexiglass between the front and the back. She took in the empty back. *They hadn't left them anything that could be used as a weapon.* Lexy smiled as she looked at the heels she'd only got to wear once. *Shit. She was going to have to wreck her new shoes. Every damn time.* Kayn was sitting next to her with her mind whirling through mortal concern and sentiment. *They'd been through so much in a short time. It was easy to overlook the fact that Brighton was barely six months out of her Testing. She should say something sisterly.* Lexy interrupted Kayn's thoughts with hers, *Change your train of thought. Emotional baggage makes you weak. There isn't time for that.* Kayn didn't appear to be placated so she added the one thing that always made her happy. *It's almost Dragon time.* Kayn's inner badass instantly surfaced. The two Abaddon had been chatting outside for a while. It felt like they were stalling. *They needed weapons. Once they were somewhere a little less public, she was going to stomp these morons out like smouldering cigarettes on pavement.* They got in, the doors closed and the engine purred. The vehicle lurched to one side as they pulled away, they toppled over giggling. A man turned back, confused as to why they were laughing their asses off about being kidnapped. Lexy winked and gave him her very best pageant smile.

Kayn gave her a playful shove as she questioned, "Are you going to tell me why we've willingly gotten into this van without an offer of candy on the table?"

Lexy chuckled on the inside as she removed her heels and commented, "Always the comedian." Lexy winked and cracked her neck as she promised, "We'll stop and get some candy on the way home." She pouted while staring longingly at her heels. *She loved these shoes. It was as though the afterlife had decreed that she would never grow attached to anything besides Grey. Her absentee Handler. She was glad he wasn't here. She'd probably end up stabbing him in the forehead with one of her heels to shut him up.* She peered up, Kayn was staring at her. *Oh, yes... She was supposed to be explaining things,* "As you know, after the Correction happens, there's a race for the survivor. These tools are just trying to stop us from interfering with their plans. They're obviously new and don't know the rules. It happens. The girl must be important." Lexy got up and began balancing as though she were surfing on a concrete sea with her palm menacingly against the see-through barrier. The man in the passenger seat noticed her as Lexy called out, "Toss me one of my shoes!" Kayn pitched a heel. Lexy caught it and winked mischievously. She smashed it against the heavy-duty shatter-resistant barrier as hard as she could while yelling a colourful list of obscenities. A fanned-out crack formed across the divider. She slammed her fist through the window, grabbed one of the men by his hair and yanked him through. Lexy tossed him at Kayn while declaring, "Snack time!"

The terrified Abaddon attempted to squirm away as Kayn swiftly pinned him down, stared deep into his eyes and declared, "You should have given me candy." Kayn put her full weight on his shoulders, immobilizing him, grasped either side of his face and drank his dark energy down like an Abaddon Slurpee.

Oh... They had a runner. Lexy climbed out the front and sprinted after their other capturer across the dusty gravel parking lot. There was a crash behind her. A door soared through the air, landing in the gravel in an explosion of dust and debris. She raced blindly through the cloud with instinct leading the way, it became a dark swirling haze and even though her vision was hindered by the rising dust of the man's feet, she knew what she'd found herself in the centre of. *Bring it on assholes.* Weapon wielding Abaddon trailing ominous black and grey mist were everywhere. *It felt like she'd just been given a gift.* "Awe, you shouldn't have," Lexy baited as the dust settled in the junkyard. There were shooters perched on top of stacks of demolished vehicles as dozens of unafraid demonic assailants sauntered her way.

Tricky but rarely impossible. She really should get that on a t-shirt. Her inner commentary was getting weird. Shit... They'd soul dusted her. This wasn't random at all. This was planned. She was going to tear these junkyard depravities new assholes. Grey was going to be sorry he missed it... Grey. This wasn't random... Grey. Where was he? She glanced at her Ankh symbol in the millisecond she had to think before tossing another demon away. *It hadn't flashed. She would have felt it.* It felt like everything was slow motion as Lexy spun around, shoving those away who dared disturb her crisis of conscience. Undragon-like insecurity rose within, slowing her descent into the emotionless void. *Who would bring her back? She was hot. Healer hot.* "Who stabbed me?" Lexy growled as she spun back to her insignificant foes. A girl with telltale blood dripping from her blade dropped it and ran as the rest attacked, slashing at her flesh with weaponized junkyard metal. Lexy was minimally aware of the other Dragon's presence while ready to leap into the rabbit hole. She snapped a demon's neck, rose to her feet next to the body, brushed herself off and announced, "Who's next?" *There were too many to half-ass her Dragon. She couldn't wait for Grey anymore.* So, she released the reigns on the beast birthed to this world, a solitary being with no emotional ties to bind her. Untameable and unhinged, she flung and booted each assailant aside as quickly as they came at her, persevering not for any person or Clan but for the thrill. Lexy hurled them through the air, stomping on the heads of those unfortunate enough to remain underfoot. She heard the whooshing of arrows a second too late. One went through her midriff. She snapped off the end, yanked it out and wiped the blood away. There were popping sounds. A bullet clipped her shoulder, another winged her. There was a burst of heat as her body expelled the shell and the wound sealed. There was a faint ringing in her ears and it was like time slowed enough to sense the path of each bullet. Maneuvering around every foreign object that came at her, she noticed Kayn peering down at blood pooling on her shirt. They were attacked from all sides in a blur of arterial spray and confusion, until the fighting ceased, leaving two Dragons standing in the wake of their destruction. They heard the ting of something falling in the junk pile. Both girls sprinted towards the noise. One by one, they hunted survivors, feeding on their energy to heal, until they were crawling through wreckage as wild creatures covered in the blood of their enemies, void of humanity. Aware of little but the sun's radiance and the metallic scent of the blood stiffening their clothes.

Lexy caught the scent of something familiar and closed her eyes, inhaling the sweet, calming fragrance. *What was that?* She found herself drawn to the pleasurable aroma.

A soothing voice whispered, "You're going to make me climb up there, aren't you?"

There was a sandy-haired male with the most magical looking aura standing below her perch trying to catch her attention. *She needed to be closer to it.* The swirling hypnotizing aura was so fascinating, like a moth to a flame, Lexy leapt from the metal heap to the gravel. The emotion in his eyes drew her in, she couldn't look away.

He whispered, "Come back to me."

Curious, she inched closer. His voice was making her eyes leak.

He opened his arms and whispered, "I know I don't deserve your forgiveness, I've been an intolerable shit, but you promised you'd always come back to me."

Her eyes were glued to his lips, where the magical voice came from. Memories of him flooded her mind as a tidal wave of love surged within her heart and washed her into his open arms. *He felt like home.*

Grey kissed her head as he vowed, "I love you more than anything. I'll try harder, I'll be more understanding."

Pulling away to look into his eyes, she questioned, "Where were you?"

He tenderly caressed her cheek as he smiled and admitted, "Off being an ignorant tool, I don't have an excuse, but I promise I'll never leave you dangling in the wind again."

Instinct gave her a split-second warning as multiple shots rang out. Lexy stepped in front of her Handler and screamed with her hands raised. The bullets froze in place, hovering in front of her.

"Holy shit," Kayn whispered.

Grey and Zach were also frozen in place. The shooters were also like statues. In awe, Lexy reached out and touched one of the hovering bullets. *Holy shit. Did she just freeze time?* From behind them, someone started a slow clap. The Dragons spun around to find their rather inept paternal figure thoroughly enjoying the show. Seth continued to clap as he marched up to motionless Grey and gave him a pat on the head.

Lexy was the first of the Dragon sisters to speak, "Did you do that?"

"No child," Seth proudly admitted. "That was all you."

"But, I can't do that," Lexy countered as she plucked a hovering bullet out of the air and stared at it in the palm of her hand.

"You couldn't do that. Now you can," the mischievous Guardian clarified as he poked the other bullet and it dropped into the gravel at his feet.

"Will I be able to do this?" Kayn questioned as she grabbed the final bullet from the air.

Seth buried the bullet at his feet with a kick as he answered, "I honestly have no idea. Stopping time is a Guardian thing, and you are part Guardian, so it's entirely possible. It doesn't last for long though, you might want to start taking those left-over Abaddon thugs out. Come see me the next time you're in the in-between and we'll experiment."

Lexy scowled at Seth as she vehemently retorted, "You left me at a demon farm for five years!"

"Are you really still on that? It's been over forty years. Get over it!" Seth retorted as he tried to come closer.

She curtly promised, "I was eleven. I may not be able to kill you, but I'll snap your bones like twigs if you take one more step!"

Seth sighed as he opted out and countered, "So, you're saying you'll need time before we cuddle?"

Lexy rolled her eyes and sparred, "Enough bullshit, black spandex man. How do I unfreeze them?"

Seth marched over and placed his hands on Kayn's forehead. Grinning like a naughty child, he whispered, "You're welcome." He vanished and materialized behind one of their assailants and rather joyously snapped his neck. "Come on you two," he declared. "The jobs not finished. The Aries group is coming. Also, you might want to keep this whole freezing time thing on the down-low." Seth disappeared and reappeared behind the next shooter and effortlessly took him out.

They were so entranced with what he was able to do, they stopped paying attention to their duties.

"We only have a few minutes here, maybe less, Lexy's new," Seth prompted. They joined in to finish the job. He motioned them closer as he announced, "Time to leave. The Aries Group is almost here." He pointedly looked at Kayn as he declared, "They shouldn't see you looking like that twice in less than a week, they'll get antsy."

Seth placed his hands on their Handler's shoulders and prompted, "We're out of time. If you want to come along, you'd better be touching them in…3, 2, 1."

They grabbed their Handler's. In a flash, they were back in their hotel room. The boys were confused as to how they got there.

Seth pressed his fingers against his lips to hush the group. He grinned at the four, then looked at Lexy and urged, "Take a chance. Come see me. I'll help you figure out that new ability." He tossed a bag of stones at her.

She was about to tell Seth off when he disappeared in a flash of light.

Grey glared at Lexy and questioned, "What new ability?"

Seth warned her to keep her newly discovered talent quiet. Lexy pressed a finger of caution against pursed lips as she dumped the privacy stones into her hand and placed them around the room.

As soon as the stones were set, Kayn piped in, "Lexy froze time! I'm starving. Dibs on the shower!" With that, she dashed into the washroom.

Brighton dropped a bomb and flitted away, leaving her to explain everything. She'd done this to her more than once now.

Grey got her started, "The last thing I remember is you stepping in front of me as shots rang out and then we were here."

"I stopped bullets in mid-air," Lexy disclosed. "It was incredibly cool."

Zach piped in, "Kayn was trying to do it. She can hover light objects but stopping a bullet is badass."

Bullets. Lexy disclosed, "I got the distinct impression this ability has to remain a secret."

"I didn't see a thing," Zach swiped the remote.

Grey was contently playing with his phone. He didn't need to say a word. They changed into less murdery clothes and left their soiled garments in a bag, intending to dispose of them later. The group opted to stay in and have drama-free bonding time, watching comedies and dining on the greasiest entrées room service had to offer. They fell asleep early and awoke to a brand-new day. Lexy and Kayn were enrolled, so the boys opted to stake out the exterior of the school, planning to head off any further complications. Even though he'd been driving her crazy lately, Lexy felt better knowing Grey was nearby. Lexy and Kayn were relieved when they spotted Carmen, knowing they'd rather epically dropped the ball the day before. The job was to stay in the background, so they'd be familiar yet unknown. If Carmen survived her Correction and recalled seeing them in passing, the odds were much higher that she'd come willingly. For days they kept to themselves, merely observing their unlikable prospect. They both wanted to leave this rotten mortal for whatever or whoever came for her next, but that wasn't the job. Their duty was to snatch her after she survived her Correction and let the chips fall where they may. At the end of each school day, they got into the car feeling like they were wasting their time, but it wasn't their job to determine who was worthy.

They tailed Carmen to her self-defence class and back to her house, pulling into the driveway across the street, trying to be as inconspicuous as possible as Carmen strolled to her front door. *The door was partially open. They all knew what that meant…It was happening.* Unlike the others, Lexy rarely felt empathy or guilt. In this case, the elitist girl had shown her nothing, making her worthy of either emotion. Carmen paused as the door shifted ever so slightly in the evening breeze. They all ducked as the spooked mortal looked back at the street. Nausea made Lexy reach for her bottle of water. She took a drink as Grey snapped his gum for the tenth time. *This was not the time to annoy her.* Her pulse raced with adrenaline. She took a deep, cleansing breath as Grey snapped his gum again. *She wasn't finding his quirks endearing today.* The air was thick with tension as she noticed Kayn's agitated state and clearly visible veins. Lexy glanced back and whispered, "Calm yourself down. Breathe in and out, until you've got it under control. You know the drill. We wait. We can only take her if she survives on her own or if Azariah gives her another chance." Lexy paused for a second before adding, "Zach, she ingested too much dark energy earlier, she might need to be weaned off. I'd feed her before she eats Grey."

"What?" Grey asked as he looked back.

"Keep snapping your gum Grey," Lexy threatened. "If she doesn't kill you, I will."

Zach was gapped out, staring at Carmen's house.

Grey snapped, "Earth to Zach! Do something before she eats me!"

Zach noticed Kayn's state and whispered, "Oh, shit. That can't be good. I'm on it." He offered her his hands.

Kayn went to take the energy he was offering and then yanked her hands away. She stammered, "I can't."

"Why not?" Lexy countered. "If you take too much, I'll bring him back. It's not a big deal."

They were debating about what Kayn did with the dark energy she ingested. Lexy's attention was drawn to the house as her warning system twisted her insides again. *This was different. Something felt off.*

Grey laughed and launched his gum at the dash.

Lexy grimaced and scolded, "That's why we can't take you anywhere." *It was too quiet.* Lexy glanced back at her sister. Kayn was poised to slice into her palm. Lexy reached into the backseat and slapped the blade out of her sister's hand. She quietly scolded, "If Abaddon's doing the Correction, they'll smell it." Their attention was brought back to the house as the lights turned on in the kitchen.

"Weird… They usually cut the power or loosen a bulb," Kayn noted.

Yes, there was something unusual going on here. The vertical blinds were partially open, but they couldn't see what was going on from their vantage point.

"I'm going to get a closer look. If I get caught, I'll improvise," Grey declared as he quietly got out, closed the car door and sprinted across the street.

Zach was about to follow when Lexy urged, "No, let him do it. This is his thing."

Grey snuck up and found the right angle to sneak a peek inside. He stepped away, strolled up the front steps and musically knocked on the door.

Lexy laughed as the door opened and he began chatting up a completely unharmed Carmen. A moment later, a teenage boy with a sketchy smoky aura appeared. He placed his arm possessively around Carmen and shut the door in Grey's face. Grey walked back to the car, got in looking defeated and said, "Let's go." He started the engine and pulled away.

"Wait. What's going on?" Zach questioned.

As they drove away, Grey explained, "There's a kitchen full of Lampir, and our Carmen appears unfazed by her family's corpses on the linoleum, this isn't our girl."

Lexy looked back at the house as it became smaller, feeling like there was something big she was missing.

Kayn confessed from the backseat, "I thought I saw another one, but she was pregnant."

Wait...What? Why hadn't she seen this girl?

"Maybe this is a test? This definitely isn't playing out like a normal Correction," Zach inferred as he grabbed a bag of Doritos from the grocery bag of surveillance snacks on the floor.

Kayn touched Grey's shoulder and asserted, "Go back. If they're Lampir, Carmen's lack of reaction is mind control. They could just be taking their time doing her Correction."

"Lampir don't partake in Corrections," Grey clarified.

"Go back, I'll dose them with pheromones and find out everything they know," Kayn asserted as she devoured a Dorito in one mouthful.

Lexy smiled at the thought of Kayn trying to seduce anyone with Dorito breath as she squeezed Grey's knee and urged, "Humour them... Job or not, rules are being broken. What's the harm in checking it out? We can't check out this pregnant girl theory till tomorrow."

Grey turned the vehicle around and smiled at Lexy as he mouthed the words, "For you."

She leaned over and kissed his shoulder as Kayn enquired, "Does anybody have a breath mint?"

Good idea. Lexy passed back a mint as she asked, "Are you sure you're capable of this right now? You haven't had the best luck summoning up abilities on command."

Kayn assured, "I can usually trigger the pheromones with Zach's help."

Lexy winked at Zach as she passed him a mint and teased, "You're on Romeo."

Zach chuckled nervously and mumbled, "No pressure or anything."

Grey glanced back and offered his services, "I'll do it."

Lexy swatted him and he giggled. Lexy recalled something Lily had mentioned in the past and offered Kayn some unsolicited advice, "Biting your lip releases serotonin. Cutting yourself also works like a charm because of the Dragon thing, but that's off the table...This is supposed to be a sneak attack."

Zach whispered, "I have an idea. You're already wearing yoga pants. Just say you were out for a jog and you tripped. Between the scent of the blood and your pheromones, this should be like taking candy from a bunch of long fanged babies." Zach caressed Kayn's hair and his lips parted as they met hers. With an erotic dart of her tongue, Kayn urged her Handler on. Forgetting they had witnesses, Kayn straddled Zach as he moved his hands intimately over her clothes. *Handler slash impromptu make-out buddy.* Lexy and Grey were sitting in the front, pretending the situation wasn't painfully awkward, until Kayn's pheromones released in an intoxicating knee-buckling wave that crazily revved everyone's libidos.

Grey began panicking, "Get out! Get out of here! Quick, Brighton!"

Grinning as she got out, Kayn slit her hand with a knife and tossed it back into the car. Casually wiping the blood off on her spicy Dorito dusted pants, she grinned and closed the door. They all ducked, peering up as Kayn marched across the street and aggressively knocked on the door. With no hesitation, she was invited in. The trio in the car were uncomfortably aroused. Grey began intimately stroking her palm making her girly bits tingly. She became aware she was turned on. Her nipples were visible through her shirt. *What were they here for again?* Lexy yanked her hand away and abruptly got out. Grey was laughing as she inhaled the pheromone free air and casually leaned against the car taking in the picturesque neighbourhood. There was a swing set in the neighbour's yard. *One of her foster homes had a swing set when she was little. When she thought back to those days, the feeling of soaring back and forth was one of her only good memories.* They joined her as she declared, "Kids live in the house next door."

"I'll text Markus and ask him what he wants us to do," Grey replied as he wandered away with his phone.

"If Kayn eats these tools, we won't have to do anything," Zach chuckled. He offered her a chip from his bag, staring at the red swing set.

Lexy's phone vibrated. She took it out of her pocket, assuming it was Markus. The message read, 'Black lace or commando?' She felt the heat of her cheeks. *It must be Orin.* She pressed her lips together to stop herself from reacting as she recalled the random naughty message she'd accidentally sent.

"That wasn't Markus, was it?" Zach jousted, feigning shock. He tried to snatch her phone.

Maneuvering out of Zach's way, she chuckled, "It definitely wasn't."

Like a naughty younger brother, Zach baited, "Which one?"

For the first time, she had multiple conquests. "There's no names attached to these numbers," Lexy countered as she slipped her cell into her pocket and smiled.

Grey strolled over and declared, "We're supposed to clear the house and text Markus with the details. Front or back?"

"I'm more of a front door girl," Lexy sparred as she snatched a stone from the garden by the side of the walkway.

Grey grabbed a garden stake and directed, "Zach, you deal with Kayn and leave the rest to us. This should be easy, twenty minutes, in and out." Zach took off as they casually strolled to the house. "Orin says hi," Grey teased as he left her side and dashed around to the back.

It must have been Orin. Distraction time. Lexy grinned as she rifled the rock at the picture window. She followed Grey's lead, snatched a garden stake from the path and strutted into the house like she owned the place. All eyes turned to her. Lexy announced, "Who wants to die first?" They came at her, doped up from Brighton's pheromones. She could hear Grey catching everyone who tried to escape out of the back. It only took a few minutes to clear the upstairs. Carmen's parents were exactly where Grey said they'd be...*Dead on the kitchen floor.* Lexy paused in front of the family portrait above the computer. *Carmen had an older brother.* She looked in the china cabinet full of sentimental trinkets and saw a copy of his obituary. It was unclear as to the circumstances surrounding his death, but knowing Carmen had lost someone gave her a touch of depth. *No witnesses...Those were the rules.* Lexy stepped over her parent's corpses, opened the door to the basement and heard some crashes. *There was a body on the stairs.* She closed the door, opting to stay in her lane. *It was her duty to make sure nothing slipped through the cracks upstairs. First things first, a room check.* Lexy opened the door to a pristinely tidy bedroom with untouched sheets and sports trophies. *That must have been her brother's room.* She tried to open the door to the next room, but it was locked. Lexy was about to boot it open when she heard pitchy singing, followed by the sound of someone going to the washroom. *Killing someone while they were on the toilet was unnecessary, she'd let them finish up first.* Lexy sat at the kitchen table and did someone's crossword puzzle. The linoleum creaked, she glanced back. *Mom and Dad weren't dead, they were in transition. Inconvenient, but on the bright side, if they completed their transformation, they wouldn't have to dispose of remains.* Lexy got up and began to look for the cutlery drawer.

Grey appeared and said, "Behind you."

"I know, I'm just looking for a knife. If I give them my blood, we can just vacuum up the evidence."

"Smart," Grey replied. He found the cutlery drawer on the first attempt and tossed Lexy a knife. "I'll start vacuuming. Are they still downstairs?"

Lexy slit her palm and dripped it into Carmen's parent's mouths as they writhed around the linoleum. "Pop down there and make sure they don't leave any evidence behind," Lexy suggested. The girl's parent's jaws morphed as they completed the transition. She methodically staked the girl's parents. Their smouldering embers turned to dust.

The toilet flushed. Grey spun around and laughed, "What in the hell? Who's that?"

"That is someone with absolutely no self-preservation skills. I was just letting him finish," Lexy explained as she sat on the couch. Feeling thirsty, she picked up a drink from the coffee table, smelled it and opted out. *After they were done here, she was going to have a nice hot bath.* Bathroom boy wandered into the room. *He was listening to music.*

He noticed her sitting there, plucked out his earbuds and said, "Where is everyone?"

Lexy got up and explained, "They're dead."

"Why?" he asked.

This one was super new. Lexy replied, "Well, it's against immortal law to turn mortals without consent." *The sound of the vacuum cleaner made things awkward.*

"Why are you cleaning?" the new Lampir asked.

"Ashes are messy," Lexy explained, unceremoniously staking the painfully oblivious house dweller. He lit up and turned to ash just as Kayn and Zach walked in. Lexy questioned, "Did you finish off the one on the stairs?"

Zach sighed, "I'll do it," as he doubled back.

Grey dumped a full container of Lampir ashes from the vacuum into a plastic bag and complained, "Lex, I was already done vacuuming, why didn't you kill him in the kitchen?"

The phone in her pocket vibrated. Grey was sweeping as she grabbed a juice box out of the fridge and said, "I'll be right back." She slipped out the back to privately check the message…Miss me yet? She pensively bit her lip. Out of the corner of her eye, she saw a guy sprinting away with Zach in pursuit. *It looks like they missed one.* The Lampir darted into the path between the garage and a stack of firewood. Lexy grabbed a garden stake, headed him off on the other side and took him out.

Zach sighed, "Kayn promised we'd let him go if he gave us information."

"No witnesses. You know better," Lexy reprimanded as she stomped on the pile of ash.

"She'll be upset," Zach answered as they wandered back.

"She'll get over it," Lexy affirmed as they strolled back in. *He was right, Kayn was upset.* Lexy announced, "The situation has been dealt with. No witnesses. The rules have a purpose. Dead Lampir tell no tales." The ashes had been swept off the linoleum but there was a fine spray of visible blood. She scowled at Grey.

"What did I do?" he chuckled.

"Come on Greydon, you know how to clean up a crime scene." They both grabbed a dish towel, soaked it in bleach and started scrubbing. Kayn was still standing there with her nose crinkled. *She despised the scent of bleach too.* Lexy looked up and asked, "What did you find out?"

Kayn stood there as she answered, "The girl we've been following is a decoy. I told you about the yellow hue around the pregnant one. I assumed there was no way it would be her. I was partially right…It's the baby she's carrying."

"Why are we even here? They can't do the Correction until the child is over the age of sixteen. Those are the rules," Grey sighed while wiping down the baseboards.

There was always fine print in any clause, they'd all learned that lesson the hard way. Lexy rinsed her pungent bleach scented towel as she explained, "Not if the pregnant mother has abilities and is scheduled for Correction. It's completely within their rights to do it in that case. The infant she's carrying would be irrelevant under immortal law." She turned to Kayn and asserted, "I didn't see anyone else with a yellow hue in their auras. You mentioned the pregnant girl, but I didn't see it."

"I'll show you who she is when we get to school," Kayn answered as she left to dump another full container of ashes out the back.

Her hands were pruned from the bleach. As Zach walked past, Lexy enquired, "You didn't put the bloody towels in the garbage can outside, did you?"

He gave her a strange look, answering, "They're in the basement with the girl."

That's right…They hadn't been told to kill her. Lexy looked for Grey, but he'd taken off. She was about to put the potent bleach-soaked dish towels into a plastic garbage bag when she noticed a spot they'd missed. She took care of it as she asked, "Was she awake?"

"She's up and bitey," Zach confirmed. "I'm not sure why we didn't gag her?"

"I thought Grey was going to do it," Lexy sighed as she became distracted by her pocket vibrating. *The scent of the bleach was too much.* She remembered what Grey was doing, "He's outside texting the address to the Aries Group. You two go downstairs and kill Carmen. Take the dustpan and the broom with you. Sweep her up and toss her out the back door."

Zach shrugged and exclaimed, "I'll go get the dustpan and broom."

Kayn turned the end table on its side, stomped on it and snapped off a leg. *Lexy rolled her eyes. They were trying to clean up the evidence, not make it obvious there had been a struggle.* Lexy collected the pieces of the coffee table and carried them out to the garage can. *They were done. Good enough.* Grey was already waiting at the car.

Grey grinned and teased, "Did you need to break that?"

"It wasn't me, she's still learning. The Aries Group is going to burn the house down anyway," Lexy explained as she smelled her hands and scowled. *She was going to be smelling bleach for days.* Kayn and Zach were done. Grey's cell vibrated as they got back into the car. He quietly read the message in his mind first, appearing upset about something.

Lexy touched her Handler's arm as she asked, "What happened?" Grey passed her his cell as he turned the key in the ignition with dewy eyes. Lexy scrolled through the messages. She looked back and explained, "The Ankh from the other continent didn't make it out of the Testing." Lexy continued to read as they drove away. Beaming, she turned again and disclosed, "The Trinity from your Testing made it out with their continent's group." *Maybe being stuck in the Testing wasn't the end anymore?* She looked at Grey and they smiled at each other. *It felt like something huge was on the horizon.*

Chapter 21

Deplorable Deeds

They'd celebrated for Trinity the night before, so the following morning the girls were feeling a little rough as they entered the high school in search of the pregnant girl. As they took their seats at the back of the room, the short-haired brunette in question strolled in looking like she'd swallowed a watermelon. *She didn't see anything out of the ordinary.* Lexy opened her book and whispered, "I don't see it."

Kayn quietly replied, "I do. It's even more intense."

The greying teacher in his mid-fifties placed his palm on Kayn's desk as he interrupted their conversation, "Miss Smith with the blonde hair, you've just volunteered. Head up to the board and answer the question."

Lexy was dying laughing on the inside as Kayn got up and sauntered over to the chalkboard, stood there for a minute and wrote, 37 on the board.

The teacher smiled and asked, "How did you get to that answer? You didn't show your work."

Kayn turned to face the class as she proclaimed, "Magic."

"Funny," the good-humoured teacher sparred. "Go sit down, Miss Smith."

Kayn pressed her lips together to stop herself from smiling as she slipped back into her seat.

The teacher placed a quiz on everyone's desk, and as he handed a copy to Kayn, he said, "You're obviously quite advanced. You should have no problem with this."

A buzzer went off. Lexy quietly opened her quiz while listening to the humming of everybody's thoughts. She narrowed in on Kayn's because she was feeding her the answers. They finished long before the bell rang. *Why couldn't she see what Kayn was able to see?* She watched the expectant teen. *It was bothering her. She was drawn out of her pity party while listening to Kayn's thoughts about never being able to have a child.* Lexy interrupted her thoughts by adding unspoken commentary, *'Don't let yourself think about it.'* The pregnant girl excused herself to go to the washroom.

The teacher razzed, "You're not going to have that baby in there are you, Emma?"

"I might," the expectant teen saucily bantered.

Kayn was clearly fascinated by the girl. Lexy couldn't allow herself to be. She'd done this far too many times to get attached to the endearing girl with the pixie cut. *A pregnant girl. How were they going to do this? How would it even work?* Kayn waited a minute or two before asking to use the washroom and made it back to class just as the bell rang. They collected their stuff and followed Emma out into the hall as a surge of students appeared. *This she could see. There were black auras…Everywhere.* "It's a distraction. You're right. That must be the girl. Where is she?" Lexy stammered. Her stomach cramped. *Shit. They lost her.* She felt nauseous as they raced through the dark foggy swarm of students. *Where was she?*

Kayn exclaimed, "They can't do a public Correction."

"Not unless it looks like an accident," Lexy answered as they continued to scour the school.

The Dragons separated as the students disappeared into the classrooms, so they'd draw less attention. *There was no way this could work. How would they train her? Maybe she should just let it happen?* She took a drink out of the fountain and felt a twinge of guilt. *She was a baby, born to a mother doomed from conception. Where in hell was Kayn?* Lexy strolled the hallways avoiding authority figures until she decided to check the lady's washroom. She shoved open the door, Kayn was sitting on the tile cradling Emma. *She saw it now…The heavenly hue of the recently saved. This was really happening.* They managed to get Emma out of the school undetected, raced back to their hotel, checked out and in less than an hour, they were on the road speeding down the highway away from the city towards the border.

Kayn nudged Emma and asked, "You don't seem to have many questions. Everybody has concerns like, why did this happen to me? My parents are going to be looking for me. Why did somebody just try to murder me?"

"I'm an empath with psychic abilities," Emma slyly confessed. "I've known someone was coming to kill me for a while. This wasn't even the first attempt. I don't have parents, they died last year in a car accident. I'm an only child. No close relatives. I've been couch surfing and living at the school because my foster home sucks. The father of this baby is an insignificant asshole. Any other questions?"

"No," Kayn commented. "This is by far the easiest kidnapping I've ever been a part of. Thanks for your cooperation."

Emma replied, "You're welcome. Thanks for showing up when you did."

They all laughed. Lexy texted the Aries group, they needed a passport for Emma. As they approached their last chance to pull off before the border, they still hadn't heard back, so she contacted the last number Ankh texted them from. *They were never going to get over the border with an expectant teenager.* After making a unanimous decision to head into Idaho, they grabbed some dinner on the go and ate their truck stop diner ham and cheese subs as they sped down the highway. Zach offered Emma a donut.

Emma scrunched up her nose as she declined, "No, thank you. I'm already fat enough and those things will kill you."

Everyone laughed including the girl as they listened to music on the radio. Here I go Again by Whitesnake came on, and in no time at all, they were all belting out the tune like road tripping warriors. Grey kept looking at Emma in the rear-view mirror as he drove. *They'd never had such precious cargo in the car. If they ran into Triad, Trinity or Abaddon, the shit would hit the fan.*

Grey announced, "Bathroom break," as he pulled over at the rest stop. Kayn accompanied Emma to the washroom just to be cautious.

As they got back into the car, Grey passed the new girl a two-litre of orange juice and awkwardly explained, "For the baby. It has folic acid. It says heart-wise on it."

"Thank you. Should I just drink it out of the carton?" Emma enquired.

"I drank some. I swear I don't have cooties," Grey flirted.

Dear lord Greydon, the girl was nine months pregnant. Their willing hostage smiled at Grey as she took a big swig from the carton. They pulled away from the rest stop and continued driving down the highway. Her phone vibrated. Lexy read the message aloud, "Our punishment must be over. We're meeting up with everyone in Montana. They're at the Edgewood Inn. Emma's new ID and passport are being couriered there. I have the directions..." Lexy's voice trailed off. *They had to brand her Ankh.*

"You might as well just spit it out," Emma sighed. "I'm not going anywhere."

Kayn showed her the Ankh symbol on the palm of her hand as she pulled off the metaphorical bandage, "We have to brand you Ankh. This symbol prohibits us from passing through the hall of souls when we die. We remain in the in-between until our bodies have been healed by our Clan."

"Alright. Let's just get it over with," Emma agreed.

Kayn took Emma's hand and whispered, "I'm sorry," as she branded her palm with her ring.

"Son of a bitch!" Emma shrieked, protectively clutching her hand against her chest. "That was not cool!" their newest Ankh complained.

"I know," Kayn affirmed. "It's done now. Welcome to Clan Ankh."

Emma questioned, "What did you mean by, our punishment is over?"

Grinning in the rear-view, Grey revealed, "During a banquet, Kayn threw her ex off a balcony, and Lexy snapped Kayn's ex-boyfriend's new girlfriend's neck."

Kayn rolled her eyes as she countered, "Come on, we're immortal, it wasn't a big deal."

Zach teased, "Don't let Markus hear you say that, Brighton."

"Brighton?" Emma questioned.

"Kayn's nickname," Lexy explained as she offered chips to her sister.

Kayn took a handful and whispered, "There's way more to the story. It'll make sense later."

Emma took some chips as she muttered, "I wish someone would toss my ex off a balcony."

That could be arranged. Kayn and Lexy both looked at the new Ankh.

Emma stammered, "Joking. I'm only kidding."

They drove through the night and into the following day until the scenery became flourishing rolling hills of green. They stopped at each rest stop to make sure their knocked-up newbie Ankh stretched her legs and got a breath of fresh air. By nightfall, they arrived at the hotel in desperate need of a shower.

"So, what are the other Ankh like? Are they as cool as you guys?" Emma questioned as they all strolled into the lobby.

Grey flung his arm around Emma's shoulder and gave her a friendly squeeze as he whispered, "No way. We're definitely the coolest."

Lexy was a little bit concerned. Grey's fascination with Emma was cute, but he knew her odds were slim. She didn't want to see him hurt. They were handed key cards at the front desk. Zach and Kayn took off up the stairs. Grey, Lexy and the new pregnant girl Emma rode the elevator up to their floor. Lexy flopped down on her bed, leaving Grey to get Emma settled. She stared at the stucco ceiling, exhausted from the drama and the drive. Someone knocked on the adjoining door. She got up and wandered over, it was the new girl. "Is everything alright?" Lexy asked as Emma slipped past her into the room.

"My room's big enough for six people. There are two queen beds and an adjoining bedroom. Are all of the rooms this big?" the new girl enquired.

Lexy peered through the open door and smiled. *They were going to put the new Ankh together.* Lexy explained, "You'll probably be sharing a room with the other new Ankh when they arrive. You'll need to get to know each other. It's a long story and one I would assume you're not quite prepared to hear in your situation."

Grey strolled in and announced, "They have us staying on either side of Emma, but her room's enormous."

Lexy watched Emma's protruding belly as she wandered around aimlessly. *She was concerned. She should be. What in the hell was Azariah doing giving them a pregnant girl? How were they going to do this? Markus was going to shit his pants when he saw her.* Emma sat on the bed. Lexy took a seat beside her and enquired, "How far along are you?"

"I have less than a month to go," Emma revealed.

Curiosity took over as Lexy enquired, "Were you planning to keep it?"

"I hadn't decided yet," Emma confessed as she rolled her shirt up over her protruding midriff and cradled it with her palms.

"Are you thirsty or hungry? Is there anything I can get for you?" Grey asked sincerely.

"Always," Emma teased, wincing while holding her stomach.

Grey was clearly fascinated by her condition. They rarely dealt with pregnant people in their line of work. The baby visibly moved. Grey knelt before her in awe and asked, "Can I touch it?"

With a strange look, Emma smiled and gave him permission, "I guess so."

Grey gently placed his hands on her stomach as the infant within her shifted and he gasped, "It's incredible. Lexy, feel this."

She couldn't. Not when she knew how this scenario was going to play out. Before Grey could ask a second time, Lexy abruptly stood up and announced, "That baby is probably hungry. I know I am. I'll text Zach and find out where their rooms are. We'll stop by on the way down to the restaurant and go together." Before she could text, someone knocked on the door. Lexy opened it. *Speak of the devil.*

Zach strolled in and asked, "Ready for dinner?"

*She was…*Lexy turned around. Grey was helping Emma up. He knew better than to get attached but she understood why he couldn't help himself. *Grey would have been an amazing father. She also wanted to overlook the caution and enjoy the novelty of the baby, but she couldn't. One of them had to remain rational, and this time, it was going to have to be her.* They took the elevator down a floor, followed Zach to his room and walked through the adjoining door to the sound of Kayn's laughter without knocking. *Awkward. She wasn't alone.*

Frost didn't miss a beat. He jumped up and sauntered over to the door, wearing only his jeans, which were now super tight in obvious places. He held out his hand to the new girl, "You must be Emma. It's a pleasure to meet you." Emma shook his hand as they all gawked at his situation. Frost looked down when he realised what they were looking at and nonchalantly shrugged. Frost pointed at Emma's protruding belly and blurted out, "How did that happen?"

Quick-witted Emma pointed at Kayn frantically, pulling up her pants and sparred, "It looks like you already know."

Frost looked at Kayn and apologized, "We're going to have to hit pause. We should be down at the restaurant for this conversation." He turned to Zach and questioned, "Has Markus seen this?"

"No, not yet. We obviously didn't know you guys were here," Zach explained.

Frost grabbed his flashing cell off the nightstand and announced, "They're down at the restaurant already." He went over, kissed Kayn's cheek and whispered something in her ear.

As they left the room, Frost began shooting random questions at the pregnant new girl. They piled into the fully mirrored elevator. Frost wrapped his arms around Kayn's waist from behind and whispered, "Just as you are." Kayn leaned against him and quietly repeated his words.

She was glad they'd made up but she was about to go into sugar shock.

As the door opened into the lobby, Emma glanced at Lexy and commented, "You know, I've made it all of the way through this pregnancy without puking."

"I like her," Frost announced as they strolled through the lobby. "The new Ankh are in the restaurant with the others. There's Dean, Samid and I got you something."

With Kayn's curiosity peaked, she turned to Frost and teased, "It's not another ring from a vending machine, is it? I already have one of those."

They were all smiling as they entered the pub-style restaurant. The table full of Ankh waved them over. It looked like almost everyone was here, that's when they noticed Molly sitting at the end of the table next to Orin.

Overcome with joy, Kayn dove into Frost's arms. He lifted her off the ground and spun her around as he whispered, "Better than a ring?"

Kayn kissed him and whispered back, "You are in so much trouble later."

"I've been in trouble since the day we met," Frost quietly admitted as the rest of their Clan got up in awe and gathered around.

The silence was deafening as Markus walked over and stood in front of Emma. Markus was in full panic mode as he questioned, "How did this happen? You're sure you took her after her Correction?"

"One hundred percent certain, she told me the lady in the light sent her back," Kayn explained.

Markus looked directly at Kayn as he asked, "Is the baby alive?"

Emma laughed as she waved at Markus and said, "You know you can speak directly to me, I'm standing right here. It's moving right now."

"I'm sorry. That was rude. This is just so unexpected. Can I touch it?" Markus asked. Emma nodded her consent. He placed both hands on Emma's rounded belly and declared, "I have absolutely no idea how we're going to do this."

Lexy strolled over to Orin. Without uttering a word, he passed her his drink. She downed it and stated, "Don't ask me anything. I wasn't even there when it happened. I showed up after the fact."

"Alright, no questions," he chuckled as they sat down. Orin obediently passed her a menu and spoke not a word.

Lexy surveyed her options and ordered. As their server left the table, she watched the newbie Ankh getting to know each other to avoid Orin's eyes.

Orin started laughing. Lexy looked at him as he admitted, "I wasn't sitting around waiting for you so let's just cut out the awkward crap and enjoy each other's company."

"I can't sleep with you," Lexy clarified, with no idea why she'd said it.

"I know," Orin revealed as mountains of appetizers were placed on the table.

They ate while chatting about random unimportant things. Lexy kept finding her eyes drawn to the new Ankh talking with Grey at the end of the table. *He was sitting so far away from her. Their bond was like a rubber band, stretched as far as it could go. It usually tugged them back together without snapping, but lately, it felt like their connection was close to being severed. There was a time when she'd believed that was impossible.* Kayn and Mel were having a deep conversation. The table became rowdier as the drinks kept flowing. *She watched Grey getting to know Emma. It felt like she was all alone at a table of friends.* Lexy did a few rounds of shots with her Clan before opting out.

Nobody noticed as she left. It felt like her universe was allowing her the time she needed. Lexy was noticeably drunk as she got into the elevator alone. Copa Cabana started playing as she stepped out into the hallway on her floor. Lexy spun around as the elevator door closed. *That was weird. Her feet were aching.* She removed her heels and carried them down the hall. She fumbled with the key until she started giggling. *Awesome Lexy, you're too wasted to open a door.* She got in and left the lights off as she tossed her shoes in the corner. *She should also lock that adjoining door.* Lexy strolled across the room. *It was already locked. Somebody must have locked it before they went down to the restaurant. It felt like she wasn't alone.* Lexy whispered, "Grey?" *There was no answer.* She felt around for the light switch. When she didn't find it right away, she decided she was being ridiculous. Lexy stripped off her clothes, slipped under the covers and snuggled up in bed. *The pillows were comfy.* She felt pressure on the mattress like someone was sitting at the end of the bed. *She'd said not tonight.* Lexy whispered, "Orin?"

Tiberius' voice whispered, "Ouch. I was third, really?"

Lexy scrambled up in bed and turned on the lamp. Tiberius was sitting there at the foot of her bed shirtless, grinning like a cat who'd just swallowed a canary. She whispered, "What are you doing here?"

"I came to see you. I swear, I'm alone," he vowed.

"You can't be here," Lexy firmly stated.

He crawled up, rested his head on the pillow next to her and whispered, "Relax. Have a conversation with me. What do you have to lose?"

Everything. Absolutely everything. "Listen, I'm flattered, but if Grey catches you here, I'll never hear the end of it," Lexy confessed, fighting the urge to touch him to see if he was real.

"I locked the door to the adjoining room. Nobody will ever know I was here," Tiberius disclosed as he reached out and touched her crimson hair.

"If you're distracting me while Triad steals our people, I'll never forgive you," Lexy whispered.

"If I promise to leave your new Ankh alone, will you trust me?" he asked, gazing into her eyes.

On any given day, she could list hundreds of reasons why this was a bad idea, but none sprung to mind.

He boldly silenced further debate with his lips. Lexy shamelessly responded as he deepened the intimacy with a delightful dart of his tongue. *She selfishly wanted this.* Her lips parted in acceptance of his vow, and they tumbled around, making out like sex-starved teenagers, touching each other and giggling until right and wrong went from blurry to inconsequential. He shocked her by biting into the tender flesh of her breast, triggering her healing ability because he knew what she needed. The white noise of everything else in the world became clouded by desire and the urgency to pick up where they left off.

He naughtily slid his hand between her thighs and promised, "I placed privacy stones, nobody's coming to stop us until one."

Lexy's eyes darted to the clock by the side of the bed... *It was twelve-thirty. He was so good at this.* She whimpered with pleasure as he rapidly stroked her until ration ceased, whispering dirty intentions. She was aching for him as he slid the length of his rigid manhood into her. Every nerve ending hummed with pleasure as he roughly gave it to her, driving her closer to the edge of sanity with each vigorous, violently perfect thrust. They rolled so she was on top. He pinched her nipples as she brazenly rode him until she began moaning his name, gasping and shuddering as the climax rippled through her. He tugged a handful of her hair, aggressively yanked her lips to his and muffled her passionate cries with his mouth and tongue as they switched positions. He brutally pounded her into the mattress until another wave of intoxicating carnal bliss detonated within her. She violently dug her nails into his back as spine-tingling euphoria swept through her entire being. Tiberius groaned her name as he kept going until they cried out in unison. He shuddered and collapsed on top of her. *She was a naughty deplorable girl. The bar would be closed. They would be back in the rooms soon.* While feeling like angels were singing between her thighs, Lexy whispered, "I don't want to seem insensitive, but you should go."

Tiberius pulled away. He gazed into her eyes as he quietly replied, "I probably should but..."

"But what?" she teased, smiling back.

Tiberius grinned and confessed, "I don't think I can walk."

She wanted more. Lexy moved beneath him.

"I really should leave before someone shows up," he chuckled.

She saucily commanded, "You can go when I'm finished."

Tiberius rolled her on top of him and with his hands possessively clasping her hips, he chuckled, "Take what you need. I'm yours."

She awoke to a pounding fist on the adjoining door and turned around. *He was gone. She was alone. Wait…Was that a dream? It was the hottest one she'd ever had if it was.* Requiring a minute, Lexy answered back, "I'm getting up."

Grey laughed and urged, "Hurry up, sleepyhead. Everyone's hungover and starving. We'll meet you downstairs at the restaurant."

She muffled her giggles in the pillow that still smelled of his cologne. *It wasn't a dream. What was wrong with her? Her enemy showed up in the middle of the night and she just did it? Shit… Jenna, Lily and Frost would know the second she walked into the restaurant. You couldn't hide deplorable deeds from those abilities. They always knew who'd been naughty and she'd just taken sinful behaviour to a new level.* Lexy showered, towel-dried her hair and quickly got dressed, downplaying her looks as much as possible. *If she was quiet, maybe they wouldn't ask questions.* She noticed a stone on the phone book. *He'd left one behind.* She recognized it immediately. *It was a bloodstone.* This struck her as peculiar because bloodstones weren't usually used for privacy. They were used for healing or as a reminder of strength and perseverance against all odds. They also had something to do with sacrifice, but she couldn't quite recall the exact purpose of the stone. She pocketed the smooth jasper stone splattered with crimson, knowing Jenna usually had answers. Lexy felt gloriously tranquil as she stepped into the elevator. The door opened on the next floor. Frost and Kayn got in. *Poof, tranquillity gone.* Frost gave her a strange knowing look.

Smiling, Kayn casually probed, "Orin or Grey?"

Lexy immediately started thinking about canned soups, trying to block even the smallest flicker of her midnight caller's identity from her mind.

"You do realise thinking of nothing but canned soup, makes the identity of your booty call more intriguing," Kayn prompted as the elevator door slid open again.

Jenna, Orin and Melody got in. Lexy rolled her eyes, looked at the ceiling and sighed, "Dear Lord."

Orin was immediately intrigued by her flushed cheeks and lack of effort in her appearance. "Hey there, Lex. You look awfully perky this morning."

He knew. Orin was quite familiar with her morning after flushed cheeks. She continued to think about soup, *Chicken noodle, tomato, mushroom, potato leek...*Orin was pissing himself laughing as they all got out of the elevator. *They were probably all assuming she'd backslid and slept with Grey. They knew he wouldn't remember, so nobody would say a word.*

As they made their way through the lobby, everyone else regaled tales of drunken shenanigans, while Lexy decided keeping her sexcapades to herself might be for the best. They all sat at the table where the others were waiting. With no knowledge of her misdeeds, Grey saved her the seat next to him. *Awesome. She was going to have to be actively thinking of soup label names for hours. Why hadn't anyone made a bracelet to block their thoughts from the others? Tomato, chicken, mushroom, potato leek.* Her eyes lit up as she slid, *minestrone* into the mix of repetitive thoughts.

Grey got up, excused himself and said, "I'm going to go get to know the new kids." He left to go sit in the empty seat next to Emma.

Lexy peered up and caught Orin staring. *Why was she feeling this guilty? Orin may look like an angel, but once you were alone, he wasn't that at all.* Her friend with benefits looked away and she suspected his romantic pursuit had been officially called off. *Fair enough. She was a horrible person. Deplorable ...that's a better word. It described who she'd become while on this journey. She belonged to a Clan. She was Ankh. He was her enemy. It was stupid and impossible but so hot it couldn't be stopped by useless ration.*

She was struggling to change her train of thought, but it just kept rolling along even with flat tires. *Lover of three...Grey, Orin and... She couldn't allow herself to think of his name, and that was becoming impossible.* Her mind kept trying to bounce back to it. *Probably so she could rationalize what she'd done.* Jenna gave her a sympathetic look from across the table. *Minestrone, chicken, mushroom...*

Lexy was tired of soup. Her mind switched gears and narrowed into thoughts anyone who hadn't gone a thousand shades last night would be having. *Breakfast. What did she want to eat?* She picked up her menu. *Bacon and eggs?* She smiled as her thoughts were drawn back to that night in Mexico. *Maybe she should just have Eggs Benny?* Orin laughed while chatting with Markus. *It was strange...All she could hear was Orin's voice.* She peered over her menu as Orin ordered steak and eggs. *That sounded perfect. That's what she felt like having today.*

Markus spoke to her, "I announced our next job last night, but you were already gone. I also have important news to share after the Summit."

"I went to bed early," Lexy innocently responded.

"We have a lead on a Venom as an insurance policy for this next group. We're off to find him while the rest protect and train our assets. We obviously have limitations until the pregnant one gives birth. We're hoping the pregnancy will bond her to the others. There's time before the next Testing but not as much as we thought. In response to extra Trinity making it out of the Testing, the Third Tiers changed this continent's schedule to every two years just like Amar's group."

What? Lexy questioned, "Can they do that?" Their conversations were silenced as their orders arrived. She watched the group getting to know each other at the end of the table as guilt crept its way to the surface, finger by finger, up through the murk and the mud. *Last night was a mistake.* Lexy forced a smile as the server placed her order in front of her. *She wasn't hungry anymore.*

As soon as their server was out of earshot, Markus continued to speak, "The Guardians agreed to the changes with one stipulation, we're allowed to use the workaround Kayn's group discovered. Lexy and Kayn, you're the next part of this equation."

Kayn snapped out of her conversation with Frost when she heard her name and asked, "Why is that?"

"You two lovely Dragons have personal relationships that can be used to our advantage," Markus disclosed with a grin. While staring directly at Lexy, he revealed, "You'll be the ones stealing the unsealed Venom from Triad."

It's a good thing she hadn't made Tiberius any promises.

The Beginning

Behind the Series

One thousand years ago, procreation with mortals became illegal under the immortal law. Any suspected immortal offspring will be allowed to live until the age of sixteen. At this time, a Correction will be sent to erase their family line. The suspected immortal and immediate family will be executed. If the partially immortal teen manages to survive their Correction or have impressed the Guardians of the in-between with their bravery, they may be granted a second chance as a sacrificial lamb for the greater good. They must join one of three Clans of immortals living on earth. Clan Ankh, Clan Trinity or Clan Triad. They will then have the symbol of that Clan branded into their flesh and with this mark, their souls will no longer be permitted through the hall of souls when they die. They must wait in the in-between for their Clans to heal their mortal shells. Once they have reached the age of eighteen, they will be sealed to their Clan. The next step is to train their partially mortal brains to survive the stresses of immortality. The next feat will be the immortal Testing where they will be dropped into a floating crypt the size of New York City. This Testing is fuelled by your worst nightmares. It is a place of magic. A personal hell, where anything can happen. Here you must die a thousand times if need be, in increasingly violent ways until you understand what it is to be immortal. All three Clans go into The Testing. They must remain together and search for the Amber room to survive. There is a catch…only the first two Clans that find the

Amber room will be allowed out. The third Clan will remain trapped in the nightmare forever...

For the reader in need of a more comical series rundown to tickle your funny bone...Enjoy.

A sexy dark comic romp through the afterlife with three Clans of naughty certifiably insane antiheroes who battle each other for shits and giggles while collecting human teenagers as they survive the exterminations of their family lines. If they've demonstrated an impressive level of badassery, they are granted a second chance at life as sacrificial lambs for the greater good. They must join one of three Clans of immortals living on earth and can be stolen at random by any other Clan until their eighteenth birthday. Plot twist... To prove their partially mortal brains are capable of grasping immortality, they will be dropped into an Immortal Testing which is basically a simulation of their own personal hells. Like rats in a maze made of nightmares and other ghastly depraved thoughts best left locked behind those mortal happy place filters, they must come out mentally intact after being murdered in thousands of increasingly creative ways.

Good news, you're not done. I'd never leave you bored till the next book in Lexy's series comes out. Check out these other titles in this universe of characters. Leave a review for the series and let me know how much you like it. They are always appreciated.

Happy Reading XO

The Children Of Ankh Series Universe

Lexy's series

Wild Thing
Wicked Thing
Deplorable Me

Kayn's Series

Sweet Sleep
Enlightenment
Let There Be Dragons
Handlers of Dragons
Coming 2020... Tragic Fools

Owen's Series

Bring Out your Dead

Fun Facts About This Series...

Correction - The scheduled execution of all partially immortal offspring and their genetic line.

Clans - Ankh, Trinity and Triad are the three Clans of immortals living on earth. You must join one of these three Clans if you survive your Correction.

Sealed - At the age of eighteen, you become sealed to your Clan.

Testing - The Testing is a floating crypt the size of New York City that contains everyone's worst nightmares. Within this crypt, you must die thousands of times to prove that your partially mortal brain can withstand the trials of being immortal.

Amber Room - Three Clans enter The Testing and race for the Amber room. Only the first two to find this room will be set free. The third will remain lost their worst nightmares forever.

Tombs - If you survive the Testing you have earned your own healing tomb.

Guardians - Three Guardians created each Clan of immortals. They are beings from the in-between.

Crypts – Home-bases for each Clan, scattered all over the world.

Dragons - There are green scaly Dragons in this series, but in most cases, the word Dragon refers to an emotional Dragon. Lexy is the Dragon of Clan Ankh. She can operate without emotions. A Dragon is used as a partially immortal hitman.

Biography

Kim Cormack is the always comedic author of the darkly twisted epic paranormal romance series, "The Children of Ankh." She worked for over 16 years in Early Childhood education and as an aid. She has M.S and has lived most of her life on Vancouver Island in beautiful British Columbia, Canada. She currently lives in the gorgeous little town of Port Alberni. She's a single mom with a daughter in University and a son who just started high school. She enjoys long walks to the fridge and listening to strange music in her minivan. If you see her just back away slowly. No sudden movements...No direct eye contact. *Can be easily distracted by hot sauce. Do not feed after midnight.*

All heroes are born from the embers that linger after the fire of great tragedy...

She slept a dreamless sleep free of Dragons for she had slain them once again...

Table Of Contents

Join us at www.childrenofankh.com
Happy Reading